VALUABLE THINGS

**Twin Sisters in Love with the Same Man
and a coin flip.
Hurricane Road # 3**

**A Novel by:
Roger C Horton**

ISBN 9781720286400

Introduction

The third novel of the Hurricane Road Series, *Valuable Things*, begins in the depths of the great depression. Beautiful twin-sisters are haunted by faint memories and dreams of a dark incident in their past. As they search for the hidden truth their lives begin to be changed by it. Raised in luxury by loving grandparents, they have been given everything money can buy. There has been two of everything until the twins fall in love with the same man. It's a story of love, jealousy, and the consequence of choices. It's about hot revenge, cold retribution, and how even a spirited woman can be beaten down by a cruel man. In old age, Asher Byran raises his great-grandson Cory. Wealth means little to Asher. He resolves instead, to give the boy his most precious possessions, valuable things that must be learned and lived.

The Byran Twins

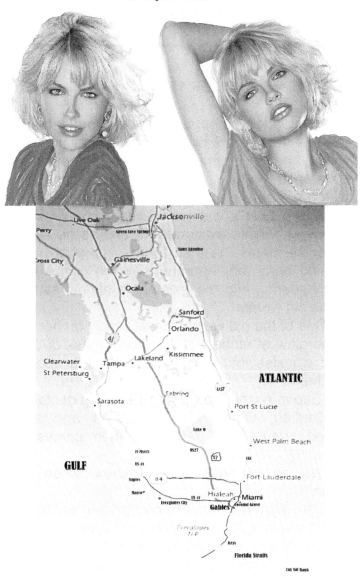

Valuable Things

CUBA, SEPTEMBER OF 1928

Two old mulatto women sat at the pier head, the pale embers of their cigars providing the only illumination. Clouds shrouded the moon and no light showed from the warehouse office. Doctor Garcia inched his car inched onto the pier, creeping past a booth that should have held a watchman. His instructions were to arrive with lights extinguished, and as he stopped and set the break, he tried to imagine what he was becoming party too. Apprehensive, he climbed from his car, peering into the gloom. He almost stumbled over the old women.

One of the old women drew deeply on her cigar, and the glow of embers lit the brown mask of deeply etched wrinkles that mapped her life. Pia spoke as she exhaled.

"*Bueno noche, doctor* 'good evening doctor'."

Startled, Garcia took a breath and asked, "*Cuando vendrás su patrone*, (When comes your employer?)"

"*No se cuando*, 'I don't know when'," Pia answered.

Garcia got back into his car, sat and waited.

After midnight, a cold wet wind blew in from the straits. Lightning followed, striking out from the rains squalls that obscured the lights of *Matanzas*. Thunder emitting from the squalls masked the drone of the big yacht's engines. Gazing out to sea, Dr. Garcia was startled by the ghostly specter as on glowing wings of spray, it rushed ominously out of the murk. The boat slowed, its bow sinking down. Only a hundred feet off the pier, its helm was put down, and its two offshore engines, backed hard. The yacht slid sideways, nudged the pier, and lay there rolling on its own wake. Men, many men, crowded her deck, and some leapt off, securing lines. They spoke in whispers and hushed voices. On the deck aft and on the cabin top, other men lay in rows, some bandaged, others covered with canvas. Handing his bag to a small man, Garcia stepped aboard. He slipped; almost fell on the wet deck. Hands steadied him. Only when only light was provided to examine the wounded, did he notice the bullet- riddled wood, the spent brass, and see what he had slipped in. The yacht was bathed in blood.

Some were dead. He passed them quickly, doing what he could for the seriously wounded, and he made mental notes of the minor cases. He gave rapid instructions to those who were competent to assist. Six men would require surgery as soon as possible, he decided. Others would need medical assistance and a hospital stay but could wait a little. Senor O'Ryan, his patron, came to him, and Garcia began to report the situation of each man.

Another man, large, a Yankee from his accent, called to someone below. Garcia continued to speak with O'Ryan as two young women were helped up the companionway by the Yankee. They appeared sick or drunk, and in the dark, Garcia paid them slight notice.

He was unaware that they had been passed to the old women on the dock.

"An additional matter," O'Ryan said, and placing a hand on Garcia's shoulder, he directed the doctor ashore, guiding him to the dimly lit office where the women waited.

O'Ryan gestured, directing Garcia's attention to the young females, "Examine them also," he instructed.

"*Putas,* 'whores'," Garcia exclaimed? He was incredulous, for he had not looked past the tight sequined gowns and heavy makeup.

"No doctor, family! My grandnieces— their abduction— the reason for this carnage," Robert O'Ryan said, his voice cold, but without anger. "Look beyond the costume for they are only children," he added, his tone becoming soft.

Garcia nodded respectfully. Confused and embarrassed by his own insulting comment, he asked diplomatically, "What would you have me examine them for?"

Exasperated, O'Ryan breathed out strongly, "Whatever can be quickly discovered, injury, drugs, you can see they're not right." He threw his arms out to the sides, his words a growl, as he spoke, "Who can know? They have witnessed death, torture, and their own mother's rape and slaughter. They were taken and for three days have been in the possession of ruthless men."

Anger had entered his voice and chilled Garcia. Without further words the doctor knelt next to the nearer of the girls, and using a penlight, examined her eyes, eyes that were somehow vacant. The pupils were dilated, and the girl barely reacted to the light. He leaned close smelling her breath, and then examined the skin of her arms and wrists. An, "Aahh," escaped him when he found fresh needle marks. He moved to the second child repeating the process before checking the pulse of both. The arm of the second girl fell limply when he released it. Her head hung loosely to one side. Pia pulled the girl towards her, resting the child's head against her shoulder.

As Garcia stood, the big Yankee entered and leaned against the door. In the light, he looked tired, and was perhaps an older man than the doctor had first thought.

"Well?" O'Ryan said, his impatience threatening.

"Needle marks on the inner arm, heroin most likely, and they were given far too much. The heartbeats are not regular," he said, shaking his head worriedly. "It's lucky they didn't die of it. There's also the smell of laudanum." Garcia paused, looked away from O'Ryan's eyes, "Do you wish a full pelvic examination, to know if—"?

"No exam!"

The words had power. They were abrupt. The Yankee at the door had given an unmistakable command that no-one dared question.

"Pia and Luca will see to them," O'Ryan said. We will inform you if your services are needed beyond this."

"And the men?"

"The boat has already departed. A few hours and they should be ashore at *Key West*."

Garcia shrugged. "Then there's nothing else for me but these two," he said, indicating the girls. "They must not sleep; make them walk and drink water, much water." He searched his bag and removed a small bottle of pills. "Tomorrow give them one of these with each class of water. They must drink water to help flush the drugs."

"We understand doctor," Robert O'Ryan said, taking the tiny bottle. The door opened, and the men went out onto the wharf, the Yankee remaining near the door.

"You have the thanks of my entire family," O'Ryan said earnestly, and embracing the doctor, he pressed on him a thick envelope.

"You would be wise to return to your home without delay," the Yankee advised from a few steps away." It is my belief, doctor that many may be in need of your skill — and soon!"

Garcia's eyebrows rose.

"Also," O'Ryan added, "It would be dangerous, even fatal, if anyone were to discover what you've seen here— ever!"

"I understand completely," the doctor said, nodding nervously.

"Go then, and take care," O'Ryan said, dismissing him.

Garcia climbed into his car, relieved to be getting away from this. "God preserve," he whispered. He wished to know nothing of what this had been about, yet he could not forget that he had just ministered to some of the province's wealthiest men. He thought, *So much, blood — a matter of family honor — The girls, yes — only over family, would these men involve themselves in such a mess."*

***

As Garcia's car pulled away, Pia Romez calmed one of the girls, while Luca washed the other's makeup away. It had required only moments to learn if these young ones had been used, but things more important could be harmed, things more fragile than the mere flesh, which was the foolish concern of men.

Pia prayed to Babalucaye, the orisha of the suffering. She prayed that the spirits of the young ones might be soothed. Later, she would offer Babalucaye aquadiente, and the sacrifice of a small animal. Then perhaps the orisha would intercede with Oludamare. Perhaps the children would be helped to live a placid life, but Pia doubted it. More likely, they would suffer from life, as did most rich women. She would pray, but most usually, the Saints only did as they wished. It was, after all, the fate of humanity is to suffer.

The girls were quiet again. Luca had finished with their bathing. They must be quickly dressed in the clothing brought for them. The men waited outside for the drive home. The men would be impatient. Pia shuddered. She thought of the great lady, a woman she had cared for as an infant, *"Tomorrow, her lady must be informed of many things, and she would suffer the worst of days."*

Chapter 1

The summer of 1934

Limbs of the great Ficus tree bent and whipped as the afternoon squall swept off Biscayne Bay and over *Hurricane Road*. The dense leaves of the Ficus sheltered the men from rain, but only for long enough toss their tools beneath a canvass and run for the house. Covered with the soil of his labors, Asher burst through the kitchen door. Paint speckled his battered hands, linseed oil stained his trousers, and sawdust clung to his shirt and hair. All were glued together with sweat. Reeking of their efforts, the four men shed sawdust and mud as they stumbled into the large kitchen.

"Aw! Cop'n Asher," the cook cried, dropping her mop on the still wet floor wax.

Abashed, George Wallace backed out onto the small porch, crowding John Peter with him.

"Damn," Asher swore, tiptoeing after them, as if tiptoeing would undo the mess.

The rainsquall was a brief one, already faltering. The men stood in the doorway dripping thin brown drops and stared skyward letting the last of it pass.

"Go on, clean up," Asher, told the three Negroes, "I'll see you tomorrow."

"Tomorrow be Fourth of July day, Cop'n Asher"

"Forgot about it," he admitted, and sniffed, suddenly aware of his own odor, and that of the other men crowded on the tiny stoop.

"Be Wednesday den, Cop'n?" Isa offered.

"Early Wednesday," he said and looked up at the sky. "And cover up the boat good before you go," he ordered.

"Be here Cop'n," George said, nodding quickly, the other two nodding in unison.

The rain had diminished to scattered sprinkles. Stepping off the porch, Asher walked around to the front of the house. He wiped his feet, and crossing both the foyer and hall, he tiptoed upstairs, intending to sneak straight into the bath. Corazon Byran waylaid him at the bedroom door. Wrinkling up her nose, She marched him to the hall laundry chute, and stood guard against the household staff as he stripped.

"My God, but you smell," she complained, now holding her husband's clothing between thumb and forefinger. She dropped them into the chute, where they sent up a small puff of dust, adding, "You promised to change in the garage."

"It started to rain," Asher mumbled kicking, off his boxer shorts.

"Inside the garage?" she chided, with a teasing smile on her face.

He pulled his robe around him and padded down the hall to their room. Moments later the water was filling the tub, and he climbed in sighing as it continued to rise. Through the thick wall, he could hear Connie and Angel arguing. He couldn't make out their words, but the tones were enough. A door slammed. That would be Angel, he thought. His granddaughters had been so close. Now they seemed to be at odds over almost everything. Remembering his twin sons, Connor and James, he sighed. The boys had been equally contentious in their middle teens. Twins were unpredictable.

Asher soaped and rinsed, then relaxed before hauling himself out of the tub and toweling. He had dressed and was combing his hair when Corazon returned to the room. Her eyes damp, she stood very still as he turned toward her.

"Mary phoned from *Charleston*," she said sadly. "Poor Kay, she finally passed on this morning."

***

The funeral service ended before noon, and the Byran's *Coconut Grove* home became crowded with many of those, who had paid their last respects to the deceased. Two days earlier a memorial service was held for Kay Byran in *Charleston*, where her mother had cared for her. She had lingered almost six years, since the Great Okeechobee hurricane took her family, health and sanity. Six years, and finally, she lay at rest beside her husband James, and their little boy. Those who knew the story, were relieved to see an end.

On a part of the verandah shaded by flowered vines, a small group of women sat about a table cluttered with plates. A partially filled pitcher of iced-tea rested near the table's center, and the women sipped from glasses as they conversed. Gathered for some time, they had been speaking incessantly. The conversation had wandered from the *Okeechobee* tragedy to gossip concerning the deaths of the remaining Byran sons in the week following. None could claim a full knowledge of the events that had cost the lives of most of what had been a large family, but a lack of facts seldom held a woman's tongue in check.

Angela Byran, a sixteen-year-old daughter of one of those sons, sat in a window seat above them, sketching in pencil. Separated by only eight feet and a flowered trellis, Angel could hear everything said. Frowns began to contort her lovely face, and from time to time, and breathed deeply, indicating annoyance at what was said about her family. It had become difficult to concentrate on what she was drawing, and she was spoiling it. There was nothing to stop Angel from moving away from the window, moving to where she couldn't hear. She knew the spasms of aggravation, caused by listening, were her own fault.

As for the women, Angel was acquainted with most of them, had known them forever. She could picture them below her, conspirators, forming a ring, leaning forward together when one recalled some shocking tidbit, all nodding in unison to affirm the truth of it. Angel's mind formed just such a picture when the elderly Mrs. Pratt suggested that for an entire extended family, children and grandchildren alike, to be taken in the span of five days, it must be the judgment of God. It must be his retribution for a life of sin. Mrs. Roper countered in a hushed voice that such had happened to Job and was Job not blameless. Mrs. Pratt returned, saying, Asher Byran, could in no way, be compared to Job, nor could his eldest son, Fred, who had outdone father in sinful excess.

Angel lifted her head; her youthful face formed an expression of absolute contempt. Had she been older, she might have realized that such matronly prattle intended no insult, that it wasn't even personal. Talk of scandal, scandal of any kind, was merely a means of spicing up the dullness of their lives. It was only a script reading, a role that each enjoyed playing on occasion.

Stiffening with resentment, she placed the drawing board aside and strode across her room to the bathroom door. A pail used for watering flowers sat beneath the sink. It took only a moment to fill it. Perhaps on another subject, she could have expressed what she felt, but on matters concerning her father, uncomfortable emotions filled her. She became resentful because of her ignorance of him, and that resentment overflowed into everything around her. The very fact that she knew so little about him incensed her. It compelled her to defend him out of blind loyalty, for if his daughter did not defend him, who would? The water, pouring down through the flowered trellis, caused a shrill end to all conversation on that part of the verandah.

Several minutes later Angel's grandmother came to her room. Corazon Byran looked rather solemn. She sat down on the foot of the bed, and gazed at her granddaughter with a concerned affection, an affection, which Angel took for, granted.

"What was that about?" Corazon asked. Hands in her lap, she waited quietly for an answer.

Angel pushed herself up abruptly, and tossing her sketchbook to one side, she swallowed in an effort to compose herself. She was quite flushed with the effort of controlling her anger, and she answered in a harsh pinched voice, through trembling lips.

"They were loathsome! The things they were saying about my father and grandpa were ghastly; that God was punishing them when all those terrible things happened and —" Angel was at a momentary loss for words. "They had no right," she ended weakly.

Corazon made the slightest smile, "Well, perhaps God chose to punish them with that brief shower."

Despite herself, Angel allowed a wicked little smirk to form on her stormy face.

"God had nothing to do with it Grandma."

Corazon searched for a way to explain human nature that would be acceptable to the girl. She said, "People, women especially, are bound to gossip, and heaven knows this family's been through enough for tongues to wag indefinitely." She smiled, "And there's a great deal that nobody even knows. We all have our secrets chica, and gossips can only guess at the truth. Now come and say goodbye to your Great Aunt Mary. She has a train to catch, and I want you and Connie with us to see her off."

She hugged the girl, thinking what beautiful young women the twins were becoming. They were identical in appearance but that's where their similarities ended. Constance had more of her mother's nature; she had calmness to her, whereas Angel was restless, owning the same hot temper she had passed to Angel's father. God knows there were countless occasions on which Corazon had given reign to that temper, occasions, which she had often regretted, and she could well understand Angel's outbursts, even if they did make life difficult.

They went through the hall and downstairs, hand in hand, to where Asher and Connie waited with the Calhouns. Together, the Byrans walked with Mary and her husband to a chauffeured car. Corazon embraced her oldest friend, took her hand for a moment through the open window, only releasing it as the car pulled away. They stood waving, and Corazon felt a sadness sweep over her. Mary, like herself, had held such hopes for their children. It had been lovely when Mary's daughter, Kay, had married her son, James. Gone now, with Connor, Pat, Cathleen, May, and Fred. Of all her grandchildren, only Fred's twins survived the tragedies of that terrible week, yet Corazon believed herself blessed with the girls. Poor Mary Calhoun had only memories.

The house emptied of guests, and Corazon went up to her room for a nap. She looked out the window and saw Asher. He was escorting their son-in-law, Chip, and her cousin, Federico, to the back of the garage to show off the big sailboat he was building. Why he was going to all that trouble to build a boat was beyond her. She lay back on her bed, at the edge of sleep, and wondered where the man found all his energy. At fifty-four years old, she was no slouch, but who could keep up with Asher? Corazon stretched, wiggled her toes and let sleep take her.

Down the hall, Constance hurriedly changed from funeral black, into old clothes, and rushed out to join the men. She ducked under the scaffolding, and squeezed up between the ketch's frames, the sort of maneuver that had become far more difficult as her figure rounded out. Climbing up through the hold, onto the deck beams, she sank down cross-legged on the fresh pine, and smiled contentedly. She was her grandfather's favorite and loved to be around him.

She also craved the attention of her stepfather, Rico, but attention from him, was something she had gotten little of in the years since her mother's death. Although Grandpa never seemed to change, her stepfather had become distant and mysterious. Rico had disappeared after mama had died. For two years, no one had heard from him. Arriving back in *Miami*, three years ago, he had immediately hired a crew to demolish the house they had all lived in. There remained, only the empty lot.

Connie had missed Fedrico, particularly with mama death but he had become so reclusive, and she suspected that he had stopped loving her. Deeply hurt, she had wallowed in an agony of adolescent self-pity, but Angel had reacted quite differently. She became irate and resentful over Fedrico's apparent lack of affection. Rico was the only father she and Connie had known and with her mother gone she saw it as another abandonment. Her real father had died before she had a chance to know him, and for reasons unknown, he had abandoned her.

Unlike Angel, Connie's hurt had dissipated, because she believed that Rico loved them as much as before. He was polite and generous, but shared his thoughts with no one, and she was puzzled by these barriers. Fedrico was a mystery like so many mysteries in her life. She determined that one day she would get past the frustrating veil of unmentionable subjects that confused her past. The aggravating phrase, *"Maybe when you're older,"* seemed to apply to almost everything from questions about her real father to going on un-chaperoned dates. On this point, she and Angel agreed. A question from Rico snapped her out of her thoughts.

"For the boat, do you have a good name to suggest, Chica?"

"Lots," she said, "but grandpa's holding out."

"Already have a name for the boat," Asher said, "keeping it secret for now."

Too many secrets around here already if you ask me," she complained.

"A surprise, then," Asher said gruffly. "Give a hand with this tarp, and we'll cover her."

"When will she be finished?" Chip asked.

"By the middle of August, and I should have her in the bay in time for us to get in some sailing before school starts."

"Gee! Two entire weeks," Connie mumbled, sarcastically.

"Quit complaining and haul on that tarp girl. What you expect from four old men?"

"I'd have thought you'd have had a yard build her," Chip said, "Labor's cheap these days."

"I can afford anything I want, but I'm tired of having things done for me," he explained. He anchored one corner of the tarp. "No fun sitting around, paying to have things handed to me. I'm enjoying this; money can't buy the satisfaction of building things with your own hands. It's vanity I suppose but then, what ain't."

Chip tied his end off and dusted his hands. "What's she for, Sir?"

"Whatever I feel like," Asher said.

Connie, who had been helping with the boat's construction since June, felt the need to communicate a territorial claim on it. In addition, she wished to be noticed by Chip, who at thirty-three, was a boyishly handsome man, not at all, what a girl pictured as a widower. She knew Chip had been married to her Aunt, but that was years ago, and she had a crush on him.

"The boat's mine to use," she said shaking the hair from her face and looking up at Chip. She grinned; "I've worked on her, so grandpa said I can take her out when I please."

"You'll drown yourself," Fedrico warned!

"Oh, phoo!" she frowned. "I can out-sail most men."

"In the blood," Chip agreed.

"It is that," Asher said smugly, and tugged on a strand of Connie's hair, as he passed her, and headed toward the house. "Who wants a beer?" he invited.

"Me!" his granddaughter cried instantly.

"No! Besides you," he said gruffly.

"I, for one," Fedrico said.

"I'm a taker."

Following them across the yard, Chip paid some attention to Connie. He had not seen her since she was eleven, and lord, but she reminded him of his wife, Cathleen. Connie was about the same age as Asher's daughter had been when they were engaged, so much alike that it unsettled him. In the house, he drank his beer and looked at his watch. It was four fifteen.

"I've got an hour to catch the *Havana Ferry*," he announced.

"You're welcome to stay over a few days," Asher invited, "plenty of room, son."

"Thanks, but I've business in *Havana*."

"I'll have Shawn run you to the ferry."

"Didn't he just leave with the Calhouns?"

"Dam'd! You're right! I'll drive you myself then," he said standing.

"I'm coming," Connie chirped, "and I'll drive."

"In that case," Fedrico said, with dry humor, "I'll stay and smoke a cigar."

Chip rode in the back seat, and at the ferry dock, shook hands with Asher, promising to visit more often. On the deck of the ferry, he thought again of his wife, children, and the hurricane. It had been the worst day of his life. Besides himself, Kay had been the only survivor, if the broken shadow could ever have been thought of as a survivor. Now she rested with all the others, and Chip did not care to be reminded of what he'd lost. Fred's daughters were also reminders to him, reminders in more ways than their resemblance to their aunt. Perhaps, he thought, his father-in-law's advice was good. Asher had told him it was time for him to move on, to marry again. Six, years, it had taken to overcome his guilt. It was time to deal with his loneliness. He was young. It was time to make a new life for himself, but not with a reminder of the old one.

Chapter 2

It was an unusually bright summer morning, clear of tropical haze and no rainsqualls loomed over the bay. It was almost fall like and quite agreeable for a launching. A fair-sized crowd had gathered to see if Captain Byran could build a boat that would float. Acquaintances, family, and local fishermen were gathered, some to watch, some for the food and drink. Hansen's tractor backed the boat down the ramp. Once the trailer was submerged, a small motor-launch made fast a line to the ketch's stern and waited with its engine idling. Connie, bottle in hand, waded out onto the trailer.

"I christen you, *Constance*," she cried brightly, and swung the Champagne bottle against the iron wood stem.

Even though encased in wicker, the exploding bottle of champagne doused her. Some of the crowd cheered, some laughed. George Wallace waved to the little towboat, and the *Constance* was dragged stern first into her element. Within moments, the little ketch nudged the work dock, and the launching party gathered around the tables of refreshments, which were set out under the palms.

A fruit punch, well laced with rum, proved to be more popular with the women than wine or lemonade, but both outlasted the beer. Angel, who had managed to slip a bottle of wine into her carry bag, would have preferred the punch, but her grandmother had been watching it like a hawk. Connie was the one with a taste for wine, but Connie would never dream of taking a drink without permission. This circumstance helped Angel to filch her bottle, because in Angel's case, the wine had not been considered a temptation.

Angel reclined in the damp shade of the dock, drowning her sour humor with a perfectly clear conscience. Her justification lay in her view of fairness. If a boat was to be named *Constance,* a second boat should have been provided to bear the name Angela. She felt absolved of all guilt by this flimsy defense. She ignored the fact that she considered sailing a bore, and that she had refused having anything to do with the construction of the ketch.

Angel plunked the cork into the bay and sipped at the wine. She looked down the aisle of creosote pilings that reached out between the moored boats. Her mind drifted; she watched crabs darting in and out of holes in the coral riprap. A gush of water driven by a hand pump aboard the *Constance* drew her attention to the voice of John Peter, who was driving the pump. Her mind focused and she became aware of the voices of the old men on the boat above her.

"Whole bottom's full of water. She leaking serious."

"She' is doing fine," George Wallace said. "Jus' need little while ta swell, dass all."

"This boat leaking pretty bad, that all I am saying."

"Dom fool, when you ever see some new boat, didn't leak some water till she swells up?"

John Peter's reply was mumbled, lost in the pump wash. Angel half listened while taking another sip and getting a bit of cork in her mouth.

"Doan see why rich mon like Cop'n Asher, he is building a boat as poor as this.

"What you saying? This here a fine boat."

"What I were saying is -- that Mon can have what boat he wants. I see dat big boat he sells. Now that were de boat for ah rich mon, not this poor thing."

"Oh, that was a fine boat, and that be de truth. There was de time when Cop'n Asher, he took pride in that boat, but at de end, it got full wit' de misery, full wit' de spirits -- That boat was swelled with blood like this one here be soaked with water. I was the fella that were sent ta fetch her home, you see. She was laying down there in Key West, and I tell you, Mon, I spend four day working ta clean de blood from that boat but never get it all. Bullet holes and scraped paint on every part you see. Up de river here, de boat yard, they work de whole month on that boat. Makes her purdy again, but de Cop'n, he never goes aboard it no more. He jus' sell de *Flyer* cheap and put from his mind how he boys die on that boat."

"Oh mon, I know de story, but talk were dat Cop'n Fred and he brother, dey killed on de *Silhouette.* Hear Cosme Fuentes there; hear that Cop'n Asher there too."

He laughed, "Nemine John Peter. You's a fella that didn't hear de right story. On dat night was de whole clan: Byrans, Vegas, O'Ryans, Costas, yes, all them and most a Fred's boys. Three boats you see, they leave ta get dose lil' girls -- they took three boats ta Veradero, but dere were two boats that didn't come back. Sunk and burned, and all those fellas what were killed and wounded, those boys end up on de *Flyer* you see. They leave de childs in Cuba. Dan Tully, he run de wounded boys to Key West. Doctor there, he takes care those fellas. Fred and Connor, they buried them here wit' de rest of de family, all buried on de same day."

"What that got ta do wit' building dis here boat, that's all I am asking?"

"Oh, dat's ah poor question. Cop'n do it 'cause it please him, why yo' think fool?"

The pumping continued, and the conversation shifted to the matter of how best to rig the mizzen backstay. Angel had quite forgotten about her wine. She had listened to the old men with rapt attention, and now her mind was a confused swirl of thoughts.

"Who were Tully and Cosme? Who were Fred's boys? Had George really meant it, that literally her whole family had been involved in some mysterious incident, an incident in which boats and people were shot to pieces, and her father killed?"

It was about little girls. Had her and Connie been the little girls old George had spoken of? Cold chills ran over her, and her skin prickled. She recalled shadows, tried to make sense of nightmares she had once had, blurs of terrifying images, visions of which had never held any sort of reality for her. She knew about their kidnapping and mama's murder, but this story was different. Were the girls they spoke of her and her sister?

Not feeling at all well, Angel scrambled from the shade of the dock, and began to walk toward home. What could be so terrible, so terrible that it had never been spoken of, and to this day was still not mentioned? She spent the remainder of the morning in her room trying to decide what it all meant and what she would do, but she was too tired to concentrate.

She was in fact, infected with a form of exhaustion brought on by the possession of too many unrelated facts. She had information but not enough, and she had no knowledge of how one thing fit to another. Without the necessary clues to resolve her mystery, she could only think in circles.

***

Early afternoon, Angel awoke from a troubled slumber, disturbed by a dream she had not had in years. In a half-panic she sat up, instantly deciding to tell her twin what she'd overheard. She went directly into the hall; the door to Connie's room was open; the Victrola was playing. Angel stood in the doorway, her face furrowed from sleeping on a corduroy pillow. Connie sat on the floor sorting her record collection. She glanced up.

"I figured you'd be in bed all afternoon."

"We have to talk," Angel whispered, and closing the door, she went to sit beside her sister on the floor.

Connie's face took on an expression of acute concern, for Angel neither looked, nor acted herself. Turning off the record player, she leaned forward, and taking her sisters hand, she squeezed it for emphasis as she spoke softly.

"What's happened? There's nothing wrong with you, is there?"

Angel's lips quivered. She fought to control, a lump swelling in her throat as the confusion of her dreams mixed with the revelations of the day. She had the feeling that everyone she loved and trusted had conspired against her. She felt they continued to conspire, and to hide a terrible secret, a secret that concerned both her and Connie. Now that she was here, she couldn't seem to express her emotions in words. Instead, tears formed, filled her eyes, and began to run down her cheeks, and then Connie was crying too, though Connie had no idea why. Twins were just that way, sharing emotions in ways that others could not begin to understand.

After several moments of sobbing, Constance pulled herself together enough to ask an all-important question. "What are we crying about?" she sniffled, while pushing back from her sister.

Angela wiped at her nose. Her tears began to recede, and the ghost of a smile began to form on her face. "I'm not completely sure, but I've lots to tell you," she said.

They both sniffed, facing each other, each seeing a mirror of her face, and both faces puffed and blotchy.

"Oh, Connie, everyone has been lying to us," she began. "Something happened, something years ago that no one talks about, and we're part of it. Maybe it's all about us."

She had said it, and the relief of saying it calmed Angela. She looked into her sister's eyes, the mirror of her own.

Connie's expression held both shock and curiosity. "What's it about?" she gasped.

"I overheard George and John Peter talking," Angel said, and proceeded to repeat the entire conversation. She confessed that just thinking about it had caused her to have bad dreams.

"They said Grandpa and everybody?"

"George said Fred's boys, and the whole clan, so I suppose he meant all the men, and why would grandpa's boat be there without him. Three boats to Veradero, but only the *Flyer* came back.

"I always wondered why grandpa sold the *Flyer,*" Connie said absently, perplexed. "What did you dream about?" she blurted suddenly, and when her twin told her, an odd, cold prickle ran up her arms, for the dreams were faintly familiar.

A period of silence spread between them, as each sorted out a jumble of partial memories. They heard the sound of a vacuum humming somewhere and a clatter of pots and pans in the kitchen. A dragonfly chose that moment to fly against the screen. Startled, both turned to look.

"I don't remember ever having that kind of dream before mama died," Connie said gravely. "I've never remembered the kidnapping, but I do remember the smell of ether. Do you remember the ether or when the dreams started?"

"I remember Grandma and Grandpa hugging me. That was after the first nightmare," Angel recalled. "We must have been at Uncle Roberts because we went to find Grandma on the beach."

"It was early morning and remember being sick to my stomach," Connie said, after a moment of introspection. That's the first time I remember having that kind of nightmare."

"What if the first time was real?" Angel gasped, somehow making an intuitive leap. "What if the first time it wasn't a dream?"

"That's stupid," Connie said, not about to be persuaded to accept such an outlandish possibility. "You're not being rational; there was nothing that made any sense in the dreams."

"Then explain to me why we both dreamed about the same things," Angel said, in her most tedious tone of voice.

The inscrutability of the question did not disturb Connie. "Because we're twins," she said irrationally.

Angel's initial impulse was to argue, but she and Connie had shared too many unexplained incidents of an extrasensory nature. She could not argue effectively or in good conscience. Restless she stood and looked out the window.

"What if we try to find out what happened, really find out? I don't believe the ransom story's true."

"You're right," Connie agreed. "We should find out why everyone lied, but how?"

Angel plopped down on the window seat and contemplated the difficulties they faced. It was human nature, she concluded, for people to talk about something if it wasn't a secret. If people could be convinced that they already knew about what had happened, they might talk about it. She explained the theory to her sister. Connie was putting her records back in a box.

"Grandma and Grandpa are too smart to fall for that. What about Uncle Robert?"

"I believe we'd have more success with somebody outside the family," Angel said with a simple logic.

"Who"?

"Like if we could find out who Cosme or Tully were—"

"How would we find them," Connie interrupted, and stood smoothing her skirt?

"Ask somebody who knew them — like John Peter."

"What would you ask him?"

"You know him better than me."

"I wouldn't know how to even begin asking him stuff like that." Connie peered at their images in the mirror. "You do it," she wheedled. "You're sneakier than me, and he can't tell us apart anyway,"

It was at moments like those that these Angel became suffused with exasperation. She hated it when excuses were thrown up to avoid doing unpleasant things that were merely inconvenient or awkward, rather than difficult. She was often guilty of the same thing, but in the mad struggle that was youth, she failed to perceive that this trait was inherent in her own being.

"You're so immature," she complained. "Think about it. Look at your hands. You've been working like a coolie all summer. One glance and anyone could see the difference."

Self-consciously Connie inspected her hands, resentfully aware of her scraped skin and short nails. When compared to her sister's smooth hands and flawlessly manicured fingers. There were those moments when she saw, quite clearly, the disadvantage of being something of a tomboy. Angel took a malicious pleasure in pointing it out.

"Well, all right, but you'll have to help me," Connie said. "I can't just come out and ask."

Chapter 3

The following morning, George Wallace was painting the masts, a job he could do quite well with the one arm, an irate husband had left him. John Peter was rigging the bobstay, a job best done with two arms, or more, if available. Connie assisted by handing him tools and materials.

At the fish dock, four men were hoisting a turtle onto a dolly. John Peter paused in his work, peering at them.

"It's awfully big isn't it?" she said, standing for a better look.

"Dat green turtle there would only be average back in de old time. When I were a young fella, I sail wit' de turtle fleet. Big turtle then, he go six, seven hundred pounds. Now they call one big if he go five, you see and that uncommon."

"Were you a captain?" Connie flattered, and sat on the gunnel cap facing him."

"No, Missy. Weren't no turtling cop'n. I sail wit' some pretty good cop'n, and I tell you, it takes many years to learn dat business. Long time necessary to become proper cop'n of a turtler. Got to know each reef and rock on de banks. Got to know the waters from *Yucatan* to *Limon*, know it like their own hand, so they kin feel each wrinkle in the dark of the night." The old man sighed. "The *Sponish Coast* be ah hard place, I tell you missy. Easy to die there. In '94, we comes up to *Key West* on the *Martha Stoneman,* to kraal our turtles. I like the place and I stay on, you know, and I'm working wit' a crew out from Saint Pete. They go about de turtling altogether different on the Florida Coast and the money better. Some mons, the use a net between boats, whiles others peg the turtles."

"What's pegging mean?" the girl asked genuinely curious.

"Use a long thin pole wit' a barbed end. Flange so it don't go deep in de turtle. Harpoon them and pull them in or tie a barrel to them iffen you hurried. Sometimes mon jumps in and get hold de shell behind the neck, put he knees low in back, and swim them up to the boat. Good money taking eggs on the beach also, both green and loggerhead.

"Are all turtles good to eat?"

"No missy. De green is de one for good eaten, but the Hawksbill it valued for its shell. Pay up to twelve dollar a pound for Hawksbill shell. You see, there is a season for turtling though. April to May and egging till September be best. Then things get slow. Lotta work and small money in that fishery in the off-season you see. My dotty, he taught me, say to go where the money is to be found, so I leave that work. Went to wrecking in '95 and was working for Cop'n W. Smith."

John Peter smiled and concentrated on his work. The port chain was attached, and shifting his bony frame around, the old man stretched himself out over the bowsprit and grasping the dangling chain, passed it to the girl.

"Tie that off to the Samson post missy."

Connie took the chain and gave it a wrap, and he inched backward over the stem.

"Grandpa did some wrecking once." Connie said, sitting back down. "He had a man named Tros Banks, who'd been a wrecker. They salvaged a ship right off Eliot Key once, I think, in 1899."

"That were about de end of the rich times for de trade you know. Hand me those pinchers," he said and mopped the sweat from his brow. "All those navigation lights, you see, they took the danger from passing through de Straits. I going to sponging round that same time you know. Mon couldn't feed himself on no wrecker's share," he said pushing his straw had down on his head, and he grinned showing off several gold teeth and a few black ones. That de first time, I was de cop'n of a boat. Oh, there were some fine fellas in de sponge boats, and some fine preaching. Was god fearing mons, back in the old-time sponge fleet, but that all gone now."

"Why?" she asked, never having thought about it.

"Dom Greeks, that why. Dom Greeks!" he repeated as if it was a nasty word, and then he spit over the side. "They ruin the beds wit' those diving rigs. Trample the beds stomping round wit' lead boots; kill the young sponge while they is harvesting the mature sponge.

"When I begin in the trade, I was on dis forty-ton schooner. Sail up round St. Marks and we is fishing, two mons in a small boat. We use a glass box to see down. One mon, he sculls and de other use dat fifty-foot pole to pick the sponge up there. Off Tampa and south, find de grass sponges. Call them Anclote sponge, and they bring the high money. Small boats harvest in the keys, but de quality ain't so high down dere."

"How long did it take to get a load of sponges?" Constance asked.

"Big boat up to three months, missy. The little boats, two week or so."

"You stayed at sea all that time," the girl, gasped. "Weren't you bored?"

"That why dey calls it work and not play missy."

"Still," she began.

"Nemine," he said. He spit over the side and took up his story again. "We rest on Sunday. Sing hymns, listen to some preaching, play a little tag," the old man smiled. "Was a God fearing" mon when I was sponging."

Connie's mind fastened on the word tag. The notion of grown men playing tag seemed silly and beginning to giggle she said as much.

"It be good way as any for men to pass de Sabbath," the old man defended. "Mons gets them self's on some lil' beach and run round, stretch out some. Get away from de smell a those dere sponge. They smell rotten.

Married me a woman in 1904, and she did not care for me being away on long trips, didn't like smell ah sponge so on me. I went to working for old Walt Smith. He had a camp at *Flamingo*, and shot birds for feathers, leastwise 'till he killed de warden. The warden was a fine young fella, name a Mr. Guy Bradley. Smith, he blames it on this farmer name of Watson. This Watson fella, he gots a bad name up there in the *Thousand Islands* -- Being, I is just ah nigger, they doan care what I saw or what I's knowing, but I gets away from all that right quick, though. Stretching of the legs be better than stretching de neck. He, he, he -- I goes to work, building on the Keys railroad then. That was about de same time, you grandotty, he was working his tugs on that very same project. Afor long Cop'n Asher, he gots three ship bringing cement for old

Mon Flagler. I am knowing George there from dose days. Then he were working on de steam tug *Bull*. George there was up to no good even then you knows." John Peter glanced up at George and winked slyly at Connie.

George, who was now painting at the base of the main mast, gave John Peter a hard look.

"Take care what tales you's spreading," the one-armed man warned, a peevish look contorting his face.

"Ain't no tale that you's was boating hooch to the construction crews."

"Just because a thing be true, it don't mean it needs telling," George complained. "There's a lot of telling I could do, telling that you's don't find so pleasant I think."

"But that was when liquor was legal," Constance said, both surprised, and searching for a way to keep them on the subject instead of niggling at each other.

"Railroad was law then and they say no spirits out there. George there, he sneaks it for a good price. He, he, he! Dam'd near get himself caught too."

"Why'd they forbid liquor?" she asked.

"Most mons they get out there is lazy no counts and drunks. They got whiskey, they don't do no work."

"Had good crews by and by," George said. "Then the hurricane a 1906 tear the place up. Blow the quarters barges out to sea and drown the mons who is on them. That was an October storm and four, maybe five hundred mons be swept to sea.

Half those, they lost. Captain Asher, he lose the old *Margarita* in that storm." George shook his head solemnly. "Good friends gone there."

"The sea, she doesn't give no nemine one way or other," John Peter remarked.

"Amen to that," George mumbled, and finished with the foremast, he moved aft to paint the mizzen.

"What happened to you in the storm?" Constance asked.

"I was at home, safe on the shore. Bein spared the destruction a that storm, my woman say, *'twas a warning of God'* — nemine what he warning of, he, he, he. Got to working on some dredge aftah den. Stay wit' that 'till aftah de war when de old woman, she passes on. Then long come prohibition and de good times." He said this smiling broadly, "Oh yes, missy, those were the best ah my days, the best days of my life."

"I heard so many keen stories," Connie said, seeing her chance to direct the conversation. "My father was a bootlegger, and he even took us on his boat once," she lied. It was called *Silhouette,* and a man named Cosme told Angel and me, it was faster than all the other smugglers' boats."

"Now that were the truth you's heard. That boat, it were very fast. It run fifty-six knots on flat water, you know. I was on her when she do it."

"I didn't know you worked for father," Connie lied, trying to act surprised. "You must have known Cosme and Mr. Tully, then."

John Peter's brown eyes lifted from his work to search Connie's face.

"What you's know bout all that missy?" the old Jamaican asked, his lips pushing out to form a sour frown as he questioned her.

"Oh phoo," she said, and giggled. Then leaning forward, she confided in a low conspiring voice, "We know all about father and grandpa being smugglers. All grandpas' people were in that trade one time or another."

"That so? and you's know all that?" the old man asked, suspiciously.

"Of course, and I know all about the big shoot out too. You know, when they went to rescue us. Do I look too dumb to remember what happened to me, what went on in my own life?" she asked, with a trace of sarcasm. "After all, we were there, weren't we?"

"If that the case," John Peter said, feeling a trifle uncomfortable with this subject. "Jus' never heared you say nothing about it."

"Were not supposed to tell anyone, but you already know," Connie said, feeling she had him snookered. "It's been so long ago; I don't see why anyone cares."

"Six year not that long a spell. Seven year be more-better, fo' de law must leave ah mon 'lone aftah seven year here but dat not de case in *Cuba*."

"I know, but I would like to thank them someday, for helping us I mean. Where does Cosme live now?" Connie asked, wearing a truly innocent expression.

"Gimme that marlin," John Peter said, pointing.

Connie handed it to him. His hand searched his baggy pants for a serving needle, and then patted his shirt as he looked down at the deck. He found it stuck through the pocket of his shirt and squinted to thread it.

"Here! Give it to me," she said. Reaching, and quickly pushed the marlin through the eye. Smiling, she passed it back, all the time considering the perplexing business of searching out Cosme Fuentes in the sprawling suburbs of *Havana*.

"Dey got some hard mons in *Cuba*, and these not the best a times there. Bad politics there. Dose fella, dey get hot, and nemine about a mon's life. You's see what some Sponish fella, he done to George there? Cut he arm off. Me, I never go back that country no more."

John Peter's eyes appeared sad.

He's old, Constance realized, old and alone. She wondered, did everyone become sad and fearful when they grew old, but her youthful thoughts were too involved with other things to dwell long on old people's state of mind?

"Got things to do at home," she announced suddenly, and stepped on the dock.

The boat rocked slightly, and John Peter looked up from his work, saying, "take a care missy."

"See you later," she called over her shoulder, and hurried toward where she would find her sister.

Chapter 4

Tuesday, following the launching of the ketch, Asher received a telegram from Gibbon MacArt, announcing that he'd be in Miami the following day. Captain MacArt was scheduled to take one of the Biscayne's ships to sea in September, but Gib had taken the train down from *Jacksonville* to advise his long-time friend and employer that he was resigning. Gib, had begun employment as an able seaman on the *Miss Fay,* and had advanced to mate and captain. Thirty-six years is a long time for one man to be associated with another, and the two had shared a good deal of life together. Each held the other in great respect.

They spent the evening at the *Surf Club* discussing MacArt's plans, a cargo venture which involved a regular run to *West Africa* with a newly purchased steamer. Asher mentioned that his friend would not be seeing much of his wife on a run like that.

"The woman's forty-four," Gibbon groaned in mock misery. "She's eight years younger than I am, and y'all think she was the elder," he laughed. "She expects me to set home and twiddle my thumbs. Hell, the woman has me pulling weeds, can y'all believe it. Besides, I'd ruther see more ah the world afor the fool politicians get us in another war."

Asher, who was more than full after fine meal, leaned back and stretched. He signaled a waiter for more coffee and let a part of his attention drift to the fight. A ring had been set up in the center of the dinning-room and two fighters were dukeing it out while the club members casually ate their dinners at ringside.

"It doesn't appear as if anything serious is going to happen tomorrow," Asher said absently.

"That depends on what piece of dirt y'all standing on."

"How's that?"

"If the troubles at your door, ya take it serious; if it ain't, well then, it's just gossip and rumor and far away to boot. Y'all know, well as me, the world's shrinking; aircraft, and bigger, faster ships."

"It's not serious yet," he said, as the waiter poured coffee.

***

Gibbon frowned. "Japanese are nibbling at *China*, the Italians at *Africa*, and the Germans will be back to the old game if that new chancellor has his way. I spec they got a right to be peevish, considering the bad deal they got handed at the end of the last war. Really cut a lot of that country away. Well, to the victor the spoils, I 'spose, but bad treaties don't keep the peace."

"Yes, to the victor the spoils, you're right. Without a just peace, it becomes easy for extremist like Hitler to gain power. Even if he is all mouth, he can still stir up trouble."

"Germans like being told they're superior. That Hitler's tells 'em what they like to hear. It's a good way to start."

"We're all like that," Asher said, grinning. "But if they begin another war, I'll be at home in my rocker. In my lifetime, I've had ships sunk under me twice.

That's more than enough to teach me, war's bad for ships and sailors. The only thing war's good for is holding the population down."

"My opinion, another big one's coming and sooner than later. Little revolutions, and a lot of old squabbles in the world — countries are picking sides again. Y'all mark my word, be another big war soon, always was wars, always will be. "Gonna be my boys in the thick of the next one."

"Where are Alan and Grey getting to these days?" Asher asked.

"Both at sea, Grey graduated in May. He's Ensign aboard a destroyer. Alan, he's still on the *Philadelphia*. He's made Lieutenant JG."

"Must suit them."

"Suits Alan, but Grey's another matter. Boy never had much patience with fools or fool rules. Hear the boy talk, Navy has too many a both."

"I had a taste of stupidity in the Army, myself. It does get under the skin. He may learn to live with it even if he doesn't like it"

"Time will tell and speaking a time passing, your granddaughters must be in blossom."

"They are that, and I expect the storms to blow in any day. Both of them, pretty as can be, and when you got real beauties, there's bound to be trouble. He yawned and stifled a sigh, thinking, time was flying, and it was wearing him down. Time grinds away at a man, same as the sea does to the coast, only faster.

"Tired?" Gibbon asked, feeling drowsy himself.

"Past my bedtime, old and lazy," he yawned.

"Could use a smidgen a rest myself."

Asher placed money on a plate bearing the check. Rising to his feet he asked, "Will you stay the night with us, Gib?"

"Thanks, but no. I'll put up at the hotel next door." He stretched and rubbed his eyes, "I have an early train to catch."

"Keep me filled in, about your venture, that is."

"I will," Gibbon promised. "Have y'all and Cori up this spring perhaps. Clare would like that. Do some hunting. Whatcha think?"

"Sounds good," he said as they shook hands.

The men parted at the front entrance, Gibbon going next door for a room, while Asher waited for his car. Gib MacArt would be close to fifty-one, Asher figured. The man was showing his age, Clare too. Will, everyone aged but the dead. Those who passed on were suspended, ageless, in the livings mind.

His thoughts went to his children, good looking young people. Cathleen had been a beauty at twenty-four and the boys, strong and handsome. May and Pat, all those who died young, always the same in his mind. He pined for them more as time passed, and he grieved for all the little ones. He sighed. Wishing for things dead and gone that was a sign of old age. Not hard to imagine how life might have been.

As a valet held the door, Asher smiled, and climbed into his car. His eyes were teary and he wiped at them, feeling that he was being pitiful. Ashamed, he pulled himself together, and told himself that the present held enough joy and misery for any man; he must leave the past buried, and the what ifs unconsidered.

He pulled out onto *Collins Ave.*, southbound toward the county causeway. Twenty minutes would have him at home. Tomorrow would present its own problems. He and Cori were due to leave for *Cuba* and at the last moment, the twins were insisting on making the trip to visit their Grand-aunt and Uncle before the start of school.

Angela's wanting to go didn't seem remarkable to Asher, but Constance had been so involved in getting the ketch ready that her interest in the trip did surprise him. Well, the two had been cozy for the past few days. They were back into that twin sister closeness. It calmed the house down when they were getting along, and it would make for a pleasant trip if they maintained the peace.

He enjoyed the company of his granddaughters. They were a striking pair. A few weeks short of their seventeenth birthday, they appeared much older when they chose to dress and act maturely. He had always taken a pride in the good looks of the Byran women, and the twins were true beauties. He intended to run off any riffraff that came courting. When it came time to choose husbands, those two would mix with the best. All but retired, he had vowed to scrutinize the young men who passed his door.

"Grandpa's home," Connie announced as Asher came through the door. "It's getting late," she warned he sister. Clothes cluttered her room; some outfits lay carefully folded in matching luggage, others were draped across the bed. Moody, Angela wasn't sure of what she wanted. Her indecisiveness was making it difficult to put together matching outfits for the trip. "Make up your mind," Connie gasped in frustration.

"No, you choose."

Connie quickly separated their things into two piles and placing them in the suitcases said, "We'll wear suits tomorrow. You wear the navy; I will wear the tan. And don't be so glum about what might have happened. Whatever the truth, it was bound to be hushed up. No one wants a scandal in their house," she said cheerfully.

Angel walked back to her room. A visit to the newspaper had left her exasperated. Research had seemed an expedient method of obtaining the information they sought. Attempting to discover the truth by reading old articles had turned out to be an improbable method. She now felt quite naïve for having approached the problem in that manner. The concept was ostensibly logical. She had merely to go there and read about it all. What she found was a great deal about the *Okeechobee* tragedy, and an article on her family's great loss in the hurricane. Another short piece was about the death of her mother in childbirth, a childbirth complicated by injuries received while defending her daughters against kidnappers.

Angel had also found the usual stories, the reporting of other crimes, murders and robberies, and a large piece covering the funeral with a picture of twelve caskets, some of them tiny. Angel had buried her face then, overcome with emotion at the thought of her mother fighting to protect her and

Connie. Her mother had died trying to protect her, yet she couldn't remember any of it. Angel had blotted her tears and abandoned the downtown office of the Herald. She arrived home tormented by more questions than she had begun with, and her mood had remained sour all evening.

Before climbing into bed for the night, Angel laid out the navy-blue suit and matching shoes, she intended to wear the following day. Determined that she would regain her positive attitude, she turned out the light, and with heavy eyes, put the entire situation out of her mind. When the nightmare came, she began twisting and whimpering. Shapes filled the dark. There was the distinct odor of liquor and hands touching her where they should not.

When the light came on, she was huddled in her bed with the sheets clutched around her. Her heart pounding and her breath was short.

"I felt something wasn't right," Connie said softly.

"I dreamed someone had me," Angel said, her voice shaky with fear, for even with the light on, the vague images lingered.

Connie crawled into the bed and hugged her. It was comforting, and her heart began to slow.

"It was awful," Angel whispered.

"I know," and then after a moment, "it frightens me, too."

"I thought yours went away."

"I lied," Connie, admitted. "They went mostly away," she confessed. After a pause, she said, "I'll sleep here."

"Good!" Angel closed her eyes and took a relaxing breath. "Together we're safe," she told herself and she felt the tension melt away.

Chapter 5

Her first waking perception was light filtering through Connie's hair. Her next was the realization her nose tickled unbearably, for her sister's hair lay across her face. She sat bolt upright and sneezed. It was a wet sneeze.

"Oh·God," Constance swore half awake, "you sneezed on me." She wiped her face vigorously, "I'm all wet," she complained, in a squeaky voice.

"I'm sorry," Angel said contritely; your hair was in my face." After a pause during which they looked at each other in a half stupor, "Thank you for spending the night with me."

"It's okay."

There was activity in the house, and a smell of frying bacon rose from the kitchen. They looked at each other for a moment, and then both lunged for Angel's robe. Connie being the quicker snatched it away and fled into the hall, shrugging into it as she ran. Clutching a sheet to her and swearing like a sailor, Angel chased after her laughing sister.

It was a quarter past eight. The cook had already taken the Byran's breakfast up on a tray, and Grace stood in the big kitchen, while Delia fried up some eggs for her breakfast. Another pot of coffee perked on the stove.

"My goodness, what smells so good?" Connie cried, sailing into the kitchen.

Grace was about to speak when Angel burst in, snatching at her sister's hair with one hand, the other holding the sheet that covered her.

"You thief," she hissed.

"Possession's nine points of the law," Connie teased, dodging to one side, only to trip over a chair.

Her twin was on her in a flash, and the two rolled laughing on the kitchen floor, pulling at each other's coverings, little that there was.

"Oh, gawd but y'all ain't the least lil' bit like no proper young ladies I ever knowed," Grace spat. "I never saw such carrying on and cutting the fool and you's coming from fine people. Get up now," she ordered, "and stop that pulling at each other for some man comes by here and see all that makes you's female. Git up now for I use the broom on you's."

Grace did use the broom, and the two did end up seated at the table, where they sat smiling over coffee with milk. Delia broke several more eggs and Grace sat down to eat with the girls, as well as the cook and the house cleaner, for the Byran household was a very casual one where help was concerned. Corazon found the twins a short while later and shooed them up to get dressed. There was a train to catch and no time to spare.

The run to *Key West* lasted five hours, and their Pullman car rolled onto the train ferry before dinner. The girls slept through the switching in *Havana* and woke a half hour before their train pulled into *Matanzas*. Robert O'Ryan's driver was waiting with the big Bentley, and he had them out to the estate for breakfast.

There was so much happening during the day that the twins had no chance to make plans before late in the evening. It was past ten before relatives and Uncle Robert's other guests departed. By bedtime, they were exhausted. Even so, Angel wanted to discuss the best way of getting to *Havana* and the *La Ceiba* district. What Cosme Fluentes might tell her was becoming an obsession -- it aggravated her that Connie was caught up in the gaiety of the day. She babbled about a bit of scandal she'd seen.

"I saw Uncle Robert with Aunt Rita's secretary," Connie giggled. "He had his hand in her dress. I saw them just as he kicked the door shut."

"Do you think Aunt Rita knows?" Angel whispered.

"No! If she knew she'd dismiss Mia, wouldn't you?"

"What good would it do?" Angel said. "I think Uncle Robert is the kind of man who thinks of all women as fair game. Half of the servants are probably our cousins."

"That's nonsense," Connie said, acting shocked.

"He's fifty-five -- I'd have thought he would have lost interest at his age."

"I suppose some men never do," Connie said. "I know grandpa certainly hasn't. I can hear him and grandma sometimes," she said grinning.

"That's disgusting," Angel huffed.

"No, it's not. I think it's sweet, really romantic when old people still have those feelings for each other, and grandpa would never be unfaithful to her."

"That's only because she'd kill him," Angel said vindictively.

"That's not the reason, and she would not," Connie defended. "I'm going to sleep."

Angel lay quietly for a few minutes before speaking again. The comment was pure mischief. "I wonder what grandpa's mistresses were like," she said casually.

"He didn't have any," Connie said derisively. "Go to sleep."

To look down on her sister, she propped herself up on her elbow. "Are you sure?" she asked.

Connie refused to be baited. She pretended to sleep.

Angel considered tormenting her twin further, because while faking sleep, Connie would be too stubborn to acknowledge her comments -- She could be teased at will. Angel's heart wasn't in it though. There was nothing to be gained, so she curled up and began devising excuses to be taken to Havana. Eventually she fell to sleep.

***

On the following morning, uproar filled the house, for Rita had discovered her husband in the intimate embrace of her secretary. Immediately she sent the unfortunate young woman packing. Angry voices echoed through the halls. This was followed by slamming doors and pounding. Muffled voices and bickering drifted from Aunt Rita's dressing room. Angel and Connie were not as ignorant of life's little scandals as their grandparents chose to believe. They hurried onto their bedroom terrace to hear what was said.

"What did you expect of me," Rita shrilled, "to allow that creature to remain in my house, humiliating me before my friends, my other servants? You might have at least had her elsewhere or paid for a whore like any other decent man. Instead, you've played the lecher in our home; worse, you've seduced my most personal employee.

"Don't act so sanctimonious," Robert, growled, "no one would have noticed if you hadn't set that old watchdog on me. Of course, I relish my little conquests. Such women exist for a man's pleasure. A man marries a wife to provide children. Rita my dear, are you interested in, or capable of, bearing more children? -- No? Well, I'm sure you have no desire to please me for the fun of it either."

"You're a disgusting goat," she shrieked, with sufficient vigor to shake the walls.

There was the sound of china breaking, the slam of a door and Robert chuckling as he walked down the hall.

Connie glanced at her sister knowingly, "See!" she whispered.

Angel wondered if men were like that naturally, or if they became that way only after their wives spurned their attentions. Perhaps it happened both ways. She contemplated this while she dressed. She had to change again after grandma came to the room. Corazon announced, for obvious reasons, plans had been made to visit their great aunt Esmeralda's home for a day of riding. Angel's mind went rapidly to other things.

At the Vega Estate, there were well over twenty automobiles. Esmeralda's youngest son, Estefan, loved fast cars, often participating in impromptu races on the open road. He was admittedly a playboy, who suffered no guilt in leaving the family affairs in the hands of his brother, Douglass. When Connie showed her admiration of a fine British sports car, her cousin had handed her the keys, and told her to enjoy it. Angel's eyes grew large as Connie started the engine. She climbed into the two-seater alongside her sister, her mind beginning an immediate assessment of distance, time, and acceptable excuses for being gone all day. She and Connie looked at each other knowingly, their minds in tandem.

"I don't have any money," Angel said.

"I do and we've a full tank," Connie informed her.

She revved the engine and eased off on the clutch. The Austin Martin leaped out of the garage. It was doing well over sixty when it passed the main gate. Connie saw her grandmother and great aunt; they were approaching the gate on horses as the car sped past the stable. She pretended not to notice them.

"See if you can find a map," Connie said, as she swung out to pass a sugar cane truck. "We need to think up something really good for being late."

"Well get the car stuck in the dirt on one of the side roads. We'll say we got lost, and then got stuck," Angel said, for she had already thought it out. "They expect women to do that kind of dumb thing; nobody will be suspicious."

The car was flying. Connie smiled and nodded in agreement. Angel knew Connie was having too much fun to give thought to what might happen later. Angel found a map in the glove box and studied it. "Take the coast highway," she shouted over the wind.

"Isn't it farther?" Connie asked, slowing as they approached a fork in the road.

"Yes, but after we're past *Matanzas*, the ocean is on our right the whole way to *Havana*. We can't get lost."

As Connie swerved right, she glanced back to the map. The road went straight through the sugar fields. It began to curve near town, then crossed the *Yumuri River*, skirted the city and swung west along the coast.

Sun and heat waves rose from the black strips of asphalt as the car flung itself past the relative stillness that lay to either side. Up one hill, down another, bright grass, yellow green, high palms bent to the sea breeze, and the sea itself glowed brilliant aqua and purple blue to the north. They tore through villages, past people on the roadside -- beings that did not seem to exist in the same realm. Other cars blew by -- blurs of hot colored metal, as separated from the earth as they -- fellow adventurers, borne on different missions, on and on.

Connie felt a spiritual release, as if free of constraints, she was hurdling toward truth. Her old world seemed far behind, and new things loomed mysteriously ahead. These concepts were shapeless abstractions, pure emotion, but she sensed them in her twin as well. They had neither consulted nor asked permission, and in making this leap, consciously choosing a path, they had become their own persons -- For good or ill, they were choosing the direction of their lives.

Angel drowsed, and soon *Cojimar* swept past, *Havana* and the bay appeared over the many-colored houses of *Casablanca*. As the road wound south into Regla, traffic slowed, and they became hemmed by heavy trucks and oppressive heat. Waking, Angel peered at the battered ships and dirty water of the inner harbor. As she opened the map to search for road signs, she wrinkled her nose at the odor of sewage and waste. Moments later, she pointed to the turnoff onto the *Central Highway*. The *Central* crossed a bridge and *Luyano* lay off to their left. In *Cerro*, they became confused, and Connie pulled off next to a small market to ask directions.

Young men conjugated; they gathered around the car, whistling, making appreciative comments, comments about both the car, and its gorgeous young occupants. Angel though animated by the attention, found she was also uncomfortable. While an old man gave directions, a darkly handsome youth made a bold suggestion to Connie and touched below her ear with the back of a finger. Tossing her head to one side, she angrily named him for a crass pig, and tires spinning gravel, she accelerated up the street.

Inland, the intensity of the blue sky was cut by smoke and dust. It shimmered a pale yellow near the horizon; white clouds floated over purple shadows. The poverty shocked Connie. She could see Angel viewed the cardboard and tin slums with a similar astonishment. Coming off the river bridge into *La Ceiba*, the neighborhood improved, and the two shared a silent relief. On a side street, the car bounced and swayed where rain had created ruts and potholes. Estefen's car creaked and groaned, causing Connie to slow to a crawl.

Their mood of exaltation had dwindled away by this time, and pulling over near a neat walled residence, the twins looked at each other with a vague disquiet. The thrust of their action had been to reach *La Ceiba*. Now, having actually arrived in the district it appeared larger than they had expected. They had developed no plan for finding Cosme Fuentes beyond asking directions to his house. Several minutes of animated discussion developed three possible solutions: the phone company, mail carriers, and asking after him in the plazas where old men gather for dominos and the sports talk. The telephone office provided three numbers without locations, but with no hesitation, a mail carrier directed them to a house a block from the river. With absurd ease, they had managed to locate Cosme Fuentes within three hours of leaving Vega land.

Connie coasted to a stop a hundred feet from a gate in the house's wall. It was a stucco wall, ten-foot high, embedded with broken bottles along its top. The neighborhood to the west was a good one, but the area to the east, backed against the river swamp and was poor. The house and its expansive grounds were once an expensive residence, but now sat only on the border of respectability. Two cars parked adjacent to the gate. Against the wall, neighborhood boys pitched coins toward a chalked line. Two young men, who had been watching this game, now shifted their attention to the sports car.

"Just pull up, say we're here to see him," Angel said, impatiently urging her sister.

"I'm nervous."

"Do it before they come over here," she hissed. Her voice was low, and her words spoken with nervous rapidly.

"Alright," Connie said, frowning. Letting the car roll forward, she pulled up alongside a parked Buick and smiled sweetly.

One of the young men, startled that such beauty had arrived at his door,

strolled toward Angel's side of the car.

"*Señorita, en que puedo servirle?*" he asked.

"*Soy extranjera,* 'I am a stranger'," Angel smiled sweetly, and continuing in Spanish said, "Can you tell me, is this the house of Mister Fuentes?"

"*Si señorita.*"

"Cosme Fuentes."

"*Si Señorita.*"

"*Usted Conoce El Señor Fuentes.* (You know him)?" she said brightly.

"*Mi tio.* (My uncle)," he announced.

"*Buen,*" she squealed. Can you tell him, the daughters of an old friend have come to visit?"

"His name," the young man said, both curious and polite.

"Byran," Connie interjected from the far side of the car. Señor Fedrico Byran O'Ryan.

"Aahh," he said, quite familiar with the name, but unsure of the circumstances. "Park the car there," he indicated. "It will be watched. Alberto," he called to the other man." Tell my uncle *Las Señoritas* Byran have come."

Connie pulled the Austin against the curb beyond the old Buick, and Cosme's nephew opened Angel's door, helping her out. He then ran around opening Connie's door almost before she could get it herself. The young man had thought them beautiful in the car, but out of it, they appeared goddesses. He could only stare. The sisters wore riding attire with high-heeled boots, chic outfits that gave them a lithe sophisticated look. As Connie stepped past the man, she realized she was taller. It suddenly occurred to her that she was tall even without the heels.

"Thank you," Connie smiled, as he closed the door.

"The pleasure is mine Miss Byran." Permit me to introduce myself. I'm José Fuentes Perez."

"*Tanto Gusto,* (so much pleasure)," she answered. I am Constance, and my sister is Angela."

"Twice a pleasure," José said with a foolish grin. "This way ladies," he said, motioning toward the gate.

Inside was a large yard overrun with small children, and in the back, laundry billowed on the breeze. Cosme waited for them on a second-floor terrace. As they approached, the old man rose from a wicker chair to greet them.

"*Muchachas, vuestra maravellas de mi dias* (girls you're the wonders of my days). Your father was my employer and my friend; I welcome you to my home."

Angela spoke first, naming herself and Constance. Connie thanked him for receiving them without warning.

"It's nothing," the old man said briskly. Sit, please, and may I have *refrescos* (drinks) brought for you?"

"A coke would be nice."

"I would prefer a beer," Angel announced sweetly.

"José see to it," Cosme barked.

He peered at them even as Connie gave her sister a piqued look concerning the beer, which she now wished she'd asked for.

"Beautiful children become beautiful women," Cosme said. "Your father would have thought you such," he added.

"Your kind," Angel told him.

"No! It is truth, Constancia."

She giggled, "But I'm Angela," she corrected.

"Who could know," he said gruffly, his eyes rolling. "You are the same."

The drinks came and as they took them from the tray, Angel said, "We came to thank you, sir, for helping to return us to our family, and also," she said, getting straight to the point, "to beg a favor."

"It's been years," he said, waving it off as nothing. "I was but one of many and your father was my patron. My good fortune came through him, and as his children, you were my concern also." Cosme paused, "Now!" he said in a hushed voice, "you speak of a favor."

"A private thing," Connie said, her eyes flickering to José, who stood at the door.

Cosme thrust out his lower lip, tilting his head. "José, should you not be at the gate?" he asked.

"Yes uncle" the young man said and moved reluctantly from the room.

Connie noticed for the first time, a large pistol, worn under his jacket.

"The two of you have stolen his brain," the old man chuckled. "There are women who can destroy men with a smile. You are such women and you are double. Be aware of this," he said with a sage seriousness. "It is a serious responsibility; you must bear it. Now this favor," he prompted leaning back in the wicker.

The twins glanced at each other and began speaking at once. Connie, who was blushing slightly at being described a siren, began to laugh, and Angel plunged ahead leaving her to listen.

"You know we were quite young when our parents died, and we knew almost nothing of our father. Very few in the family knew him since he was a boy, and we have the hope that you and others who knew him well could help us to learn more about him. We are curious about the man he was, and about the life, he chose. We're curious about how he lived and the events that caused his death. *Por favor puede dicerme,* (please can you tell me)"?"

"And you are old now?" Cosme chuckled.

He smiled, took a sip and sighed, thinking, "*it was always so with the young ones, the hunger to learn the secret things. They believe that to know a man's history is to know a man's heart.*" *Cosme doubted if there were many persons, who knew their own heart. And, truth, what was truth? Truth was a different thing for each person. There was nothing Fred's daughters could be told, but very much they could not understand.*" He would speak. After all, it was a small thing to tell of the past, and old men were more comfortable in the past than the present, anyway.

"I can speak of those things I know," Cosme offered, after a brief moment of silence. "Some things you may have heard, but then you will hear them twice," he said. He gave them a gap-toothed grin and reached for a cigar already burning in a tray. "Your father had only a few years more than you when I first knew him. He was tough, a hard man for one so young, and a sly fox. Fools did not live long in our business. He was also a man who kept his mouth shut about his work. He was also quick to judge the character of other men. This is a gift. Because of these things, he survived and prospered when many did not."

Cosme puffed his cigar and launched himself into an explanation of how the smuggling trade was conducted, with highlights concerning Fred Byran and the dangerous events that at times threatened to finish him. With pleasure in his voice, he related how his boss had duped both the competition and the Coast Guard, seldom losing cargo, and never giving up a paying passenger. Cosme showed anger at the loss of a boat named *Shadow* to a Navy destroyer. It was not fair to hunt businessmen with a war ship. The boss had understood it to be unfair. He had not held the loss of his best boat against its captain. Finally, he explained that their father had grown rich but tired of bootlegging, he had begun to separate himself from the business. He began to sell the boats and became a club owner. This was in the last year or two, Cosme explained. His great friend, Tully, he was gone, mostly to *Miami*, and your father began to enjoy other things, to travel more, to court a respectable woman.

As Cosme's cigar dwindled and as he lit another his narrative faltered. The girls had devoured every word, but they knew little more about their father than before. They had acquired facts about him, and facts the things he had done, but nothing of his reasoning, or inner being. Nothing a daughter could hang an emotion on. Both wished to know about their father, not about the things he did.

"What did he do for enjoyment," Connie asked, not posing the question properly for what she truly wished to know.

"Has not your family spoken of those things? I remember — was he not close to his family in *Cuba*? I know he played the polo, and he was among them often."

"The family was divided over him," Angel said, "Because of my mother. He didn't want a wife and family. Mother finally remarried."

"I suppose he disliked women," Connie offered.

Cosme chuckled then laughed deeply, a laugh that became a cough. When he controlled it, he spoke with amusement in his eyes.

"Your father was very attractive to women. He spent much of his time with them; he enjoyed women but had no sympathy for them. He had no respect for a woman who did not stand up to him. He could be very cruel with his women, and if they were weak or foolish, he made them suffer. Such is often the case with young men, for to them a woman is a prize, a thing to be acquired, to be played with like a fast car or a good horse. Men often believe a woman should be used, enjoyed and kept in her place. Your father had many pleasures; women were one of them."

Cosme noticed the twins shared a disturbed expression, perhaps a burgeoning resentment. He wished them to understand how it often was with men. Some became responsible with women only after many years, some never. Later they would learn. As women, they would suffer because of a man, suffer like all women; perhaps someday they would understand. For now, they could at least hear.

"You are upset. I see this. I tell you about myself. I tell you, so you can learn of life. You are young; the young suffer from life, women more than men. May I tell you?"

Both nodded; Angel's face held a trace of impatience.

"I became a man with less than your years; it was on the coast near *Mariel*. I cut cane, I fished; I had my eye on a handsome young girl who was respectable. I would dress myself well and walk past her with my hat pulled down; I held my head low, so she could not recognize. I ignored her, which made her curious for pretty girls are accustomed to receiving attention. Because I paid her no attention she came to wonder why. Courting is a game you see, played in different ways in different places, but always a game. For humans, life is full of tricks.

At a fiesta, I kissed her, and when she did not run away, I went to her house. I spoke with her father. I had a place but only a mat and a log for a pillow. Carlota Suarez Montanya, she was named. It was the custom in my village for the parents of a girl to provide things for their daughter, and they brought a bed, table, stools, and a cabinet. For the yard, they provided chickens, and a pig. We were married in the chapel behind the church, and I took her twice before the sun set."

Smiling at the memory, Cosme poured rum and drank a little. He said, "You think I understood love — No — Carlota, she was a good girl who did as I said, cooked and gave me pleasure when I wished it. I got her with child, and she was proud and loved me. Carlota understood love. To a woman, the love of her man is everything. To a man, you see, a woman and love is only a small part of life.

When the Revolution came in '95, I left her alone, one infant in her arms, another life within her. I fought the Spanish with Gomez. War is an adventure; men will choose war and death over the love of a living woman. It is our nature. Sometimes I thought of her and missed her company. Alone, she starved, died in one of Wyler's reconcentration camp.

I married another woman after the peace. This was in *Regla*, when I worked the docks. In those days, I gambled. I had many women then and treated her badly. We fought much, and she cut me here," he said pointing to his chin. "She loved me very strong though," Cosme, explained, "Yet to me, she was only a handsome woman, who belonged to me. I did not understand love. Clara was my wife for three years before she got with child. She caught me drunk then -- in bed with her sister, and hung herself where, in the morning, the neighbors would see and understand it was my responsibility — I suffer a great guilt for it, a greater guilt than she — no matter what the priests say."

Cosme crossed himself, drank rum. The girls sat frozen, totally still, Connie with her arms wrapped around herself. They looked much younger to the old Cuban now.

"With Margarita I have ten children, and over thirty grandchildren. I was thirty years old when her brother took me to the Perez house. I was not a good man, but I had suffered guilt, I knew loneliness. In a year, she became Margarita Perez de Fuentes, and soon gave me a daughter. I had learned love was a state in which one thinks first of another. This comes to a man when he forgets to be selfish."

Cosme leaned forward in his chair, and the wicker creaked. A baby cried in a room downstairs, but he paid it no mind as he gazed at the pair. Like seeing double, he thought. Beauty causes much pain and these two they shared true beauty. The clear green eyes were not usual, and the old Cuban tried to remember if he had known anyone with those green eyes.

"A proverb," he told them, still leaning forward, *"The Devil is not wise because he is the Devil. He is wise because he is old."* He leaned back against his chair, said, "Wisdom, most often it comes with mistakes and age. Your father was not a saintly man, nor was he evil. Toward the end, different things had become important to him. He was, I believe, a man who was forgetting to be selfish. To save you, his children, he spent much of his fortune and gave up his life. He did this without hesitation."

Connie's eyes teared, "He really loved us then?" she said in a weak voice.

"Who can know another's mind, Chica? Still, what father does not somehow love his child?"

"But why were we taken," Angel blurted. "We know it wasn't for money," she said. "Why?"

Though both twins were touched with emotion, Angel was obsessed with the need to know what had taken place. She wanted the dim specters haunting her dreams revealed, exorcized and the veils of secrecy parted, so she might see the truth, understand the reasons behind the lie.

Cosme looked thoughtful, adjusted himself in the chair; "You have asked your people this question?" he said cautiously.

"No!" Angel said resentfully. "We know they wouldn't tell us."

"But you expect it of me?"

"We had hoped it, sir," Connie pleaded.

"There are reasons --- when truth is not revealed — perhaps the truth is not known — perhaps — this truth is too dangerous to be known."

"But it was so long ago," Angel argued.

"Six years child, long ago for one so young, but yesterday for us old ones," Cosme looked out the window thoughtfully. A little would not hurt he told himself. "You will not repeat what you hear?" he cautioned. "People would die. People you love."

"Only to someone, who already knows," Angel promised.

"We'd be very careful," Connie, added, "never a word."

"Okay. I will tell you a story, but I do not know the whole story. Only dead men know this entire story."

A cat had entered the room. It pushed itself against the old Cuban's leg, and he leaned over and picked it up. He placed it in his lap; stroking it absently, he began to speak.

"Men — who knows their names, they were hijacking boats in *Florida Bay*. With his own well-armed boats, your father went to catch them at it. We followed a boat going north, waiting to see if the hijackers would try to take it. They did. They were shooting it up good when we surprised them. When we finished with the hijackers, we boarded the boat they had assaulted. It was not full with liquor, but full with children, many of them wounded. A ruthless man would have left them. Even a wise man, he would have left them, but your father would not see children die. He sent some to a hospital and took others to a safe place. The crew of this boat was dead, and the family of these men, they believed it was your father who killed them. Your father, he retired, he quit for this business sickened him. The family owning the boat with the cargo of children, they wanted vengeance but were stupid. They thought your father responsible, Thought your mother was still wife to your father. When they killed her, they also took you. It was a thing of vengeance. You were given to a powerful man. You were to be made whores as an insult to your father. That it was all because of the mistakes of careless men — that meant nothing. Could your mother be given back her life? No. You could be found though, yes, and he began to search."

Cosme could see the shock in the faces of the girls. "Good," he thought. Perhaps they would see that life was neither simple nor just. Young girls should know that life can be dangerous and cruel. Young girls should be cautious. The cat yawned and stretched in his lap. He scratched under its chin and continued.

"Your father's secoundo, a bold man and friend named Tully, he discovered who took you. With the men of your family, Tully followed by sea, with your grandfather and uncles from the north. I came from the south with your father's men. We took the ship you had been placed aboard, but you were already gone. On shore that night, many men died to discover where you disappeared. The grandee, to whom you were a gift, this man, he was far too important. He was not a man who would give you up. For him you would have caused embarrassment. Your father understood that you would be secretly killed. Your father, he was no fool when it came to such matters.

The old Cuban coughed and sipped rum, to loosen his voice. "Many men came, all the men of your family, and all those who had been employed by your father, hard men. By force, you were brought home. It was not a fight, but a small war, with many killed on both sides. Even the Cuban Army became involved, and we were lucky to escape to sea. People important to the government were killed and wounded, but it was made to appear the responsibility of *insurrectos*." Cosme leaned forward, disturbing the cat. "You see the need of the lie. These are not things one relates to small children. You are no longer small children, though. *Es Verdad?* 'Is truth'? If truth were known, many of us would be hunted to the death, and your family held responsible" the old man said, a note of warning in his voice, "You now bear the weight of many lives. I and my children are in your hands."

The twins, both subdued by what Cosme had told them, nodded in a sort of stunned acknowledgment.

Connie, the first to find her voice, thanked him.

"How did he die?" Angel asked.

"An artillery shell, one of many fired by the army. He and your uncle together, it struck almost as the *Silhouette* crossed the reef. They spoke with each other until death took them. It was not a bad death, I think."

"I still don't know my father," Angel whispered, more to herself than Cosme, "How he was."

"Only Tully, I think, knew him. They had become true friends. Dan Tully, he lives across an ocean since that time. On an Island to the west of *Inglaterra*, *Ireland* it's called."

The cat rubbed his head against Cosme's wrist, a reminder he was to be petted, but instead the old Cuban pushed him gently off his lap. He glanced at a clock, seeing it was nearly three in the afternoon.

"Where have you come from," he asked the now quiet twins.

"*Matanzas*," Connie said.

"Alone, you came from *Matanzas* alone?" he worried. "It's becoming late, and there could be road blocks. Batista, the pretty mulatto, he still hunts his old friends. It is not good for young women to be without the protection of family men."

"But we have a car."

"Even worse," Cosme said irritated.

He walked stiffly into the hall, calling for a Gerardo, leaving the sisters looking uncertainly at each other, while he disappeared into other parts of his house. Connie was for the first time becoming apprehensive about being so far from home on her own. Now that she had succeeded in doing what she had set out to do, she worried about the possible trouble she could be in. That, and the level of Cosme Fuentes' worry, led her to suspect a drive across sixty miles of *Cuba* and through the districts of *Havana* might be more hazardous than she had realized.

"Where'd he go to?" Angel asked in a hushed voice.

"How would I know?"

"We should leave, but I need to use a lavatory first."

"So do I," Connie said impatient with both herself and her sister. "Just wait."

"I can't," Angel, said fidgeting. She had not even noticed the pressure while Señor Fuentes was talking. It was just there when he left the room.

Moments later Cosme returned with two older men, introducing them as Gerardo and Carlos. These two would drive to *Matanzas*, and the girls would follow closely. If they departed now, Cosme explained, they would make the drive before dark, even with the traffic.

Angel asked if they might use the lavatory first, and Cosme had one of his granddaughters show them the way.

Gerardo took the *Carretera Central* East, and the trip was uneventful. Connie grew tired outside the city, and Angel drove. She stayed close behind the Buick, her brain attempting to sort out what she had heard, while her emotions made her too confused to think. She wondered how her sister could sleep at a time like this. She wished she could sleep.

Three miles from the Vega estate, Angel blew her horn to attract Carlos's attention. She pulled off the road. The Buick stopped and backed up to where Angel was causing the sports car's tires to spin themselves into the loose sand on the roads shoulder.

Stupefied by the girl's actions, Carlos leaned out his window, and called, "*Que Pasa?*"

"An excuse," Angel explained, shutting off the engine, "For not returning home on time. We'll need a ride now," she added opening her door.

Carlos grinned, gleefully at Gerardo, shaking his head. He got out onto the road, opening the Buick's rear door for the sisters to get into the backseat. The sun was low, almost below the mature cane that lined the road. It was also hot, for the cane blocked the wind. "Young girls are sly," he whispered leaning toward his friend. He grinned again. "I will remember when my own daughters return home late."

Esmeralda, accompanied by one of her housemaids, came out to meet the strange car. She made a fuss over the girls and thanked the men for bringing them from their disabled car. The women were already entering the building when Asher returned from his search.

Chapter 6

School began two days after the twins celebrated their seventeenth birthday and continued through the fall without an interruption due to hurricanes. Angela had never cared for the structure of school or the duty of learning according to the expectations of others. Mathematics and the sciences, all subjects that Constance mastered brilliantly, Angel detested.

She believed that individuals should be educated in the things that interested them. What Angel enjoyed was literature, philosophy, history and the arts. She like foreign languages and was a hungry reader, who had devoured the classics as a child. In the past few years, Angel had attacked histories, political philosophies, and books discussing human functions: sociology, psychology, and relationships.

She had behind her bookcase, *The Complete Manual on Human Physical Relations,* by: Everhart and Price, a book which she had read several times. Not everything stated agreed with what other experts wrote concerning sex and psychology. So diverse were the opinions that it was like trying to reconcile the teachings of the Catholic Church with those of Brigham Young, or Buda. She knew that eventually she would have to deal physically with the subject which was more frightening than on an intellectual basis. She found the physical mechanics difficult to imagine as pleasant, but romance novels helped.

Angel had reached a plateau during the summer, a point where the confusion of viewpoints exhausted her. In the fall, numerous sought-out books lay unread and neglected in her room, for lately she had been reading poetry for pure pleasure, for its rhyme and flow. Why should she burden her mind with contradictory information concerning the world and herself? There were too many theories she had no way to prove. At least not without experimentation, she was unprepared to attempt experiments involving physical relationships.

She often envied Constance, whose choice of curriculum at school gave no cause for self-doubt. There was little confusion in science; calculus is straight forward, and physics is anchored in irrevocable law. Avoiding the debate club, Connie opted for sports, tennis and softball. On those occasions when Connie joined friends for picnics and softball or went riding, she was at her happiest. Connie, unlike Angel, took a simple uncomplicated view of the world, and when confronted by a problem or contradiction of life, she was usually quite willing to let time clear the thing up.

For instance, after reading the same sex manual as her sister, she had frustrated Angel's attempt to discuss the subject by saying, "Gee! Ask me after I've tried it. This answer may have been practical, but Angel wanted to know ahead of time. Somehow, she just needed to know; for Angel there was a security in knowing.

This had been the problem when they had returned to Aunt Esmeralda's estate. Connie had learned enough from Cosme to satisfy her curiosity. She remained a little curious but felt the rest of the story would come in time. Angel could not rest without all the facts. Despite her better judgment, Connie had let Angel push her into more intrigue.

Uncle Robert had gone to *New York* on business, a tactic that allowed time for Aunt Rita's wrath to dissipate. Unable to question him, Angel had insisted on approaching their cousin Estefan. When questioned, Estefan had gazed at them in a quizzical manner, and asked what they were talking about. Connie backed off, but Angel, ever impatient, pressed on trying the same tactic with Douglass Vega, only to get a scolding when she awkwardly broached the subject of *Veradero*. He refused to speak with them during the remaining day of their visit. Connie had counseled Angel to keep her mouth shut after Estefen's reaction, and as a result, Connie became indignant when her twin aggravated their cousin, Douglass.

"I suppose you're satisfied," Connie had snapped.

Angel glared back in frustrated outrage, then mumbled, "Oh go squat." She had stomped out into midday sun, walking toward the stables. She knew her sister was right, and had wanted to apologize, but her pride wouldn't allow it. Of course, they had continued to talk about the past, and though they continued to be intrigued by the story Cosme Fuentes told them they'd also been frightened by the ruthless violence of it. The lack of detail gave run to their imaginations, concerning not only what did occur, but also what might have. After the strong reaction of their cousins, they were subdued to the point that neither saw any point in approaching their grandparents.

Angel suggested they try to get something out of Uncle Chip, but Connie had argued that according to Cosme Fuentes, only Dan Tully knew everything. She later suggested they find his address and write him, but Connie considered the idea idiotic and refused to discuss it. Angel became discouraged and unable to agree, they did nothing.

Soon the routine of school and the distractions of an active social life absorbed even Angel's attention. Their interest in the past temporarily receded. It resided at a level reserved for projects such as essays and term papers, important things, but things which could be dealt with later. This was their senior year, and for the first time, un-chaperoned evenings with groups of friends were allowed. Even double dates were possible.

***

With the repeal of prohibition, the mid-thirties were wonderful years to be young in *Miami*. Evening entertainment blossomed; all the big bands played in *Miami* and dances were held everywhere. The twins were out on the town, wearing heels, and lovely gowns, dinning, dancing, and even sneaking a few drinks. It was rich and romantic. Everyone, it seemed, was wealthy, but then *Miami* did have more millionaires than any other place in the nation.

When they shopped, Corazon took them to *Lincoln Rd.* where chrome and marble fronted stores provided for the discerning rich, and sleek limousines lined the palm-shaded curbs. Champagne was served while gowns were modeled. When accessories were shown, it was one by one and on black velvet frames. Each establishment vied with its neighbor to supply the finest. Cost was never a consideration.

Here, the casual observer would never suspect the nation was locked in a great depression, or that a substantial portion of the population lacked food and shelter. It wasn't noticed that jobless men deserted their families and took to the road in search of work. To the twins, the depression was only a word. Poverty was an abstraction, an article in the paper, a voice on the radio. It lacked reality. Blue bloods, gangsters, movie stars and sports figures peopled their world. A mix of wealth and fame that rubbed shoulders at Hialeah racetrack, bathed in the warm surf, dined, danced, and played roulette at the many casinos. Miami was an exciting party, a party where the world's rich came to play and be entertained.

Even though the twins spent every moment out of class being entertained, they somehow managed to keep up with school. They were both bright and good students but, as twins, found occasional advantage in taking each other's exams. Angel and Connie soon discovered advantages in addition to taking each other's exams: boys could not tell them apart.

It all began as good fun when they swapped just to see if they could get away with it. By thanksgiving, they had begun to switch dates frequently. Often the twins exchanged identities before leaving home, and occasionally, while on a double date, the switch was made by a simple exchange of clothing on a trip to the lavatory. It became more than a good joke, it was often a favor that one twin could do for the other, or even a practical method of comparing notes on boys.

The major difficulties in their social life stemmed from restrictions imposed by their grandparents, particularly their grandfather. Asher kept his eye on them constantly. They were always chauffeured, and the driver kept watch. Being alone with a boy was nearly impossible. Even worse, it seemed, the most exciting boys were the ones grandfather most frequently discouraged. Grandma could be fooled, but grandpa seemed aware of every infraction to the rules, almost a sixth sense. Angel was twice confined to the house for being caught drinking; Connie, once, when she was sailing on the ketch with a freshman from *Miami University* and arrived home past dark.

Contrary to her nature, Angel had apologized meekly on both occasions, but Connie was defensive, complaining that she had been becalmed. Her grandfather told her that she knew dammed well, the wind fell off at sunset, and besides, one boy is not a double date. Asher gave her a week at home to remember. The Bryans had no real problem dealing with local schoolboys who wished to become involved in their granddaughter's lives. Their problems started with a young man.

Chapter 7

During the Easter holiday of 1935, *Miami* was assigned the liberty port for three U.S. Navy destroyers. Ensign MacArt received an invitation to the Byran home within an hour of his ship's arrival in port. Five years past, Grey MacArt had gone off to *Annapolis* as a beanpole, seventeen-year-old. This was his first visit since. The broad, athletic young officer who knocked on the door could hardly be recognized as the boy who had last visited the Byran home. The housekeeper answered the door and escorted Grey to the garden. Asher and Corazon were playing croquette. It took Corazon a moment to realize, who the young man was.

"My goodness, Asher" Corazon exclaimed, and leaving her husband standing in the middle of the yard, walked directly towards the young officer. "Look at this handsome thing that dragged itself ashore?" she said. Smiling, she gave him a motherly hug.

"Welcome back to *Miami* Grey, and back to *Hurricane Road*" Asher said, approaching and extending a hand.

"Good to see you again, sir," Grey said, firmly shaking the older man's hand. "It's swell of you to have me here. Five years is quite a stretch'

"Come, sit down," she invited. I have lemonade, Grey, or would you prefer wine.

"Actually ma'am, a cold beer would go down really well if you don't mind."

"Not at all, we have plenty cold in the fridge," she said, and started for the kitchen.

"Make that two," Asher called after her as he plopped down onto a large rattan rocker. He indicated the chair opposite his and said," take a load off son." He paused as Grey sat, then continued. "What's this, your old man tells me that you don't care for navy life? Was it just the academy you disliked, or does that destroyer your aboard leave something to be desired?

Completely unprepared for such a direct inquiry, Grey's answer was somewhat vague. "The work's okay sir; it's the system that frustrates me. Most of us come to terms with it. I'll just have to wait and see how I do," he said and smiled.

"Well, if you don't — uh — come to terms with it that is, you can count on a berth on one of my ships,

unless your daddy grabs you first. By the way, how is
—"

The sound of squealing tires and a horn interrupted Asher. Car doors slammed, almost together, punctuating the sound of two irritated feminine voices, voices that drew rapidly nearer.

"That'll be the twins," Asher said, wincing." They tend to disagree quite often these days."

The voices of the girls became clear as the front door opened.

"You said you would, and now after I've made all my plans you're, backing out," Constance complained angrily, as her footsteps rapidly ascended the stairs.

"That was last year, and I have every right to reconsider," Angela called after her, in an annoyingly pleasant tone of voice.

Corazon, who was walking brusquely toward the French doors with a tray, called to her granddaughter, "Angel, come, you'll never guess who's here."

"Should I try to guess?" she called back, as she approached the door.

Though the Byrans had been mildly surprised at Grey's change in appearance, the solidly tall young officer was pole axed when he saw the twin. The girls had been gangly twelve-year-olds on his last visit. The young officer, now a veteran of academy social life, had in his short career also caroused in more than a few seaports. Though he was far from being a shy lad, few would have guessed it from the way he reacted.

Grey gawked. He was unaware of it. He rose abruptly from his chair jarring the adjacent end table.

Unconsciously, he smoothed his uniform as Angel approached. By chance, the sunlight framed her as she walked onto the patio. To Grey, she appeared animated, golden, somehow both wholesome and siren. The soft honey hair that flowed past her shoulders, shared the translucent glow of her lightly tanned skin. Grey's eyes focused first on her lips when she smiled, warm, pink orange, and then on the sparkling green of her eyes. Whatever she said was fine because he didn't hear it anyway. For the moment, he was deaf and dumb.

"Grey, your beer," Corazon's voice pierced his moment of trance-like preoccupation.

He turned, reached awkwardly for the bottle, misjudged the distance and knocked it sideways. Very quickly, if not adroitly, he snatched it from midair. Unfortunately, the rapidity of action caused foam to spray from the bottle, wetting his uniform.

"Sorry ma'am," he said apologetically, "clumsy of me." His eyes darted back to her granddaughter, and suddenly, schoolboy shy, he couldn't even meet the girl's gaze.

"Oh! That'll stain," Angel, gasped, grabbing a towel from the back of a chair. "Beer will make a mess of your whites. Here," she offered, stepping close to him, "let me blot some of that out for you." Slipping a sideways glance at her grandmother, she asked," Why didn't you say Grey was going to visit?"

"Your grandfather never mentioned it", Corazon answered tersely.

"Didn't know until today," he said, and then it slipped my mind."

While this short exchange of words took place, Grey's gaze slipped downward, focusing on Angel's breast, now partly exposed as she leaned forward blotting the beer from his blouse. His head jerked to the side, and though he smiled sheepishly at Asher, the image of two perky young breasts and a nipple burned into his memory.

"Will you be in port long?" Asher enquired.

"Sir?" Grey answered. He was wretchedly hoping his host had not noticed him looking down his granddaughter's dress.

"Will you be in port long?" Asher repeated. "If you're going to be in port long, we'll plan something."

"I have the mid-watch tonight, sir." The faint scent of perfume and Angel's nearness was making concentration difficult. "Uh, after, uh after that I'm free for two days," he stammered.

"Perhaps he'd like to go dancing," Angel suggested, glancing up, drawing his eyes to hers.

"I'm keen for dancing," Grey said hopefully.

Recognizing Angel's blatant hint as a ploy for possession, Corazon replied, "I'm sure Grey will have some suggestions. Now, Chica, go tell your sister we have company. Go!"

"There's some on your trousers yet," Angel indicated placing the towel solidly in his free hand. If you'll excuse me I'll be back in a jiff," she promised, and flashing back a quick smile, she left the room.

"Perhaps we could go to the club later," Asher suggested. "I'll have Shawn run you back to your ship, or you can take one of our cars if you'd prefer."

Asher took a swig of beer, looked up at his wife, who was pouring herself a glass of wine. He grinned;

the young man was obviously smitten. It had taken Angel about five seconds to be-dazzle the young officer, not that it would have taken Constance any longer. Asher had only lately begun to realize just how attractive his granddaughters had become too young men. Hell, they were very attractive to men in general. The thought of them going away to college unsettled him, but he had been a parent long enough to recognize the limitations of the office. A parent was similar to a modern-day potentate; he had a great deal of influence, but very little control over his subjects.

Grey finished dabbing at his trousers. He straightened and placed the towel neatly across the end of the table. As Corazon turned toward him, sipping from her glass and he said, "You know I really do enjoy dancing."

Meanwhile, upstairs, Angel opened her sister's door without warning, but only wide enough for her head. Connie, undressed except for panties, stood in the bathroom stuffing her hair into a shower cap.

"You could have knocked," she said snappishly

"Sorry," Angel lied, "but Grandma said to have you come down right away".

"I'm almost in the shower," Connie complained, managing to imprison the last golden strands of her hair.

"She said right away," Angel, insisted, barely managing to keep from giggling. Closing the door, she hurried a few steps to her room, where she applied a touch of her favorite perfume. A glance in the mirror reassured her that everything looked fine, and she ran back out into the hall, just as Connie emerged wearing a robe and slippers.

The sisters descended the stairs together, Connie, remaining silently aloof, choosing not to speak to Angel.

"Don't you want to know what's up?" Angel said, setting her up for the, 'you would not listen to me', defense. As they crossed to the French doors, Connie continued to ignore Angel, and she timed her words for the moment her sister stepped onto the patio.

"Well, we're to have a guest with us for a few days, "Angel said innocently. She sped up, moving ahead of her sister, and over her shoulder added, "Grey MacArt is here; his ship is in port, Grandpa's asked him to come by."

For once, there was no doubt concerning which twin was which. Connie, in robe, shower cap and fuzzy slippers was appalled at being seen this way, particularly by a very handsome young man. Too late to retreat, she made the best of it, and while appearing blithe, inwardly, she seethed with fury toward her sister.

"My goodness, Connie you needn't have come down this directly," Corazon told her granddaughter.

The touch of disapproval in the comment gave Connie even more reason to loathe her twin. She colored and began a nervous laugh but checked herself. "Angel surprised me with this Grandma." Turning to Grey she smiled and pulling off the shower cap, pushed her hair over one golden shoulder. "A good surprise though. Gee, we haven't seen you for so long," she said, not able to control the blushing.

"Well, I've got a few days," Grey said, becoming less tongue-tied, faced with a bathrobe. "We can all catch up on each other's adventures. Boy do I have some sea stories," Grey boasted, as he began to loosen up.

"Suitable for young ladies," Asher asked?

"Mostly" Grey replied, as his eyes returned to Angel, who now stood holding her grandfather's arm.

"Please excuse me. I was about to get under the shower", Connie explained, searching for any avenue that might offer a quick escape. "It won't take a minute and I'll be back down," she said already moving toward the French doors. Upstairs, she yanked off the robe and turned on the water, holding a hand in the stream until the temperature suited her. The hiss of the water, the hot barrage of droplets against her skin, released the angry tension. The soreness of her mood rinsed away, leaving her normal good spirits and sense of humor in place. Constance left the bathroom, toweling herself, and sat nude before the mirror of her dressing table, brushing out her hair. She applied a touch of powder to her face, only enough to dust the shine from bathing, and then chose undergarments and a sundress from her wardrobe. In her improved mood, Connie found the prank pulled by her twin amusing; in fact, she saw it as an excellent excuse to exact just payment with a stunt of her own. Revenge could be yummy.

Stepping into a comfortable pair of sandals, she left her room, and descending to the patio, found the others in a round gathering of rattan furniture. Their faces were warm and relaxed. Corazon was relating to Grey the details of the week spent with his parents over Thanksgiving. Constance took a seat next to her sister, and soon joined in the conversation, laughing and reminiscing with the others.

The air cooled suddenly, and a few large raindrops spattered the tile. A gust of wind and the crash of thunder booming overhead announced a sudden squall.

"Dam' it! Where'd that come from," Asher swore, surprised by the approaching rain. "Here, Drag this stuff back under the roof," he ordered, marshaling the others in a manner, which never doubted compliance.

The furniture was hustled into shelter, and with a rush and a roar, the rain swept down in a silver curtain. Laughing, they fled through the French doors, turning into the high ceiling living room. The thunder crashing around them was so loud; they could not understand each other's words though they were half shouting. The storm passed as suddenly as it had appeared, leaving the house cool and moist. Grace appeared and quietly informed Corazon that the cook had dinner ready if she wished it set out.

When they moved into the dining room, the soup was on the table as was a large salad bowl, while the other dishes sat on a buffet adjacent the table. Corazon only glanced at it. Instead, she observed the twins suspiciously, sensing undercurrents in their apparently amicable behavior. She could never be quite sure how they would go off. At least it could be said fairly of Constance, that her bursts of ill humor were short-lived, whereas Angel's evil bouts of temper tended to lay dormant, smoldering long after the initial explosion. Putting her thoughts aside, she became a proper hostess.

"If you men aren't satisfied with wine, you may find a beverage that suits you at the bar." Corazon said pleasantly.

"Fine with me," Grey said, pulling back a chair for Constance, who had maneuvered for a seat next to him.

"Wine's good enough," Asher said, while pulling back his wife's chair. "We like this mild red. Order it up every year, Grey, from *Argentina*," he said. Taking a bottle, he drew the cork as he spoke, and moved around the table to fill each glass. When Asher sat, he took up his own glass and toasted, "to family, to friends, to loyalty."

"Family, friends, loyalty," they repeatedly in unison and emptied their glasses.

Grey unconsciously made a pleased ticking sound between his tongue, and pallet as he finished, and grinned sheepishly, when he realized the twins were staring at him. "Old habit," he said, explaining himself.

"My yes!" Corazon said, with a short laugh. "You used to do the same thing when I gave you lemonade. That was at about five years old I'd guess."

After a prayer was said, the soup was passed around and then the salad.

"Grey, might you carve the roast," Corazon asked as Delia brought in the platter. Sit it there," she said gesturing to a place beside her guest.

"How do you like it," he asked, taking up the carving knife.

"Thick and red," Asher answered without hesitation and Grey began to cut.

"Medium," Angel informed.

"Rare but thin," Connie instructed, then, "here, let me help you," she added, slipping out of her chair to get the plates.

"I'll get the sides," Angel announced.

Rising gracefully from her seat and turning to the buffet behind her, Angel bent, just slightly more than was necessary to pick up the mashed potatoes.

Grey, directly behind Angel, and separated only by the table, had an excellent view of some lovely curves. So much so, that he allowed his knife to slip and rap loudly on the platter. Barely had he begun to place his attention back on the carving, when Connie putting the plates next to the platter, leaned against his left shoulder. The scent of powder and freshly scrubbed young female filled his nostrils.

She had hardly moved away when Angel appeared on his left with the potatoes. Angel placed them on the table, turning back briskly so that her hair brushed his neck, leaving goose flesh and the faint scent of perfume in her wake. The piece of medium fillet flopped onto the tablecloth.

"Gee'z! I'm sorry," Grey groaned, watching the stain spread, even as he maneuvered the meat back onto the platter. "I'm usually quite competent when I carve," he explained.

"It'll wash out," Asher said, scooping potatoes alongside his roast.

He knew exactly why the lad had become suddenly maladroit but was enjoying himself too much to let on. He smiled as Connie placed a dish of asparagus in the center of the table in such a way as to make sure she received as much attention as her sister. Corazon's mouth opened to speak, but Asher nudged her under the table before she got a word out. His eyebrows rose slightly; she gave him a prickly look. It spoke a great deal concerning what was transpiring at her table.

Eventually, the meal was eaten, and the table cleared. They sat over coffee and cake, enjoying small talk. When the subject of nightlife was introduced, the level of competition rising between the twins, threatened to become obvious. Corazon did not find it amusing. Regardless of her husband's wishes, she decided to put a stop to it before real trouble started.

"Asher, why don't you show Grey the boat you're so proud to have built. The girls and I will freshen up a bit and be right with you."

"Is that alright with you, Grey?" Asher asked his face lighting.

"I'd love it sir. What kind is she? "

As the two men began speaking about the ketch, Corazon shooed the girls into the kitchen, beginning to speak as the door swung shut.

"I was shamed by your behavior," were the first words out of her mouth as the kitchen door latched. "You've been raised as ladies. I do not expect you to reflect every ridiculous convention of etiquette, but I do expect you to honor the values of this family. Grey is a guest in this home, and he will not be fought over by you two cats, like some unfortunate rodent." Corazon paced, wrapped quite tight after being constrained from interfering earlier. She calmed herself and began anew in a motherly tone, "you know quite well the opinion men have of girls, who, well!" she left it unsaid.

Connie, red-faced, stared at her feet. Angel, gone pale, was fiercely defensive. Corazon forced herself to remain placid.

"Now," she continued and with a firm gentleness, "tell me about this, Angel, you first."

Angel was prepared to be sarcastic, but wisely decided that her grandmother was in no mood for cheek. "I find him very attractive," she said. "I'll admit that I was flirting."

"Connie?"

"I've always liked Grey, Grandma. It's just that he's so different now, he's matured. What gives Angel the exclusive right to him?"

"I saw him first."

"What's wrong with sharing?"

Corazon remained exasperatingly patient. "Men cannot be shared," she said, amazed that she should have to explain this. "We haven't time and I've suffered enough of this foolishness. "Here," she said, taking a quarter from the milk money on the counter. Flipping the coin and covering it in her palm, she said to Connie, "Choose! The loser leaves the young man in peace for the next three days."

"Tails," Connie called, but it was heads.

Chapter 8

The lights came on in the small compartment and the exuberant voice boomed, echoed off the steel bulkheads.

"Alf — hey Alf!"

Felton moaned, and put up a hand to shield his eyes from the light. Grey had pulled the curtain open on his bunk and was shaking Alf's foot ruthlessly.

"Huh! What?"

"Put your feet on the deck, now!"

"Why?" Ensign Felton said wearily. He twisted, getting his legs over the side of his bunk, and sat hunched, eyes squinting, blinking against the light.

Grey's blouse lay over a chair and he was hopping on one foot as he kicked himself free of his trousers.

"You're going dancing, double date, so shake a leg."

"I just got to sleep, buddy," he grumbled, shielding his eyes with his pillow.

"Hell! It's only 19:00 hours," Grey informed him and snatched the pillow away.

"I had the watch, plus I've been ashore all day," Felton whined. He propped himself up on an elbow and rubbed his eyes. Finally, beginning to act more like his self, he asked, "Well, now that I'm awake what does she look like?"

"Blond, classy, beautiful beyond description, and your date's every bit the knock out mine is. However, it's strictly hands off. They're friends of the family. It's, officers and gentleman, we must be." Grey stopped what he was doing, and looking his buddy squarely on the eye said, "I stress the gentleman, Alf. Our families are close and they're schoolgirls."

"Aw for Christ sakes, for this you woke me up," he grumbled.

"You looked lonesome," Grey said, pulling on a clean pair of pants. "Now get a move on. People are waiting, and I have the mid-watch."

In a matter of minutes, they were hurrying down the gangway. Grey pointed to a new Corde roadster, parked a few feet to the side. He said, "Nice, huh?"

"Gee'z, where did you get your hands on that?"

"Our date's grandfather loaned it," he said, getting in.

Felton climbed in. He smelled the new leather. He ran his hand over it. "You have any idea what one of these things cost?" he asked, as Grey started the engine.

"None of my business, but I doubt if Capt. Byran has any worries over making payments."

"What is he, navy brass?" he asked, his voice suddenly less sure.

"Merchant Marine! He owns Biscayne Shipping," Grey explained as he drove out onto the boulevard. "My old man was a Captain with Biscayne for 30 years. We've all been like family."

"This date's a little incestuous then?" he joked, in a lame attempt at humor.

"Lay off that kind of crap," Grey warned, with an edge to his voice that advised him he was over the line.

They crossed the causeway, swung left and raced north on *Collins Avenue*. When they pulled up in front of the *Surf Club*, Grey turned the roadster over to a parking attendant, and hurried up the wide coral stairway. To the doorman, he presented the guest pass given him by Captain Byran, and he asked if the Captain's party had preceded him. Pleased to find that he had arrived early, Grey asked the doorman to tell Capt. Byran they would be waiting inside. Alf picked a column to lean on, and began observing women as they passed by, appraising each by some private standard. Grey sat on a bench, eyes on the door, like a loyal watchdog.

It was nearly 8:00 pm. Members in evening attire filled the *Surf Club*. A band played, and the dance floor was crowded with couples. Alf's attention was on the dance floor, when he heard Grey's voice and the snap of shoes on the tile as Grey sprang back to his feet.

"They're here," Grey, said moving toward the Byrans.

"Wow!" Ensign Felton blurted as he turned and saw his date.

He had no idea which of the two young heartbreakers she was, because he could not see any difference in them. Just inside the door, the Byrans exchanged pleasantries with the Burdines. The two young officers stood at ease several feet away, waiting.

Finally, turning to the young men, Asher said, "I see you wasted no time getting here, Grey. Hope we didn't keep you waiting long."

"Not at all sir, and may I introduce my fellow officer, Alfred Felton. Alf, this is Captain and Mrs. Byran, and these are their granddaughters, Constance and Angela. "

"My pleasure, Captain, and ladies," Felton said, coming briefly to attention and nodding his head. "And thank you for having us as your guest, sir."

"My pleasure, Mr. Felton," Asher said.

"And if you'll excuse us," Corazon said, tugging at Asher, "The Hertz's are by the big doors of the veranda. I haven't seen Myra since last season," she explained. "Have fun," she called over her shoulder, as she moved off with her husband in tow.

"We know you're confused," Connie announced matter-of-factly, re-directing their escorts attention. "Everyone is confused, so we've decided to make it easy. I'm Connie," she said, taking Alf's arm. "And remember, Alf, I'm wearing the black gown and Angel is in white."

"White is Angelic," Angel said making a proprietary shift toward Grey, "so now that the matter of who is who, has been cleared up, gentlemen, lead on."

"Ma'am," Felton said, bowing slightly, "would you care to dance,"

"Why certainly," Connie said, smiling and taking the proffered hand, allowed herself to be drawn toward the dance floor.

"How about you," Grey asked, "a dance, or maybe I could get you a drink."

"A drink would be nice; they have a nice Rum Punch here, but do you think we could get a table first," Angel asked, giving him just the slightest hint of a smile.

"Sure, absolutely," he agreed, looking around for a waiter.

When Grey managed to get a waiter's attention, he pointed to an area to the right of the band, near doors that opened onto the beach. The waiter seated them and went for drinks. Grey made a conscious effort not to stare. Nevertheless, he found his eyes coming back to Angel almost before he managed to tear them away.

"Your dress is lovely," he complimented, wishing he could come up with something clever, but she thanked him and said his uniform suited him, as well.

The number the band was playing ended, and some couples moved toward their tables while others waited for the music to begin anew. A slick olive dark man, Angel knew to be an acquaintance of her sister, led his date from the dance floor. He and another couple stopped at the table when they saw Angel.

"Connie, kid," he laughed, "where you been? Wait, you don't have to answer that, kid. I can see — the Navy's in."

Grey was getting to his feet, and Angel introduced them, "Paul, this is Ensign Grey MacArt and Grey, Mr. Paul Benetti and that's Don Lumas there behind him. By the way Paul, that's Connie over there on the dance floor," she pointed, "with that other uniform."

"Oops," Paul grimaced. He extended a hand to meet Grey's, and squeezed hard, surprised when the pressure of Grey's grip equaled his. "Good to meet you, but I gotta go," he said, gesturing toward a party coming into the room.

Lumas shook Grey's hand as Benetti moved away. "This is Miss McGraw, "he introduced, giving his date a little tug with the arm he had at her waist, "A fellow scholar at U of *Miami.*"

"Delighted, ma'am," Grey said, with a slight nod of his head. "We have drinks coming, could I order you something?"

"Sure, our table's packed anyway; looks like Benetti's crowd sort of took over," he said, glancing toward a mob of young socialites. He pulled a chair back, seating Gail, then reversed his own and straddled it, leaning forward against the back. "Some crowd tonight, huh? Its college break week. That's why we outnumber the old fogies for a change.

"I assume you're off one of those warships," the date said to Grey. "The ones we saw this morning. How you men stand being cramped up in those things for weeks at a time, I'll never fathom."

"One gets into the routine of it," Grey said, "and they do allow us ashore from time to time." He winked at Angel.

The drinks arrived; more were ordered, and soon Connie and Alf turned up, snatching chairs from a third table to join the group. They began talking with the new couple, who set each other off stylishly, and spoke easily with a chatty amusement that drew others along. She was a small pallid girl, with a thin, starved appearance. She had fine hands with long nervous fingers, straight dark hair that she cut above the chin to shorten a narrow face. She had penciled eyebrows, connected by a thin nose to a wide thin mouth that spoke carefully chosen words. It was as if at any given moment she was aware of what she would say and was determined to appear stylish while saying it. She lacked beauty but carried herself with an assurance that made her attractive in an intellectual way. Relating a humorous bit of gossip, she was subtly disparaging Paul Benetti's family, as Italians and gangsters. As they chatted, Angel became jealous of the girl's sophisticated confidence. She disagreed with her statements, and thought the conversation in general to be uncivil, but she lacked the confidence to challenge it. Angel knew, herself to be far more attractive, and equally intelligent, but was frustrated in her inability to hold her own in the discourse. Connie managed easily, but Angel found herself silently sipping her drink, resenting the attention being paid to the older girl's cute banter. When the band struck up a new tune, she used the music as an excuse to separate herself from what she considered a bore and unfair competition.

Excitedly pressing Gray's arm, she announced, "Oh I love this; can we dance?"

"Nothing I'd like better," he said, relieved, and pushing back his chair, he led her out onto the dance floor with a grin. He held her quite properly, not exactly at arms-length, but not body to body either. Soon though the tempo quickened, and a jazzy number loosened them up. They danced four in a row before Paul Benetti cut in. Then Don cut in, followed by Alf, and Grey was lost in the whirl. When Angel spied him again, he was only a few feet away, and dancing with Miss skinny. The moment Angel realized his eyes were on her instead of his partner, she was elated. When he winked, she blushed, her body filling with giddy warmth.

There was more conversation, more drinks, and sometime after ten, Grey danced her out onto the veranda. The night was mild, with a three-quarter moon hovering over the ocean. They sat at a round concrete table under a beach umbrella, letting the breeze cool them as they talked. Angel felt compelled by convention to ask questions concerning Gray's career and interests. She would rather have been more herself and asked about personal the things: philosophies, passions, the small intimate details that form a personality. Being objective was difficult, though. His closeness, his scent, somehow differed from the kids she had dated. It stirred in her an awareness of masculinity, a power that was somehow hers to control. It brought up within her a physical response, a quickening that came as a surprise.

Grey checked his watch and sighed reluctantly, "Gotta go, mustn't be late for watch."

"I've enjoyed myself," she told him honestly, not ready for the evening to end.

"What about tomorrow, how about the beach?"

"Yes, I'd love to", she answered, sounding suddenly like an excited ten-year-old.

"Late morning, I'll be by before noon, lunch on the beach."

Plans made, they went inside, searching the crowd until they found her grandparents at a table with friends. Grey thanked them for their hospitality and the use of the car. He informed them; he had to get back to the ship. Laughing, Asher told him he understood and to hold onto the car. He would see him tomorrow. The departing officer took a possessive look over his shoulder at Angel.

She remembered him that way, and understood that he had selected her to dance, choosing her each time over dozens of possibilities. Grey had singled her out during the evening, and he had asked her out tomorrow. For the remainder of the evening, Angel danced only reluctantly, and never twice with the same partner. It seemed to Angel that she was about to become Ensign MacArt's girl.

They lunched the next day under umbrellas at the *Roney's, Cafe de la Pax*, and swam in the gentle surf. In the late afternoon, they played doubles against Angel's grandparents on the back-yard tennis courts and were beaten soundly. That evening, they went to the movies to see, *It Happened One Night*. It was Angel's first real date, allowed because of the MacArt, Byran family ties. The Romantic comedy set the day off perfectly, and at the front door, Grey took Angel in his arms and kissed her. It was not Angel's first kiss. It was, however, the first time a man had kissed her, and the difference was astounding. In that, moment she was only aware of strength in the pressure of the circling arms, and a hot rush that surged up from her middle as the softness of her body was held to the hardness of his. Later, she remembered details: the brush of stubble on his chin, the mixed scent of old spice and perspiration, the taste of buttered popcorn on his lips. She suddenly knew what it was all about. Not just words but also the heat, the rush, and she understood finally, why double dating was necessary.

***

Grey attended Easter services with the Bryans, and later escorted them on a tour of his ship, open to the public Sunday afternoon. Angel, who had often been aboard passenger and cargo ships, was shocked by the cramped closeness of the destroyer. It was narrow and cut by seemingly endless bulkheads. The passageways were cramped with pipes and bundles of wire that ran everywhere. Even the officers were jammed; two to a tiny cabin, and equipment seemed to be stowed or bolted every place she looked.

If the maze of technology bewildered Angel, it interested Connie, who asked endless and surprisingly intelligent questions, which Grey seemed to enjoy answering. Angel began to see herself as lacking, and followed quietly, insecure in an environment that made her feel inadequate. She despised her sister's mechanical intellect and hated Grey for the attention he paid Connie. Her confidence was not helped by the fact that he kept getting their names confused. No matter where they went on the ship, young men eyed the girls. Angel in her growing distemper received their longing gazes with a cold contempt, a contempt that remained with her even after she returned to the privacy of the car.

On Monday night, the city hosted a ball for the officers of Grey's squadron, which the twins attended. The affair, offering two bands and an open-air bar, was packed. By late evening, the place was really warming up, and more than a few in the crowd were staggering drunk. Angel had no intention of becoming intoxicated. She had no intention of making a fool of herself and hated the ordeal of being hung over. She also had no doubt that her grandfather would strip her of privileges if she overindulged again. Angel drank only enough to take the edge off her inhibitions and irritability. She was irritable because the place was a madhouse and she kept being separated from Grey. She would have liked to dance more often with Grey, but the crush of men cutting in on everyone was frantic. It made no difference who danced with whom, and though it was fun, it was also impersonal on an evening that Angel wanted to be very personal. Cheek to cheek, or being flung around to a jumpy swing tune, it was all the same without the partner she wanted.

For Connie, the evening was much the same. She had literally danced until her feet hurt. Hot and a bit out of breath after a wild swing number, she leaned against the wall of the terrace letting the breeze cool her. She gasped when strong arms grasped her. She found herself pulled tight against a man who gave her a very thorough kiss, a kiss that she returned with the similar vigor.

"My god, you're a scrumptious female Angel," Grey whispered, against Connie's lips.

"I am not," she laughed.

"I'll be the judge of that," he argued, starting to kiss her again.

"I am not," she giggled. The word Angel muffled by the kiss.

Over his shoulder, Connie caught sight of her sister moving towards the door. Reluctantly she pushed Grey back, seeking to disengage, and at the same time giggling against his lips.

"You got the wrong twin," she gasped finally, turning her head, "not that I didn't enjoy it."

He jumped straight, letting go of her. "Gee! I'm sorry."

"Not your fault. Oops", she called gaily as she turned."

Out of the corner of her eye, she saw Angel several feet away, wearing a shocked expression. Ducking past Grey, she slipped back into the bustle of the ballroom. Connie knew her sister was furious, but it was an accident. Anyway, the deal was three days, and the three days had been up for over five hours. Besides, Connie reminded herself again. I was an innocent victim of mistaken identity.

***

At noon on Tuesday, the destroyers slipped their lines, and one by one, steamed seaward. As the ships passed, automobiles on the county causeway blew their horns, people waved, and by 1:00 pm, the ships were mere smudges, bound south on the *Gulf Stream*, towards *Panama*.

Angel had said goodbye to Grey on the dock, had in fact kissed him goodbye on the dock. She watched him leading a detail of sailors as they got in the stern lines. As the ship moved and the aquamarine waters spread between them, she placed a kiss on her fingertips and tossed it towards him. The second ship slid past amid a racket of whistles and bullhorns, flags whipped in the breeze, and its deck was filled with activity. It fell in behind its sister, and Grey disappeared from sight.

On arrival home the previous evening, Angel had delivered a caustic sermon. The subject was disloyalty and man theft. She had neither spoken to Connie nor acknowledged her since. It seemed the very temperature in the house had plunged, so cold was Angel's treatment of her sister. Wednesday morning frustrated and irritable, Corazon decided she had put up with as much of the foolishness as was necessary. She ushered the young women into her sewing room, having the express intent of presenting them with an addendum to the facts of life.

The twins avoided looking at each other as they entered the room. She, pointed to the loveseat, ordered them to sit. They did, each girl crowding her respective end, to create as wide a gap between them, as that piece of furniture would allow. Corazon sat opposite, and in an even dignified voice, began a lecture, which her granddaughters resented before the first word was spoken.

"This business over Grey — no, you'll keep your mouths shut until I have finished." Angel's lips had begun to move, and Connie's eyebrows had risen at the mention of Grey. "You are both very young and no matter if you see this or not, you're both playing games. Half the souls on this earth are men. You, on the other hand, each have but one sister and a twin sister at that," She sighed, her eyes rolling momentarily to the ceiling. "This is partly my fault because I've spoiled you, and others have spoiled you as well. Look," she said, extending a hand. "You have two of everything. Whatever you have ever wished for you have gotten and you've never shared a thing outside of your mother's womb. You're both miserably selfish."

Corazon looked at them directly, one and then the other, each sullen, each wishing this to be over. Well, she was far from finished.

"You're beautiful young women, each with independent wealth. At a time when half the world is begging for bread, you're fortunate, beautiful, and healthy. You have outward beauty, but that's not such a good thing when you're also selfish and immature. You've become so used to getting what you wish, you don't recognize what's right for you." she huffed, "Desire is one thing children; life with a man is another matter entirely. You must understand and be able to accommodate each other. Love and desire are not enough; desire and love bring disaster to the foolish every day."

Corazon paused, introspective for a moment; she recalled a moment of thoughtless naivety from her own youth, a tragic moment. "There are endless passions to understand and weigh against each other when you choose to engage in adult relationships. Consider not only your own feelings and those of the person you're interested in, but the feelings of your family and friends. When I was only a little older than you, I failed to take the passions of others seriously, the passions of jealousy and hate in my own family. In a careless moment, with a single innocent kiss, I created a circumstance that ended in the death of one cousin and the injury or another."

"Your cousins fought each other over you," Angel blurted, suddenly big eyed with curiosity.

"No!" Corazon corrected, and breathing deeply, continued with an odd sadness. "They fought your grandfather. Duels were considered necessary then, and they challenged your grandfather, one after the other, because I was seen kissing him. It was at the end of a war in *Cuba*. Our men fought on opposite sides. Some of them hated Americans. I had been apart from the war, protected; like you spoiled, and I failed to seriously consider the passions. Hate is a passion, a strong passion. Natan died on your grandfather's sword; it might have been the otherwise." Corazon smiled softly. "Had either Natan or Louis won, we would not be having this talk.

"Swords," Connie said, incredulous.

"Understand, children, Corazon said, suddenly annoyed with herself for airing this tragedy from another era, "Circumstances can quickly spin beyond our control, take us to places we never imagined. When you seek to form an alliance with a man, it gets complicated. You mix different families, friends, morals, religions, and politics, even food. It is an endless morass but the more alike your people and outlook are, the better the fit. Desire is only a part of planning life with someone, and desire has nothing to do with what is best for a woman in the end. It's as easy to desire a bad man as it is a good one. Desire can be a miserable trap, and you'll find that many a poor woman has come to ill through her desire for a rotten man."

She paused once more, determining that she now held their full attention. She leaned forward, grasping first Angel's hands and then Connie's. She noted that they were slowly becoming more tolerant of each other.

"Looking at you, a stranger sees only two lovely girls, each the mirror image of the other. An incredible likeness, but I know you are alike only to the eye. I know those things that make you individuals, your temperaments, fears, your personalities. I know you as a blind person would know you, and this is how a man, the man that you would trust to share life with must come to know you. This is how you must come to know him." She tugged at both their hands. "Flesh," she laughed, "A necessary suit that serves us from birth to grave. Your suits are beautiful, but beauty can be a curse if those who we desire come to love the suit without knowing the soul within it. You see," she said, shaking both of the hands she held, "even if you both want a single man, the poor fellow at first sees only one woman. What does he know? Like it or not, he must come to know the difference between you before he can choose, and both sexes have to choose and agree. Be honest, be rational."

She stood, releasing the girl's hands, and walked to the door. "Grey's ship is on its way to the *Pacific*. He must be away for over a year, and for you to fight over him is absurd. Which man will you be fighting over next month? Or have you both decided to give up your social life until he returns." She opened the door, "I expect you two to conclude your hostilities as of now. If you wish to be treated as adults, stop acting like adolescents."

As Corazon closed the door, she noted the twins looking at each other with a shared embarrassment. How long would a truce last this time she wondered?

Chapter 9

After graduation ceremonies, in late May, the Byran's took the girls to *Europe*, booking cabins on the *Queen Mary*. The six-week excursion was a success, and in mid-July they arrived back in *Florida*. Angel had enrolled for a month-long watercolor course at Ringling and needed to be driven to *Sarasota* almost immediately after their return. During the time she was gone, Connie spent most of her time sailing on the bay, or

enjoying evenings out with friends. Nine days before her planned departure for *Radcliff*, where she was to begin her college career, she decided instead to attend the rural *Florida State University at Gainesville*. If it had been up to her grandfather, Constance would have gone to college in *Miami*, and remained at home which is what her sister planed. *Gainesville* was closer, though, near enough that she could return home on holidays and though he didn't say so, Asher was pleased by the change of plans.

***

In the last week of August, on a Monday, they loaded Connie's trunks into the Packard and took the *Dixie Highway* north, reaching *Ormond Beach* by dark. An early start allowed them to cross the *John's River* at *Palatka* and cover a hundred and twenty miles of piney woods before noon. Connie's enrollment took less than two hours. A school porter hauled her trunks up to her quarters in the confusion of the dormitory.

Amidst the bustle of parents and students coming and going, Connie, was quickly recognized by friends, and forgot her grandparents. It was obviously time for them to leave. Corazon closed the car door, and pulling a hanky, dabbed at her eyes. Asher started the engine.

"It's so hard to let them go," she sniffed. "I'll worry about her."

"Kids have to make the own stupid mistakes," Asher said, his voice gruff over the engine noise. "We certainly made ours."

"You're a terrible man," she said, looking away from him, and towards the school, knowing he was worried to.

Not in a hurry, they enjoyed a few days getting to *Sarasota*, by visiting *Silver Springs*, and later *Tampa* where they had been introduced in 1898. The heat and humidity of late summer was oppressive, and in those periods of time when the breeze did not blow, perspiration would saturate clothing. It sprang up through the pores of even the most refined women. Fans were present everywhere.

Hot moist air drawn from the sea on three sides, blanketed the state. The land was fed vapor and this unstable air rose in pillars to form the towering column-nimbus clouds, which marched majestically across the landscape as great blue-black squalls. Cool air preceded them, followed by thunder, lightning, and wind driven rain. Then came the return of the miasmal heat, and that was cycle of the weather of summertime *Florida*.

Being a native, Asher knew to travel early before the worst heat of the day set in. They reached

Sarasota before noon, and checked into a hotel before fetching their granddaughter from The *Ringling School of Art*. After lunch, they took a tour of the *Ringling Museum* and attended an exhibit of work done by Ringling students. One of Angel's pieces had received the award for second place, and that evening, after dinner, she spoke excitedly with her grandmother about the exhibits and the work that she hoped to do in the future.

Before turning in, Asher listened to news transmitted from a local radio station. There was commentary on Germany's growing confidence under its new chancellor; a memorial was being organized for Will Rogers, dead two weeks in an Alaskan plane crash, and there was plenty of political give and take concerning Roosevelt's new policies. Many of his opponents were, in fact, calling him and out an out communist. The weather report was what got Asher's attention. Cuban weather officials had notified *Miami* of a minimal hurricane two days earlier, but the U.S. weather bureau had been unable to track the erratic course of the storm. A warning was now up for *Miami* and the Keys.

He phoned Fedrico in *Coconut Grove*, asking him to have the house closed up and the boat moved up the river. He informed the women, and the three of them made plans for an early start home in the morning. September 2nd was Labor Day. The traffic was so light it seemed to Asher that most of the West Coast had slept in. He pushed the big Packard hard, averaging almost seventy in overdrive, eating up the country roads and actually passing *Fort Myers* before 9:00 a.m. When they stopped for gas in *Naples*, the air had a hazy sheen. The sky was a blotchy gray to the southeast, and Asher studied it while the station attendant pumped his tank full. The *Okeechobee* storm of '28 came to mind, and he quickly pushed the memory away.

"Heading for *Miami* I spose," the man said, and gave the sky a suspicious look.

"Had it in mind," Asher said, looking at the southeastern sky, dubiously. "Looks like that hurricane's moving up fast, though."

"Thought so myself and sent my boys to get our boat up in those mangroves about an hour ago." The man spit tobacco juice and turned back to Asher. "More in likely be crossing *Florida Bay* sometime soon. *Everglades City* get a taste of it more en-likely."

"That's what I'm thinking."

"Wouldn't be the first time — that'll be a dollar sixty for the gas Mister."

He paid the attendant as the women returned from the lavatory. He looked at the sky once more. "Where's the telephone office?" he asked the attendant.

"Closed for the holiday but y'all might use the phone at the sheriff's office. The deputy, he'd be pleased to take your money."

"Thanks," Asher said, and got behind the wheel. "The storm might be coming across the *Everglades*," he told the women, "I'm going to check."

"You mean we're going to be stuck in this car until tomorrow." Angel complained. "It really doesn't look bad at all, Grandpa."

"*Tamiami Trail* is no more than three foot above the water in the *Glades* Angel, and that water can come up fast."

Asher turned the car and drove back toward the Sheriff's office talking as he went. "I'm going to make a call to Pan Am, in *Miami* and see what the wind's doing there. If it looks good, we can be home in four hours, give or take. If not, I'll phone Shawn to have the house shuttered, and we can run back by way of *Fort Myers.* Hell, I grew up there."

"I'd thought your people were from *Charleston*, grandpa".

"They were, but my daddy decided to grow oranges in *Fort Myers*. To get away from his in-laws as much as to get away from the Yankees I think. *Florida* was a hard place in those days Angel, and between fever and the harshness, it killed everyone, excepting your great Aunt Fay and myself. When my uncle died, she hauled me and the furniture back to *Charleston* and enrolled me at the *Citadel*." Asher stopped the car.

"But that's an military college," Angel exclaimed as her grandfather got out.

"Yes, it is that," he agreed, closing the door and he went inside.

"Your grandfather was a very dashing Army Officer. I saw him for the first time at a ball in *Charleston*. We were very nearly married before I ever saw him out of Army uniform," Corazon laughed. "By then he was dressed in naval garb. I was shocked the first time I saw him in strange civilian clothing."

"I knew he was an Army Officer, but not that he went to a military college. What was grandpa like then?" Angel asked, seeing the pleasure her grandmother had in the memory.

"He had steadiness to him; no matter what might happen, one could feel his calm. He could be fierce when he chose, but even at those times, when he was the most-fierce, one could sense that he measured his violence. He controlled it so that his heart remained calm. Aahh, you have no idea," She gasped, rolling her eyes. "When I met him, other men seemed to shrink, and the men I speak of, the men of my family, they were not weak men or cowards. I have never had a second thought about my choice of a husband; never saw his equal in another man. That's what your grandfather was like, is still like," she said, her voice dreamy.

"Was my father like grandpa," Angel asked suddenly, for she had not planned a question, rather it simply popped out of its accord.

"Yes!" Corazon answered, equally surprised. "They were mostly alike in temperament; too much alike to get along with each other, but then your father was also a selfish man, an angry man. Like a small child, he hurt people, often without thought, certainly without guilt. Had he lived, he might have grown up." Corazon looked wistful. "They were signs you know, that he was changing, but then," she sighed a deep breath, "we will never know, and that is how life is. He was my first child, a life from my own body, and I loved him. No matter what, he was my child and I loved him."

The women were startled as Asher opened the car door. "Winds are east at twenty-five in *Miami*, so the storm must be to the south. We have time to make the run. I'll chance it anyway."

"It'll be good to sleep in my own bed," Corazon said, as the engine started.

The car accelerated southeast into the *Everglades* and towards *Miami*. In deep thought, Angel rode in silence. She pictured Grey, so handsome in his uniform, and he was calm and competent like grandpa. She found herself wondering about her father, the conflicting stories, stories about what he was like and who he really was. She remembered Tully's name and wondered what he could tell her. Grandma had said her father was angry and selfish, vices that she reluctantly admitted to sharing. Perhaps I'm like him, she thought, before the road lulled her to sleep.

***

Much too much happened after they returned to *Miami* to allow Angel time for delving into the past. The hurricane that had been worrying Asher had made its landfall at the *Matecumbe Keys* on Monday, the evening of their return. The tragic results included the beaching of the Biscayne tug, *Tom Strong*. The ninety-foot vessel was not merely aground; it was ashore some three-quarters of a mile and laying broadside to the embankment of Flagler's ruined rail line. Fortunately, the *Tom Strong's* crew had survived, which was more than could be said for those poor souls inhabiting the adjacent keys.

When the winds had begun to blow, late on Labor Day morning, federal officials had ordered a special train out of *Miami* for the evacuation of residents and the 600 laborers, veterans were working on the overseas highway project. Bureaucratic red tape delayed the process, and by the time, the train departed *Miami,* late that afternoon, winds were already near hurricane force. When the train finally reached the *Islamorada Station* at 8:00 pm, conditions were so severe that it steamed blindly past, never seeing the station or the crowd waiting to board.

Within the hour, the cars of the train were blown off the tracks. The barometer plunged to the lowest mark ever recorded in *Florida*, 26.30, and the winds rose well above 200 miles per hour. Leaves were stripped from the trees, and then the trees were stripped from the earth. Roofs flew from buildings and buildings themselves disintegrated. The Stygian darkness was lit by static electric charge, as millions of granules of sand left the earth swirling, colliding in a mixture of wind driven water and salt air. Those unfortunates left clinging to stonewalls and foundations were sandblasted. First their clothing was eaten away and then their skin. Bodies became raw lumps, left wearing only leather belts and shoes. Some were impaled or dismembered by flying debris. Those who had tied themselves to the tracks or ruins were beyond identification with their faces sandblasted to the bone. Most, though, were swept to sea by the surge, a twenty-foot wall of water that roared over the islands sometime before midnight. By morning some 500 had died. The writer Ernest Hemingway arrived from *Key West*, aboard his boat to find the water clogged with bloated corpses. The article he wrote for a Socialist magazine was scathing. It placed the responsibility squarely on the backs of inept bureaucrats. The search for bodies went on for weeks on *Florida Bay* and in the mangrove forest that lined its shore.

***

Angel had, mostly out of curiosity, asked to accompany her grandfather when he went to survey the tug on Tuesday. She regretted going more than Asher regretted taking her. Neither had imagined the magnitude of destruction. North of *Islamorada,* Asher turned the car around. He loaded dazed and exhausted survivors and drove them directly to a clinic in *Homestead.* Angel did her best to comfort the injured as her grandfather drove, but there was little she could do. Leaving *Homestead,* she rode in shocked silence. When Asher returned to the *Matecumbe* on Wednesday, it was without Angel.

As horrendous as the hurricane was, Miamians were used to them, and business continued as usual in the Magic City. Angel began her first classes at *University of Miami* and was soon absorbed in the studies and social aspects of the university. Perhaps the plight of the hurricane's survivors had shocked Angel to a new level of social consciousness; maybe it was the mix of opinions that academia exposed her to. Suddenly, knowledge she had held in the abstract became a vivid reality. She found herself in the endless debate concerning human equality, freedom, and the rights of man. Daily, Angel vacillated between states of elation and outrage over matters concerning the human condition. With her friends, she was constantly engaged in serious dialogue concerning ways to improve the plight of man.

Asher caught up in spirited discussions covering a broad spectrum of subjects. He was sometimes shocked, more often amused, but occasionally he found himself interested in their youthful perspectives. What he found impressive was that this generation saw the world as a whole; they instinctively understood that isolationism was no longer viable for the *United States.*

Asher, whose career had been in the maritime trades, saw the world as a single market. When the students argued against the Smoot Hardly act, the Ottawa conference, and isolationism, he could not have agreed more. He also agreed with them on the Roosevelt administration's new programs, the new deal. Though he supported Roosevelt, it was not without reservation, for he was not liberal to the degree that he could go along with the Democratic administration's support of communist inspired labor organizations. He'd sworn to sell off his own ships before he'd be forced to bargain with his crews. He'd always paid a fair wage and fed well. If a seaman was not satisfied with his job aboard a Biscayne ship, he was welcome to find another ship. This was how Asher felt about it, and to be practical, these days there was dam'd little profit in operating a ship anyway, He was of a mind to sell the business for the aggravation certainly out-weighted what little income was generated.

Angel's favorite cause became human rights. She was soon convinced of the duty to share in the burdens of governing, and the need for a fair distribution of the world's wealth. In late October, she was quoting from Karl Marx, and planning to join the young communist league. Only a week later, she quit in dismay after learning of the millions exterminated in Soviet labor camps.

Daily, the Byrans were informed in detail of the world's inequities: famine in *China*, color bars in *South Africa*, chain gangs in the south, Klan lynching, and the mistreatment of the masses in general. In November, Angel was aghast when she learned of Germany's Nuremberg laws. The code passed only two months earlier was already making life difficult for German minorities, particularly the Jews. Each day more racial and religious restrictions were enforced. She read to her grandparents' accounts of persecution from the Freedom Society's newsletter and was incensed when Asher pointed out the level of anti-Semitism in her own community.

While volunteering in a medical clinic for the poor, she caught the measles. This was a week before Thanksgiving and the illness demanded that she remain quarantined, in a curtain-darkened room, for two weeks. As a result, Angel was unable to attend the funeral of Gibbon MacArt two days after her quarantine began.

Chapter 10

The early morning service was a simple ritual. At fifty-three years of age, Gibbon MacArt was brought down by Dingy-fever. On the far-off coast of *Cameroon*, his body had been committed to the deep. There being no body, only a small box with Gibbon's captain's hat and a lock of hair remained to be buried next to his headstone. The graveyard was neither large nor crowded for *Green Cove Springs* was neither large nor ancient, and its cemetery had not the time to grow.

Mourners had gathered under a shady oak, and the early morning air was soft with the perfume of flowers. As the preacher spoke, Connie was conscious of birdsong, distant laughter, and from the road, the tingling of a bicycle bell. These things were reassuring, proof for her that life continues even as death is acknowledged. The prayer ended and the figures beneath the great oak raised their eyes to observe shimmering light, trickling down through the leaves and moss. Clare's eyes, red and miserable, reached out to her son. Grey's arm pulled his mother gently to him, and he walked her towards the gate. In pairs and bunches, friends and family followed after them.

Connie walked ahead of her grandparents, just behind Grey. She had taken the train from *Gainesville* yesterday, getting into town only an hour or so after Grey had arrived by plane from *San Diego*. Her grandparents had met the train and together, they had paid Clare a short visit before going to a hotel. Connie genuinely liked Mrs. MacArt but was astonished at the bitterness the woman expressed at her husband's death. It was as if he'd gotten himself killed to spite her. After a life spent mostly alone, Clare had looked forward to his companionship in her old age. She perceived herself as a wife who had been robbed or cruelly cheated.

Grey's presence soothed his mother considerably. To attend the funeral and settle his father's affairs, he'd been given 21 days of emergency leave. With his older brother assigned to the Asian squadron, all the responsibility fell on Grey. Though his mother put her trust in Grey's judgment, he lacked experience in marine commerce. Completely out of his element, he asked advice from the Byrans. Asher got his attorneys involved, and matters were cleared up before Thanksgiving.

Gibbon MacArt's major interest in the venture had been his expertise, and his participation as master of the vessel. There had been very little capital ventured on MacArt's part, and virtually nothing to get back other than a share of profits. Clare was otherwise, financially secure thanks to investments Gibbon had made over the years. The estate was quickly settled.

***

When the Byrans returned home the day after Thanksgiving, Grey found himself with over two weeks on his hands. He had sixteen days in which to do whatever pleased him. On the first day, he volunteered to drive Connie back to *Gainesville*. It was clear and cool, a perfect day. He owned a Ford convertible, and on the near empty rural road, he traveled fast with the top down. As wind whipped around them, he watched as Connie buttoned up her jacket. She sat erect letting her hair stream in the wind.

He kept glancing to the side to study her. She was disconcertingly lovely, and he had to remind himself that she was only one of the two such beauties, the wrong one. He grinned to himself, remembering what kissing her had been like. No! That had been Angel, but then he had kissed Connie as well, once, he knew that he'd kissed her that one time.

Connie caught him looking, frowned and then laughed, an expression of enjoyment spreading over her face. "What's so funny?" she inquired.

"Nothing," Grey lied, looking abruptly guilty.

In the several months since his visit, Connie had almost forgotten the pull of this young man's presence, but here, for the first time alone with him, she found herself acutely reminded of the attraction. She liked his look, his ruddy, tanned, squarish face and sun-streaked hair. His eyes were blue, set over high cheekbones, and got all squinty when he smiled. Mostly though, she liked the way he reacted to life, to the world and to those around him. After the fuss Angel had made, Connie had willed herself to remain aloof, to keep a certain distance, yet her large eyes glowed, and she found herself responding to Grey despite her best intentions. How could she help it when he looked so boyishly guilty?

"Come on," she insisted, "You're grinning like the Cheshire cat. You had something on your mind sailor. Own up, Spit it out."

"I was remembering what it was like to kiss you," he said, trying to look serious, "and then it occurred to me, it was your sister I was remembering, but then there was the time that I got you mixed up, understandably of course, and that was Ooo-la-la." He flashed a foolish grin at her and turned his attention back to the road.

"Oh, brother, I might have guessed it," Connie said, acting a little miffed. She looked away, quiet, just long enough to put him off balance. She had a flicker of guilt concerning her sister but assured herself that sufficient time had passed since April. He was fair game. She took a breath then said, "I did enjoy that mix-up, you know. And really, I'd hate to leave you undecided over who's the better smooch in the family. Why don't we pull over right here, and let's get this sorted out." Connie had felt her voice shake, she held her breath, shocked at what had come out of her own mouth but it was done.

Grey felt his face flush and he gawked like an awkward smuck. "What?" He said, his head jerking around.

"You heard me," she said, in a soft, seductive voice that made his heart skip.

He lay on the brakes, almost skidding sideways, and pulled off onto the shoulder. Connie looked at him, big eyed with amazement and a little uncertain, then bit her tongue while smiling in the most mischievous manner.

"Now" he said, sliding towards her on the front seat, "shall we settle this in the name of science?"

"That might take some time," Connie warned, tilting her head.

They both laughed, and he took her in his arms. Her lips met his, soft, hesitant at first, then moist, and open as she fit herself into his arms. The kiss seemed to go on for some time, until they both shifted at the same instant and their teeth clicked. Her eyes opened to his, making them both cross-eyed, and suddenly they burst out laughing.

"Wow" she gasped and taking a huge breath of air, pushed back from him. "What you got should be bottled. You'd better stay on your own side of the car for a while. I'm a good girl you know."

"Yes ma'am, but that won't be easy," he said, and feeling prickly all over, rubbed his scalp with both hands. "Well that settles that."

"What," Connie said, turning the mirror to check her lipstick, as an excuse to look away from him and to let her heart stop racing.

"Science," Grey said, starting the engine, and twisting around to check traffic.

"And?" she said, quite pleased with herself in the kissing department, and quite prepared to be complimented.

"Well, it was close, but."

"Just drive," she said, cuffing him on the shoulder, "I wasn't warmed up yet."

For a few minutes, they clipped along, both thinking their own thoughts. On the outskirts of a small-town Grey all of a sudden said, "Hey! Have you ever eaten alligator?"

"That's a twist. No! Why would I want to eat an alligator?"

"A lot of people do," Grey said defensively. "Really," he added, when Connie's face screwed up. "The tail is solid meat and the steaks are great."

"You're not kidding me, are you?" She said, thinking the idea uncivilized when perfectly good beefsteak was available. Then on the other hand, adventure was what made life interesting.

"Nope, honest injun, it's absolutely delicious. Place right here in this town, serves it up with fried spuds and cold slaw, cold beer to wash it down with." He smacked his lips, rolled his eyes, and looked ridiculous.

"I'll try a bite for the beer's sake," she laughed. "And the gator's mama had better not come looking for me, either."

"I won't tell," he, promised, his blue eyes taking on an amused glint.

He turned onto a shell road, shifted down to second and drove down to the shore of a large lake. A sign sat on the roof of a rough shanty-like structure, built out over the water's edge. The sign read, Calhoun's Bar-B-Q, best oysters, fish, and gator in the county. They climbed the steps onto a large deck and entered. The place was nearly empty, and with a choice of seats, they sat by a window looking out on the lake. Grey fetched two beers, and a plump girl came and took their orders. Connie sipped her drink and looked out on the wind ruffed water.

"Nice view, huh?"

"It's okay," she said, "but it's dull, it lacks brilliance."

"You miss Miami?"

"It's the brightness there," she said brightening up herself. "I miss the color, the dazzle. I miss that, and the heat, and I miss sailing on the bay. It's nice enough up here and I've friends; still, I've been thinking of transferring to *Miami University* next year." She looked down, embarrassed. "I suppose I miss my family, too. Angel and I are always at each other, but we have an understanding between us, without words, I mean. We share feeling, know things about each other that can't be explained. I crave that closeness even if we do squabble. Oh, look at me. Here I am, Miss Independent, homesick in her first semester away."

"I know what you mean," he said. He slouched back in his seat holding his beer in both hands over his stomach. "My first year at *Annapolis* was torture. Half the time snow and rain, always cold, I never did get to like the climate. My brother was an upper classman. We really couldn't associate. I was a sorry case."

"Just the weather you couldn't get used to or was it the Navy and the weather?" she asked, sensing a reticent air in the way he spoke.

"I didn't really care for the weather, and I don't care for the navy. To tell the truth I would have rather gone to sea like dad, or to an ordinary university. My brother, he thrives on the Navy. I don't care for it, too many restrictions. The system just seems nuts at times. They do it all the hard way. At least it seems that way to me, but then, I'm no authority."

"Why do you stay then?" Connie asked, leaning forward." Why not leave the service?"

"Oh! I hate to quit something before I've given it my best shot, and I promised my parents I'd give it a couple of years. Mom likes the idea of her sons being officers and gentlemen. She's quite socially conscious. Her people were well up in the social pecking order before the civil war broke them. Her grandparents still had a big house and pretensions when she was a girl, and her uncles were in politics. She has never said so, but I think she feels, it was a step down when she married into the MacArt family. She was always putting on the dog, and always trying to knock the rough edges off my pop. Made us all sit at the table and use just the right utensil; we had to eat each course in the proper order. I found the socials skills to be useful, but pop never did see the point." Grey chuckled, "He'd take just so much, and then he'd go off to sea. Mom got terribly frustrated. At heart, she's an antebellum lady, who was attempting to make gentlemen out of a bunch of crackers."

"Gee! My great grandfather's fortune was confiscated after the civil war, too. I think grandpa is still sore at northerners over that," Connie said. "What did the Yankees do to your mother's people?"

"It wasn't the Yankees! It was the Confederates. Mom's people put all their money into a railroad that ran from the *Atlantic Coast* all the way to *Mobile*. It was just finished when the war broke out. The Confederacy needed rails, so they tore the whole line up, and put it to better use elsewhere.

"Lots of ways to lose out in a war," Connie said, thoughtfully.

"Then, there are people who get rich." Grey smiled, "Opportunity, timing, or just luck."

"Or ruthlessness," she added, "Eat or be eaten."

"Speaking of eating," he said pointing, "Our lunch is here."

In a moment, the food was on the table and Connie tried a small piece of the fried gator. "This is good," she exclaimed and quickly popped another, and much larger, chunk into her mouth. Between them, the food disappeared rapidly. Connie washed the last of her meal down with a gulp of beer, a little of which trickled out of the corners of her mouth. She belched and pressed three fingers of her hand up over her mouth, as Grey chuckled with satisfaction.

"Excuse me! I'm so greedy. My sister would have died before she'd burped in front of someone she was out with."

Grey watched as she dabbed at her mouth with a paper napkin. "This is a date then?" he said, in a teasing tone. He enjoyed the look of amusement on her face, and the way she shifted her gaze when she was searching for a worthy retort.

"A date — this was an escort, as in back to *Gainesville*, as I remember. Of course, if you're asking for a date — are you asking me for a date, or to change this to a date — officially?" she said, boring straight in, without taking a breath.

"Well, uh, yeah!" he said, caught off guard.

"You're so eloquent Grey. Well, uh, yeah! Those words just sweep a girl right off her feet. Well, uh, yeah, is this going to be our date or are we discussing another occasion?" she teased.

"Both!" he said, suddenly sure that he wanted to spend more time with her, needed to spend more time with her.

"I must seem like a pushover; one kiss and I'm putty in your hands," she laughed.

"Two kisses and I'm the one that's putty," he said seriously, gazing into her laughing eyes with an expectant intensity. He added, "I'll grovel if it'll help."

She laughed loudly, felt her face burning and brought her hands up, covering her mouth. With him looking at her this way, she felt a ridiculous giddiness. Somebody had put money in the jukebox. A number from some Broadway musical began blaring but she hardly noticed. "Where are you taking me on our date?" she asked, her hands falling away, one finger left touching the center of her chin.

"Where would like to go?" Grey asked, anxious to please.

"You decide what we do today, but tomorrow I want to pack a picnic and go sailing. There has to be lakes up here with sailboats for rent, and I haven't been sailing in months."

"If there isn't a place, I'll haul you back to *Green Cove*, We'll go out on the river in my cat boat," he promised. "As for tonight, have you ever been to a square dance?"

"I've seen them in the movies, but no, I've never been to one."

"Well tonight's the night. Are you ready?" Gray said standing.

"Yes, but I would like to use the lady's room first."

The plump waitress was mopping tabletops with a wet towel. She pointed toward the lady's room, then moved towards Grey, as she pulled out her check pad. When Connie opened the door to the women's privy, she began to giggle. A wide polished plank stretched along the wall with four evenly spaced round holes cut into it." Ten foot below, waves lapped against the piles of the building. She pulled up her skirt, wiggled her panties down and sat, quite self-consciously over the ten-inch circle. There was a breeze blowing up through the hole, which made her feel even more exposed, and she could just imagine someone peering up from a rowboat or something. It took a moment to relax sufficiently to pee, and she was unreasonably embarrassed when she met Grey at the front door.

***

The remaining 40 miles to *Gainesville* took about an hour to drive. It was an hour past noon when they pulled up to the front of her dorm. As Grey waited by the car, she hurried towards the entrance on a course that converged with two of her friends. One of them was Bonnie Jean Gates, called BJ. BJ was her roommate.

"Hi!" B.J. called to her. "Where were you? You missed the game."

"Oh — Out-of-town," pushing the door open with her backside. "I went to a funeral, a friend of the family who lived east of here."

"Isn't that your sister's boyfriend?" Gail asked. She glanced over her shoulder as they went through the door, "The Navy guy she was all gah, gah over?"

"Yes," Connie answered tersely, both annoyed and guilty at being reminded of Angel's prior claim on Grey.

"Well," Gail said.

"It was his father who passed away, and he's given me a ride back to school. I've offered to show him around while he's here," Connie answered evasively.

Bonnie Jean's eyebrows went up, but she said nothing. She had been to school with the twins since kindergarten and she smelled a rat. Gail went on her way down the hall, while Connie and BJ went up to their room. BJ walked to the window and peered down at Grey MacArt, who sat on the fender of his car playing with, of all things, a yo-yo. Connie was hurriedly changing into her tennis outfit.

"Do you mind if I borrow your racket. We're going to play some tennis, and Grey doesn't have his with him?" Connie asked breathlessly, for she was bent over tying her shoes.

"You're welcome; it's behind my chest of drawers."

"Thanks," Connie said, and standing, she wiggled and twisted her skirt around straight.

"Was Angel up for the funeral?"

"No," Connie said and began to brush her hair back. "Of all things, she caught the measles. She's locked in her dungeon in *Miami*, quarantined."

BJ gasped, "Why you little thief," she exclaimed, wagging her finger, "and your own sister's boyfriend."

"She only went with him for three days, and that was over seven months ago," Connie shot back defensively. "Angel does not stay that serious for seven months. She's been on dates and he's fair game now."

"That's a lie, Connie May Byran, a black lie. Maxine's brother took Angel out last month, and she only let him kiss her on the cheek. She's crazy about that guy and you know it."

Connie's brows knitted, and she pouted. She was basically honest and had never been comfortable with even a small fib.

"Oh! Drat," she mumbled, trying to tie a scarf around her hair.

"Let me help," BJ offered, moving over to her, and thinking it was unlike her roommate to be deceptive or to go overboard where boys were concerned.

"I like him too," Connie admitted, as her roommate tied her hair back. "We've all known one another since we were little, but when he came back last year it was different. Both Angel and I were attracted to him. We were from the first and we've already fought over him. Angel won a three-day coin toss and got a head start. He left before I got my chance at him, and I know my sister is jealous. Grandma said that, in the end, he'd make the choice if we were both serious."

"Serious — are you daft?" BJ burst out. "You're just starting to have fun. College lasts four years."

"I said if, but there is something about him, it's electric when we're together. Gee, it's — WOW-ZAP."

"You're crazy, kiddo."

The door popped open and Joan Broward leaned in. "Hey! Isn't that your sister's boyfriend down there?" she asked, innocently.

BJ smirked.

"He's not anybody's boyfriend," Connie exclaimed in an irritated voice.

"Whoa! Gee, I think I may take a shot at him myself then."

"Just try it and I'll snatch you bald," Connie flared.

"That's what I figured," Joan snickered.

She took a deep breath and burst out laughing. "I'm such a little bitch all of a sudden. My god what's coming over me?"

"Him," Joan said, pointing out the window.

"Say," she gasped, "don't you square dance?"

"Yes, though not much lately. I used to go a lot when I dated Dave."

"I'll have a couple of hours when I get back from tennis. Could you give me some pointers," Connie pleaded? "Just teach me enough so I don't make a complete fool of myself?"

"Heck, I'll even loan you a dress for it. Joan looked at BJ. "She might as well have a little fun before Angel kills her."

Connie had retrieved the tennis racket from behind the dresser and pulled her own down from the wall. "Thanks," she said, bolting out the door.

The two friends watched her skip down the steps and hurry toward the tall young man.

"This is going to cause of a real cat fight," BJ said with a grin.

"Angel will never forgive her," Joan said, gravely. "Never!"

Chapter 11

The county fairgrounds and the farmer's market backed up to the rail line that separated them. Each week, a warehouse was cleaned and swept for Friday and Saturday evening dances. Hot dogs, cokes and beer sold off to one side of the building; and moonshine was sold out back for people who hadn't brought a bottle of something along with them.

It was a townie atmosphere with families present. Outside, kids were always running up a rumpus under the lights of the ballpark, while inside the grown-ups hooted it up. There were two bands on Friday night. The ones with the straw hats and bib overhauls, they were up on the platform, playing hot and fast, when Grey led her inside. At tables, all around the dance floor folks stomped and clapped. Farmers and ranchers mixed with students and townies. A caller shouted instructions to the dancers. He called in a poetic, chanting flow, and they bowed and bobbed, turning round and round to the hillbilly rhythm. Gents whirled their ladies, teeth flashing, skirts flared out above bare legs and prancing boots.

There were two empty seats at a big round table near the wall, and Connie sat while Grey went for drinks. She watched for a time, mesmerized by the character of the place, the crowd's laughter, the rowdy yells, the blue smoke snaking up through strung lights, to disappear in the dim black rafters. It was entirely different in form and atmosphere from dances and dancing places, she had known. Quickly, the caller picked up his cadence, more calls, different calls, square after square, breaking down, until only four panting dancers remained, and then a great whoop of applause went up for them.

Three couples shared the table where Connie sat, and the women who appeared well acquainted with one another, were joking about their men. In lowered voices, they were telling what those men did that got them all bothered.

"Ward," said the first girl, "he up an brought home wildflowers, no reason at all, right out of the blue, and he was grinning like some schoolboy. I just got all hot and faintly for him, right then and there. It's those silly little things that get to me," she said laughing. "How about you?"

The youngest of the three giggled. She looked side to side then leaned toward the other women cupping her mouth. "Norm has a way of teasing and whispering things, y'all know, and when he gets out of the bath, all hairy wet and says stuff, gawd, I just melt. Gawd he makes me hot."

The oldest of the three women chuckled loudly, winked at Connie, who sat next to her. "Hot, I'll tell you hot," she blared over the music, not caring who heard. "My Homer comes home all drunk with his money gone payday night; now that gets me hot, real hot."

The two young wives squealed, and Connie burst into laughter with them. The band struck up another tune, and Grey arrived with two beers in paper cups. The heavy, older woman leaned close to Connie and whispered, "The good-looking ones are more trouble than they're worth honey. All the other girls are after em, and you can't never relax. You best shuck him off right now." Connie looked shocked, and the woman gave her a little push. "Go on now child. I'm just funning y'all. You can throw that un my way anytime."

The woman's husband was up and dragging on her arm. Giving a little yell, she sprang up, allowing herself to be handed out onto the dance floor.

"What do you think?" Grey asked.

"Are they all like this?" she whispered in his ear.

"Pretty much. My uncle Desmond, he used to live over this way before he was appointed judge in *Palatka*. I used to come here a lot, live it up with my cousins. You know how it is when you're from a bitty place like *Green Cove Springs*," he said, just a little embarrassed. "Anyways, at some dance places, the crowd can get pretty rowdy. It's mostly a married bunch here though, less trouble. Well, girl, speaking of dancing, are you ready to try it?" Grey asked, nodding toward the dance floor.

"I'll mess up for sure. Do you mind if I watch a little longer? Just a little longer," she begged, more than a little hesitant at being thrust into the melee. At least before, she had some idea of what she was supposed to do.

"Sure, but don't worry. Why everyone messes up when they're learning. My brother got me dancing by feeding me three shots of white lightning. Shy as I was, after a few snorts, I didn't care how silly I looked or how often I broke up my square. Fell flat on the floor after my fifth drink."

"What does it taste like?"

"Depends, the good stuff is pretty smooth, but most is pure fire. Not too bad if you mix in a little something, some favor molasses. The second swallow doesn't burn nearly so much going down. Prohibition and all, shine was all we could get back then, so we weren't too fussy, and it does have a kick."

"Well, I may need a taste. I'm not brave enough to make a fool out of myself without help."

Grey laughed. "Square dancing isn't all that hard to learn, and they do some easy calls, basic steps for beginners.

"If you say so"

The next few dances were simple. With what Joan had shown to her, and what she'd learned by watching, Connie did pretty well. That is, until she turned the wrong way, and collided with a burley farmer in another square. Grey pulled her up from the floor, and he wasn't the only one laughing. She brushed off the sawdust and advised him, she was ready to try a little of the shine. He brought her some in a coke bottle. Connie held her nose and took a generous gulp. She gasped; mouth and eyes wide open and clutched her throat.

"This batch isn't one of Luke's best," Grey said, clicking his tongue.

"Holy cow," she squeaked when the burning eased up enough for her to generate sounds.

"It is an experience, isn't it?" Grey chuckled.

"One that will last me a lifetime," she promised, wiping the tears from eyes and feeling the heat of the corn liquor spread to her stomach. "Do people actually like this stuff?"

"Well most people cut it a little. The women put a little bit in their Coke you know. To down a big slug neat like you just did, it takes a real tough number." He said this, trying to keep from laughing as he spoke.

"You jerk," she spat. She laughed just as quickly and leaned against him. "I certainly asked for it, didn't I. Whew!" She giggled again. "Goes right to work doesn't it?"

The other band, the four men dressed like cowboys, began to play, and Grey took her in his arms. They danced to a mellow old tune as the floor filled with couples cuddling and turning about each other, swaying to the sad old words. One dance followed another, square dancing began again, and Connie caught onto the calling. She drank too much, played the fool and had a wonderful time.

Late in the evening, some fists flew, men got their faces slapped for one thing or another and a car backed into the beer truck. One young woman fled past Connie, only to be overtaken by her husband. He shook her by the shoulders, until her hair came loose and fell around her face. 'I'll slap slop out of you girl, I ever see you kissing him again. I'll slap you rosy," he shouted. Men pulled him away, and as he shrugged them off, Connie could see the tears in his eyes. "I'm going to kick shit out of him," he threatened and went off to settle accounts with his brother.

Grey brought her back late for curfew, and she had to climb in through the window. She woke up nauseated; she was fuzzy mouthed; her head throbbed, and she hated BJ for opening the curtains. She got up, though, swayed a little and made her way towards the bathroom, but only because she really had too. With eyes half shut, she shuffled down the hall, wishing she were still asleep. Feeling sorry for herself, Connie sat on the toilet with her head resting against the wall and moaned. Afterward, she took a long shower. It made her feel better and eating a slightly stale donut found on her roommate's dresser helped settle her stomach. Finally, she looked at her clock and gasped. He was picking her up at ten, and it was half past nine. She rushed to make herself look human.

Grey had not driven back to *Green Cove Springs*; instead, he had taken a room. He'd got up early, shopped for clothes, asked about a boat rental, and got the name of a delicatessen. He arrived with a thermos of coffee, a box of sweet rolls, and gave a toot on his horn, because men weren't allowed in the building. Connie was impressed with his energetic efficiency, and happy to share the coffee and pastry. At the deli, they put together their picnic and raced east toward Newnan's lake. It was a great day for sailing, and not a bad day for necking. They had dinner in town, went to movies again, and necked in his car until she had to run to make curfew. He stood out in front until she waved from her window. She watched him get into his car and wave, watched as he pulled out, and drove northeast towards home. She was already impatient for him to return. He did. He was back every night that week. On the weekend, he invited her home.

***

Clare MacArt, through officially in mourning, was well over her loss; she was prepared to worry about other matters. She played checkers with Pearl until nine, but the black woman preferred turning in early. Clare sat up by herself Sunday night, waiting for her son to return from driving Connie back to *Gainesville*. Clare did not approve of what Grey was up to, not one bit.

"Come in the kitchen and sit with me," she called when she heard Grey at the front door. She smiled as he came in, his cheeks red from driving with the top down. He bent down to give her a peck on the cheek. She spied lipstick under his ear and she smelled Connie May Byran's perfume. "Pour some tea and sit down here," she said sweetly. "Your mother wants a few words with you."

Grey sighed. He knew the tone of voice. He only wondered what she was going to get on him about. He poured some tea, took a few cookies off the counter, and then sat across from his mother. He sipped and put the coffee cup carefully on the table.

"What's on your mind, mama?" he asked, getting right to it.

"Grey," she said earnestly, "y'all know I hate a busybody and I hate butting in, but there are times when it's a mother's duty to speak up. I'm only being frank," she said, sitting straighter. "I believe you're being unfair to those girls. First, y'all went out with Angela, and now y'all are chasing after Constance. The courting of two sisters at the same time is neither wise nor proper. It's not a good idea to court sisters at all. Why look in the Bible son, and you will see that almost every time a man became involved with sisters, it led to misery or tragedy, and those were

God's chosen men. Sure, as God above, involvement with sisters is going to bring a man trouble. Every time it will cause trouble, and I will not sit mute while my son brings himself to grief. I will not remain silent while he trifles with the daughters of friends. The Byrans have been our friends for thirty years," She said, looking him hard in the eye, "and I won't have it, Grey."

Clare's sweet smile had faded. She was fuming. "If you're serious, y'all choose out which ah those young women y'all intend court and let the other know how she stands with y'all. And do it right quick." She muttered, shifted around in her chair, and looked at the phone. "I'm of a mind to phone the Byrans myself, just to give them warning of what sort of troublesome things, y'all have been up to."

"For crying out loud ma, gimme a break. I only went out with Angel for a few days, and that was months ago, besides—"

"Shut up," Clare ordered in high moral indignity. "Y'all been corresponding with the young lady have you not? Well —" she prompted, when he did not answer fast enough to suit her.

"Yes ma'am," Grey mumbled, fidgeting.

"Y'all were kissing on her when you were in *Miami*, telling her she was a sweet thing —. Well you were, weren't y'all?"

"Yes ma'am," he confessed, squirming in the intensity of her glare.

"That's courting and that is leading a young lady on, if and when y'all are doing it with more than one young lady at a time," she lectured. "And y'all had best get this mess straightened out and the sooner the better. "Now which sister is it going to be?"

Grey looked up at the ceiling, attempting to associate two personalities with a single image. At first, it had been as if he was dealing with the same woman in different moods, but he had gotten a far better grasp on their differences in the last few weeks. Angel was the deeper person. She was far more complex and sensitive than her sister, but she lacked Connie's confidence and love of life's physical side. Both had attributes of which he found himself drawn.

"Hell, mama, now there's a question," he said, already pretty sure of the answer.

"Don't y'all swear in this house."

She was upset, and Grey could see the blood pulsing in the veins of her neck.

"Settle down mama. I like them both. I'd take either one over any other girl I've ever met, but of the two, I'm more at ease with Connie. We think alike; you know right where you stand with her. Angel is more intense, mysterious. She's the kind of girl who tries to make a fellow feel special. It's as if Angel's always trying to say what I want to hear instead of what she thinks. With Connie, it's all out in the open, take it or leave it. There's no show to her. I'd do better with Connie, even if she shows me up once in a while. We'll probably battle, hook and tong, but with her, when a thing is settled, it's settled. She not the kind of woman to throw the past at you, and, she's a sport."

"Are you in love with her?" Clare asked, rising from the table, agitated and needing to do something. She turned to put her saucer and cup in the sink.

"I could love them both, but yeah, I'm in love with Connie," he said grudgingly. He said it as if he had only just become aware of the fact.

"Have you told the girl?" Clare asked. She turned the tap, rinsing the dishes. Grey's voice was barely discernible over the running water.

"No ma'am."

Clare shut off the water. She shook her hands dry as she turned to face him and reached for a towel. "When do you intend to tell her?" she asked in a far gentler tone.

"I was planning to go into *Jacksonville* and shop for a ring tomorrow, then sort of wait for the right moment, you know. I can't wait too long, though. My leave's about up." Grey looked up at his mother, who had moved close to him, and saw her eyes had gone teary. She put her arms around his head, pulling his head against her bosom, and he was aware of the musty smell of dishwater and onions on her hands and apron.

"Son, y'all best call Angela and tell her how you feel about her sister. She's bound to be terrible hurt by this. She's to be y'all sister and y'all going to be dealing with her for a lifetime."

Clare rubbed her son's hair and held his head back away from her as she looked down into his face. She prayed to God that Angela Byran did not have strong sentiments for her boy. A marriage had more than enough problems without jealousy in the bargain.

"Y'all must be a gentleman Grey and treat both of those girls like the ladies they are. Good manners have smoothed over many a bump on the road of life," she counseled.

Chapter 12

Grey found the ring sets he wanted at the second jewelry store that he visited. He went to another shop to be sure, then came back and bargained. The jeweler came off his price substantially. The little theater in *Gainesville* was presenting, *A Comedy of Errors*. He had made plans with Connie to catch the play that evening, and sometime after the performance, Grey intended to ask her to marry him. He drove directly to *Gainesville* stopping only to fill the gas tank and add a little oil. He noted he'd put almost 1600 miles on the car in the last several days, and figured he'd wear it out, if he kept up his long-range romance. He checked into the same small cabin he'd rented the week before and showered and changed for his evening out. He decided to wear his uniform and took particular care to polish up his brass and put a shine on his shoes. He brushed his hair using a second mirror to make sure it looked right from behind, and then realized that his hat would mess it up anyway. Well, he'd carry the damn hat.

Grey closed his eyes and pictured the evening ahead: first the play, then dinner at a restaurant he'd chosen. He'd ask Connie right there, or perhaps on a walk in the park afterwards. They might even have time to go dancing, but no, not with a weeknight curfew of 10:00 pm. Well there was always the window. He chuckled to himself, remembering how he stood on a trashcan, boosting her up over the ledge. Her legs were kicking as she wiggled through the window. She had really nice legs.

Grey arrived at the dorm and stood in the small waiting room inside the front door, while someone went up to inform her that her date had arrived. Suddenly self-conscious, he checked his reflection in the glass. Trying to look sharp, he tucked his hat under one arm.

Connie had been watching at the window for at least twenty minutes waiting for Grey to arrive. BJ had spent hours helping her prepare for the evening. The fact that he had only a couple days left of his leave weighed on her. She'd been unable to concentrate in class; in fact, she might just as well have stayed in her room. Homework— she hadn't done any in a week and couldn't imagine trying. She was determined to look her best tonight, so that if he did leave, another woman, any other woman, would have one hell of a memory with which to compete.

The prospect that Grey would be gone for a year was frightening. It was particularly frightening, considering that, he was uncommitted and fair game for any female who was willing to throw herself at him. Her own behavior, with respect to her sister, was not lost on her and if anything, it caused her even more worry. Love was awful when you weren't sure you had it in return. It was wanting the commitment, wanting it so badly a woman thought she would wither and die if she didn't get it. However, as a woman, she was not allowed to ask. Be delicious and wait, that was the credo. It was maddening; it was unfair; it was painful, but there it was, and as a woman, Connie had to deal with it. She knew in her bones, this man she was meant to marry, and as she went downstairs to greet him, she hoped that he would recognize it.

"Grey."

He started and turned to greet her. He hadn't noticed Connie coming and was a little embarrassed at being caught gazing at his own reflection. She walked toward him, confident of her appearance. One arm raised, she made a complete turn, once around for his inspection, and waited for some form of compliment. Grey was caught for a moment without words, for in the soft light of the evening, she was, if anything, more beautiful than usual. She had chosen to wear an evening dress of the latest fashion: an off the shoulder creation of black silk. It fit tight to her high waist, and then flowed down over the perfect curve of her hips, to cling and flare in chiffon trimmed pleats behind her knees. Her hair was done up, exposing the classic line of her neck and shoulders, and secured with pearls, matching her earrings and necklace. Connie also wore a new perfume, and the combination of sight and scent made him dizzy.

Finding his voice, Grey said, "You look fantastic."

"You don't think I'm overdressed then?"

"Other women would hate you no matter what you wore."

"It's just that up here, there's so little to dress up for, and people aren't really very fashion conscious. I wanted to knock you out. I'm glad you're pleased," she said smugly.

"Pleased cannot possibly describe it," he said hungrily. "Come here."

She took two steps, and he enveloped her in his arms, kissing her, carefully so as not to disturb her elegantly arranged hair. Her lips and breath tasted like spearmint gum, and her body felt amazingly soft beneath the silk. She pushed him back, gently smiling up with warm humor in her green eyes.

"Settle down, sailor," she whispered softly, "or everyone's going to be talking about me."

"They probably already are. You look like a Christmas package Connie, one I'd enjoy unwrapping," he whispered.

She gave him a jab below the ribs with one finger and said, "Dream on, sailor." She turned away from him before he could see her blush.

The little theater version of *A Comedy of Errors* was humorously romantic, if somewhat slapstick. The characters of the play were totally confused, and all falling in love with the wrong person, until in the end, Master Shakespeare got it all worked out. After the last curtain, Grey drove them to Dominick's, for dinner. There was a piano player and they danced between cocktails and the first course of dinner. It was only natural that all eyes were on the young couple; Grey tall in his officer's uniform, Connie's stunning beauty framed in black silk. None of that mattered because, as they danced, their eyes held only each other, with the effect that they might have been alone in the room.

It was nearly curfew when Grey realized he had forgotten the engagement ring. They were walking towards his car, holding hands in the dim glow of a street lamp. He'd intended to continue into the park, where he would seat her on a bench, drop to one knee and proffering the ring, while beseeching her to become his wife. He now pictured the ring on the dresser in his tiny cabin and groaned inwardly.

"Would you mind if I stopped by my room on the way back?" he asked. "I only need a moment to grab something."

She glanced at her watch. "We've time," she said.

It was quiet when they drove in. It was also dark, for the owner saw no reason to waste money on outside lighting. Grey set the emergency brake and gave her a peck on the cheek. "Back in a jiffy," he said.

"Wait! Do you mind if I use your bathroom? I feel an emergency coming on."

"Come on in then." He hurried around the car, opening her door, and together they walked to the tiny cabin. He reached up under the eaves for the key, and fumbling with it in the dark, finally opened the door. Connie noticed the window shade in the next cabin open a crack, and she stepped quickly through the door.

"Tongues will be wagging tomorrow," she said, amused.

Grey closed the door and flipped the light switch. There was a flash as the bulb burnt out, and then more inky darkness. Connie stifled a giggle and stumbled over a chair, steadying herself on the end of the bed. The lights of passing car on the highway showed her the bathroom door.

"Excuse me," she said and moved toward the opening, one hand out before her.

As the door closed behind her, there was a click in the velvet dark, and then a rectangle of light outlined the door. Grey swept the top of the dresser with his hand, and finding the tiny box clutched it. He sat on the edge of the bed, waited, listening to faint sounds from the bathroom, his eyes growing accustomed to the dark. When the door opened the flare of light blinded him. It was off just as quickly, followed by a thump and the sound of the springs. The bed swayed.

"Oh drat," she giggled pushing herself up. "I'm blind and there's no room in here at all."

"Sit where you are for a second. Let your eyes adjust," Grey said, taking the ring out of its box. He reached toward her, finding her hand. She placed her other hand on his. He could just make out the pale glow of her face in the dark. He said, "I love you darling. Will you marry me?"

She could feel him tremble as he asked the question, and a sense satisfied warmth passed over her. "Yes," she murmured, "of course." She could not see the ring, but felt it being slipped onto her finger, and she was filled with elation. She had been sought after and claimed. She would belong to this man. She leaned toward him, felt his hands through the thin silk of her dress, and in the dark, his moist lips.

"I'll be a good wife to you," she promised. Her arms around his neck, she pulled him down, her breath against his throat.

"I'll make you a good husband too," he promised.

As she lay there, he kissed her again, her mouth, her neck, her breasts above the line of her dress, and she responded warm and accepting. Her breath deepened, became fast, seductive and he knew that she was his, he only need to take her, but on this very edge of passion, the ethics of his upbringing spoke to him and he drew back. This was not some brief encounter, but the woman with which he'd be sharing his life. He wanted to honor her. Connie's strong young arms were about his neck, and he gently disengaged himself.

"My uncle's a judge," he reminded her "and I've only two days of my leave remaining. Marry me tonight?"

"Why not? You've made me miss my curfew," she answered, at the same time serious and joking. She breathed in deeply, sucking the air through her teeth. "Let's hurry though. I don't know how much longer I can wait for you."

The drive to *Palatka* took over an hour and Judge Kirk was sound asleep when his doorbell began ringing. The sleepy colored houseboy recognized the judge's nephew and opened the door. At Grey's insistence, he went upstairs and woke the judge, who hurried down expecting that his nephew's arrival was to announce some family tragedy. Advised of the true nature of the midnight visit, he fetched Grey's aunt down as a witness, and grudgingly married them before returning to bed. Halfway back to *Gainesville*, the newlyweds ran out of gas.

***

Dawn soaked into the oak forest slowly, pushing the darkness west. Connie was aware of the birds first, the sound mainly, for in the upper branches, their quick movements were obscure among the roof of leaves. She listened, and it seemed as if their calls complained of the disturbing light. She felt the warmth of flesh at her back. She curled against a warm mass, whose hand dangled over her breast. She sighed with satisfied remembrance; she was a married woman.

She lay still for a time, ignoring the prickle of pine needles, savoring the sensation of lying nude in a man's arms, and not with any man, but with her man, with her husband. Her husband, god how wonderfully strange that sounded. The first rays of sunlight caught the branches and painted the leaves and Spanish moss a brilliant gold. Somewhere nearby there were voices. A tractor motor backfired and started. Suddenly she remembered that she lay naked, except for a picnic blanket, in the middle of pasture. Alarmed, Connie nudged her husband with her elbow.

"W—what's," he stammered.

"Get dressed, somebody's coming," she cried.

"Oh," he mumbled, sitting up and stretching.

Connie pulled the blanket around herself; her eyes went to her husband's groin with a certain amount of dismay. It had been dark last night, and this was the first time she had seen him in the altogether. He'd awakened fully aroused and seeing him caused her to feel both embarrassed and excited. She had never imagined quite how big it got. Pictures and sculptures, it seemed, had failed to properly depict the aroused male organ, and she was amazed that would fit into her. Well it did, and it had, and she turned red remembering just how well it had. My God, she thought, everyone would know what she had been doing. He was pulling on his pants and had to wiggle and stuff himself down to one side to get them zipped. She giggled despite herself, because he looked so foolish, and he turned his back trying to adjust things.

Finally situated, he said, "Climb into the car honey and I'll put the top up, so you can get dressed. The sound of the tractor engine was near, and he looked into the wall of trees. Grey had pushed the ford a couple hundred feet off the road, and he guessed that there must be a farmhouse right on the other side of the trees. "Sounds like there might be some gas to be had over there," he suggested.

As she climbed in, he latched the top, at the same time admiring the curves of her bottom, as she tried without success to keep herself covered while retrieving her slip from the backseat. Connie could not help noticing his pleased interest.

"You go on," she ordered, pulling the blanket around herself modestly. "I can get dressed by myself." As he walked into the trees, she began squirming into her panties. "Oh God," she gasped thinking of it for the first time. "I've got to call grandmother."

Grey bought two gallons of gas from the farmer and had the car on the road within a few minutes. Connie snuggled drowsily against him, and as he drove, Grey contemplated the difficulties their elopement was certain to produce. His mother was going to be shocked. He had neglected to ask Captain Byran's permission. Where would his wife reside when he departed tomorrow. Would she want to continue at school, or follow him to the west coast? They would need to let their friends and families in on the news, and then he remembered. He had not called Angel as he'd promised. He cringed inwardly. That call would not be easy!

Chapter 13

Angel remembered holding her eyes open with the terrible determination to avoid sleep and her frantic dreams. Her conscious mind was separated into parts. One part aware that the images in the darkness were not real, and another terrified part, which was reluctant to fall into sleep. Wanting only to be held, she wished for her mother, for her grandmother, and for her sister, but instead she remained alone in the dark. Her exhaustion defeated her, sliding her back into sleep and tenacious nightmares.

When next she woke, Angel knew she had been asleep for quite a while. The door had opened with no other warning than the click of the latch. It was as if she was blind, and she turned her face into her pillow. Corazon shut the door quickly and came directly to

Angel's bed, sitting on the edge. She brushed her granddaughter's hair back, pressing her hand to the girl's forehead. It was quite hot.

"How are you feeling, darling?"

"Oh, Grandma," she murmured," I feel dreadful. I've the worst headache."

"You wouldn't take your medicine Grace said, and you've given the nurse nothing but trouble. That's why you're worse now."

"It made me vomit, and she tied mittens on me," Angel sobbed miserably. "And they wouldn't let me read."

"The light is bad for your eyes, it could make you blind, and you were scratching. The mittens are for your own protection, or would you rather have ugly scars." Corazon put her arms around her granddaughter, and hugging her tightly against her, she began to rock. "I'm so sorry your sick sweetheart, and sorry that I went away and left you alone. Dr. Ritchie says you have a very virulent strain of the measles. We had no concept of how sick you'd be."

Angel sighed in the comfort of being held. "I love you," she whispered softly.

"I love you too and we're going to make you feel better. Grace is running a bath for you. A bath will help to lower your fever and soothe your blisters."

Tears were in her eyes and she said, "I've got red spots and scabs all over and I itch. I must look awful. I know I look awful," she whined.

"It will clear up as long as you don't scratch. Your Uncle Connor had a terrible case of measles when he was little. I was worried to death, but it never left the mark on him, nor did it bother his eyesight."

She lowered Angel back onto her pillow and dampened a cloth, placing it on her forehead. "How does that feel?"

"Good," she said, and reached weakly for her grandmother's hands.

"First were going to bathe you. They're putting blankets over the windows to darken the bathroom. Afterward you'll get some broth. You must drink it even if you throw it up."

"But I don't want anything," she said, nauseous.

"I don't care. You will keep eating until something stays in you, or would you rather be at the hospital being fed through a tube in your arm."

"No! Not that."

"Then don't act like a child. You're a grown woman now; you must help yourself."

There was a knock at the door, Corazon pulled the cloth over Angel's eyes and called out, "come in." Asher opened the door, entering with ginger ale and crushed ice on a tray.

"Shawn has returned from the pharmacist, and Grandpa's brought up your medicine, let me sit you up so you can take it."

Angel, hot with fever, was in bed without a nightgown but too ill to care. As Corazon propped her up, her hair dangled in crazy knots over her bare breasts. Her normally creamy skin was flushed; it was dappled with countless tiny fiery red bumps, and some that had scabbed over where they'd been scratched. Asher, without a word, but with a very worried expression, poured ginger ale over the ice. He stirred in her medicine. Squatting beside the bed, he placed a hand behind Angel's head, and held the glass to her mouth. She drank, choking and spilling a little. The cold liquid dribbled down her chin, off her breasts and pooled in her belly button.

"That's cold," she gulped, beginning to shiver and retch.

"Hold your chin up and swallow," Asher ordered. "You won't get over this by gagging on your medicine."

Corazon dabbed Angel dry with a towel, while giving him a nasty look of repugnance. "Don't you bully her; she's doing the best she can. You go see if they have the curtains hung. Go on now — Thinks he's on the deck of a ship, dam'd him," she muttered under her breath."

The bathroom was ready, and Asher returned. He lifted his granddaughter from the bed as the three women hovered around. The heat she radiated concerned him; she was burning up. He had lowered her in, and as weak as she was, it took all three women the keep her in the cool water. Asher, a coward under the circumstances, fled downstairs and away from the commotion, and poured some scotch. He'd seen Indians this sick and dying from the measles on the *Spanish Coast* but had thought European stock was more resistant. In Angel's case, he'd been proven wrong. He felt guilty for the three days he'd stayed over in *Green Cove Springs*. "Well hell," he told himself, how was he to know?

Soon it was quiet upstairs. They succeeded in getting Angel's fever down and put her back to bed under a light blanket. She even managed to hold down a cup of broth. For an entire week, she slept, waking for only short periods of the time when they fed and bathed her. Slowly, the spots and scabs began to clear.

On Monday, she sat in a lounge chair before an open window in her room. The first sunlight she had seen in two weeks poured down on her from an intense blue sky; flowers outside her window offered a profusion of lustrous color. She had been in a dim twilight state for far too long, and it had seemed this day would never come. Filled with an exuberant appreciation, she worked with pastels, managing to capture the beauty of her window of light.

Grandma had brought a mirror and face-cream and had brushed out her hair after breakfast. She looked at the fading pink spots where the scabs had left new skin; noted the slight hollowness in her cheeks, dark circles beneath her eyes and the dullness of her complexion. She wanted to cry. Could this be her face? She was told that she had lost twelve pounds and would need to eat well in order to put it back.

She thought of Grey. She had spoken to him the evening of his arrival from *California*. Then she had worsened, become so withered and shamefully ill, that she had been aware of nothing until now. Now she realized he would be leaving soon. She wanted terribly to see him but appalled by her appearance she was ashamed. How could she face him looking like a diseased corpse? She had looked a mess when she saw herself in the mirror, but after her grandmother had applied a little cream, a little powder, a dab of rouge, she had improved remarkably. "You'll be yourself in a week," grandma had promised her.

With renewed confidence, Angel had called the MacArt residence in *Green Cove Springs*. Pearl answered and told her that the Mrs. was in town and Mister Grey had driven to *Jacksonville*. Angel had asked that Pearl inform them that though she had been ill, she was very much improved, and hoped to catch them home the next time she phoned.

The pastel completed, Angel took a nap after lunch, and then grandfather came up to play chess with her after dinner. She had expected a call from Grey but had forgotten about it by bedtime. Early Tuesday morning, Dr. Ritchie made a house call and proclaimed her cured. On his way out of the house, he removed the quarantine notice from the front door. Fedrico made a rare appearance, inviting them for breakfast at a *Coral Gables* restaurant. Afterward, he went off to his office and Corazon took Angel to the beauty salon for pampering. It was near lunchtime when they returned home. Grace was answering the phone as they entered the house.

"Why yes, she is Lieutenant MacArt," Grace spoke into the phone, winking at Angel, who pointed to upstairs. "Just one minute, she's going to take the call upstairs."

Angel flashed her grandmother a happy smile and climbed the stairway as quickly as possible in her weakened state. The door slammed, and Grace put the receiver down. The women went into the kitchen, both inwardly pleased with how the day was going. A short time later Asher came up from the yacht club with a big dolphin he'd been given. He filleted it, while Delia began to make up a lunch.

"How's Angel doing today?" He guzzled down his entire glass of iced-tea and sighed.

"A world of difference," Corazon answered, quite pleased to inform him. She pointed upstairs with a newly manicured finger. "She's on the phone. Grey just called."

"That should perk her up," he said, smirking, and he stretched and yawned. He stretched out of pure pleasure, like an old cat. He had begun thinking lately that it would be nice having grandbabies in the house again. Yep, he thought, those girls are ripe and ready.

"You look smug enough Asher Byran."

"Well, Cori my love, I expect wedding bells and babies aren't far off. Probably would have happened already if the boy hadn't been off with the Navy.

"It's been so long since we had a wedding here. You remember how lovely Cathleen looked on her wedding day. I do look forward to doing all those things again, but they seem so young."

"Scuse me ma'am," Delia interrupted, "you's want me to set up a place for Angel?"

She glanced at the wall clock: twenty minutes. She should be off the phone. "Yes! Set a place. I'll run up and get her," Corazon said standing. "What do you bet Grey comes down for a visit before leaving for *California*?" she said gaily over her shoulder, as she headed upstairs. Angel's door was closed. She opened it a crack and called cheerfully. There was no answer, so she opened it further and entered. The room was dim, lit only by what light passed through the closed curtains. As her eyes became accustomed to the shadows, she realized Angel was nowhere to be seen. Puzzled, she turned to leave, and then heard a muffled sob.

"Angel," she called. Seeing that the door to the closet was open, she recalled that her granddaughter had fled into that dark recess as a little girl. She had hidden there when she was upset. She went to the door, peered in, and saw her curled in the corner. "Why, chica," she said softly, "whatever's the matter?" Angel said nothing, and Corazon kneeling down next to her, heard her trying to smother her sobs in a pillow. "Darling, you're crying, what's happened?"

She raised her face, a mask of hopelessness and spoke, her words a flood of misery. "I'm so ashamed; he didn't want me Grandma. B — but I don't understand why, because he called me his sweetheart and h — he wrote to me about the things we'd do when he came back. W — what's wrong with me?" She stuttered. "We look alike, h — he couldn't even tell us apart, and I tried so hard to be perfect for him."

Angel's nose was running, and Corazon wiped it with her hanky, as astonished, she gasped, "What has happened to make you think that Grey doesn't like you darling?"

"B — because," she stammered, trying to get the words past her trembling lips, "he's married Connie," and again Angel began her disconsolate weeping.

Corazon lost her balance and plopped onto the hardwood floor next to her heartbroken granddaughter. As she gazed into the tear-filled eyes, Corazon was, for once in her life, speechless.

Chapter 14

Distraught to the point of illness, Angel sequestered herself in her room for another three days, ignoring phone calls; one was from Wayne Ross with an invitation to a dance on campus. She felt unlovable, betrayed, and was unable to bear any mention of Grey or her disloyal sister. By the fourth day, her agonized self-pity turned to anger, which she took out first on a packet of Grey's letters, and then her sister's room. Afterward, sitting amidst the wreckage, she brooded. Finally, becoming suffused with moody guilt, she sighed and stared blankly at the wreckage.

Realization fermented in her that now that she was not to be Grey's, she knew neither who, she was or what she wished to become. It was as if she'd sought a revelation of herself, and in the very moment of discovery, had forgotten what had been revealed. What was to be her reason to exist amidst life's chaos? At this particular moment, she was reluctant to give the question weight. On an intellectual level, Angel understood this to be a condition of adolescence, but resented this explanation of her mood. She was no child. Her concern broadened. She must decide on a course of action. She must accept things, as they were, at least those things that were beyond control.

She observed the destruction she'd caused. There was a satisfaction to be had in smashing things, but she recognized it as childish. She wouldn't be childish. Physically destructive behavior was futile. It was beneath her. She began to put the room back in order.

As she swept up the glass, she gasped and dropped to her knees. The shattered pieces of a statue her mother had made lay next to the dresser. The figurine was a guardian angel, its wings wrapped protectively about a small child. May had crafted one for each of her daughters. Angel's was still in her room. Carefully, she gathered the pieces, searching out each sliver and placing them in a cigar box. She was deeply upset, for what she'd destroyed was not merely a gift, it was the irreplaceable work of a wonderful artist, who had imagined it, and had then given her vision form. As an artist herself, Angel had a deep appreciation for works of art. She put the box in a drawer in her room, and carefully picked up her own figurine. She walked quietly down the hall and placed it lovingly on Connie's dresser.

In a positive frame of mind, she returning to her room, stripped off her nightgown, showered, dried, powered and applied a touch of makeup. Intending to go forth with a new resolve, she flung open the closet looking for something in her wardrobe that expressed the image of that new resolve. On finding it, she dressed herself to go shopping. She would pull things together. She would begin by replacing everything she'd broken and extend her good feeling to the purchase of Christmas gifts. There would be a dance at the University tonight. She would attend.

Angel slipped quietly out of the house and into her car, planning to drive first to Burdines, the downtown store. Not used for three weeks, the engine did not start immediately, and backfired when it did. "So much for slipping away unnoticed", she thought backing past the startled gardener, she made a mental note to address Shawn's failure to properly maintain her car.

The December air was cool without being cold and she felt suddenly good at being out, getting a grip. Even if her thinness embarrassed her, there would be some who liked it. There were other men. The world was full of men, men who would beg for just a chance to date her. Well, at least after she had a little time to fill back out. What a fool she'd been, hanging on to a three-day memory for nine months. She had ignored males in general, given the cold shoulder to any man who showed interest. She couldn't deny an attraction to Grey, but there was other game in the forest, and it was time she strung her bow. The dance would be fun, a chance to sharpen her hunting skills.

In the past, Angel had been confident of her own sensuality, her ability to deal with the opposite sex. She had been dumbstruck by Connie's coup. Her sister was a tomboy, who went out in the sun without a hat, ran around in boy's clothes, treated men like playground chums, and liked nothing better than beating them at their own silly games. Connie, even if she was good at math, had never had an intellectual or creative thought in her life. Connie could not have stolen her sweetheart, unless a tomboy was what Grey wanted.

Or, had Connie started paying more attention to glamour than she had to baseball scores? The thought that her twin would deliberately move in on her beau hurt terribly. Even grandpa had refrained from defending Connie this time. It was doubly injurious because Angel loved her sister, was a part of her and had dreadfully missed her when she went up north. Despite their little spats, Angel shared unspoken feelings with Connie, feelings that no one else understood.

Admittedly, Angel also saw her twin as a competitor, an adversary who must be bested whenever possible. If Connie did a thing better, Angel was irritated. When someone preferred Connie's company, Angel was eaten up with jealousy. Connie probably never noticed Angel's jealous streak. She wouldn't have cared if she had noticed it. Angel was as aware of her envious streak as she was of her short temper. The sin of envy was a sin that she mentioned when she confessed. However, acknowledgement and confession had done little to shorten her fuse or to curb envy's power. The revelation that her sister had also been envious, envious to the point of snatching her sweetheart from behind her back, well, it was more than a shock. It was almost beyond dealing with.

At Burdines, Angel shopped for over an hour, during which time she did not think of Grey for an instant, but leaving, she ran into Bonnie Kohl at the door. Suddenly she felt exposed.

"Angel," Bonnie gushed, "Word is your sister eloped with a sailor."

"She sure did," she confirmed. "But it's not much of a scandal! An officer, a family friend, we've known him since we were kids."

"Not the dreamboat you were dating last spring," Bonnie said with a knowing little smirk.

Angel nodded with a stiff smile. "The very same," she said with a shaky laugh. "Good looking but not my type," she lied. "He must have rung Connie's bells though. Gotta run girls," Angel chirped, turning toward her parked car.

Ignoring traffic, she bolted across the street, ignoring a blaring horn. She wanted to call out a cheerful goodbye, but the words hung on her tongue. She opened the door and threw her purchases in the back seat. Blinking away hot tears that blurred her vision, Angel climbed behind the wheel. She was humiliated; she could barely stand her own company. They knew Grey MacArt had thrown her over for Connie. They were probably laughing behind her back this very moment, which was so unfair, because she was miserable already.

Starting the car, Angel pulled out into traffic, and drove fast toward the beach. The tears were tears of resentful anger, and she told herself this would all turn around quite soon. She pulled up to the Winsor Hotel, turned her car over to the valet, and walked through the lobby to a café adjacent to the pool. She ordered a sandwich and a rum punch. When the sandwich came, she ordered another drink and a third, which she carried to the pool.

As the alcohol mellowed her, Angel lounged under an umbrella. She watched the surf pile on the sand. The breeze cooled her and moved the flowered vines on the wall. Soothed by the rum, she considered what colors she would use to reproduce the brilliance of the flowers against the Gulf Stream blue. She was at peace thinking about it, beginning to compose the painting in her mind when a voice startled her.

"Connie Byran, I didn't know you were back in town, babe."

Angel turned, angry at the mention of her sister's name, and shielded her eyes against the sun. She saw Paul Benetti standing over her.

"You've got the wrong sister again, Paul, and its Mrs. Connie MacArt these days."

"Married— Gees, you're kidding me. College guy?"

"Navy!"

"Navy, the guy she was out with last Easter?"

"The same," She said, not bothering to correct the details of Benetti's assumption. "They eloped a few weeks ago. The happy couple should be settling into navy housing in *San Diego*."

"Quick work! Dam'd salts don't waste time. I was still trying to get a date out of your sister when she left for *Gainesville*."

"Oh Paul, Don't be discouraged, I 'm sure somebody will go out with you eventually," Angel said feeling perverse.

He laughed. "Don't kid yourself sweetheart. I beat em off with sticks. Selective, that's me. Your sister was a fun kid." He gave Angel an appraising look. "Play your cards right and I might reserve a little time for you."

"Why I'll start working myself up to your standards tomorrow, Paul," she said with a note of sarcasm. "I'll phone when I think I'm ready."

His sharp black eyes glared fleetingly. There was a mean antagonism in his eyes, even as his mouth smiled. Paul snorted with apparent humor.

"Do that," he countered, and walked toward the cabañas without a backward glance.

Angel sat, annoyed, more at the loss of her focus than the man who caused it. The composition she had begun to put together in her mind and her sense of peace was gone. Without caring, she finished her drink and went home. She was determined to regain what pride she could, and decided again, as she drove, she would begin acting like a reasonable adult, rather than a distraught child. "After all," she told herself for the hundredth time, "you haven't seen the man in months, and there's certainly no shortage of men in the world."

Angel parked, and with her packages, hurried up to her room to compose her thoughts before sitting down to dinner with her grandparents. Again, she bathed, and for the first time in weeks, spent time on painting her fingernails. She arranged her hair in just the way it would appeal to a man. She began to renew in herself that delight a female feels in dressing for men. She chose a dress that was smart rather than pretty. She chose, instinctively, a dress that hung fashionably elegant on her slimmed frame. Angel stroked it downward, over her stomach and thighs, and thought that she looked very much in vogue. Perhaps she should remain thin.

Restless, she walked to the French doors and studied the effect of the light on the bougainvillea. The late afternoon sun angled in beneath the clouds enriching the colors. The sky itself was active, clouds rising, boiling into thunderheads, their tops overhanging patches of intense tropical blue. On one level, she considered how she might catch the effect on canvas, while on another, she weighed the advantage of returning Wayne Ross' call. Should she accept his invitation, or of just go to the dance unescorted? Both offered advantages. She smelled jasmine drifting up from the garden and the scent recalled to her consciousness, a memory of dancing in Grey's arms.

In an instant, Angel became both sad and petulant, and the prospect of attending a dance seemed far less desirable. The idea of a campaign of male conquest disgusted her; the whole system of relationships between men and women disgusted her, and she didn't understand why. She didn't understand why her mood fluctuated so abruptly. She was at once drawn and repelled. She both longed for a formless comfort, she instinctively knew would be born of a relationship, and feared the pain that seemed an inevitable product of emotional closeness. She had been touched by both but understood neither.

From downstairs came the tingling of the dinner bell. Suddenly, Angel knew she was hungry. Hunger— she was undoubtedly hungry, and with that one sure thing as a catalyst, Angel decided she would go dancing, and she would go unescorted, and she would enjoy herself. She was determined to enjoy herself, determined to be seen enjoying herself.

She recalled the look of the thin dark-haired girl; McGraw, the sophomore who had been at their table with Don Lumas. She had had such a sophisticated air. Angel changed her hair and make-up after dinner and studied herself in the mirror. She saw a haughty unapproachable young woman, a woman who emitted a subtle daring. She was pleased with effect of her new look, but despite her pleasure, was somehow uncomfortable, for it was not her. The sophistication of her new look was striking, even severe, but that was not it. She turned side to side and regarded the image through a pair of troubled eyes. Unconsciously she began to transform her own inner image to match that cool nonchalance she perceived to be the characterization of the woman of the mirror.

As Angel reached the foot of the stairs, Grace called to her from the dining room, telling her that her grandmother wanted a word on the veranda. Angel walked through the French doors, stood before her grandmother, and posed, one hand on a rattan chair, already assuming her new role.

"What?"

Corazon put aside her magazine and stood smiling, "I only wanted to see you off, darling. My, aren't we snappish?"

Angel melted, "I'm in a mood," she apologized.

"Well you're getting out again and I hope you have a nice evening with your friends. Very stylish," Corazon observed, aware of her granddaughter's change in appearance. "A trifle severe for your age, but striking all the same," she said. "Turn so I can see," she commanded and stepped back.

"You like it?"

"Yes! Perhaps a little mature, but you must please yourself," Corazon said with a dismissive smile, and changing the focus, continued, "You'll be home at a reasonable hour of course?"

"Like everyone else," Angel replied evasively as a feeling of irritability rose up. "Eighteen with a married twin, and I'm to be treated like a child," she thought. A flicker of resentment crossed her face.

"Call if you're to be late, or if you'd like us to send Shawn," Corazon said, exasperatingly patient. She gave her granddaughter a kiss and watched as the girl walked to her car.

On campus, Angel parked and walked toward the building, merging with other students. She joined in a light banter with Julie and Meg Parks as she entered the building. The place was strung with colored lights; Christmas decorations covered walls that surrounded a mass of dancers and reflected the rhythmic blare of a big band. To the side, young people were mixing, laughing, and drinking punch, much of it laced with something brought along to loosen up with. Angel moved among them, talking, receiving sisterly smiles from girlfriends, and the fresh hoots and whistles of unattached men.

By nine, she had allowed herself to be cornered by a tall sandy haired senior. He was square jawed with determined blue eyes, and a confident insistence that she dance with him. She did for a while, one number after another. When she finally brushed him off, he gave a great sigh for an audience of friends.

Clutching his heart, he staggered against the wall crying, "Darlin, I'm gonna die if you don't say you love me."

She turned back, a hand on her hip, the other fingertips to her cheek. With a pleasantly sarcastic expression, Angel promised to send flowers.

"Baby, baby, it hurts; your killing me," he cried after her. "I'm dying here," he insisted, and everyone laughed; and she laughed as she moved off with friends. It felt good to tell a man where to get off. By midnight, she was exhausted and a little drunk. Meg drove her home and she was hung over on Sunday.

Chapter 15

School and its extracurricular activities kept Angel busy. New Year's day, the *University of Miami Hurricanes* faced off against *Bucknell* in the Orange Bowl Tournament. She had a date with a halfback for the dance that evening. She attended the lectures of Robert Frost at the Fourth annual *Winter Institute of Literature*, and after attending the Winter Arts Festival, she began to paint again. Study and the social whirl became a blur, for she was involved in the family's calendar of activities as well as her own.

The week before Easter, two separate events took precedence over school in Angel's thoughts. First, her grandmother announced that Connie was pregnant and began making plans for a late spring visit to *California*. The second was that on the same day, Angel was introduced to her father's old partner, Dan Tully.

It was in the winner's circle at *Tropical Park*. One of the Tully horses had won, and Angel had been with her grandparents when they went down to congratulate him. The old curiosity of things concerning her father had bubbled to the surface of her mind, and a reawakened jealousy at Connie having Grey's baby, momentarily lost its importance. She'd decided to get answers to the questions that had obsessed her only two years earlier.

Mrs. Tully had been warm and Tully, himself charming. Strangely, Tully frightened Angel a little. Even though his face was filled with jovial good will, she sensed in him an underlying menace, a lethal directness that was out of character with the grinning image of a fond upper-class race-horse owner. This observation was reinforced when she overheard that Tully found an extended *Miami* vacation necessary. He had, it was rumored, once more embroiled himself in *Irish Republican* politics. She was introduced and complimented in his pleasant Irish brogue but with the opportunity at hand, decided on some unconscious level to leave questions wait.

Celebration, and champagne followed the race. Angel, still sulking at news of her sister's pregnancy, and feeling betrayed in affairs of the heart, imbibed more than her share. She knew she was probably an embarrassment to her grandparents, not that she allowed knowledge of their displeasure to make more of a difference than the promise of a hangover. She made her own decisions. Though it was a façade Angel's crafted persona of sassy independence had become a well-worn suit, and she was seen as flirtatious, outspoken, even daring, but above all a cool customer, a girl who knew what the wolves wanted, but knew that they would not be getting it from her.

It was a week before Angel worked up the gumption to approach Dan Tully, and then it took an hour to turn the conversation to the subject of her father. What Angel gleaned from Tully's words was a sense that though her father was a man with many faults, most had grown from a rebellion against authority. Her father was a heroic figure, a natural leader, crafty and romantic.

It didn't occur to her that she was hearing about her father from a man who recalled Fred Byran as a best friend and chose not to remember or mention his brutally rough edges. Tully related some of the better parts of their history and did so with a certain humor that made Fred's bad boy character seem appealing. For better or worse, and more often than not, women are unconsciously drawn to men who remind them of their father.

In late May, while her grandparents were visiting Connie in *California*, Angel attended a private party on the beach, a senior graduation party, and it was the first occasion that, Angel had found Paul Benetti to be anything other than irritating. A rude group of outsiders had tried to crash the party, men pulling her and some of her girlfriends, roughly out onto the dance floor. The revelry had come to an abrupt halt when the interlopers became loudly resistant to leaving. Paul had handled it personally, talking to them, and forcefully evicting three who refused to listen. He was surprisingly powerful and quick with his fists. Angel was reminded of her father's tough guy persona. Paul was also a very flashy dancer and the floor. Before midnight, Paul and a couple of cars packed full of kids, drove up to the casino at *Hallandale Beach*. Everybody at the club knew the Benetti family. What Paul asked for he got. Angel drank champagne as she played roulette for the first time. At craps, she won a little playing at a table alongside Paul, who won a lot. She found herself feverishly screaming the jargon of the game as the dice flew and the drinks kept coming. The atmosphere was charged; the risk, the excitement of it was infectious.

Angel was far too drunk to remember anything concerning the sexual encounter she had with Paul Benetti. It had taken place on the beach behind the casino, and to her credit, even if she didn't remember, she had repeatedly said no. She had even made a feebly drunken attempt to defend her honor. Paul Benetti however, like her father, was not a man who took the word no seriously.

***

Angel woke up a little past noon, suffering a terrible hangover. It was a half hour before she could even manage a shower. Grace had just brought up some tea and toast when Meg Parks phoned asking if she were all right. Angel had no idea what Meg meant, but the question worried her. She didn't even remember how she'd gotten home.

"What do you mean?"

"You don't remember?"

"I Must have passed out. The last thing I remember is playing craps."

"Oh, God Angel, you were dancing with Paul and then you were out back. I had too much to drink myself, but you two were doing some heavy petting, and then he hauled you into a cabana. I was trying to deal with my own date, and later I noticed you didn't come out. Julie and I had to dress you and bring you home."

"Dress me?"

"All you had on were your nylons."

"Oh my god Meg, I don't remember."

"Well you seemed pretty enthusiastic, I mean, the way you were kissing him earlier."

"But I don't even like him."

Meg sighed into the phone, "That's the problem with booze. I sure learned the hard way."

"What!"

"New Year's Eve, but Bill was drunk out of his head too. We just got carried away, but I remember it all — It just isn't going to happen again."

"I didn't Know."

"Bills all right, but you be careful around Paul — Benetti's not like the other kids. I've heard stories about his family."

"Oh Meg, I've got to go — I've got to think."

Angel hung up. Did anybody else Know? Know what? She wasn't sure what.

Grace's knock startled her.

"Yes!"

"You have a message from Mr. Benetti. He says he sorry but he's going to be a half hour late for your dinner date."

"Thank you," she told Grace, her voice sounding far more calm than she was for she had no memory of making a date. He first impulse was to call and cancel, but it occurred to her that her self-respect demanded that she privately confront Paul, He was the only one that knew what had happened, and from what Meg said, she had thrown herself at the man. She fell across the bed, feeling a mixture of dismay and anger, at Paul, at herself, for what she suspected had transpired on the previous evening. She was disgusted and at the same time strangely anxious. She shuddered, fearing she would be considered a slut, a tramp, if anyone were to hear about it, no matter what she had actually done. She needed to ask him, to know — how far she had gone. Yes, she needed to deal with the issue of what had taken place.

When Paul arrived, he brought a gift-wrapped box of chocolates and a card on which he'd written that he was crazy about her. Angel was polite but nervous for it seemed that though she didn't really know him, he had a claim on her. She hurried into the car without waiting for him to get her door.

"Why did you ask me out?" she asked him, meaning to be confrontational, but not quite pulling it off.

He laughed, disbelieving what he'd heard, and flicked away his cigarette. "After last night, you gotta ask me why we're going out to dinner. If we hadn't already had a date, I would' a phoned ya, babe. Gimme a break!" he grinned suggestively, "I like you."

"That — that's it?" she stammered, feeling suddenly naked in his presence, embarrassed at having asked at all.

"Well —" he countered, turning his eyes boldly where they should not be, and said in his deep syrup sweet baritone, "I liked what you gave me, and I'd like some more of the same. Whew! You were more than a little enthusiastic, and I've been around."

She let out a gasp, followed by ragged agitated laughter, "Really!" She stared at him incredulously and began to laugh again. Inside she was growing both sick and furious with herself because she couldn't remember, could not be sure any part of what he said was entirely true. She faintly recalled kissing, rubbing against him, but she couldn't sort them out. "*God*," she thought appalled, "*look what drinking has brought me down to.*"

Paul chuckled, not grasping the nature of her reaction and said, "I wouldn't have believed it of you babe. You always came across as the original snow princess." He turned the car onto "*U.S.1*" and sped up. "I'm going to take you to a little place in the Gables. First class chef and the pastry is something else, best outside of *New York*."

Angel was thinking, *'now that I know how stupid I was, what am I doing here?'* She couldn't blame it all on him, and so she said nothing, choosing instead to stare at a freight rumbling past it the opposite direction.

The evening sun was low in the trees, but the heat still shimmered up off the asphalt. June was hot, humid, and the air rushing past felt good. The cool air was the only thing that Angel could think of at that moment for her mind seemed frozen in a new and confusing reality. Though Paul unsettled her, even frightened her a little, it was as if she had somehow become bound to him by that most intimate act. She was temporarily helpless to remove herself from the power it invoked.

At the restaurant, there were people they both knew, and they were invited for drinks at a table filled with lively conversation. Time was spent ordering, and more time debating the wine, though it was obvious the waiter considered them barbarians. That proved to be true, for they continued to order more liquor, and consume it with the meal. The food was good, though Angel picked at it with little appetite. Afterward, they went to a dance club, and more drinks appeared at the table. Now that Angel had become acutely aware of the pitfalls of drinking, it seemed as if alcohol was appearing everywhere. She reached out her hand for a drink, but intending to control her intoxication, she only sipped it. She was determined to drink no more than was necessary to soften her resentment.

The music started back up and she danced with Phil Fry, who tried to ask her out. Angel danced one dance after another until the band would break, and they would sit, chat, and have another drink. Surrounded by the hot pulse of the club's music, she danced one guy to the next, cheek to cheek, body pressed to body or apart, fast and loose to swing. Partners were anonymous. Some she knew, but mostly she danced with Paul.

As the evening grew late, he danced her into a dark corner a few times, and kissed her aggressively, each time in the same manner, tilting her head back and pressing his lower body against her. Breathless, he would chuckle, and in his soft deep voice say, "I'm a wolf baby, yeah, but ya gotta gimme a break here. Ya got me hot babe, hot," he would say, as if it were her fault that he couldn't keep his paws to himself. It was ridiculous, him acting apologetic with a lecherous gleam in his eye. She could have laughed in his arrogant face, but at the same time, he was so confident and handsome, and Angel half believed him when he said he liked her. Besides — the thought of cooling a man like Paul off, it frightened her.

Later, a guy asked her to dance and Paul backed him off. She was silently pleased, until she noticed no one else was asking her to dance. Paul danced three numbers with a blowzy redhead and disappeared outside. Angel sat alone at the table, feeling suddenly feeling hurt, after staring to warm up to him. The confident image of herself, she had spent so many months constructing was obliterated, and she finished two drinks. She was a woman who sat trembling, unloved and insecure. She only wanted to be recognized as a human being' and treated with consideration. She suddenly loathed Paul Benetti, loathed him with a cold contempt that spread to a passionate hatred of men in general. To celebrate this new understanding, Angel ordered another drink. She had just taken the first sip when Paul showed up with a bundle of flowers.

Confusion! She felt the silence. Other people were watching, and as her spirits soared in a contrite wave of elation, for he had not abandoned her, he did like her. She cried, "Oh Paul, they're lovely." She laughed. It was a laugh of release and a little shaky, for she remained uncertain of her own judgment.

"Let's go babe," Paul said, as the band started up with a fast-rhythmic number. Pulling her up from the table, and grinning, he flung her out onto the dance floor. He swung and spun her to the beat, head bobbing and his thick black hair falling in his face. He called out, "Go babe, go."

Angel did, smiling brightly, trying to anticipate him, to match his moves, while within that critical part of herself, she analyzed her moves and thought, *"Am I good enough, am I doing this the way he likes?"* The next number was slow, and when he danced her out of the main room and into a hall, she went with him easily at first.

"It's dark," she said nervously, after he kissed her.

"Come with me, babe," he said, his voice low and urgent.

"Where?"

"There," he said indicating a door. "Manager's office, guy's ah friend of mine."

She glanced nervously back toward the group at their table. They were laughing about something, and for the moment, were unaware she existed. She thought of running.

"Come on," he said impatient, "they're okay."

He pulled her arm, and when she hesitated, he picked her up, carrying her to the door and into the room. It was a strange and humbling sensation, being swept up and carried so lightly. Without putting her down, he kissed her again and kicked the door shut. Angel felt both dizzy and alarmed, but before she could protest Paul kissed her again. When he carried her to the couch, she was swept by a sense of helplessness that absolved her from protest.

"Don't worry, babe," Paul crooned as he looked down at her, admiringly. "It's locked," he said, for he'd noticed her eyes dart toward the door.

Hand braced against the couch, he bent to kiss her. His eyes were dark, approving, his face flushed. She shut her eyes, the alcohol preparing her to let herself dissolve in the kiss, but it was hard, demanding, his mouth boring down on hers lips so that they hurt, and she came awake, aware, soberly telling herself that this was not the way it was supposed to be. He lay down, pressing against her his knee forcing its way between her thighs. His hand fumbled under her dress, circled her breast, and he pinched the nipple.

"No!" She stiffened and tried to sit up, demanding angrily, "What do you think you're doing?"

He pressed her down, "God dam you're a number, babe. What do you think we're doing?" He laughed against her ear; his hand slid under her panties.

It was an entirely rhetorical question, which she seriously considered answering, except that his finger had slid into her, and that invasion required her entire attention. He had gotten both her wrists in one big paw, and his weight bore down on her, making her twisting struggles less than futile. Angel tried to bite, but he buried his face against her throat, kissing. He got his mouth on her breast and around its nipple, all the time his finger moved inside. Her struggles heightened the maddening sensation, and her growing exhaustion added to the fever creeping up from a traitorous body. She was furious, with him, with herself, with what was about to happen. She could feel herself growing moist, open, and he could too, for suddenly his hand came away. He pulled it toward the front of his body, undoing his pants. She twisted again, trying to squirm away as, hunched kneeling, he began to position his big body, spreading her knees even wider apart. He held himself, rubbed the smooth head against the base of her mound and she trembled.

Tears welling in her eyes, she stared at him incredulously, and said, "You're completely disgusting," but even as she spoke, she felt herself the hypocrite, for she had done this before.

"Sure, babe, and I like you too," he said grinning.

As he began to push himself into her, Angel watched his jaw clench. She watched the features of his strong face become hard with pleasure, and she resolved to freeze, to offer no response. It took no more than a minute for that resolve to crumble and she gasped. She gasped again and began to move with him. He released her wrists then, increased the pace and power of his thrusts, and when she clung to him, he laughed low. He laughed, and she hated him, but she couldn't stop. Tears of shame and anger ran down her face, and she moaned and gave herself up to act.

"God, I wouldn't have believed it of ya, kid, I never would have believed it."

He threw one of her legs up over his shoulder and drove into her grunting. It went on and on, and time became abstract. She began to cry out, and Paul clapped a hand over her mouth. She couldn't breathe. A red haze, black spots, floated before her eyes as it went on and on. She was going to die but she couldn't stop the wildly powerful thrusts, and then it was over. His weight sagged down, crushing her, his hand slipping away. She gasped, sucking in great gulps of air, her body limp, and her feelings strangely tender.

"Your perfection hon', perfect," Paul said, rolling off her onto the floor. "You act like a lady and screw like a whore." On his knees, he was stuffing himself into his pants, shaking his head with approval. "You're my kinda broad. I like you babe."

His words shattered the fantasy she had begun to create to explain what had just taken place — they exploded any soft or romantic notions that might have blossomed. In a desert of reality, the logical part of Angel's psyche knew that Paul Benetti was a callous brute, but meek, the coward traitor in her, still, he likes me. She pulled at her dress trying to cover herself, and realized he'd torn away her underwear. She hadn't noticed until now.

"You've torn my clothes," she said, as if that meant anything at all when measured against a scale of his other crimes.

"Hell, Angel, I'm sorry. I'm a clumsy gorilla, but it's your own fault," he whispered in his soft croon, and he pulled her up from the couch. "What do you expect from me when you give the come on? You drive me crazy when you act the way you do."

"What part of the come on is the word no?" she asked, rubbing herself as if she could rub away the memory. She had not known she was going to say those words.

"Don't give me that," Paul grunted, and handed her a shoe. "Tease, give the come on and then turn it off." He snorted. "That crap doesn't work on me Angel." His laugh was mocking. "I've been in you babe, and I know what you want. Let's blow this place."

It seemed unlikely she would win this debate, and managing to get her shoe on, Angel brushed past him, moving quickly toward the door. He grabbed her upper arm so tightly that she squealed with pain.

"Settle down," he said, forcing a smile on his face. "Don't go running out of here embarrassing me in front of my friends," he said, masking his annoyance. "Were together, see." He opened the door to the hall.

"I want to go home," she said, looking down, shrugging her arm free.

"Sure, why not?" he agreed, walking her to the now vacant table, "I'll get the tab."

Angel sat. She was emotionally numb, but acutely consciously of her body. She was very different from the young girl of two days before. She wanted a drink and finishing her own, she gulped another left unfinished on the table. Paul returned, and she saw his eyes move over her. She forced herself to seem unconscious of his scrutinizing gaze and made an abrupt and angry movement as she stood, only managing to lose her balance. His hand went to her shoulder to check her, and she looked away from him, uncomfortably. Together they walked out, and the ride home was silent.

"Lets us get past this little mad miffed act," Paul said, as he pulled into her drive, and when she went to get out, he grabbed her wrist. He crooned, "Settle down sweetheart," and dragging her back across the seat, he kissed her, running a hand back under her dress.

She honestly fought him this time, but he only laughed in his mocking way and in no time, he was in her again. Half way through it, he pulled her out of the car, bent her over the fender, and took her from behind. Slapping flesh, grunts, the sounds of crickets, owl, wind, smell of jasmine and sex, were all part of those dark moments. That, and Paul's low laugh, and his voice calling out, "see you tomorrow, babe," as she fled up the front walk.

In her room, Angel was so ashamed she could not look at herself in the mirror. He would find her again tomorrow or the next day. She would have no choice but to spend time with him and it would begin all over because the word "NO!" meant nothing to him. She couldn't imagine telling anyone about what she'd allowed to happen or how she had felt. The thought that her grandparents might find out after their warnings about drinking made her sick. She showered and sat with the light out. She trembled with fear, real fear of Paul Benetti for she was alone in this. She was unable to shake the feeling that through a physical act this man now owned her. He had gained an immeasurable power over her, for detest him as she might, she could still feel him within her.

Chapter 16

The sounds Connie made, whimpering sobs, fractured the walls of the nightmare, but she didn't wake. Grey's comforting hand woke her, not awake in a true sense, rather a dazed, other dimensional, half consciousness, for a part of her remained engulfed in the conflict of the otherness that had tortured her sleep. Connie came up fighting. She reacted with astonishing violence, and Grey found himself clawed and bruised before he could retreat from his bed. The light woke her. In her dream she had already been awake and on her feet, ready to fight, to run. Grey watched as the flash of the light struck her. She was panting. Eyes wild, hair tangled, she was crouched against the headboard like a cornered tigress. Adrenaline, driven by a pounding heart, coursed through her arteries.

"Christ," Grey said soberly, "Are you alright honey?"

Connie blinked, waking with a start. Before, disoriented, she'd seen her husband as a stranger. He was now standing at the foot of the bed; one hand lingered on the light switch. Her breath took a deep shudder, and she began to relax as reality and recognition came.

"Connie, honey," Grey said softly, his hand falling from the switch, reaching out cautiously.

Otherness and reality were separate now, and she realized there was blood running down her husband's face, angry scratches on his neck and chest. One eye was beginning to puff up.

"What happened darling?" he asked as he sat on the foot of the bed. "Was it a nightmare," he asked, and leaned forward to put his arm around her.

Connie drew back, palms up; her fingers spread a wall between them. An emotion deep within her warned of contact with a man, any man. "I was there. Something's happened," she blurted, her voice shaking. "Something's happened to Angel."

"It was just a bad dream," he said rationally. "We're here in our bedroom honey."

"You don't understand," she cried, a note of hysteria in her voice, "I was there."

"Connie," Grey argued, gesturing, "look honey, were in our bedroom. You've been beside me, right here in bed."

"No!" she screamed. "You don't understand. I was there, in her mind, with her in her mind. It was terrible," she sobbed.

"Shhh! Shhh! Settle down," he pleaded, "You're gonna wake the neighbors, honey. Tell me what it was it that happened, honey?"

"I don't know," she wailed, and sprawling across the bed, she buried her face in a pillow and sobbed.

Grey sighed deeply and put a comforting hand on her shoulder. She shrugged it off. "Okay!" he said.

"What can I do?" He was becoming exasperated. "Should I call the house in *Miami*?" he suggested. "How about I phone the hotel? You can talk to your grandmother, honey, how about that?"

Grey saw her head move up and down to the affirmative, and glad to have a course of action, he went directly to the phone. The base operator got the hotel's number, and the hotel operator rang the Byran's room. Asher's sleep dulled voice answered. Grey explained, and Asher put Corazon on. Stretching the cord, Grey handed the phone to his wife. Within minutes, Connie had calmed down. She hung up the phone and let him put his arm around her.

"Grandma's going to phone home and check on Angel," Connie told him, as she allowed herself to be cuddled. "She's promised to call right back." Connie glanced up at Grey, seeing the scratches. "I did that? Oh god, I'm sorry, darling. Let me put something on those," she said pulling him toward the tiny bathroom.

She was just finishing with the peroxide when the she heard the first ring. Putting the bottle down, she ran for the phone. "Grandma?"

"Everything's fine. I reached Delia. She went upstairs and checked. Your sister was asleep in her bed. It was only a dream darling, a bad dream."

"But it was so real grandma. It was more real than— I can't describe it."

"But it wasn't the first one that's upset you. Now you go to sleep now, and we'll come in the morning. We'll take you for breakfast."

"Tell grandpa goodnight and tell him, thank you," Connie said fondly.

Corazon laughed. "He's asleep and snoring already. You can tell him yourself tomorrow."

"Well?" Grey asked as Connie placed the phone back in its cradle.

"Everything's alright." A puzzled look crept over her face. "It can't be though. I was there, with her and something terrible happened."

Grey sighed and put an arm around her. "Come to bed honey. I have the deck tomorrow and its past 1:00 am already. Bad enough I gotta go aboard looking like a barber's pole, I don't want to be dead tired, worn-out to boot."

"I'm so sorry," she said as he turned out the light, and she wiggled back against him.

"Maybe it was because you're pregnant." The nightmare I mean."

"Maybe," she said, not really believing it.

Connie forced herself to lie quietly in her husband's arms, fighting a sense of menace she knew to be unreasonable. She felt his breathing change as sleep took him. She tried to remember details of the nightmare, but there was only a residual feeling of helpless, hopeless dread. The sun was up when Connie woke. Grey was gone to the ship and grandpa was banging on the door.

They had a pleasant breakfast and a wonderful week. When the day of departure came for her grandparents, Connie bid them farewell at the airport. Connie was already lonely for them, missing them terribly before their plane had cleared the runway. She loved Grey, loved her husband madly. Her college classes here were interesting, as was her life, but it was so difficult separated from her family, particularly with a baby coming. She wanted to share the experience, share the wonder of it, and she wanted, she needed, to be supported in those moments when she would become afraid.

Again, Connie thought of her sister and was immersed in guilt. Each day, it seemed that her love for Grey grew. The more precious he became to her, the stronger her guilt became. Watching her grandparent's plane lift she had thought of her twin.

"Time cures hurts she whispered," and she hoped it would.

***

The morning after The Byrans' return, Angel woke early to bright streams of light through the French doors. She kicked off the covers and stretched, letting the rays warm her flesh. A lazy well-being crept over her, and she felt fresh following the first night of sound sleep in a week. She could hear her grandmother's voice, and in that, instant was completely and at peace. At breakfast with her grandmother, she had pastries with coffee and orange juice. She laughed at humorous stories about the two days spent on the airliner and the problems with the toilet. She was called to the phone just as they were finishing coffee. The sound of Paul's voice ruined it all.

Afterward, grandfather had found her and grandma on the veranda. He began to press her for a decision on her plans for *Europe.* He was astonished to find her completely unprepared. Angel was unable to give her grandfather a straightforward answer, and he was unwilling to go without one.

He asked her again, "Do you or do you not intend to travel to Italy as planned?"

"I don't know," Angel repeated, wavering, between temper and tears. "I — well —until last week I intended to, but Italy seems so remote, and besides I've come prefer the French style."

"Considering the width of the *Atlantic Ocean*," Asher said, "there's little difference in the distance between *France* and *Italy*. Your ship is to depart in four days. If you'd rather study art in *France*, say so and I'll make the arrangements. Well?" Asher urged his patience slipping.

"It's not about the painting, grandpa."

She stopped, for she was unable to express pure emotion in words, and her own indecision confused her. "So, you want me away, you want me to leave home?" Angel accused pathetically, and tears began to glisten in the corners of sad green eyes.

"Aahh hell, Angel."

"That's enough. You let her be," Corazon said standing, and she crossed to her granddaughter, who instantly buried her face against the older woman.

"But, I never meant anything of the sort," her defended hopelessly. After a pause, "You take a while and let me know in time to cancel the tickets. I've a few things to do," he said standing. "Be in the library."

Corazon hugged her granddaughter and watched Asher disappear into his lair. She could imagine the sound of his teeth grinding out of frustration. It was generally so with men, more so with a sea captain. They had a need to seize upon a problem. They needed to provide a solution with utter dispatch, to command the solution be put into effect and see an end to the problem. Women, of course felt compelled to talk a problem over in length, discuss its nuances and understand every possible outcome of a decision. To a woman, the process itself offered satisfaction, and the process was often more important than the finding of a solution. There were times, of course, that a woman had no inkling of what a problem consisted of, only the surety of its existed. This was the case with Angel and this required talking about, too.

Corazon believed Angel was over her disappointment concerning Grey MacArt, but since their return from *California,* she had been less sure. Only ten days ago, at the end of spring semester, Angel had seemed fine. When they had arrived home yesterday, Corazon sensed a change in her Granddaughter. It was immediately evident. Angel appeared animated and nervous one moment, moody and lethargic the next. This was out of character for Angel, and it bothered her that she had no clue to what was going on inside the girl's head.

"My, but aren't you becoming a softy chica." She pushed Angel back, so she could look into her eyes. "Tell me, why do you hesitate, why do you change your plans? It's a young man perhaps, one that you don't wish to abandon for the summer?" Angel's eyes flickered, and she looked down, a sure sign to Corazon that she would rather not provide a truthful answer to the question. She laughed, "So tell me about it," she coaxed.

"Grandma!"

"Tell me."

"No!"

"Please. A little bit at least, a hint."

Involuntarily, Angel blushed, and turned her face away, as the possibility of an answer hung on balance. She thought, "What can I say." It would be impossible to describe her feelings. Not for the first time that week, she asked herself what she'd been thinking when she allowed a man like Paul Benetti to take possession of her, for that's what he'd done. He ordered her about and she obeyed. When he made physical demands, she complied. There was no logical answer for her behavior. One moment she was desperate to be free of him, the next she feared that he might no longer want her. She was one moment flattered and the next frightened by his jealous need for control. She had lost her sense of self. If she went to Europe, if she just got away from him for a few months, would that be enough?

At moments, she was excited by the animal strength in Paul, but she was always frightened of it. She was more terrified than she could admit to herself, for she had experienced the violence in him; saw what happened when he had turned it on others. She had witnessed the beating of a man who welshed on a bet to Paul's uncle. The welsher had been beaten half to death. It was Paul's job to make these examples, but he had enjoyed doing it. She saw it in his eyes, in his body, in the way he strutted.

Angel had some relief since her grandparent's return the day before. With them home, Paul couldn't just barge in on her. She suspected he might have some hesitancy concerning her grandfather. Grandpa was old, but he had a certain reputation in the community. Her respite wouldn't last long though. Paul had already asked her when he was going to meet the family. He'd hinted again, this morning, when they spoke on the phone. She was becoming adept at reading inflections in his voice, and she had read the irritation, the masked anger, in seemingly pleasant words.

What, she wondered, would he do, if she announced that she was going to Europe? How would he react if she refused to introduce him to the family? What if she ran, escaped to *Europe* without telling him? Angel was afraid to find out. When Paul was angry or wanted something, he didn't seem to consider consequences. Understanding this, Angel had grown apprehensive about challenging Paul, and fear of his displeasure suddenly boiled up in her. Looking out the French doors Angel spoke.

"I've been dating a man, Paul Benetti. He just graduated. His family has hotels on the beach." Fear and need had caused the words to burst out of her, unbidden. The sound of her voice, the content of her words surprised her, for until that instant, Angel had not intended to say a word concerning Paul.

Corazon reached out her arm slowly, put a hand gently on Angel's cheek. "This is what you've kept from us? I knew it was something like this," she said, with the deepest sound of relief in her voice.

"You knew?"

"Of course, we knew there was something. So quiet and suddenly inconsistent, it was obvious something had changed," Corazon said softly. "Why haven't you said something?"

Angel wanted to explain, but she was so ashamed that it was impossible. She wanted to cry but she didn't dare start. "I'm not sure about things, about him," she lied. "It's been no time at all really," she, added not really a complete lie.

"You must feel very strongly about this young man to consider canceling your plans for *Italy*. Does he want you to cancel your plans?"

"I haven't mentioned my plans," she said truthfully, and she began to fidget. "I expect he might become upset about me leaving."

"You don't sound as if you know him well enough to be serious. Would you like to ask him to dinner? Let us have a look," she said smiling. "Perhaps that will help you decide about *Europe*. Decide, before you grandfather has another of his temper tantrums."

She took a deep breath. "Yes, but grandma, lets don't mention *Europe* just yet."

"Would tonight be too soon? For dinner, I mean. After all, darling, you have only a few days to decide. You'll have to take train in three days to meet your ship in New York.?"

"I suppose tonight would be good if he agrees," she said flatly.

"Darling, you sound so unenthusiastic. You're sure you want us meet him so soon?"

"Yes!" she smiled, trying to put a positive face on things. "It's just that I'm not sure that he'll be able to make it on such short notice. I'll try to reach him at the hotel," she said, feeling increasingly uncomfortable, almost panicked. "I can drive over to the beach, in fact."

Even as she suggested these things, Angel felt ill. She was appalled at the prospect of entertaining Paul Benetti in her home. She pictured herself introducing him, watching, as he acted charming, as he became friendly with her grandparents. In the fabric of her being, her relationship with her grandparents was the remnant, the last threads that remained free of Paul's grasp. Instinctively, she knew this invitation to be a mistake, but could think of no plausible way to avoid it. What if he told people what she'd been doing? No! In truth, Angel lacked the courage to refuse Paul an invitation. In her heart, Angel knew that there were always choices available to those who had the courage, but somehow courage had been lost to her. As she dialed Paul's number, she wondered how she'd become such a coward.

Chapter 17

"It ain't personal Paulo, but cha know how it is," said the bald man. "Were speaking of two-grand 'dat cha put on ponies what couldn't run, and now you're telling me you're light. The word your uncle put out was no more credit, no bets on the cuff, and here ya went and wagered wit' cash ya din't have. Shit, Paulo, you're a collector yourself. For Christ sakes, what cha doin' here kid?"

"Two lousy grand," Paul snorted disdainfully. "Look, Sticks, with a little time, I'm good for it anyway, but you tell Fats I've got things in the works. Big money, a sure thing," Paul winked with assurance. "Tell em, no sweat and I'll cover the interest in the meantime."

"Fats, he's a bird in the hand type kid. Don't know how much time he's willing to spot cha. Man's got no patience where his money's concerned." The bald man sucked on his cigar, and flipped the butt away, blowing smoke. "Best cha calls him yourself, work it out so I don't gotta come back ta see ya. I'd be bringing help ah course," he added with a sly smile, "you being a tough cookie, but Paulo, even tough-cookies gotta pay up when they lose."

"Tonight, Sticks, I'll phone him, and don't you worry old man. We won't have to tangle. Not that I could make that mug of yours look any worse."

"Humph," the bald man grunted, and closed the door to Paul's room behind him.

Paul sighed, looked in the mirror, smiled, and flexed his muscles. Pleased with what he saw, he moved to the closet and chose a suit for his dinner engagement. He'd felt a lot more confident discussing business with Sticks after receiving the call from Angela Byran. Dinner with the grandparents was tonight, and it was about time. Things were falling into place. If you had it in mind to marry a rich chic, you could do one hell of a lot worse than Angel Byran. Good looking and hot under the sheets, hot even if she was a slow starter. The trick was going to be getting past the old people. That was the key to getting her down the aisle.

Paul shrugged into the suit and took a moment to select a tie. He stood before the mirror as he tied the knot, then smoothed his hair. "*Good behavior, manly but respectful,*" he thought to himself. He felt confident about the girl. Hell, he'd bowled her over. He couldn't decide if she was in love or just scared shitless of him, not that it mattered. What mattered was he had control of her. Her family was another matter.

Paul knew a guy needed to have a broad's family on board if he wanted to get a handle on the money. Satisfied with the knot, he smiled. One way or the other she was going to marry him though. Hell, he'd been banging her three times a day for weeks, and if she wasn't knocked up by now it wasn't for the lack of trying on his part. He splashed on a little cologne, and picking up his car keys, he headed for *Coconut Grove*. It was time to go to work.

Paul thought the dinner went pretty well. He could see Angel was a bundle of nerves, but he was on his best behavior, buttering up the old broad and smiling a lot. He figured he'd made points with her, but old man Byran was another matter altogether. Pleasant enough old fart, but not the kind of man you brought around at one sitting. Paul sensed that he would have to watch himself around the old man. The old prick was no fool. He'd heard stories about Captain Byran, most likely bullshit stories, but you never knew, and his kind of money could buy trouble.

Paul had been having an after-dinner cigar with old man Byran when the subject of Angel's trip to *Europe* was mentioned. The information had filled Paul with a barely concealed rage. "The lying little bitch," he seethed inwardly. So, she was trying to pull something, trying to get away. He'd see about that. When it was time to leave, he got her to walk him to his car.

"I enjoyed myself," he said wrapping his arms around her. He nuzzled her head and said, "Your grandparents are nice people. I liked them."

"They really are wonderful," she said honestly.

"They seem close; my grandparents are like that." Paul sighed, "Ya know, babe, I guess I come on rough and tumble. I'm a bulldozer, see, no class, but that's just me. What I want though, it's like your grandparents have. I want somebody I'm crazy about that I can count on. I want somebody like you Angel. I want you with me. I'm crazy about you, kid."

"You are," she said timidly, "really?"

"Hell yes. I figured you'd have the picture by now, babe. Gee'z, haven't I been all over you for weeks?"

"Sometimes you frighten me, Paul." She felt an involuntary trembling as she continued, "You can be cruel."

"Gee," he said softly, "I'm sorry if I come across that way. Maybe you can knock the corners off," he laughed, "smooth me out some. If anybody can gentle me down, it's you babe. Just tell me when I'm being a brute. I'll be putty in your hands."

At the thought of Paul malleable as putty, she sniggered despite herself. "That'll be the day."

"Seriously kid, I'm crazy about you. I can't imagine being away from you. If you ever left, I'd track you to the ends of the earth. This is sudden I know, but I can't help it. What if I get you pregnant? I want this on the up and up. I want to marry you, Angel. I want you for my wife."

"I — I don't know Paul. I've got school, and —"

"What difference does that make," he asked, cutting her off and giving her a squeeze at the same time. "So, if we're married you can still fool around with school. Come on Angel, you're gonna make me crazy if you say no."

"How about I'll think about it," she said feeling panicky. "Give a girl a little time."

"What's to think about? We're great together."

She felt his fury, as what had seemed to be a loving embrace, tightened. "You said to tell you when you're being mean," she said looking into his intense eyes. "I need to think about it."

"Yeah, yeah, I'm sorry. You're killing me here, you know that don't you?" He released her and gave her a quick kiss. I'll call — tomorrow," he said getting into his car.

"Paul! Come on — I didn't say I'd have an answer tomorrow," she complained, trying to keep her voice light and steady.

"Guess I can wait," he said and laughed. "Neither one of us is going anywhere, right?"

Angel stood still as his car pulled away, and she watched until it turned the corner. Returning to the house, she chose to sit on a wicker chair on the veranda rather than go up to her room. She hadn't noticed Grace sitting there in the dark. The black women's voice startled her.

"Its fine out here in the cool of the night, don't you think?"

"Yes, cool and dark."

"I sit out often you knows, when it pleasant like this."

A dog barked down the block. The sound carried perfectly in the stillness. Someone laughed in the house next door.

"Sitting out here one night when that fellow brings y'all home. What I heard — will it been troubling my sleep." Grace could see that Angel had frozen in her seat, but Grace couldn't stop her own words. "You's a young woman now, Miss Byran. Spose it ain't my place saying, but a man that treats a young woman like that troubles me. I'd be afraid for my own child being round a man like that. Spose most womens has the poor luck to come across a mean man sometime or other. The lucky ones, they win free of them. They wins free afor de real misery comes to them."

Grace paused, and when Angel said nothing Grace added, "Surprised to see that fella invited here tonight." Grace stood and said softly, no more than a whisper. "Comes a time y'all needs to talk missy, you's just come visit wit' me." When Angel said nothing, the servant sighed. She rose slowly and went to her room by the kitchen.

Tears running down her cheeks, Angel sat perfectly still, paralyzed by opposing emotions. She was horrified that Grace knew, and at the same time relieved that she was not alone with her dilemma. She felt entirely confused, frightened and confused. Was it her imagination that Paul was threatening her? He seemed so sincere, so sweet when he spoke about his grandparents and wanting closeness, and he'd been such a gentleman tonight. Could it be true that he cared so much about her that he couldn't control himself? Maybe Paul had a temper like her. He lashed out when he was hurt or upset.

The possibility of pregnancy flickered in her mind, but conception, like death was a thing of the distant future. She was amazed it had not at least occurred to her through all this, but she refused to dwell on a remote possibility in the madness that her life had become. She couldn't make a judgment based on mere possibility; she couldn't trust herself to make any judgments.

She did not have to decide. She didn't have to marry him, and she didn't have to tell him to leave. There would be plenty of time for things to clear themselves up, for her to be sure of herself again. There was tomorrow, and the day after that, and she was safe here with grandma to protect her mind and body. She wouldn't go to *France* where she would be alone. She'd stay here in the shelter of her grandparent's love. Calmed within, Angel dried her tears and went to bed.

Over the days and weeks that followed, Angel's state of mind and confidence improved, at least up until the second she suspected she was pregnant. Paul's trap had sprung.

Chapter 18

In the first weeks after returning from her honeymoon, Angel submerged herself in the organizing of her home, a pleasant two story on the beach. Through the doors of this airy assortment of rooms, furnishings flowed in and out like the tides. She had assembled this grouping and that, sometimes building on a single item, or moving on to yet another article in the attempt to achieve an ambiance, a quality that suited some unformed image. The obsessive nature in which she pursued this project was, in a sense for her, like the creation of a private world. It was a temporary escape, a false security at best, but it kept her occupied for long stretches.

Her decorative activities would begin late in the day, always after Paul left the house. Unless she was expected to meet him during the evening, Angel had a good deal of time, which she spent more often by herself. Paul had disapproved of her friends. The scenes he caused made a non-existent social life the solution of least resistance. Angel's relationship with her grandparents was also altered. A little had to do with her pride, but primarily Angel was too fearful, and ashamed to confide in them. Instead, she acted happy, and slowly a wall had risen around her, a wall of her own building, a wall of fear, misery and deceit.

Late in her third month, an all-consuming lethargy infused her, leaving her uncomfortable, limp and sick for days at a time. She actually found herself clinging anxiously to Paul, dependent on his company, and when he had gone, she would accuse herself of gross stupidity, piteous behavior, and she would dream of divorce.

One night, a total exhaustion overwhelmed her, a weary fatigue at which her limbs had grown so heavy, she could not drag herself from the chair to her bed. Angel woke knowing she'd not slept well. Any number of times she'd half wakened with the knowledge that Paul would expect her to be waiting for him in bed, no-matter what time he came home. She stood just as the bedroom door burst open; the lights flashed on, adrenaline burst through her system. Her ruffled and slightly unsteady husband came straight for her, swept her up, and fell with her across the bed.

"The boys wanted me to hang around for a few more hands, but I told 'em I had pleasures to pursue at home." He repeated the specific pleasures he had described to them, ground her against him, and as a possessive grin covered his face, he began to yank at her clothes. He'd laughed and said, "I'd have some of that now."

Heart racing, she tore herself suddenly away from him, angry and embarrassed. Standing next to the bed, her back to him, hating him, she undressed flinging off clothes in silence. Naked, she turned and placed one knee on the bed, playing her part in this farce, the female instinct to please an survive overcoming her disgust.

To Paul, her resentment was not apparent. To Paul, a naked woman was both invitation and compliment to his ego. Pulling open his pants, he drew her back onto the bed and heaved himself on top. It went on for a quite a while and Angel was far too tired and angry to achieve anything beyond dizzy exhaustion, but she dared not stop responding. Her attention strained to any change in his movement, for she knew better than to disappoint him in bed. The end came as a surprise for her.

"Ah yeah," he groaned, rolling off her. "Good stuff."

Angel had not replied. Hard lessons and instinct were teaching her to pretend pleasure, fake fulfillment, and to mask her feeling of loathing. She lay panting. She sensed when Paul fell into sleep but remained silent though she wanted to weep. If he woke, she might have to explain her weeping and she couldn't. She'd never been coaxed or wooed into bed, never loved, merely assaulted. She was now caught, caged and used at will. Her independence, her freedom to rule her own mind and body were lost. She had lost those taken for granted rights that had been hers only months before. To trade independence for love, that was one thing, this was another. In her bout of self-pity, Angel thought of Grey, and in turn came an emotion of pain, a jab of hateful jealousy toward her twin.

A time came in August when Angel's temper began to overtake her caution. She was nearly five months and showing it. Paul had lost interest in her. At first, it was a relief to be free of his attentions, but with him openly discussing his girlfriends in front of the help, it became an insult. The remnants of her pride led to an ill-advised boldness on her part.

The first time Paul smacked Angel hard was at breakfast, four months into the marriage. She had mentioned that the amount of money in their account was fifty thousand dollars less than the three hundred thousand dollars her father had left her.

"I made investments for us," Paul said, looking up from his racing form.

"What were they?"

"Investments," he repeated, hard eyes confronting her over the table.

His voice was level and pleasant, incongruously timid compared to the intimidating message of his eyes, and Angel was not misled by his voice. Her own ill temper caused her to be a bit bolder than was wise around Paul.

"What did you invest it in?" she snapped with an obvious tone of disgust, "horses."

If Paul had any ear at all for revulsion, he would have recognized it in his wife's voice. He was not concerned with Angel's disgust. He was however concerned with control, and the backhanded slap came far too fast for Angel to flinch. It rocked her back in her chair.

"Unless you watch your mouth, you're going to get more of that -- Show a little respect -- Mind your own business and we'll do just fine."

Paul smiled at the maid, who had backed against the dining room wall. His smooth voice and concerned expression bore no resemblance to the violence in his eyes, and Angel sat shaken. Despair had swept her; despair and loathing for this man, this husband, comforter and protector of a wife. She felt fear and rage, but the fear won out, and she found herself mumbling an apology for her disrespect. Not that the apology served to improve her condition for afterward, excuses for inflicting pain became easier to find.

***

In early October, Grey MacArt's squadron had put to sea and Connie had returned home to have her baby. Reunited with her pregnant sister, Angel became, for the first time, excided over her own pregnancy. Paul was out of town and the twins were nearly inseparable in the weeks that followed.

On November 7, Connie gave birth to a boy, Cory Byran MacArt. The family brought baby Cory home to *Hurricane Road* where they joyously celebrated his arrival as the first member of the next generation. Midst this happy activity, Paul Benetti returned unannounced, except for his wife, to *Miami*.

Granted, Angel was surprised to see her husband, but more than that, she was shocked silent to see the state he was in. Bruised and dirty, Paul was in need of a shave; his suit was torn, his collar bloody, but most telling was an obvious nervousness, immediately apparent as his trembling hand spilled the whiskey he was pouring.

"What, no big smile, babe, no welcome home," he said, half turning toward her.

"My God, Paul,' she said weakly, "you look like you were thrown out of a boxcar."

"Dam'd near." He looked at his wife's pale face, her swollen stomach, and hated her for what he had to ask. "Come and sit," he said, sloshing his drink on the tile as he motioned toward the sofa.

She walked carefully past the bar, and he reached out pulling her to him. It was an instant when both hid the distain they shared. Paul leaned over, flashing his smile and she responded by brushing past his lips, kissing his cheek. The danger of her instinctive response frightened her, and instantly she shifted, allowing him to kiss her on the mouth. They sat turned slightly toward each other and Paul began to speak.

"We have a problem, one that you can help me solve," he began.

"What kind of problem," Angel asked, puzzled?

"I'm temporarily light on cash, and I'm into a guy who's to big too skate on."

"How much," she asked innocently.

"Twenty-thousand."

"That's a lot but we've got more than enough to cover that in the bank. Why not write a check," she suggested?

"I did, but the funds are tied up in another deal and it's going to bounce. This guy isn't someone you pass bad paper off on."

"But we have a quarter of a million dollars in savings," she gasped in confusion.

"I told you, our money was invested," he lied, "tied up in another deal." He swallowed some whiskey and pushed down his annoyance. He looked straight into her eyes and thought, "dumb bitch."

"But Paul," she said, trying to be reasonable, "Who is he? Couldn't you contact him, explain the situation."

"The man's name is Ben Siegel," Paul said, resisting the urge belt her. He was so pissed that he would have liked to choke her until her eyes popped, but that wouldn't get him money, wouldn't get him off the hook. "He's not an understanding man," Paul explained with a forced smile, "Particularly not where cash is concerned, and he never lets a welsher slide."

Angel's mouth hung open. "Ben Siegel the gangster, the one they call Bugsy, my god Paul how did you end up owning him money," she asked, incredulous? Angel's mind raced. Siegel was famous or infamous, even worse than Al Capone. His job was killing people, and Paul had written him a bad check. Her own name was on the checks. Would he come after her?

"Cards, and I'm not proud to say it, but I was too drunk to know what I was doing." Paul was telling half a lie, and not letting it show on his face. "We got a day, maybe two, to cover that check. Your grandparents have it. You gotta get em to loan us the twenty grand or we're dead meat Angel. Tell em it's for a few weeks. This guy does not screw around. It's our only way out of this kid, ours and the baby's." He said the word 'baby' purposely, drawing out her fear, her maternal sense of danger.

Stunned, she sat nodding in affirmation, so swept up in worry that she completely forgot about the happenings of the past few days. All Angel could think about, focus on, was how she would approach grandpa for the money.

She had made a request for the loan the next morning using Paul's explanation that their funds were temporally tied up. Her grandfather had told her he would think about it, and to have Paul stop by to explain about his investments. He wanted to know how long it would be before Paul's funds would be free. It was Friday and Angel was feeling panicky, for the money would have to be deposited before the end of the banking day. She lied; she explained that Paul hadn't gotten back into town. She smiled, tried to wheedle it out of Asher, and finally threw a minor tantrum, which accomplished nothing.

Having dealt with a lifetime of Angel's pleading, Asher was not about to hand over twenty thousand dollars without some reasonable explanation. He had grown stubborn and the way he saw it, her husband was the one who should have been approaching him with this request. Had Angel told the truth, she would have most certainly received the money, but what little she did know about Paul's affairs, she'd been forbidden to divulge.

For three hours, Angel hurried about town trying to find her grandmother. Her last hope was that the money might be secured behind her grandfather's back. An hour past noon she returned home, nauseous and trembling, to confess her failure. Facing Paul wasn't easy for Angel. First, she sat in the car. Then she stood outside her own front door, too weak with dread to enter and admit that the money wasn't in the bank. When she did manage to enter the house, Paul rushed toward her.

"Gee'z, where in hell have you been? Did you get it?"

Afraid to look into his eyes she spoke at the floor, trying to explain. "Grandpa said he needed to see you before he'd loan us anything. I explained you were out of town, but he wouldn't budge. I tried everything, but he insisted you call him."

"That took since nine this morning," he snapped, the sarcastic anger rising up out of him.

"No Paul, I've been trying to find grandma," she said defensively. Her voice quivered now, even though she fought to keep it steady. "There was a chance she might write me a check without asking grandpa, but I couldn't find her."

"And you didn't think to let me know what was going on. You dumb bitch." Nostrils flaring, his eyes round with fury, he grabbed her arm. "Have you any idea what time it is?" He squeezed so hard she gasped, "The banks are about to close for the weekend."

"I tried," she blurted, her eyes beginning to tear, but I couldn't find her. "What if we sold my jewelry, the car, mortgage the house," she offered.

"I already did," he yelled six inches from her ear. "Jewelry, jewelry," he thought. He considered the possibility of getting his hands on the old bitch's jewelry. He calmed himself, lowered his tone, "You know where your grandmother keeps her jewelry don't you — don't you Angel?"

Angel's eyes grew large in disbelief and she looked up at him.

"You go over there tonight and you either bring me back a check or bring that jewelry. You understand?"

It burst from Angel, straight from her heart, "Oh Paul, I could never steal from her, I — eeow."

He gave her arm a vicious yank, snapping her head back. "Shut up. When I ask you a question that is when you talk. Now, I didn't ask you to bring me the jewelry, I told you to bring me the jewelry — told you."

"No!" Angel said the word without time to consider its consequence and had no chance to take it back.

Paul's body emitted pure aggression, and the fist lashed out before the conscious mind ordered it. The blow was yellow orange, then white, then black as Angel's knees buckled, and she slipped to the floor. Paul, still gripping her arm, pulled her back up. He pushed hard against her abdomen, banging her into the wall, arm high and pinned, dangling by the arm, and his face inches from hers.

He shouted, "No! You're telling me no." There was the sour taste of bile in her mouth as she fought to hold down the contents of her stomach. His shouted words did not register as she formed her own. "The baby," she whispered, "Paul, be careful with the baby."

Paul smelled weakness like a shark smells blood and he swam toward it. "The baby," he mocked, running his free hand around her distended stomach. Then in a voice so cold, "Angel, you get me what I gotta have or so help me, I'll kill that baby right inside you, kill it so you feel it die. Gone before it sucks a first breath, and I'll see you don't have another." He grabbed a hand full of her hair jerking her head around until her eyes looked into his. "It's yes now isn't it?" he cajoled in sweet baritone as he nodded the correct answer for her.

The word 'yes', as her lips formed, and her breath pushed, was barely audible, but Paul recognized total capitulation. He released her, letting her slide down the wall as he walked away. Angel hunched over, urped and threw up. She drew her knees up to stop the pain, and curled gasping for breath. Later she crept like a mouse to the bathroom to assess the damage and attempt to look presentable. Just after 3:00 pm. she slipped out of the house, avoiding Paul, and drove toward *Coconut Grove* to steal her grandmother's jewels.

Chapter 19

Paul Benetti was not a solitary man. To remain alone at home was not in his nature, even in the face of dire consequence. This was not a matter of boldness on Benetti's part. It was simply that he was easily seduced by any vice. He indulged his appetites on whatever the moment offered, and having always escaped the consequences of his actions, he saw no reason to restrain himself. By dusk, he was driving to a spot he frequented, a club that specialized in very young girls.

He was let in through a dim vestibule where the hatcheck girl took his Fedora. It was too early for the traffic inside to be anything but light. A few men hunched against the bar, and only half the tables were occupied. Pretty barmaids, in ten-inch skirts, served while on the stage another girl stripped to loud music. Paul picked a table and sat. He squeezed the butt of the waitress as he ordered his drink, and looking around, nodded to a few acquaintances. Relaxing, he watched the stripper.

In the shadows near the back wall, four men shared a burn-scarred table usually reserved for vendors. One balding man held his beer mug with a three-fingered hand; he was tall, had thick arms and barrel chest. A second was squat, with a fist scared face. This man, Dino he was called, appeared fat at first glance, but was all hard flesh under his shabby coat. The sharp dresser was obviously the brains of this group; the other two were bone breakers. The forth was merely the snitch.

The snitch, a slight fellow with a clerkish look, pointed toward Benetti, "That's him, he said to the dresser.

Frank Lasco leaned toward the snitch with a scowl, "You're sure, sonny?"

"Absolutely, sir."

Slipping the snitch two twenties, Fast Frankie said, "Disappear." He turned his head to take a good look at Paul and let out a humorous snort. No matter if the screwball had big brass balls, or was too dumb to shit, it was a very poor move to pay Bugsy off with bad paper. Siegel's banker had known it was rubber twelve hours after the bum wrote it, which was the reason for his own hasty trip to *Miami*. Adding to it, word was that the bum tried to cheat the game.

"We gonna follow em home," Baldy asked?

"Nah, the bum's married into some swell family; they're pillars of the community. We are to reimburse Mr. Benetti in a public setting, dark mind you, and quiet, but public. There is to be no doubt, what the beef was over. It being a business matter, the message is meant to circulate in the right crowd."

Frank thought it over for a bit. The guy probably drove his own car. Screw up his car and take him on the road when it quits. Better yet, pay the valet to take a powder. They could jump Benetti behind the joint when he goes for the car. Maybe do both just in case.

"Evening boys," it was a middle-aged doxie dressed to the hilt. "Got the best gals back here, they're young, they're the primed."

Frankie scowled, took a drink, "later maybe," he said.

***

Paul was pissed. The valet wasn't in his box or anywhere else in sight. Paul paced for a few minutes thinking, "Just like a dam'd Cuban, probably humping some broad in the back of her car." Finally, he searched the board for his keys and started for the back lot. He spotted his car, and he was squeezing between it and a Packard sedan. The Packard's doors flew open, trapping him between the cars. He glimpsed a pistol.

Paul hadn't been expecting anything, but he'd come up in a rough crowd and had good reflexes. He dropped to his belly just as the gun went off. He wriggled under his car, rolled and came up running for the alley; his ear stung and blood was running down his neck. Baldy was stepping out from the wall, ready to take a two-handed swing with a pipe when Paul saw him. Unable to check his momentum, Paul dove under the swing. The pipe scuffed his hair, burning like hell as his shoulder plowed into the leg Baldy had planted to swing. The man fell on top of him, snarling as his knee popped. Hurt but still full of mayhem, he got a fist full of Paul's hair and busted him in the nose, but the angle was bad, and he did no serious damage. On the other hand, the stiletto blade that Paul slipped between his ribs did a lot of damage to Baldy's heart. Feet were pounding on the pavement. Paul sprung up running like hell. He heard two shots; one chipped the brick as he was turning the corner, and he fled for his life.

The Squat man was not equipped for chasing an athletic type in his mid-twenties, and Frank had little incentive to run after Benetti alone. Fast Frankie Lasco was no pussy, but experience had taught him that sometimes, in the commission of a hit, there was an instant that you knew, if you didn't back off you were screwed. Well, his shot between the cars had taken a chunk of the kid's ear off. That was a start. He'd been warned, Benetti was a tough Wop, and the condition of Baldy Schmidt confirmed it. So much for working the guy over before they finished him, he'd do it the other way around. Who'd be the wiser? 'Let's don't, and say we did', the saying went.

Back in the alley, he stood looking at Baldy and a hell of a lot of blood.

"Wadda we do, put em in the trunk?"

"Mess up the car and besides, I ain't getting tagged to a stiff. Canal is about fifty foot the other side of the fence. C'mon, grab a foot."

Four blocks up, Paul had kicked in the door of a beach cabaña, and dropped into a lounge chair, panting. "Can't go home," he thought, "can't go back to the car.' He was amazed at how fast they'd run him down. He'd figured he was in the clear until Monday at least. Paul flexed his shoulders some to ease the tension. With nothing, he could do, and in a safe hole, he relaxed. Angel would have his ticket out of this mess in the morning. Holding on to that thought he slept.

Paul woke with the early morning sun in his eyes and the clatter of a hotel worker setting up beach chairs. He slipped away, walking down the beach, and got coffee at some Jew's bagel shop on *South Beach*. On the wall, he dropped a nickel in the pay phone and got one of his wife's servants. Angel hadn't come home last night. He didn't know if this was good or bad. What if the same people that hit at him had grabbed her? If she had the goods on her, he was really screwed. Maybe she was still at the old folk's place in the Grove, still watching for her chance at grandma's jewelry case. Paul dropped another nickel and the housekeeper picked up.

"Byrans residence, Grace speaking."

"This is Paul, Grace. I just got back into town and I was wondering if my wife was there."

"Why, yes sir. She was feeling poorly, and they had her to stay over. The house is still sleeping Mr. Paul, but they' s entertaining this afternoon, so they be up soon. I can pass the message when they gets up."

"Just tell Angel, I'm in town but not at home. She's to stay there and I'll phone her later."

"Be sure ta tell her, soon she's up.

"Thanks," Paul said, and hung up with one less thing to worry about. A least he knew they hadn't got the jewels. The question was, had his wife gotten her hands on them yet. He needed a place to disappear for a while. He decided it would be best if he were away from his usual haunts and near his wife. He caught a cab to *Coconut Grove* and rented a room on *Dixie Highway*, just off *twenty-seventh Ave.* The 'Palm Motel and Trailer Park" was a place he'd used a few times in college. He sent the housekeeper down the street to buy him a bottle, and he settled down to worry.

Chapter 20

Somewhere near a baby cried in short hungry wails, each separated by a gasp for breath. Finally, the crying ended mid-wail, as the baby found mother's breast. Angel thought of her sister and smiled. Light poured into the room and through the leaves and the flower petals beyond. Filled with an unfamiliar sense of well-being, she sighed. A tiny but sharp kick caused the side of her stomach to bulge; Angel felt the baby inside her move, and she let out a joyous laugh. It was then that she remembered her baby's father and she began to cry softly

Essentially, she was torn, divided against herself. While the instinctive and physical parts of her were consumed with the developing infant within, the conscious mind was engaged in a chaotic defense without. Millenniums of maternal instinct urged her to submit to any demand, avoid every danger. A younger but no less powerful ethic demanded truth, honesty, love of family. Frozen by competing loyalties, Angel was locked into an inevitable process that dragged her toward a spiritual, moral abyss.

Connie was tapping on Angel's door. The knob turned, and she slipped in cradling little Cory in the crook of one arm. He smelled powdery and faintly sour as Connie leaned over the bed.

"Wake up," she said, smiling. "Come on lazy bones, let's go eat."

Angel rolled over, wiping her teary face against her pillow to erase evidence of her misery. She sat up awkwardly and stretched. "The baby woke me a little while ago," she said. "I was just enjoying a few last moments of indolence."

"Enjoy while you can." Connie said looking down at her sleeping baby, "Moments are all you have once their born,"

They continued to talk as Angel dressed, and they went downstairs together. Asher was already plowing into a stack of pancakes. Corazon, enjoying her first coffee, laughed as they arrived.

"Look Asher, see how easy it's become to tell them apart in the last week.

He smiled swallowing. "Back to a matched set in a few months," he joked.

Connie stuck out her tongue as they as they sat, and Delia asked what they would like. The baby began to fuss, and Corazon called Grace to come take her. As Grace took little Cory, she remembered that Paul Benetti had phoned, and repeated the message to Angel.

"He said to remain here, and he'd call?" Angel repeated, puzzled.

"Yes ma'am, exactly."

"Well," Asher interjected, "If he's back in town, he can get together with me on that matter you asked about."

"Yes," she replied, making no further comment, but realizing her difficulties were even more complicated than before.

Breakfast finished, Corazon gave the cook orders for a late lunch. Asher took Shawn down to the Yacht Club to ready a boat for the afternoon of fishing he'd promised Dan Tully. The sisters wandered about, conversing lightly now and again; Connie preoccupied with baby, Angel, tense and fearful of her inability to accomplish what her husband demanded.

The Tullys arrived early afternoon and everyone partook of a light buffet on the verandah. Afterward, Dan and Asher went fishing, while the women sat discussing pregnancy and babies. Kim was expecting her third in March and was hoping for a girl this time. Connie unabashedly swore she'd never have another, which drew knowing laughs from the older women. Corazon admitted that she'd said the same after the birth of her first.

"You'll change your mind after a bit," Kim said. "After all, 'tis the first that's hardest, and the next one is a walk in the park darling."

They chatted on, sharing experiences, and time escaped them. They were surprised to realize it was dusk and to hear the men returning. It was then the phone rang.

***

After a lousy night and a morning spent with a fifth of whiskey, Paul slept soundly into the late afternoon. The multiple slams of car doors woke him. He sat up and peered out the bottom corner on the window. It was just as well that he did, because he recognized Sticks Harper's baldhead, among a group of six men headed straight for his door. Not even taking an instant to grab his shirt, Paul scrambled out the bathroom window, and sprinted through the trailer park. He didn't slow down until he reached *Biscayne Bay*, five blocks to the east. There on the narrow beach, he crouched, hands on his knees, panting.

Almost being nailed last night had been enough of a fright. Them spotting him there was understandable. He'd been cocky. He'd thought he had more time. This was different. They must have called every motel and flophouse within twenty miles to locate him. They weren't playing games. Paul considered catching the ferry to *Havana*, but that would be a temporary fix. No, he needed the cash to pay off Siegel and he needed it yesterday.

Paul walked alone down the beach, feeling the pinpricks of eyes as he crossed open spots. Passing the Yacht Club, he picked up a straw hat and cane-fishing pole. His appearance altered, he continued toward the Pan American terminal. It was getting dark and he broke the light in the booth before making the call. Again, it was Grace that picked up, and she immediately called his wife to the phone.

"Have you got the dough," he blurted into the receiver.

There was a second of silence and a hesitant, "No."

No!

"Not after you called and announced you were back in town."

"Shit! What about your grandmother's jewels? Can you get them tonight?"

"I don't think so Paul. They're in the safe. I don't know the combination," she lied.

"Look bitch, I almost got rubbed out twice since last night. I hadda kill a guy to save my own skin. I'm on the lam with half the dam'd city out for my blood. You do it, and do it quick or I'll have your ass, Angel."

Paul slammed down the receiver. He thought about it for a moment. He pictured the jewelry case on his mother in law's dressing table. Safe, shit, there was no god dam safe. "She's hanging me out to dry." He shouted it aloud. She lied. The two-faced slut is lying to me.

What he felt for Angel was beyond ordinary rage, for she had not simply defied him, but betrayed him, refused him his way out of a lethal situation. A denial of his ownership, an escape from his control was what she was trying to pull off. He was possessed by a need to rip and tear, to pound and destroy, and he began to walk inland, fists clenching and unclenching as his mind teemed.

Connie must have noticed the stress in her twin's face. Perhaps it was more; perhaps it was a sixth sense they shared. "Come out on the verandah with me," she coaxed, taking Angel's hand. "There's something private, "she said quietly.

"What?"

"Shush, outside I'll tell you."

They walked to the far end and sat in their grandfather's swing chair. The air was chill, and they tried to pull the material around them, but it was caught. Connie giggled.

"What is it, "Angel asked abruptly, her tension amplifying annoyance?

"I want to know what is going on. You know you can't fool me. I've felt something hasn't been right for a long time. I've even had nightmares."

"Everybody has nightmares."

"I'm talking about the nightmares," Connie said. "I was feeling something you were feeling, like it was happening to me at the same time and it was horrible. I've been very concerned."

Angel became very quiet. She looked down at her knees as the chair swung back and forth.

"What is going on, what is it?"

"When did you have them, the nightmares?"

"The first was in May, when Grandma and Grandpa came to visit. It was the worst. I almost scratched Grey's eyes out when he tried to wake me." Connie paused and when her sister said nothing, she added, "There have been others since then. You know what it's like."

There were tears in the corners on Angel's eyes now, and she looked away, ashamed to meet her sister's eyes.

"It's your husband isn't it," Connie guessed, the inflection of anger in her voice. "I heard things about him years ago," she continued with, growing conviction. "What's he doing to you?"

Angel sucked in her breath, her dammed up emotions burst, and she acknowledged her plight.

For several minutes, Connie listened, expressing anger and disbelief in a string disconnected but supportive comments common to women.

"Oh my God, He raped you — That was when I had the nightmare — I'm so sorry Angel — Pregnant — And I couldn't understand why you agreed to marry him— Oh, he didn't — Oh My — How could he? I knew he was a bastard but that's cruel — All your money's gone? No, not your house too?— Bugsy Siegel? Steal from grandma — I thought he was out of town — Kill his own baby; no one could be that inhuman — Killers after him — After you?"

"I'm so terrified I can't think," Angel finally said, as her sister hugged her.

"You're home now. Once grandpa knows, he'll protect you. He won't let anything bad happen in this house," Connie assured her sister. "We're going to tell grandma," she said standing, "right now."

"I can't tell it again right now," Angel sobbed."

"Then I will," Connie, said decisively. "Come on," she said reaching for her hand.

"Not with the Tullys here."

"Then I'll bring her," Connie said, and turned walking briskly toward the French doors, passing Grace, who was setting the table.

***

The light was dim as Paul cleared the wide aircraft taxi area, but street lamps were already on. In the time it took to walk to the Byran place, darkness was complete. He climbed the slight slope of the coral ridge and stopped in the shadows at the edge of the street to watch. As he settled into the notch of two trees, he noticed Shawn, the chauffer, cleaning fish by the garage. Paul was still, only his eyes moved as he peered through the windows. He could see old man Byran and another larger man in a front room. The old woman and another woman were in the living room. The help moved about within the house. They had company, and there was no sign of his wife.

He decided she might be in her room, a room with windows opening onto the rear of the house. Paul circled the block, entering the alley and, peered through the fence at the rear of the garden. There were no lights in the upstairs windows, but he could hear an exchange of words, voices, very low and very near. Both sounded like his wife. He could hear the squeak on the swing and moved to see in that direction. A woman stood silhouetted against the lights of the house. For an instant, Paul thought it was his wife, until he realized the woman wasn't pregnant. She said something Paul couldn't quite hear, and turned, walking toward the house. His wife was still on the swing. He saw his chance and quietly opened the back gate.

By the time Angel heard his feet on the gravel, Paul was already between her and the house. She stood then, but remained frozen in place, alert but mute. He was reaching, ready to spring, and she started to cry out, but it was too late, for his hand closed over her mouth. She twisted, but his other hand got hold of her hair, and she felt herself dragged backward. She thought, I will not let him, she struggled futilely, then as he shifted his grip, she bit down on his hand so hard that he loosened her teeth as he yanked it free. She managed a scream, but it was short and muffled as his forearm tightened under her chin. She kicked, fighting him, as she was hauled back toward the alley.

"Go ahead," Paul, whispered into her ear, "kick, squirm, wiggle you faithless bitch." Here's what you were promised if you crossed me. He spun her, then and with all his strength slugged her full in the face.

The cedar fence along the alley was old and not as sturdy as it appeared. Angel was propelled into it with such velocity that an entire section collapsed. She found herself on hands and knees, unable to breathe through a broken nose. It was then that he kicked her in the stomach. She was astonished at the violence of the pain. She was swallowed by the pain, which gripped her back and front like tightening steel bands. She was in the fetal position when the next kick landed in the small of her back. There were others. She lost count. There was finally a blaze of white as she was kicked in the head, and unconsciousness.

Paul had a peripheral impression, something coming quickly at him from the side. As he turned, it swarmed out from a dark shape into his eyes, his nose, even his throat. Now, it was him rolling on the ground choking, rubbing at eyes sockets that held hot coals. Almost blind, he tried to run and slammed into a telephone pole. Dazed, with his throat and lungs on fire he began to sneeze. He crawled into a mud puddle, and splashed water into his red streaked eyes. He sneezed again, blowing snot everywhere. He heard shouts and a woman's piercing screams and pushed himself up. Ablaze with pain, his mind frazzled with fear, Paul stumbled into the dark.

Only Grace had heard Angel's first muffled scream. Preparing the table, she stepped to one side to see who was fooling around. She caught a glimpse of something struggling, a flash of blond hair. Grasping the first thing that her eyes fell on, she turned, hurrying toward the alley just as the fence came crashing down. At first, in the poor light she saw only Angel on hands and knees, then to her horror, Paul's first brutal kick. Grace rushed toward them as he kicked repeatedly. At the last instant, he had sensed Grace, turned toward her, turned just as she pitched the bowl of cayenne pepper into his face. She had yelled then and kept up the yelling as she bent over the young woman. Shawn had arrived first, then Tully; the rest seemed to come all at once. Corazon Byran had screamed and fainted at the blood. Connie had dropped to her knees next to her sister and wept. Kim Tully took charge.

Kim sent Shawn running for the car, and Asher for towels. She did what she could for the girl and tried to slow the bleeding, while Grace tried to revive the grandmother. Dan Tully, in the meantime, raced uselessly up and down the alleys, shouting angrily, as he searched for Paul.

Shawn brought the car around; Angel was placed across the back seat, and Kim climbed in beside. As Connie tried to get in, Kim told her to look to her baby and closed the door. Asher leapt behind the wheel, tearing out of the alley so recklessly he nearly ran down some of his neighbors. Fortunately, the hospital was not distant.

Chapter 21

Asher sat brooding in the hospital waiting room. He had debated calling Fedrico but decided to wait until he knew the outcome. The last time one of the women in his life had suffered something like this Fedrico had gone a little crazy. Not that it wasn't understandable, but Asher thought it would be best to wait. Dan Tully returned from the phone and passed Asher a flask. Asher sipped whisky and gazed at a wall. Years before, he had prayed that he would never again experience days such as this. Well, here he was, Angel surrounded by doctors in surgery; Corazon sedated in a room down the hall, Connie, her face tear streaked, sipping orange juice after giving two pints of blood.

His wife had completely lost her composure, had collapsed, fainted. Both the women had become hysterical, not that he could expect otherwise when confronted by such a tragedy. Simply put, Asher had never imagined his wife could break down so completely. He supposed a part of it was self-blame, a questioning of her part in promoting Angel's marriage to Paul Benetti. Perhaps it was the sum of many tragedies. Why his family should be so marked by tragedy was a mystery to him. He had tried to care for and protect them. Benetti was his fault though, entirely his fault.

Truthfully, Asher had not been pleased at the surprise announcement of his granddaughter's engagement. This was specifically due to her choice of a husband. Asher had been uncomfortable around Paul from the start. He had expressed these feelings of discomfort privately to his wife, who had then promptly reminded him of her own father's opinion of the young fortune seeker she had chosen to marry. He was advised that the choice of a husband was Angel's to make. When he continued to argue the point, Corazon, in a moment of high temper, had declared, "At least Mr. Benetti has not slain a few cousins as a prelude to the nuptials." Her throwing this up to him was not fair and he resented it. Nevertheless, he was long accustomed to the futility of debating with his wife while her temper was up, and he had retreated to consider his options. That had been two weeks before the wedding. Seven months had passed since.

It was in his gut that he had been wary of Benetti. On the surface, Paul had seemed a pleasant enough fellow. He seemed brash perhaps, and a little uncultured for a college man. You could describe him as crude at times, but that was nothing to hold against him. Deeper and far more subtle traits had set off alarms in his subconscious. Asher Byran had spent a lifetime commanding men and playing poker. Success in both endeavors required a keen ability to judge character. Paul Benetti had certain mannerisms that bothered Asher, not the least of which was a barely concealed temper, and a look of eye that threatened even when the man smiled.

Members of Paul's family belonged to the same club as the Byrans. At functions, Asher had been aware of the young man as a face among the many, as a member of the crowd with which the twins socialized. Yes, Benetti's name had been familiar enough. Before Angel invited Paul to dinner, Asher never had reason to give him a moment's consideration. Yes, the invitation to dinner had changed all that. Afterward, Asher had made prudent inquiries. He'd not been pleased with the results of those inquires, but on the other hand, Angel hadn't seemed to be overly found of the young man anyway and — well, Asher had cursed himself for not becoming involved earlier, although he had no idea how he could have affected the outcome.

He had some opportunities. He should have suspected something on his return from *California*, when Angel canceled her trip to *Europe*, and again when she had rushed the wedding. He had not been surprised when only six weeks into her marriage his granddaughter announced she was pregnant. His error was in not being more than suspicious at Angel's need to borrow money less than six months after receiving an inheritance, her half of her father's estate. That had been only two days past.

In retrospect, he should have agreed to give her the twenty thousand while he looked into the matter. It was a insignificant amount. Moreover, he should have been alarmed Friday night when he noticed a bruise on her cheek, should have guessed its cause to be other than a slip due to the awkwardness of pregnancy, should have, should have! He felt deeply that this tragedy was, in a large measure, due to his complacency. He was, after all, the patriarch of his family. He understood that the blame for this tragedy rested squarely on his shoulders.

The phone rang down the hall and Tully hurried to answer it. Tully conversed for a few minutes, hung up, and returned to sit next to Asher. "Tis it a proper time captain, do ya think, for us to have a word in private?"

"What about?"

"Tis about what you'd wish to do about that bloody bastard. Seems the cops ain't got much chance of getting him.

"Why not," Asher asked as he stood.

"Cause according to an acquaintance of mine," Tully whispered, as they moved down the hall, "he's about due to die of lead poisoning."

"When?"

"Sooner than later. There is serious people that have been after him for a couple days. If their job had been done proper, he would ah never got to Angel, God curse the incompetent Bastards."

"I'd prefer to attend to it myself," Asher said.

"As would I."

"I assume the problem was over a sum of twenty thousand dollars; that's the sum Angel asked me to loan her." Asher stopped and faced Tully, "Could we cover the debt? I'd prefer seeing him suffer our justice rather than theirs."

"'T'would be a pleasure to share in your justice sir, and 'tis a man I know; one that could look into the possibility," Tully said, with a cruel grin.

"Dan, I'd appreciate it," Asher said somberly.

"'Tis ah part in this that's rightly mine. You'll understand me rights to place, captain?"

The motion of the waiting room door caught Asher's eye. He saw Kim Tully shifting Connie's baby to her shoulder, as she stood to face a doctor. "Your place here, It's always been understood, Dan," and he hurried down the hall.

The Doctor was brief and sympathetic. There had been no hope for the baby, but barring complications, Angel would survive. She had suffered a fractured skull as well as broken ribs and some damage to her liver and a kidney. Both should heal. The damage to her face could be addressed when she was stronger. Kim had asked the only pointed question, would Angel be able to conceive another child. The doctor thought it possible.

Asher went to Corazon's room. He spoke with Connie and held her for a short time. Kim brought in the baby. It was awake and hungry, and he left the women alone. Tully was on the phone, and Asher leaned against the wall, waiting.

"Done," he said, putting down the phone. "Twill cost ya the twenty-grand and five more for the pleasure, plus a bit more for the boys that put the glove on him to keep him alive. Bonus pay, so to speak, for the same mugs as was working for Paul's *New York* problem. They will be watching all the terminals and the roads north. Watch gas stations coming off the long stretches, ya see. Deal is

Benetti's to be breathing, though a few nicks and dents might be expected."

"No one mentioned in this family, no names."

Tully smirked. "No names involved, save me own Captain, and me own name — why it lost its shine some years back, and the terms — 'tis unspoken of course, but it's well understood what you're paying for."

"First we even things up personally. I don't want the women to guess I had a hand in this. When we're done with him, we see he ends up behind bars," Asher emphasized, "Permanently behind bars."

"Kill the bastard and 'tis no more harm he'll do; that's if ya want my advice," Tully protested. "He's too vicious a dog to trust with life. Kill him and be safe."

The women will want it," Asher said sadly. "They'll be reassured by seeing it played out in court. They will witness the public condemnation. A man spending his lifetime, dwelling in misery on his evil deeds, now that is a woman's vision of justice."

"You'll need ta lay something heavy on Benetti. Wife beating won't cut it. You need something more serious than a bloody assault charge, and you need to make dam'd sure it sticks. Getting the law involved in personal matters can be tricky. Better ta rub the bastard out and be sure."

"Let's see how it plays out," Asher said tiredly. "Lay hands on him first and see how we feel then. Whoever said, 'Vengeance is a meal best eaten cold,' had it right."

Chapter 22

Three hundred yards south of the seaplane hangars, Paul lay on the slightly mildewed berth of a moored sloop. The invincible feeling, he experienced as he gave his bitch wife what she deserved had been subdued. The agonizing pain and temporary blindness, he suffered had balanced him out. He survived though; he'd got clean away. He told himself he was okay. He was good. He was alive and free; had fresh clothes on his back, and a couple hundred in his pocket. No one would bother him on this boat either. He had swum out and boarded. The old drunk who'd owned it made the mistake of showing up a couple of hours later. Paul had used the stiletto. Aided by a spare anchor, he had disposed of the body.

Things would be different now, no going back. Nothing here for him anymore, nothing but guaranteed death. He'd be rubbed if any number of people caught up with him. Even with his family, he was a pariah. His own mother refused to talk with him, refused him money. Paul reminded himself of the rules of survival; he resolved to heed them in the future.

Hungry, he rummaged through the small galley, finding sardines and a tin of crackers. The sardines were Japo, Chinese, or something eastern. He studied the label and surmised that if an inanimate sardine could travel here, he could get there. The world was wide, and for a tough remorseful and intelligent man such as himself, easy to vanish into. The difficult part would be getting out of *Miami*. He scratched the idea of using *Havana* as a haven because an island was a trap. Besides, he didn't fit in, didn't speak the lingo. Trains and planes were out; they were too easy to watch. That left the road, but he didn't dare go near his car. He supposed he'd have to highjack one. Grab the car and driver so there'd be no police report; bump the yokel, take his I.D. and leave him for gator bait. He liked it, head for the *West Coast, Canada*, yeah! Feeling confident, Paul rummaged in a locker for canned fruit, found none. He did find a rusty shotgun and a quart of rum behind the ceilings. He set the gun aside, pulled the cork, and sniffed. It would do.

Half-drunk and sweaty, Paul awoke in the dark. He sat up and stretched, felt blindly for the bottle and took a drink. He began to move aft, to the cockpit, but the boat was rocking, and he fell, cursing under his breath. In the blurry black, he wobbled back to his bunk and sat. Time to get moving he decided, while there was plenty of traffic on the streets. He drained the last of the rum and put on his shoes. As an afterthought, he lit a candle and rummaged for shotgun shells. He found a stained box with two shells inside; he scooped them into his pocket. Seconds later, he dropped into the dingy with a thump, pulled the shotgun down with him and cast off.

Hijacking a car was easy. Paul sat down next to a hedge in the Pan American parking lot and waited for someone alone to come for their car. He wanted somebody he could pass for, and he let several men pass him by before deciding. The person he picked had a late model Chevy that would do. Paul was sliding into the passenger's seat before the stooge knew what was happening. First irritated surprise, then fear covered the driver's face as the shotgun pressed into his side.

"Know how to get to route '41'?" Paul asked and leaned back, one shoulder against the door, pulling his hat down. At gunpoint, the man drove west through the *Gables*, and past the racetrack into the outskirts of the city. Once onto the narrow macadam of the *Tamiami Trail* proper, there were no lights. Through the pitch-black swamp, the car sped west behind a luminous cave of headlamps. Twice the driver had started to say something, and Paul told him to shut up. Just short of the *Everglades City* junction, he ordered the man to pull over.

"Gotta take a piss," he explained. Leave the lights on and stand in front of the car," he ordered.

"Gotta go too, Mister," the man said.

"Be my guest,"

Paul waited for the man to start unbuttoning his trousers and shot him in the face. The roar of the shotgun echoed in the distance. Nearby, a flock of startled birds took flight. Paul stooped, began rifling, the still-twitching man's urine-soaked pockets. He slapped at mosquitoes. Wallet, pipe, jack-knife, small change, and a pouch of tobacco. The wallet held about eight bucks. "*Big spender*," Paul thought.

The drivers-license identified the man as David Elmo Schimminar, twenty-eight years old.

Paul's faced soured; "*A kraut, what a shit name*," he thought. He removed the cash from his own wallet and shoved the wallet into Schimminar's pocket. Grabbing the feet of the now motionless body, he dragged it to the canal bank and rolled it into the water.

"Goodbye Paul Benetti," he called pleasantly.

The mosquitoes were swarming now, and he ran for the car, starting the engine. He drove smoothly for perhaps another six miles before the engine began to sputter, buck, and then die completely. He looked at the gauges. The gas registered below empty. Shoving open the door, he leapt out of the car, cursed, threw rocks and pounded his fists on the hood. The mosquitoes found him, and he tore a blanket from the back seat and wound it around his head and shoulders. He was about four miles past the turnoff. It would be another fifteen miles to the first diner and gas station near the *Marco* turn-off. It would take three hours to walk if he stepped out fast, and even at this god-forsaken hour, there was always the chance of a ride. He pushed the car to the side of the road, took the shotgun and began to walk quickly, west on the centerline.

Water, warm vapor from the *Gulf Stream* rose in the east and the dawn was red orange. The old truck was heading north to *Naples* with some twenty migrant workers. The farmer had offered to carry him a way, if he didn't mind riding up back. Paul minded but he was in no position to turn down the ride, so he climbed up with the crowd of blacks.

***

Jack Bellis was inside the screened dining area, avoiding bugs when the farm truck stopped to fuel up. He was reading the sports page of the *Tampa Tribune* and didn't give the shabby outfit a second look. The hick that walked in and sat at the counter didn't catch his attention either. Jerry wasn't looking for someone dressed like a yokel and needing a shave, but when the yokel mouthed off to the waitress, Jack gave him a quick second look. That had been a smart mouth city boy talking, and yeah, it could be his man. When the guy asked what time, a bus was scheduled northbound that settled it for Jack. Thirty seconds later, he was dialing Frank Lasco.

Frank listened to Bellis blabber for a second and cut him off. "Is his left ear messed up?"

"I was on his right."

"Well go look, smuck."

"Hold on." Jack walked to the counter where Paul had just begun eating and asked the waitress for a buck's change for the phone. He glanced at Paul, smiled and said, "It's my mother's birthday. You know mothers, they like to talk." Change in hand, Jack returned to the dangling receiver. For credibility, he dropped a quarter in the slot and said, "Left ears got a new grove."

"See ya in two hours," Frankie said. "And Jack, keep an eye on him."

***

Paul woke to a cold pressure at the back of his neck and an instant of fear.

"Keep your hands where they are Paulo," said the voice. "Lay still or dam'd if we don't finish you now."

Paul was dismissive of fear and had always kept a check on it, but in the last days, people had been scaring the hell out of him. He hated the feeling. He started to turn his head to one side, tried to see who had the drop on him. He didn't fancy ending up dead in some shit hole.

"I said freeze, or I'll put one in your brain, kid, you deaf or something?"

Paul froze.

"Sit on his feet Jack. Dino, do his hands, tight"

"I know how to tie a knot," the squat man said.

Paul had been sleeping on a bench. The gas station attendant was supposed to wake him when the *Tampa* bus came in. Goddamn them! How'd they find him? He suddenly recognized the man at his feet, the man who was calling his mother on the phone. The Bastards had been laying for him. How would they know?

"Pat him down," Frankie ordered, as the squat man finished with his hands. "Check him good. He likes to play with knives."

He patted him down and out came the wallet and jackknife. "Kiddy knife," Dino smirked.

"Get him on his feet and in the car," Frank ordered. The station attendant and a couple locals were giving them the eye when Sticks pulled up in the Lincoln. Frank flashed a fake badge. "Police business," he said tersely.

Dino shoved Paul into the back of the car and climbed in after; Jack got in on the opposite side.

Frank climbed in next to Sticks Harper and motioned him to go.

"Who's this Schimminar?" Dino asked, holding up the driver's license.

"What about it, Paulo," Frank said?

"Found it under the bench—guy must have lost it," Paul answered with a surly tone.

"Yeah, I'll bet," Sticks smirked.

"Right, the wallet plus his ass," Dino laughed.

"Dino, wanna shot," Sticks asked and passed a flask over his shoulder.

Dino tilted his head back, appeared to take a sip. "Good stuff," he said lowering the flask. "Wanna slug kid?"

"Yeah," Paul said and holding the flask with two hands, he took a long pull.

They all smiled at him funny, which made Paul nervous. He'd got a good look at Frank's pistol. It was fitted with a silencer. Why hadn't they just shot him? Were they going to work him over, beat him to death? "You going to kill me," he asked straight out.

Frank snorted a laugh. "Hell no, kid, we're gonna drop you off. Turn ya over to some old chums. Not to be scratched."

"What about Siegel?"

"No sweat with Ben, your wife squared you with him on Saturday."

Paul was stunned. "What time Saturday?"

"How in the hell would I know?" Frankie was tired after a late night, and an early morning. He was in no mood to answer questions.

"Where are we—?"

"Shut your yap," Frank shouted— "Gee'z!"

Paul felt sleepy, suddenly dizzy. While he was wondering about it, he passed out.

"That was fast," Frank said.

"Put enough in there to knock a horse over," Sticks said. "He'll be out for five, six hours anyway."

The car sped east into the glare of the morning sun, its occupants mute.

***

At his home on *Miami Beach*, Tully took the late morning phone call. The caller asked one simple question, where did he want his package delivered? Tully gave him the address and went to meet them.

The place was a closed butcher shop near the *Liberty City* neighborhood. In a cooler, Dino tossed Paul on a table, one of the big wooden cutting tables, and went with Frankie to buy lunch. Half an hour later, Tully opened the door and let in a large, well-tanned man with a black bag. The veterinary doctor remained inside for an hour. Late afternoon, Paul was dumped two blocks down in an alley.

Within minutes, anonymous phone calls had brought both the police and the ambulance, which had rushed him to the hospital. Benetti's crushed hands were set and put in casts. They operated on his left knee. He would walk with a stiff limp, but never run. There was nothing to do about the full castration. The staff did remark that it was a neat procedure, which was certainly accomplished by a professional.

The police recovered the wallet and I.D. of Dave Schimminar from his pockets. Paul's fingerprints were later taken from Schimminar's abandoned car. Schimminar was the father of three, and a Deacon of his church, and well-liked by his fellow workers. Schimminar's abduction and murder led police to *Dinner Key*, where Earl Blanchard's bloated body had been discovered floating next to his sloop. Paul's fingerprints, some of them bloody, were found throughout the victim's boat. Later, a witness who saw him running from and alley tied him to a knifing behind a *Miami Beach Club*. In the end, the assault on Angela Benetti turned out to be no more than a footnote in the charges brought by the *Dade County* prosecutor. The papers called Paul Benetti a one-man crime spree. Framing had not been necessary, only a little finger pointing.

Chapter 23

With the day nearly gone, the light had changed. Angel studied her work critically. To catch the midday light just so, to apply highlights and deepen the shadows, her painting needed another hour's work here on the mountain. A painting was rendered poor or wonderful in the final hour of work, and a return to the mountain was necessary. That would be an hour on another day, though, for she had to give the canvass time to dry, and besides, she would be away, off to *Rome*.

She slid the canvass into its case, closed her palette box and strapped them both to her motor bike. The motor buzzed to life on the second kick. She let out the clutch and started down the winding road. Over the roofs of *San Remo*, the *Mediterranean* filled the horizon. The view from her little house was lovely, but up here, it was grand. Angel had grown to love the landscape, and light of the *Maritime Alps.* They had made an impression on her when she first traveled from *Toulon* to *Genoa*, and even after visiting all the great cities of northern Italy, she found her mind dwelling on a return to this coast.

She acknowledged her affinity for the sea. Her first choice had been a strip of *Spain's* northern coast, the *Gulf of Gascoigne*, near the French frontier. Her familiarity with the language had brought her to *Spain*. The wild violent beauty of the coast and the mountains had kept her painting in a village north of *Bilbao*. At least it had kept her until Spain's Civil War drew near. On September 4, 1936, fascist rebels took *Irun*. That was the day Angel boarded a French ship for *Arcachon*. She had been in *Bordeaux* on September 12, when *San Sebastian* fell. She was relieved to be in *France*, in *Aquitaine*, and relieved that she was safe.

Angel knew no one in *France*, and made no friends, nor did she wish to burden herself with friends. Through the fall and winter, she toured the country, like a beautiful ghost, often seen but never touchable. By spring, she had visited *Monaco* and was on to *Italy*. The month of May found her back in *San Remo*.

She had owned the house above the town for almost two years. It was a square building of two stories, with a small courtyard at the center. It encompassed a great room, a dining room, a kitchen. Several rooms could be used for any purpose, but she used them for her art. At ridiculously low wages, Angel had hired a cook, housekeeper, and a gardener. She seldom spoke to anyone outside her residence and accepted no invitations from the large expatriate community. Riding about on her motor bike, she was a curiosity, even a mystery, and of course, a topic of gossip. Angel had no conception of her notoriety. All she cared for was her art.

After the loss of her baby, Angel's physical recovery had been rapid. The procedures performed by cosmetic surgeons were completely successful. There were deep hurts to her mind and spirit though; these were not so quickly healed as the flesh and bone. For three months, she had remained at home, leaving the house only for stays at the hospital. She chose to see no one. What she wished was privacy, anonymity.

In February, the Byran women had gone west by train, traveling together for a portion of the distance. Connie was returning to *San Diego* to join Grey, while Angel, accompanied by Corazon, was bound for *Reno, Nevada*. The quick *Nevada* divorce was granted in April; the day before Paul Benetti's death sentence, and to her family's astonishment, Angel refused to return home. Instead, she announced her intentions to go to *Europe*. She had the means, because Corazon had created a trust for her, a trust with a generous monthly allowance. With independence, Angel could do as she chose, and she told her grandmother that she chose to go to *Europe*. She had kissed her goodbye, and since that day, had written home monthly. Beyond that, Angel had ignored society and to whatever degree it was possible, she had ignored the world.

***

To the people of San Remo, the death of the Pope came as a curious surprise. Angel's house was abuzz with the servants talking about the election and the coronation. Angel merely decided she would see it. It was as if she had suddenly woken to a curious noise and looked out the window. It was a whim. A trip to Rome for the crowning of Pius XII might seem strange; after all, Angel was hardly religious these days, but that's what whims were about. With Agata, her young housekeeper, she took a boat to *Genoa* and then the train south to *Rome*. Though the cities' accommodations were overwhelmed, the wealthy seldom find crowding a problem. Angel's room in a five-star hotel was secured without effort.

Outside, the streets swarmed with pilgrims, processions and parades passed everywhere. With Agata, she viewed the ceremony at Saint Peter's from a rooftop. It came almost as an anti-climax. Suddenly the idea of an immediate return to *San Remo* seemed foolish to Angel, for she had never been to *Rome*, and might never return. Why not see more of the city?

Through her hotel, she arranged for a guide and car, and set out to experience the ancient grandeur of *Rome*. On the third day of explorations, as they were moving at a crawl in the tangle of a traffic circle, her driver struck a young man on a motorcycle. He seemed not to be seriously hurt, and he picked his motorcycle up. In fact, he appeared more embarrassed than injured. He had waved her driver off, speaking in English. It seemed strange to hear English spoken, at least English with a brash American accent.

***

The Invitational International Exhibit opened on Saturday night. Including the work of contemporary sculpture from all over the world, it held several hundred pieces, done in varied styles and mediums. Angel found herself drawn to the bronzes. One life size bronze absorbed her. It was of a small girl, frightened and clinging to a confident, smiling mother. It transported Angel to a forgotten moment in her own childhood; a garden snake in her sand box had terrified her. Oblivious to the din around her, Angel could at this moment, hear her mother's voice laughing lovingly, telling her that it was a friendly kind of snake.

Gazing at the statue, she stood alone amidst the human throng, and shed her first tears since the loss of her baby. Remarkably, she was mourning all that she had lost or never known: the father who had never held her, her young mother, her unborn child, the family she had abandoned three years before, and her own innocence. Somehow, the genius of this sculpture had brought it all back to her, and as wonderful as it was, it was terribly painful.

Jed Russell leaned against the wall, watching the reaction of the astonishingly lovely young woman, who stood completely absorbed before his piece.

When he saw the tears running down her face, he didn't know if he should feel elated or embarrassed by the strength of her emotional response. Her expression seemed a mixture of joy and pain and he tried to memorize it. He wasn't sure if he could capture it or if it could be reproduced, but he would try. What Jed did know was, she was the most beautiful mortal in the world, and that he'd seen her before. Her driver had knocked him off his motorcycle two days before.

A photographer was passing, and Jed whispered to him. The burst of light from the flash bulb broke the spell. Startled, Angel turned away from the flash. She turned toward Jed, still unaware of him, but realizing her face was wet, she dug into her purse, searching for a napkin.

"May I offer you my handkerchief Miss?" he asked. "My fault, your makeup's running," he added quietly.

Angel saw his hand first. It was extended slightly, offering the handkerchief. It was a big hand, strong and calloused, a hand that understood work. Though the voice was quiet, its timber was low and strangely gentle. It reminded her of grandpa. Even beyond that, the voice was otherwise familiar. When she looked up, Angel had the instant uneasy impression of physical power. She pushed the fear away, and recognized in the way this man carried himself, not the aggressive power of a Paul Benetti, but a benign strength, a useful worker's muscle. She accepted the handkerchief, dabbed away her tears, and smiled briefly up at him.

"Thank you," she said looking away, "but how is it your fault?"

"Well, I assumed it was my entry that made you cry."

"You did this?" she asked, turning back to look at the *Mother and Daughter*.

"What do you think?" he asked with a concern he couldn't have explained.

"It's wonderful." She turned to face him. "You've captured something, an emotion I feel strongly but can't describe." She said this softly, looking up at him. She could face him now. He seemed somehow shy, vulnerable. He was tanned, and despite his freckles, ruggedly handsome, with blue eyes and sandy hair. Angel realized she knew this face. "Gosh," she blurted, "You're the one Pietro knocked off a motor cycle."

"The same," he laughed. "May I introduce myself? Jed Russell. I'm from Ohio."

"Miss Byran," she replied, for the first time in years, not hesitating to think. "I'm from *Florida* but I suppose I could be officially described as an expatriate. I've had a home near *San Remo* for two years." 'Why did I let him know that?' she wondered, with inner alarm.

"I'm not much of a traveler, only here for this exhibit," he said, turning and gesturing to the many works in the hall. "It's farming that pays for the luxury of being an artist," he chuckled. "Have to get home before long. There's the spring plowing, you see."

She noticed that he favored his right leg. "Were you hurt when we knocked you down?" she asked."

"Sprain's all," he said, as if ashamed to admit any injury. "What brought you to live in *San Remo*, where-ever that is?" he asked, attempting to keep the conversation moving.

"The light and the landscape," she answered.

"You're a painter?"

"I try," she said modestly.

"Perhaps someday I could see your work," he suggested.

"*San Remo* is pretty far from here, and then there's the spring planting," she laughed. She picked her words to hold him at a safe distance. "Perhaps we'll meet on another day, when I'm ready to unveil my work."

"Perhaps," he said smiling. "I'm sure you'll get your show. When it happens, I hope you're a great success. I've been promised my own show, the summer of next year, *New York City*, in the last week of June." He paused. "Perhaps you could make it. That's if you find yourself in *New York*," he added, uncertain.

"If?" she said smiling.

"If," he replied. "A terrible word — we never know, do we?"

"Well, it's been a pleasure Mr. Russell," Angel said, disengaging herself. "I've the rest of the exhibit to see, and friends to track down," she lied.

"Well then Miss Byran, until we meet again," Jed told her, smiling and hiding an unexpectedly deep regret.

"Goodbye."

She moved away from him, and as he watched the gold of her hair vanish into the crowd, Jed fought down the urge to follow her. She was from a different world, and his own world demanded his return. He sighed. They had met twice. Perhaps there would be a third time. Jed remembered the photographer and set out to find him. He wanted her picture.

Chapter 24

At the last possible moment, Connie remembered she hadn't phoned grandmother as promised. The phone was two feet from the door on a table. Looking at it had reminded her that she had promised to call the minute she knew. However, once on the phone, her grandmother enjoyed talking, and it would take time she did not have now. The babysitter was in the house; Grey was going to the car, and all their friends would be waiting. She would call her later, she thought, then remembering the time difference between *San Diego* and *Miami*, she groaned and vowed to call her in the morning.

Grey was starting the engine as Connie climbed in. She slid across the seat to press herself against him, wiggled her feet out of her high heels, and curled them up beside her. He was intent on backing out on the driveway and shrugged her off when she nibbled his neck.

"Gee'z Connie, you're going to get us in a wreck," he growled.

"There's nothing coming," she said smugly. His ship had only come into port three days before, and it was like the third day of a honeymoon. Touch was important to her.

"Were late," he added, putting the car into forward and accelerating.

Connie snuggled against him again, this time abstaining from tasting his neck. It wouldn't hurt if he were few minutes late for his own surprise party.

"Grey MacArt," she scolded," grow up. Arriving at Commander Evans party a few minutes late is not going to make one bit of difference, especially with you leaving the Navy. On top of that, buster, the SP's are going to ticket us. That's another on the list if you don't slow down."

"Common Sugar, you know, I hate being late," he complained. The Ford convertible was flying now.

"Don't be a jerk, lover. You don't want Cory growing up an orphan, do you?"

The car began to slow. She could hear him take a deep breath, that sigh of capitulation and she hid her grin. It took a long time to learn how to exercise a smidgen of control over a man. It was even more difficult when he was gone for months on end, because he got into the habit of having his own way. She turned on the radio. There was a song playing that she loved.

Excited, she said, "Listen Grey, this song reminds me of you." They turned onto *Lincoln Boulevard* and the power lines caused the station to go to static.

"See if you can get the sports news honey," Grey asked, without commenting on the song.

It irritated her, both the static and the lack of interest, but she leaned forward and began the search for a sports commentator. When Grey pulled up in front of the Officer's Club, Connie was still fumbling unsuccessfully with the radio dial. Under the shade of an awning, a valet took the keys. Grey put his arm around her waist, and they started up the steps.

Inside, they'd just begin to mingle when one of Grey's shipmates dropped a banner, '*Bon Voyage Lt. MacArt*'. In an explosion of male exuberance, the drinking and ribbing began in earnest. The Officer's Club was a large enough building, but the private room Evans had reserved, was only a small part of it. The destroyer squadron had a lot of officers, and after a ninety-day cruise, they were primed and ready for any excuse to party. It got close and noisy in there. At some period during the last few years, Connie had grown to dislike a claustrophobic atmosphere, particularly one made up of too many loud drunks occupying too small a space. It was worse perhaps for a good-looking woman. She had to endure stepped on feet, spilled drinks, brushed breasts and other accidental groping, while listening to the din of a hundred men enthusiastically discussing other drunken parties they'd attended.

She found herself trapped in a corner by a brand-new Ensign. The goof somehow thought she would be impressed hearing that he was ninth in his class, a prodigy at gunnery, and was loved by women on three continents. When he turned to respond to a question, she instantly ducked under his arm and made her escape.

Connie found herself sitting in a bay window where at least she could breathe. A problem with attending a party with the guest of honor was you could not simply leave. To bail out on your husband was poor social conduct and defiantly not Navy. She stared gloomily out over the bay. God was she sick of the navy. A pair of legs in dress whites was suddenly in front of her. She looked up fearing the return of the Ensign, but when she looked up it was Commander Evans. He had a drink in each hand.

"I thought you might like another drink, Ma'am."

"Why thank you," she said accepting the glass.

"Mind if I sit?" Evans said, "unless you prefer being alone of course."

"No. Be my guest," she said gesturing toward the sill beside her. "Less smoke near the floor," she added, only half joking.

He sat on an angle to her and nodded toward a bar where Grey was involved in a jovial conversation. "Your husband is a talented officer, and his paperwork for promotion to full Lieutenant is already approved. I hate to see the navy lose him. I expect — well — you're ready to be free of it all."

"Yes, I am," she said without hesitation. "But Grey's ready too. Before we married, he told me that he didn't think the navy was what he wanted, but he was going to give a shot. He'd promised his parents, you know."

"I didn't."

"His father was a captain with my grandfather's shipping company. Our families have been close for years. Grey's brother, Alan, was a year ahead of him at *Annapolis*, loves the navy. Grey prefers the merchant fleet." Connie smiled a little sadly, and said, "He'll be away from home and hearth, navy or not, but at least I'll have my own home, and I'll be close to my family when he's at sea. Byran men have been at sea for generations Commander. Like it or not, we Byran women know what to expect."

"You sound like my wife," he said, his eyes crinkled with amusement, "Supportive but disapproving. I'm supposed to give promising young officers a pitch to reenlist, and of course it helps to know where the wife stands."

"The loyal opposition stands opposed sir." She said this with a deep voice and mock seriousness.

"Ah well, I suppose there's not much hope for my pitch then."

"From my direction, not even faint hope."

"Well I appreciate your candor. It'll probably end all the same anyway, the resignation issue that is. War's not far off. When it comes, the navy will be calling its lost sheep back to the fleet. In a war, it's best to be on a warship; my opinion of course, but the record shows that merchant ships are pretty much sitting ducks.

"My grandfather's ship, the *Biscayne,* it was torpedoed and sunk in the last war. I'm sure you two could have some fine discussions on the subject, but I, Commander, I am going home in eight days as the wife of a civilian." Connie raised her glass, "To freedom from navy housing," she toasted and drained it. "Now, how are your wife and children?" she asked Evans. "Are they still living back home in Iowa?" She winked.

Connie spent most of the evening in an adjoining room with some other wives. Grey had vanished into a drunken pack of stomping, shouting young officers, who sang and danced inarticulately in pagan tribute to Pan. The party held until the club closed, but by then few were able to walk properly. Connie asked two Pilipino stewards to put her husband in the car. At home, she left Grey in the back seat to sleep it off and called a cab for the babysitter. She had expected a little companionship, a bit of fooling around when they got home, but that was certainly out of the question now. Too irritated to sleep, she began to pack for their move home to *Florida.*

***

The week had gone quickly, and the train ride was actually a pleasure. They disembarked for a day in *New Orleans,* where Grey had an employment interview at the offices of *Lykes Line.* He got the job, which was an excuse for celebration that night, dinner and dancing in the French Quarter.

Green Cove Springs was their next stop. They stayed with Clare MacArt during the first week of June. Clare cooked big meals, spoiled her grandson, Cory, and fussed about Grey's leaving the navy. Connie, who was enjoying herself, wouldn't have minded staying a little longer. However, Grey quickly grew annoyed. Having Alan's promotion and, decision to make the navy a career thrown at him daily got under his skin, and he finally told his mother that four years of academy and six years in the fleet was enough. They boarded the sleeper for Miami and woke Passing Palm Beach. The dining car was brilliant with light and coconut palms flashing past during breakfast. It would be good to be home again.

Cousin Estefan was visiting with his wife and five-year-old son. Fedrico Vega dropped by each afternoon, and other old friends came and went. As they were welcomed home, the Byran house filled with laughter and happy conversation. The little third cousins, Cory and Ramon, ran squealing through the house with the Tully's twin girls. They were a small mob, knocking things ajar and disturbing all sense of peace. The cook served up special dishes, the women shopped, and the men went deep-sea fishing on Dan Tully's new boat. It was a happy time for Connie, but amidst the joy of it, she found herself missing her twin more sharply than usual.

Grey, who had been talking to Tully, broke the news to Connie concerning Paul Benetti's death sentence. It had been altered to life without parole. It was an arrangement made with the Feds two years before and only just confirmed. Paul had agreed to name names and tell what he knew about some very dangerous people. He was ready to testify in court for the first time. According to Tully's sources, Benetti had been transferred to a federal facility in *New York* in order to keep him alive long enough to be useful. When the news broke a few days later in the *Miami Herald*, this Federal intervention incensed not only the Byrans, but also the community as a whole. The women were far angrier than the men were, some showing their fury while others wept. Dan Tully put it clearly in perspective. He explained the facts of it.

"He's a convicted murderer you see, but he's also a snitch and ah informer to boot. I am telling you friends, being a bloody informer in Paul's world 'tis a far nastier thing for a man than murder. Most lads are fine with killing you see, but an informer is a danger to all and cannot be tolerated. Every hand is turned against him, you see. To survive he's gotta live guarded. 'Tis round the clock in gloomy isolation he sits and breathes. 'Tis big money that's offered, and 'twill be paid, for the spilling of his blood. Ladies," Tully said "'tis surprised I'd be, if the man lives out the year."

***

On a Saturday, Asher had taken Connie and Grey house hunting. He'd shown them some beautiful places on the beach, homes that in the depression could be had at bargain prices. Grey had commented that the beach was nice, but he couldn't stomach living with a bunch of Jews. This comment did not sit well with Asher Byran. Connie noticed a difference in her grandfather even if Grey did not. Grandpa had remained pleasant, he continued to make suggestions and to be helpful, but she wasn't surprised when he left them on their own the following day.

By the end of the week, they found a place they both loved, and they'd found it all on their own. It was a modest two story built on an acre lot, atop the *Coral Ridge.* The bay was visible from the upper windows, and the house was designed to bring any breeze in under the porch roof. It was the house of her dreams, and Connie had endless decorating ideas to make it come alive as a home. She began to choose the furnishings immediately; Grey balked at the cost. The domestic battle that followed concerned the use of her money. He refused to be seen as, or made to feel like, a kept man.

Even after Connie told him off and described what he could do with his backward pride, his selfish sensitivities, she remained filled with extraordinary resentment. There was no love making that night nor for a few nights thereafter. She was determined that he understand the enormity of his error, and he would be given time for it to sink in. Her own desires ruined the lesson earlier than she had intended but----. When she first awoke on the morning after, Connie felt herself curled against his lean body, sensed the heartbeat in the warm flesh beside her. The lesson she'd meant to instill seemed quite unimportant.

She had shared the new house with him for only two weeks before Lykes called, and he went to meet his ship as a second mate. Grey was at sea four months but returned in time for Cory's fourth birthday. He was gone again a month later with a promotion to chief mate. This time he was out for six months. He'd spent more time with her when he was in the navy, Connie told herself, and she struggled to contain her loneliness. When her grandmother had proposed the trip to *Europe*, it had seemed a good idea.

Corazon and Asher planned to leave for *Europe* in the spring to visit Angel, and they wanted Connie to accompany them. In April, though, the war began to heat up and spread to more countries. German U-boats were active in the *Atlantic*, and Asher put a halt to the trip, insisting it was far too dangerous. Corazon argued that the war had ended in *Spain*, and *Italy* had vowed neutrality. Within days, Asher was proved right with the German invasion of the Nordic countries. Through the spring, the women worried about Angel, alone in Italy. Grey arrived home on vacation in June, and the next day a telegram arrived. Angel was returning from *Italy*. The family was overcome with relief.

Chapter 25

Through the spring and summer of 1939, *San Remo* was little touched by the world's troubles. One day Agata had shown Angel an article in an Italian paper. She asked her, "Was this not her home?" A ship, the *St. Louis*, carrying 930 Jewish refugees had been denied entry into *Miami*. Angel told her yes.

Agata had smiled, "Jews — God's curse on them," she said.

Angel felt uncomfortable with this, but refused to dwell on it, but soon the echoes of political tribulations reverberated even in *San Remo*. In September, news of the invasion of *Poland* by German forces reached Angel's doorstep on the day it began. News of subsequent international upheavals filled the papers each day, and for the first time in years, Angel began to read and pay attention. Through the winter of 1940, the war was mainly one of rhetoric, but with the first airs of spring, armies began to move. By June, *Western Europe* was aflame with war, and the rest of the world smoldering. Italy's Mussolini had declared neutrality, but few believed it would last. Angel was apprehensive. She suddenly realized how out of place she was, how alone. She needed to return to the *United States.*

It was in the first days of June that she made the decision to leave Italy. Once decided, the preparations did not take long. Her servants were invited to stay on at the house, and she advanced their pay for the year. The clothing she wished to take fit into a single chest. She would only take those few clothes and her paintings. There were over a hundred canvasses. Each was removed from its frame, carefully rolled, and placed in a tube. Agata's brother drove Angel to *Genoa* where she booked passage to *New York* on an American Ship.

With the growing population of refugees, obtaining her papers and exit visa had taken all day at the consulate. Preparing to board her ship, she rummaged in the side pocket of her purse where she had shoved her Passport. She hadn't used the purse since Rome, and in the corner was a handkerchief. The monogram was "JR", Jed Russell. She hadn't thought of him in some time. What beautiful work he did. She pictured him. What was it he'd told her? A show in *New York* in June, if she happened to be in *New York*, he had said. The line moved, and she presented her papers. "If?" she had answered.

***

The ship was new, painted black with huge American flags painted on her side so she would be recognized as neutral in wartime. She was also luxurious, and quite fast, making the passage to *New York* in only eight days. Angel used those eight days, getting used to speaking English again. *"Has it been Four years?"* she asked herself again.

Disembarking on the *Hudson* side of *Manhattan*, Angel was struck by the harsh noise, the rush of traffic, and the sheer size of the buildings. She hailed a cab and directed the driver to the Waldorf Astoria. After checking in, she sent a telegram rather than phoning her family. Somehow hearing their voices would give them too much power over her. She wasn't ready yet. Perhaps she would be ready tomorrow. In her room, she relaxed. It was a refuge and a place to think and plan. She wanted to go home, yet she could not. Four years, it was difficult to believe it had been that long. The memories and shame of her life with Paul were still raw. However, she missed her family. She would go home — for a visit perhaps, but there was no rush. She would experience *New York* first. She could shop for a new wardrobe, take in the galleries, visit the museums and sample music in the nightclubs. Then, there was Jed Russell. His one-man exhibit was to be showing somewhere in *Manhattan* this week. She would have the front desk make inquiries.

News of the war in *Europe* covered the papers. While she was at sea, the British forces had been driven into the sea at *Dunkirk*. Loses of thirty thousand were reported, but three-hundred and thirty-five thousand allied troops had been rescued in a heroic sealift. Italy was in the war on *Germany's* side. *France* and *Belgium* had fallen, and the Germans occupied *Paris.*

Angel put the papers aside, trying to comprehend the rapidity of all that had happened. In the end, *Italy* and little *San Remo* remained untouched. Mighty France was on its knees, and *England* stood against the Germans, bloodied and alone. Angel had taken passage on a ship, and the world had changed. She was no longer a part of Europe, of that world she told herself. The *United States* was safe and remote from the insanity of European politics. Tomorrow, she resolved, tomorrow she would make a new beginning, a new start and enjoy what life offered here. Tomorrow she would go shopping.

Wednesday morning, her first stop was at a chic *Fifth Avenue* dress shop. From there, she went on to buy shoes, gloves, and hats, all of which they delivered to her room by the time she returned from lunch. There was also information at the desk concerning her request. *Holms Gallery* would be exhibiting Mr. Russell's work for two weeks, starting this Friday evening. This was Wednesday. There was plenty to keep her occupied for two days, and the opening night of any event was the most exciting. She changed to casual attire and caught a cab to the *Metropolitan Museum*. The afternoon went quickly, as did the next two days.

***

Holms Gallery was on a side street, one door off *Fifth Avenue*. It had once been a small warehouse, which allowed for the high ceilings and spaciousness. When Angel arrived at 8:00 p.m., there was already a good crowd, and some serious buyers. The *Mother and Daughter*, the piece she had admired in *Rome*, was one of almost fifty pieces in the Russell collection. Its impression on Angel remained as strong as in *Rome*. It had a twelve-hundred-dollar price tag; she decided to pay the price before it occurred to her that she had nowhere to put it.

One of the salespersons found Jed speaking with one of the critics. She stole Jed away and informed him that another of his pieces may have sold. Summoned to meet a potential buyer he came immediately, because a word or two with the artist is often what it took to close a sale. Angel was already writing the check when Jed saw her. He was dumb struck. For over a year, he'd had this woman in his head, and she shows up at his opening.

"Was she interested in him," he wondered, or just his art?

"Miss Byran," he said, smiling, perhaps too broadly, "I'm astonished to find you here at my opening, let alone acquiring a piece."

"Oh splendid, you're acquainted then," the sales person said, backing away. "I'll just leave you two to chat."

Tilting her head coyly, Angel responded, "I was invited, was I not?"

"To see a one man, show — it's a long way to travel from Italy," Jed said jovially. "I'm honored."

His grin was infectious, and Angel smiled. "Well, in all honesty," she said in a pretend whisper, "the war in *Europe* did prompt me a bit, and the only ship available was bound for *New York*. I see it as a fortunate turn of fate though. My ship only arrived Tuesday, and here I am, the owner of a lovely work of art." She paused for an instant and added sincerely, "To be honest Mr. Russell, I've loved this piece. I felt a connection since the moment I saw it in *Rome*." Again, her tone changed, became light, "But now that it's mine," she added, "I've no home to put it in."

"For now, I'm sure the gallery can find a corner to store it in. I'll see to it, and please — call me Jed," he said hopefully.

"Thanks, Jed. I'm Angela, Angel to my friends." Again, the expression on her face changed in an instant, she said, "I'd only had the chance to see a half dozen pieces before I decided to acquire the *Mother and Daughter.* Would you mind showing me the rest, Jed? Of course, I'll understand if you're called away."

He gestured toward the front of the gallery and said, "I'd love to Angel, and shall we start where you left off?"

What Jed was thinking was that he would have tossed everyone out and given her, a private showing if she'd asked. He could not believe this was happening to him. God was good. They spent over an hour looking at various pieces, and while discussed his sculpting and casting methods, they sat sipping wine for a while longer. When he was called away to meet other patrons, Jed got her to promise not to disappear and he kept an eye out to make sure she didn't wander off on him. Finally, he asked her out for a late dinner or at least a snack, for the gallery closed at eleven, and it was almost ten-thirty.

He took her to a jazz club a few blocks away, and finally, around three, back to the Waldorf. Jed Russell very nearly levitated on his way back to his hotel. He had met and dated a stunning and classy woman, more important she understood his art, was an artist herself. Besides that, Jed really, really liked her personality. The one stopping point was that he couldn't quite imagine Angel Byran on a farm. Jed went to sleep promising to think on that.

***

Angel lay sleepless in her hotel room for some time. She had broken her vow to be wary of men, but this man seemed warm and considerate and he had gentle eyes. She then warned herself that the way he seemed meant nothing. It was one thing when men wanted a woman, another when they had her. She ran her fingers over a faint scar at her hairline, reminding herself how quickly Paul could change. She remembered the desperation, and how being possessed by a man had made her feel less than a slave.

Yet, this man seemed so different, so sensitive. She thought, "Could a man, who could put such emotion into stone and metal, be a brute?" She questioned, debated with herself. "Yes," she thought. There were many great artists who had treated their women cruelly. It was impossible to know the heart of a man, impossible, no matter how nice they seemed. Grey had seemed so sweet, so loyal, and had deserted her for Connie. No. That was not fair. Connie had been the prime mover in that. She knew her sister far too well to think otherwise. Well, Jed was interesting though, and she could leave *New York* any time she became uncomfortable. Reassured, Angel allowed herself to sleep.

The next morning Angel called home. It had been almost a year since she had spoken with her grandmother, far longer with everyone else. She was nervous and held back at first, but within moments, her reticence was gone. She drank in the family news with a thirst she had not realized was there. She was surprised to hear Grey was out of the navy that he and Connie were living nearby. She was astonished they had been on the brink of a surprise visit in Italy.

When Corazon suggested they take the train to *New York*, Angel panicked. She wasn't ready yet, and she lied. She told her grandmother of plans to go to *Long Island* with friends. Corazon pressed Angel; she would not let go of the issue and, finally Angel promised to come home for a visit in a few weeks. The call was a long one, well over an hour, and it left Angel apprehensive and elated.

Not in the mood to dress or to deal with people, she ordered breakfast from room service and took a shower while she waited. After coffee and an omelet, she felt better, even energetic. She began dressing to go out. The phone rang, surprising her as she did her eyes. She jumped, smearing her mascara. Mumbling under her breath, Angel lifted the phone.

"Yes?"

"Good morning Angel. It's Jed," the newly familiar voice said. "Would you be up to visiting a few galleries with me this afternoon— if you'd like, perhaps a late lunch."

"My, what time is it," she asked knowing it was past eleven. He'd caught her by surprise. She needed a moment to consider the implications of accepting. *"He's from Ohio and we're both leaving town,"* she told herself reassuringly. She had after all, been going out to do the very same thing, and so far, Jed had been pleasant company.

"Eleven-twenty," he said. "Be dark soon if we don't get a move on," he joked.

"Why not?" She had been thinking the words. She was shocked that she'd spoke them.

"I'm not far from your hotel. Would thirty-minutes be too soon?"

She thought Jed's voice sounded both pleased and a little shaky. Maybe it was the connection. "Thirty minutes, Jed," she promised in a friendly tone. "In the lobby."

"Until then," he said, and the phone disconnected.

Angel returned to her dressing table and began to reapply her eyeliner, which was difficult because her hand shook. Angrily, she supported one hand with the other and did a proper job of it. "I don't need this," she said aloud, believing that she had done perfectly well without men, without anybody. It opened a person to hurt when they became too involved with other people. Nevertheless, she didn't have to become involved. She reassured herself that this was merely an afternoon out with a pleasant stranger.

Angel remained a little hesitant right up to the point that Jed met her in the lobby. Afterward, it was so nice that she forgot to be concerned at all. For the two weeks that followed, she spent every day with the calm smiling man from *Ohio*. She learned about the family farm near *Harpersfield*, and about his mother and brother. On weekends, he was an aircraft maintenance officer in the *Army National Guard*. She allowed him to see her artwork, and he in turn insisted she allow him to show it to the gallery owners, he did business with. Almost immediately, she had her work hung on consignment in two respected establishments.

On the final evening of Jed's show at the *Holms Gallery*, he took Angel to dinner. They had had wine with dinner, and after that another bottle of champagne to celebrate. Jed was exuberant. The gallery had sold thirty-two pieces, and by his standards, he was a wealthy man. He told her he could pay off the debt on the farm, send his younger brother to college, and have enough to buy the small house in town that his mother wanted. They walked in *Central Park* and for the first time, they kissed. A rush of physical desire consumed Angel. At that moment, she could not think of anything but the warm softness of his lips, heat, and the security of his arms.

"I love you Angel; I love you," he whispered.

The stark realization of her weaknesses woke her to a litany of hard-learned lessons. She had been drinking. She made terrible mistakes when she drank. She was a sensuous woman, who was vulnerable to men. She was the victim of her own desires, and she must always be on guard. Like an ice bath, cold memories and unreasonable fears flooded her mind. She pushed back from Jed. She felt cold chills and nausea.

"I'm sorry," she said attempting a weak smile. "Suddenly I don't feel well. Perhaps it's too much champagne."

"Your hotel is just over there," he pointed.

The concern in his voice was evident and, though she felt inclined to run blindly, Angel allowed herself to be escorted toward the Waldorf. She bid Jed goodnight at the elevator, and entering her room, went straight to the lavatory and threw up. She tore off her clothes and showered for long minutes before collapsing on her bed without bothering to towel.

"I cannot deal with this," she said aloud.

Angel did not take Jed's calls the next morning. From *Pennsylvania Station*, she sent a note by messenger, and boarded the *Southern States Special*. Angel settled down to read a book chosen for the trip. The train pulled out at eleven; she would be home in *Miami* in eighteen hours.

Dear Jed: I've had a lovely two weeks. Thank you so much for the help in placing my work, and I wish you the utmost success with yours. Sorry I couldn't see you, but I've had to hurry away on family matters. When I return to the city and get a place, I will give Holms a call and have them send over my sculpture. Thank you, Jed, for capturing such emotional beauty. Until we meet again.

Farewell, Angela

Chapter 26

Asher found the sight of Angel coming up the front walk disconcerting. At first, he assumed it was Connie, but was puzzled at why Connie would be arriving by cab instead of driving her car. Then he noticed the change in hairstyle, and how pale she was. He mentally processed her complexion as the result of some new makeup and a visit to the beauty salon. The truth struck him when he saw no wedding ring. Whooping, he threw open the door and gave her a dam'd good hug.

"Grandpa," she gasped, "you're squashing me, grandpa."

"Dam'd right," he replied, "and after all this time I'm not about to turn you loose," he added twirling her to the point she lost one of her high heels.

"I've missed you too, grandpa," she said as he put her down.

"I would have never known it from the number of times you came home to visit," he grumbled. The cabbie was coming up the steps, struggling under the weight of a steamer trunk, and Asher stepped aside, holding open the door. "Sit it right inside," Asher said. Grace was standing with her hands over her mouth, and Asher waved at her, "Go tell Cori we have a surprise."

Grace ran up the stairs; Corazon ran down the stairs; Angel ran up, meeting her in the middle. This took place amid piercing female screams of joy. Asher paid and tipped the cabbie. He stood watching the women for a moment before phoning Connie. Five minutes later Connie's car slid screeching into the driveway, and there was more screaming and crying. Asher, knowing better than to think he could get a word in, sat back and listened. It went on for some time and then others arrived. By afternoon, it was an out and out gathering, complete with children, who got into everything not placed above their reach. When the ice cream truck came around, Asher treated the kids and himself. Delia, the cook, put out trays of snacks, and Asher had more than his share. By evening, Asher was as tired as the children were, and he sat rocking little Cory, who had worn himself out. The little boy curled against him in limp exhaustion. Asher was content. His granddaughters were both back under his wing, and friends were nearby. Life was good.

A few minutes before nine, Corazon went to wake her husband. Connie had extracted her sleeping son from his old Pap's lap without waking the child or the old man. Corazon, who had ignored her husband all afternoon, now wanted his attention. The company was gone. Asher was exhausted and getting ready for bed, but Corazon was full of happy energy. When he mumbled and balked at being roused, she put the chilled wine bottle against his neck and called out, "All hands-on deck."

Asher started, coming fully awake and to his feet, as the rocker flew back across the floor. Wide eyed he swore, "Son-of-a-bitch, what in God's name did you do that for, woman?"

She giggled. It was an uncommon response for a woman of sixty. "Because you were ignoring me, and I wanted to talk and drink some wine," she said holding up the bottle.

"Ignoring you, I was asleep Cori."

"Exactly!"

He grumbled, and his heart stopped racing. He breathed deeply and allowed himself to be herded toward the garden, where he sat on a swing. She had not brought glasses so, like a couple of crackers, they sipped from the wine bottle, and gazed at the stars as they talked.

"Is she home to stay?" he asked.

"No, only for a visit I think, and then back to *New York*. Yes, New York I think, not *Europe*."

"I can understand why she's not going back to *Italy*. She may be a little eccentric of late, but the girl is not crazy enough to put her foot back in that nest of fascist lunatics. Nevertheless, why *New York*?"

"Art! She has put her heart into art since the divorce. Art is both a refuge and a passion for Angel. *New York* is becoming an artist's mecca, even more so with *Paris* under the German boot. I believe too, it's the sheer size of the city. I feel the girl wants to be invisible, lost in the crowd."

Asher swallowed some wine and passed the bottle. He said in his matter-of-fact tone, "With looks like hers, she's never going to be invisible. I'll tell you that for a fact."

Corazon frowned, "You know what I mean."

"Yeah, I suppose. How long will she stay — what do you think?"

"A month maybe, a lot will depend on how she gets on with Connie."

"What's the problem with Connie?"

"Nothing — just that Connie has Grey and little Cory, and I don't know if Angel has ever gotten past that.

Asher snorted, he was running one hand up his wife's thigh as he said, "Grey was Angel's school girl rush and six years ago at that. The girl is long past that. I can understand her being distressed at losing the baby, but she's only twenty-three. She has time to marry and bear a dozen yet."

"Asher Byran, for a supposedly intelligent man, you can be so dense at times." Corazon leaned away from him and pushed his hand away. She needed a little separation to air her irritation. "It would be reasonable to expect a man of your advanced age might have grasped a little of how women feel about such things. A girl seldom forgets her first love, and sisters are inherently jealous of each other. These things never change, my love."

"Well if that is the case, its plain hopeless."

"No, not hopeless, but I don't feel she'll be at ease around her sister until she has a family of her own."

"What if we invite some of her old boyfriends by?"

Corazon drew a sharp breath and got up from the swing dismayed; teeth clenched, she shook her head in frustration. She thought to herself, "It would be easier to explain the desert to a fish than this sort of thing to a man." She extended a hand to pull her husband up and said, "Let's go to bed, darling. The day's catching up with me."

He grunted, and as he stood, put and arm around her. Together they walked toward the house.

"What," Asher suggested, "if the boy converted to the Church of Mormon? They could both have him."

Corazon elbowed him in the ribs and laughed in spite of herself. They both laughed.

***

Angel and Connie were close during the following weeks. They were at the beach one moment the tennis court the next. When the bay breezed up in the afternoon, they sailed, at night they went to the movies. Toward the end of July, the great-grandparents looked after Cory, and the sisters took the ferry to *Cuba*, spending a few days in *Matanzas* with their aunts, uncles, and cousins. The girls had intended to spend a week there until Connie received word that Grey was in *New Orleans*. He was due home on Tuesday. Abruptly, Connie was in a mad rush, returning to *Miami* in time to meet him.

Angel saw nothing of Connie on the day of Grey's return, and when the MacArts arrived for lunch the following day, there was a subtle correctness to the twins' behavior. Angel smiled warmly at her sister and greeted her brother-in-law with a sisterly hug and kiss on the cheek. She joined in spirited political conversation during the meal and afterward on the terrace. Corazon however, thought Angel was spending entirely too much time gazing at Grey when others were speaking. Connie was equally engaged in topics that stretched from the Republican's choice of the Willkie, McNary ticket, to Britain's chances of holding off the Germans. Though Connie showed no outward signs, Angel's interest in Grey was not lost on her. Although nothing was said, an underling tension existed by the evening's end, a tension that had not existed a day before.

A few days later, Grey took Connie and Cory north, to see his mother, and Corazon was relieved. It was she, who spent time with Angel now. Horseback riding and or walking, they wound through well-known trails in the Gables and down toward old *Cutler Ridge*. Often, they talked of serious things, themselves and the war. Just as often they were silent, each woman with her, own thoughts. Corazon could see that her granddaughter had become restless. Both women recognized the nature of Angel's varied problems. Neither could bring themselves to broach the subject.

The day before the MacArts were to arrive home, Angel announced her intention to return to New York. She felt compelled to find a place of her own and return to her work. She had thought it out and planned to get a room until she found a large place that suited her. She wanted a loft for the space and light. Her intention was to become a successful artist, a known artist, and New York was a city where people appreciated the arts. Corazon and Asher saw her to the train station and extracted the promise of an address and phone number at the earliest possible moment.

Asher watched as the train shrank into the heat waves. He tugged at his wife's waist, and said, "Looks like we'll be spending some time up north, Cori."

"Not in the winter," she replied.

Chapter 27

Angel had bought several papers before coming out of the subway, and tucking them into a bag of groceries, hauled them up the stairs to her loft. The elevator was out again, and the stairs were a struggle, but she supposed the walk up kept her fit. In San Remo, she had done far more climbing and had hardly noticed it. By far, the most objectionable thing about New York was the cold. New York in February was far colder than Italy, and when the wind blew, it rushed between the buildings like a gale.

Placing her purchases on the table, she cut a slice of cheese, another slice from an apple, and began to nibble at them. She selected a paper from the pile and began to read. There was plenty of news from Europe. The Romanians and Bulgarians had joined the Hitler club, and it seemed Churchill's government was to remain in power. In Washington, Roosevelt was trying to get a bill passed. Something called Lend Lease. Angel moved quickly to the Art and Entertainment Section. She had begun to read when the phone rang.

She picked up and cautiously answered, "Yes."

"Angel, you must help. I'm about to have a complete nervous breakdown."

"What's wrong, Gay?" It was Gay Dereker. They had met at a political discussion group. The members had turned out to be a bunch of uninformed Communists, but she and Gay had become part time friends.

"My mother is coming to see me," Gay cried. "What should I do?"

"See her, of course."

"Yes, but she can't come here. She doesn't know I'm living in sin," she sniffled. "Billy isn't going to move out of his own place, and I can't have her here with him," she whined.

"What do you want me to do Gay, recommend a psychiatrist?"

"No, of course not, but you've a huge place; you could let me stay for a few days."

Angel was thinking, "this is a perfect example why it's was unwise to let people get close."

"She'll be gone in a few days. Please, Angel, please, please, please," Gay, begged.

"Three," Angel said feeling herself weaken.

"Four," Gay said her voice already brightening.

"I guess four days will be okay, but no one comes in except your mom. That includes Billy Angel said coolly." She had met Gay's boyfriend once and could not stand him.

"I'm on my way," Gay squealed.

The mother fell ill on the second day, and Angel's guests were with her for over a week. That was how he got back into her life. Late one afternoon she had come in out of a wicked snowstorm to find

Jed Russell sitting on her couch drinking coffee with Mrs. Dereker.

"Angel," she called sweetly, "Your friend from *Ohio* has come to visit."

"Jed Russell, my God how did you ever find me?" The words just spilled out with the surprise of it. It was so unexpected. Angel didn't know if she was pleased or disturbed.

"I got the address from *Holms Gallery,*" he said standing, "From when your bronze was delivered. I hope you don't mind."

"No, of course not, are you in the city for long," she asked, unbuttoning her coat.

"It depends." Jed hesitated. He said, "Fact is Angel, I've been offered a contract by the *Metropolitan Museum*. It's to work on an *Egyptian* exhibit, a combination of sculpture and bas-relief. It has to be painted, and there will be murals, too. Some of it will be fresco and I'm not much of a painter unless it's painting barns. I need a colleague, a painter who's, good and you're better than good."

"I don't know what to say." Angel turned and hung her coat. "What length of time are you talking about, Jed?"

"Two months, perhaps longer. The money's good, too, but the money isn't it. Millions of people will see this." There was excitement in his voice. "It'll be fantastic to have done something this grandiose, to have brought a lost world to life."

Jed's enthusiasm was infectious. "You make it sound exciting," Angel said.

"I would love to see it," Mrs. Dereker said.

Jed grinned with delight. He pointed to a large tube leaning against the end table. "Would you like to see the project sketches?"

Within five minutes, Angel was hooked. The uncertainties that had caused her to flee this man's presence a year before did not apply. This would be her first real job, artwork, and it was to be a collaboration.

Their schedule was tight. The museum wanted to open *The Egyptian Exhibition* in June and the carpenters would not be finished and ready for them until April. To get a head start, they began setting up a workshop in the museum basement, and Angel was at work a week later. Jed began by making plugs out of wood and clay and then forming molds. He cast pillars and sections of stonewall that would later be erected and fitted together. Angel was able to begin the basic under painting and some bas-relief fresco. Early on, it became obvious they would need additional help. Jed hired two art students, Jake and Greg, to work part-time, and his younger brother, Kurt, came up from college during Easter vacation.

Kurt was far more talkative than his brother, Jed. He was one of those people who saw the funny side of everything and answered questions with humorous stories. Angel had been surprised to learn that their mother was almost sixty years old.

"Yep, she married pretty late," Kurt, said, "Thirty-four, I think."

"That's a bit late to start a family," Angel remarked.

Jed, who was pouring plaster into a mold said, "Mom was pretty feisty as a girl. Most of the boys were a little frightened of her, I heard. Sweet as can be after she married dad, though."

Angel said, "I suppose love makes changes in people."

"Uncle Wilt told me a story about Mom's wedding day. Wilt pretty well explained it," Kurt said. "You see it was back in '1912' they got married, and there weren't too many folks had cars you see. Well they left the church in *Harpersfield* and headed toward home in a horse and buggy. Well, going up-hill the horse balked. Dad got out and he led the animal to the top of the hill, and he stood in front of the horse. He looked into the nag's eyes, shook his finger and said, "That's once." When they came to a stream the horse balked a second time, and dad had to get his shoes and trousers wet leading the animal across. He stood in front of that horse, looked into its eyes, shook his finger and said, "That's twice." Mom must have wondered what kind of odd quirks her new husband had, but she kept her peace for the moment. Dad got in, snapped his whip and away they went until they came to a bridge, and the horse shied and would not cross. Uncle Wilt, he told me Dad walked around front of that horse; he said, "That's three times," and pulling his pistol, he shot it dead. Well they were some distance from home, on a muddy road, and mom stood up and yelled, *Jed Russell, you fool, what have you done? It is six miles to the farm and now were going to have to walk. Are you some kind of a crazy idiot?* According to Uncle wilt, dad holstered his pistol and walked back to the buggy. He looked Mom in the eye and said, *That's once.*"

"That's baloney," Jed snapped, obviously hot under the collar.

"Ah yeah, but it was a good story," Kurt chuckled. "You have to admit it's a good story."

Angel enjoyed the banter and the light humor. It was comfortable and as the work progressed, it was almost like being with family.

Soon it was June and the project was coming together. In a few days, the real artifacts would be moved in. The effect would be spectacular. Angel was amazed at what they had done together. She'd never worked so close, or so long, with another human. The closeness resulted in the inevitable intimacy that Angel had tried so hard to avoid. She had argued with herself, told herself that it was a fling; she could break it off when the project was completed. When the realization came that she had fallen in love with Jed Russell, it came more as a sorrow than a joy. On June 1, the Day of the opening, Jed asked her to marry him. She asked for a little time to clear her head and went home to see her Grandmother.

***

Alone with Corazon, The emotional dam that had held back years of Angel's secret misgivings and restraint burst. She spoke of betrayal, of drunkenness and her conflicting fears and desires. How she loved her sister, and at the same time resented her for having Grey. For the first time Angel explained the details of how her relationship with Paul had begun, how Paul had made her a victim through her own shame and pride. She tried to explain the difficulty of being two women in one skin. One woman was passionate and like a child, wanted to run ahead, to see and experience. The other was a watcher, always-dreading injury, cautious, drawing back, questioning, judging. At times, Angel felt as if her inner debates would drive her mad. How could these two parts of her inner being reconcile. How could she be brought to trust herself and others? The women were both teary-eyed at that point. When Angel broached the subject of Jed Andrew's proposal and their relationship, she began sobbing almost uncontrollably, though.

"How can I be sure of myself?" she blubbered.

Corazon laughed. The girl was so pitifully sincere, and her runny makeup gave her the look of a sad clown.

"Only our death is sure, Chica, and we don't know the when or how. Marriage is a leap of faith tempered with reason. Love and hate are the mirror image of each other and either one can rule on a given day. There are other things in marriage, things more important than a fickle emotion like love." Corazon handed Angel a tissue. "If you aren't sure of how strongly you love this man Angel — what about him are you sure of," Corazon asked? "Do you respect this man? Do you like him, like to be with him? Is he kind; is he honest, does he hold your welfare above his? Would he be a responsible and loving father to your children? Above all Angel, is his love for you — from the heart?"

Angel discarded a tissue and took another. "He's a wonderful man grandma, and I have to admit, I have to believe that he truly loves me. It's me — I can't trust myself. One minute I want one thing, the next I want another. Even if I accept Jed's proposal, I'm not sure I can be what he deserves."

"What he deserves — Don't be foolish. When a man marries a woman, he gets what she is, not what he deserves. You think too much, Chica, worry too much! If you like, I know of an utterly brilliant psychiatrist. You can be analyzed, and in the end, he will tell you, life is not fair; he will tell you, life is not sure, and he will tell you that you worry too much. Stay with us a while, rest your mind. If you want, you can invite Jed here, and we'll look him over. I promise a better job than last time."

"I love you, grandma."

"And I love you, too, now get yourself together. Your sister and her husband are coming for lunch"

Connie and Grey were already on the patio with her grandparents when Angel came downstairs. Cory was in great-grandfather's lap and Connie was complaining that they'd found termites in the house. It would have to be tented.

"If only we'd discovered them before we went up to visit Mother MacArt; it could've been done while we were away," she said.

Grey, trying again to sooth her said, "We'll only be out of the house for a few days, honey. What if we borrowed the *Constance* from your Grandfather, and sailed down to the keys for a few days?"

"After May, it's too hot and buggy to be anything but miserable," she said.

"You're all welcome here of course," Asher said.

"We appreciate that, sir, but maybe we'll get a place on the beach for a few days."

"But Grey, my sister's in town, and I'd like to spend some time with her. Let's take grandpa up on his invitation."

Grey shrugged, everything he had suggested for the last week Connie had wanted to do otherwise. "Why not?" he said.

Angel appeared in the doorway, and Connie jumped up to give her sister a hug, "Speak of the devil," she said. God, Angel, the phone calls are okay, but it's so good to look you in the eye." Why the sudden visit?"

"I finished the job at the Met. It was the perfect time for a vacation."

They sat side by side on the rattan love seat, and Grey was astonished at how much alike the twins still looked. The only real difference was Angel's northern pall. A few days in the sun, and that would be gone. He looked over at Asher, "It's been some years since you came ashore. Do you miss it, sir?

"Not at first," Asher said, "but, lately I've been thinking of it quite a bit, not so much the steamers, but the sail. In fact, old man Thompson asked me if I'd like to relieve on one of his ships for a month, now and then. The idea has some appeal. I'm running out of diversions around here. How long are you ashore for?" Asher asked.

"Another month and a half, sir, and it's good to be ashore with all the U-boat activity, it makes a man nervous. Mistakes happen, like the *Robin Moor*. She was marked, a big American flag painted on her sides, and they still sank her. I'm surprised to see so few problems, with neutral shipping being sunk," Grey added.

"You've heard the British have been driven off *Crete*."

"No!"

"Three days ago."

Corazon stood, "They want to discuss the war, girls. Come; take a look at my early birthday present. It's a Packard convertible and you won't believe the things it has built in."

The men smiled politely as the women left but never stopped talking. Grey said, "The navy's ramping up the Caribbean Patrol Force since they gave it fleet status. I've carried three military cargos to *Caribbean* ports in the last four months. Navy has new ships being built every place there's a yard. They're getting ready."

"War's coming all right," Asher said. "Congress has okayed fifty thousand war planes, and with all the new gadgets, it's going to be worse than the last war. The Germans are already trying to steal our military secretes. The FBI got thirty spies up north just this month, one down here. Hel,l the man has been running a sight-seeing boat here for years, called himself, Captain Jack Post. He was a Voters Registration clerk for crying out-loud. Real name was Carl Schrotter."

"Never know, Sir. We are a country of emigrants."

"Things sure don't look good. You think you'll be called back to the Navy, Grey?"

Grey finished his beer and sighed, "If I'm still sailing first mate, yeah. As a master, I doubt it, but truth is I'll go back into the navy on my own if we get into the war. The navy is short of experienced officers.

I have ten years navy experience, plus my merchant time and I owe it to the country. They'd probably raise me up a notch in rank, and it's far and away safer than merchant shipping in wartime."

"You told Connie?"

"No, and I won't. No use in stirring the pot before it needs to be stirred." Grey smiled, "Let 'her worry about termites and her own little problems for now. Be plenty of time to worry when it comes," Grey said.

"Amen," Asher replied.

Cook rang the dinner bell and both men went to have lunch.

Connie and Grey moved into her old room for the week, and the twins began to plan a Sunday birthday party for their grandmother. A summer squall blew the tenting off the house, and to Angel's discomfort, the termite extermination was set back a few more days. Being in the same house with Grey was becoming difficult for Angel again. She argued within herself. Told herself that she loved Jed Russell. Still, she could not get her brother-in-law out of her thoughts. She avoided Grey as much as possible and made plans to fly back to *New York* after the weekend.

The birthday party was a success. Corazon had expected only a small family party, but the girls had managed to invite almost fifty of her friends. The cake was a masterpiece, and there was a lot of champagne. After the party wound down that evening, the mood in the house changed with Connie's blow up.

Grey told Connie that he'd gotten a call from the company. The Captain of the *Wilber Lykes* had suffered a heart attack in *Port of Spain, Trinidad.* Grey had been offered the job, providing he was willing to fly out and take immediately command, for the *Wilber Lykes* was a fast-refrigerated ship with a partial cargo of meat products. Connie objected and the two had a huge fight. Unable to have her way, Connie had taken Cory and driven to a friend's house, while Grey packed, his gear and began to get very drunk.

Grandma and Grandpa were in the library with the door closed in order to remain clear of the verbal battle. Grace was standing wide-eyed by the dining room wall when Connie stamped out of the house. Angel was astonished at the ferocity her sister had unleashed on her husband. She emptied her wine glass and exchanged an uncomfortable look with Grace.

"Well," she said merrily, "We've all had a little more to drink than we should have, but I certainly wouldn't have sent him off to sea with nothing but a piece of my mind." She wiggled and winked, and Grace could not help but grin.

Angel took a bottle of wine and some cheese to her room, where she read for a while. Some-time after midnight, and more than a little tipsy, she decided she wanted more wine; she started down to the kitchen. Grey must have heard her footsteps for his door came open. He reached out and took her hand.

"Connie," he said, and pulled Angel against him, kissing her.

Angel said nothing. His embrace, his kiss, unhinged her, it sparked the tinder of the years of wanting, dreaming.

"Connie," he whispered softly, "I'm so glad you've came back."

Angel could smell the whisky on him; she started to explain — almost, she almost did, but his lips were against hers, and his hands were opening her robe. The excitement of his touch was so intense that she could not stop her response. *Just this one time,*" she thought. *"He was mine once,"* she reasoned, and gave herself up to him, up to him and to her own overpowering desire.

Chapter 28

Angel woke before dawn. The smell of alcohol seeped from her skin and her head hurt. Grey slept beside her. The realization, the horror of what she had done washed over her. Surely, she could not have done this; surely, it was a nightmare; but it was not!

Holding her breath, she slipped from the bed, and on hands and knees, collected her underwear. She shrugged on her robe and eased open the door. She had only just closed the door to her own room when Grey's alarm clock went off.

Angel locked her door and lay across her bed. The shame of what she had done surpassed any shame she had ever known. It was an unforgivable act, to allow her sister's husband to make love to her while thinking she was his wife. She felt Connie would know by simply looking into her eyes. After all these years of wanting him, Angel realized in the most precipitous manner that it had been all illusion. She was such a fool. Somehow, she must make it right.

Dawn was breaking; in the next room, she could hear Grey getting dressed. His door opened, and his footsteps went toward the stairs. She heard Grace tell him good morning; she heard him ask where Connie was. Grace told him, at Silvia's house.

Grey laughed and said, "If she's at Silvia's — then I had one hell of a dream. Drank too much I guess."

After that, their voices disappeared into the kitchen. Angel laid thinking until his cab pulled away. He didn't know. Connie didn't know. Angel could still be a part of the family and be accepted without the terrible stain of adultery.

"I must confess," she said aloud and immediately began to dress. Angel couldn't remember the last time she had been to confession, certainly not since before her marriage. Drinking was a thing of the past for her now. She vowed never to drink again. Terrible things happened to her when she drank. She slipped out the front door and walked four blocks to the church. She had to wait a while before a priest entered the confessional. Unburdening herself was a wonderful relief, and the stern words of reprimand,

and warning the priest had whispered had been far less than she deserved.

Angel knelt and prayed and as a penance, she did the Stations of the Cross twice. For the benefit of her soul, she paid for a mass to be said. For a while, Angel felt better, but when she was walking home, guilt and nausea began to eat at her again.

Connie had returned to the house while Angel was at church, She was crying hysterically to her grandmother that she had allowed her husband to leave on bad terms, and without even a goodbye.

"I didn't know his plane departed so early," she wailed. "He never leaves that early. I would have been there to apologize, to see him off. Oh, grandma, I'm so ashamed. I knew what a command of his own meant to Grey, and I made that awful scene anyway. I'm so selfish."

"Shush now," Corazon, said. "Your man knows you by now. Good and bad, he knows you, Connie. He understands, so you just go down to Western Union and you send a good long telegram to his ship. Moreover, you remember, a captain can take his wife to sea with him. I often sailed with your grandpa." She held out a napkin for Connie to wipe her face. "Go on now. We'll keep an eye on Cory."

Angel saw Connie's car drive away as she walked up *Hurricane Road*. She was hung over and her mouth felt like cotton. She felt as if she deserved to be sick, but she needed coffee. She poured it while her grandmother was speaking, and unable to face her, she started for her room.

"Where have you been?"

For a walk grandma and I stopped by the church," she said over shoulder.

With Connie already gone, Corazon's attention went to Angel with every alarm going off. She had not dealt with her granddaughters for twenty-three years for nothing. There was something going on. It was all over the girl's face. Even more extraordinary, Angel had gone to church. As a child, yes but she had only gone to church to confess when she had done something despicable. She never went to confession unless she was unbearably guilty. Leaving her own breakfast, she buttered two pieces of toast, smeared them with jam and climbed the stairs to Angel's room. She entered without knocking. Angel was sitting on the floor with tears dripping into her coffee.

"You missed breakfast," she said. "I brought you toast." Looking down, she thought, "Does it never end with these two? I am growing tired."

"Thank you," Angel said reaching up with her free hand. She attempted to wipe away her tears and slopped a little coffee on her dress.

"Connie has just stopped her crying and now you start. What is it that has you upset so early in the day?"

"I'm feeling down that's all." She munched on the toast, little bites.

"I'm going out to the Gables to shop later. Do you want to go?"

"No thank you. I'm going to go back to *New York*. I need to pack."

"That's rather abrupt. Have you decided what your answer is to Jed?"

"Probably — no," she said softly. She looked up; there was jam on the corner of her mouth. "He deserves better than me," she said, dully morose.

"Angel Byran, what is this self-pity all about? What has you all sad eyed when you've been fine for a week?"

"Nothing," she lied, although she was aching to confess it all. She was torn between her shame and a spiritual need to confess and receive punishment.

Corazon sat stiffly on the floor opposite her. "There is Jam on your face," she said tersely, "But there's not enough of it to cover the lie. What have you done that has you so guilty-faced?"

"I'm a grown woman," she said bristling. "I'm entitled to my own secrets, a modicum of privacy in my life."

Corazon started to push herself back up to her feet and said, "When you can't live with your guilty secret come and see me. I'm going to take Cory shopping."

Angel watched as her grandmother got to her feet; she was showing her age. Only when the older woman started to open the door, did Angel's need to tell become unbearable. "Wait," she cried.

Corazon sat, this time on a chair, and she asked, "What was so terrible, Chica, that you had to go to confession before seven in the morning?"

She began to speak, and actually stuttered.

Fighting back the urge to laugh, Corazon said, "Take a breath and start again slowly.

Angel could not say it directly. "Grey made a mistake and I didn't correct him," Angel said, looking at her toes.

"For this you had to go to confession at the break of dawn." She had engaged in this exercise with Angel for a lifetime. She would have to dig it out. "What kind of a mistake did he make?"

"He thought I was Connie." Angel was tangling a lock of her hair with one finger.

"That's happened before. When was this?"

"Last night, but he was drunk."

"After Connie had left?" Corazon asked cautiously.

Angel nodded.

"How long after Connie left?"

"It was late grandma. I had drunk a lot of wine and went to the kitchen for a snack. He opened his door and grabbed me."

"Why didn't you say something?"

"Because he was kissing me."

"Angela Byran! You let your brother-in-law kiss you without saying a word?"

"He surprised me, and I'd had a lot to drink." She looked up, "It's hard to talk when you're being kissed, and I did say his name. I said, 'Grey'. I was going to say, 'Grey, I'm Angel', but he kissed me again before I could finish." She hung her head and said, "And then I forgot."

"And what did he say when you told him."

Angel lowered her head and mumbled, "I didn't."

Corazon gasped. She suddenly suspected where this was going.

"I was going to, but then he kissed me again and pulled my robe off. I almost said something but then I couldn't and —."

"Angel, you didn't," Corazon gasped. The fact that Angel hung her head, unable to look her in the eye gave her the answer to her question. "Does Grey know?"

"He was so drunk that he thought he was dreaming," she said in a squeaky voice. "He doesn't have the slightest notion. Oh, grandma, I want to tell Connie how sorry I am."

"That is absurd."

"But I need to —."

"You need to shut your mouth and listen," Corazon snapped. "You need; you want; you feel — do you think you're the center of the universe? You do but you are not!" She had lost both temper and patience, and she leaned forward, finger-wagging, eyes flashing. "Bad enough that you've been lusting after that poor man for six years, but now you've gone and tricked him into adultery. Well, he may be guilty of being a drunken fool, but then a large part of that is being a man. That's all he's guilty of, and you are not going to ruin his life and your sister's marriage merely to ease your conscience."

Corazon recalled her own fits of jealousy, and the disasters of close friends and relatives. The one thing she was sure of was, there are those times when the truth did no one any good.

She said, "Angel, at some level, Connie would always believe that Grey knew. If she thought he did not know, she would be crushed because he couldn't tell the difference. The very fact that of all the world's women, it was her sister, who slept with him, would break Connie's heart forever. Even if she forgave you, she could never feel the same about you." Corazon paused, and reaching out, took hold of Angel's chin, forcing her to look her in the eye. "Do you understand, Angela; you must do as I will, and take this secret to the grave." She nodded and repeated, "To the grave — Yes."

"Yes," Angel whispered.

"Swear it."

"I swear I'll never speak of it," Angel promised.

"And your man from *Ohio*, Do you love him?"

"Yes!"

"Then phone him today and tell him, yes. Marry him and go live your life. Put an end to your foolish-self- doubt and self-absorption." Corazon smiled; she gave a good-natured snort for her temper seldom lasted. "Be happy, Chica, and bring me great-grand babies. Life's too short for all this misery and drama."

She waited while Angel made her phone call to *New York*. It was a long conversation, and she helped Angel pack afterward. The girl looked calm now that her decision was made. They would be married at the courthouse in *New York* and honeymoon at *Niagara Falls*, on the way home to *Harpersfield*.

She told Connie that Angel was under the weather, and took her to lunch, for the two should not be together for a while. Angel flew out early in the afternoon. A peaceful quiet settled over the house.

***

Angel called them three days later to announce she was Mrs. Russell. She called again from *Niagara* and then from the farm outside of *Harpersfield*. Each time she sounded happier than before. When she called in early August, the voice on the phone was far more somber.

"I wanted you to know first, grandma. I'm pregnant."

"Ah, that is so wonderful, sweetheart. I'm so happy for you, when?"

"I'm due in February grandma."

"You sound a little down Chica, are you frightened?"

"It's not that, it's — it's that — Grandma," she said with a troubled voice.

"I'm not sure about who the father is."

"It makes no difference." Corazon said hurriedly. "The baby will be yours and will be a proud member of this family. That it might be Grey's is so slight a possibility Chica." She laughed more to make a point—more than from honest humor. "Now stop this and remember, *'TO THE GRAVE'*," she reminded. "Don't even worry about the possibility. It's too silly."

They spoke for a while longer, covering other subjects, asking about loved ones, and finally said goodbye to each other. "Twins were such a trial. For now, it was a blessing that they lived far apart."

Chapter 29

Connie was in the best of moods, for her husband had been at home since late September, a full six weeks, and soon she was to sail with him. Grey's ship was bound to *Rio de Janeiro* and back, with stops in *Port of Spain, Maracaibo, Cartagena* and *Colon.* Grandfather was against her going. He was concerned that any ship might be mistakenly torpedoed or caught at sea by the outbreak of war. Asher told Grey he was a dam fool for taking his wife along, with an escalating global war. Grandpa argued, but he had no say in the matter. In Connie's opinion, her grandfather was growing overly cautious, even paranoid, where the war was concerned. There had been years of conflict, and the *United States* remained neutral. The Germans had their hands full with the Russians and wanted no trouble with the *United States.* Editorials in the big papers said as much.

On the other hand, in September, Asher had been at sea as a relief captain on the *Utila.* He argued that there were U-boats in *American* waters. He'd seen subs in the *Caribbean,* and even spotted one in the *Florida Straits* that he was sure was a U-boat. He argued that, statistically, wars came most often to neutral countries as a surprise, and the USA was not acting very neutral, anyway.

Nevertheless, Connie's plans were settled. She would join Grey's ship in *Galveston* in only six days, and while she was gone, Cory would stay with his great-grandparents. She was keeping secret the one bit of information that could nix the entire adventure. She suspected she was pregnant. She wasn't sure, only kinda sure, and she would visit the doctor when she got back home. It would be a good time to have another baby. Angel was due in four months, and the cousins would be close in age if her baby came in July. That was always nice.

They departed a week early and Asher and Corazon traveled up to *Green Cove Springs* with them for a visit with Grey's mother. The early November weather was lovely, brisk at night and pleasant during the day. The men took Cory fishing on the river, and Connie enjoyed her time with the older women. It was relaxing to be in a different place with no responsibilities.

Her son was her major responsibility. Cory was a handful, ever talkative, spoiled and into everything, he detested the word 'no' and loved the word 'why'. Grandpa was largely accountable for spoiling him, so grandpa could deal with him. Although she loved her son dearly, it was going to be a relief to leave him behind for a while. For two whole months, she would be a carefree girl again, alone with her husband, the honeymoon she never had.

Grandma was excited about Angel's pregnancy and showed Clare pictures of Angel in a maternity smock. Corazon was coaxing Angel to come south to have the baby, but Angel didn't want to be away from her husband or her doctor.

"I suppose I'll have to get some warm clothes, and visit before it gets too cold up there," Corazon complained.

"Maybe I'll go up to *Ohio* after I get back," Connie said. She was jealous of the attention and dying to announce that she was equally pregnant but knew better than to mention a hint of it before her ship sailed. "Maybe I'll go up to *Ohio* after I get back," she continued. "Grey will have a couple of months to go yet. We could go together grandma."

"Connie, you and Cori can leave the boy right here if you want," Clare offered. "Boy ain't used to that cold."

"I may do just that mother, if grandpa can't handle him."

"The last place you'll get Asher to go for the winter is a farm in *Ohio*," Corazon said. "I don't look forward to the cold, myself."

"God knows, we agree on that," Clare said. "As a girl, I spent a winter in *Chicago* with my great aunt. I don't know as I've ever been warm since. Alan is the only one that likes the cold. Loved the winters when he was at *Annapolis*."

"Where's he now, Clare."

"Flight school in *Pensacola*, he's commander MacArt now. Be on carriers by springtime or least as soon as he graduates."

From outside came high-pitched squealing and laughter, "They're back from the river," Connie said.

"Fish to fry," Grey called.

"I caught the biggest, and I want to eat the one I caught," Cory yelled.

"Cooks to the galley," Asher chimed in.

***

On the day she left for *Galveston*, Connie spoke with her sister on the phone. Angel seemed so happy and excited about her marriage and pregnancy that Connie could not help telling her that she was going to have another baby, herself. First, she made Angel promise and then told her, it was probably Grey's first night back. She told Angel about her list of places to-see, and how exciting it would be. It was the most pleasant talk they had shared in a long time. Connie hung up feeling very happy.

The family celebrated Cory's fifth birthday early the following day and Asher drove the MacArts to the train station. He wished them a safe passage. Grey shook his hand and Connie gave him a hug and kiss. The whistle blew, and they boarded, leaving Asher alone on the platform. By the time they'd found their cabin, the station was far behind, and when Asher got back to Clare's, they had poor little Cory weeding in the garden.

By week's end, the Byrans took their own train south, and Shawn brought the Packard to the station to pick them up. Asher had him drive them out to Joe's Crab Shack on the beach for dinner.

"I love to travel," Corazon, sighed, and as she had said countless times, "but then I love to come home."

Cory began to fidget and Corazon gave him some crackers to keep him occupied. They ordered, and while waiting for the food, Asher opened the newspaper. The Russian armies were being driven back, and in the *Crimea*, the Germans were about to surround *Sevastopol*. The Japs were advancing all over *Asia*. Hostilities were flaring up all over the world and the loss of shipping was at an all-time high.

"Anything interesting?" Corazon asked.

"Good time for everyone to stay at home," he had answered dryly.

Three days after thanksgiving, Jed Russell had phoned from Ohio and Grace had taken the call.

"The call is for you Mam. It's long distance," Grace said.

Expecting Angel, Corazon picked up in the library. It was Jed. They had met once and spoken on the phone only a few times, but she perceived a strain in his voice.

"Is everything okay, Jed?"

"Angel slipped on the ice and it was a pretty good spill. We're hoping it's nothing serious, but Angel's Doctor insists she take it easy. Rest and stay off her feet.

"Has she someone to look after her, Jed?"

"Our regular help ran off to get married. I've hired a woman from the next farm, Mrs. Palmer's here to help out, but Angel is frightened. After losing her first, well, you understand."

"I understand completely. What do you want me to do," Corazon, asked keeping her voice steady?

"She's not asking; I am. Would you come up and stay with her? I'd send her down to *Miami*," Jed explained, "but she's not supposed to travel, and she's so dam'd stubborn about not leaving."

"Jed, I'll pack right away, and I'll phone you back when I've made travel arrangements."

"I really appreciate this, Ma'am."

"Jed Russell were family now, so you just expect that I'm going to come when needed, and I'm your grandma, not ma'am."

"Yes, Ma'am," he replied, "and we'll be waiting."

"I'll call right back," Corazon promised, and hung up. "Grace," she called, "get my winter clothes out of the attic. Have Shawn bring down the luggage."

She called the train station and discovered it would take three days to reach Cleveland by rail. She decided to fly. She booked a flight to *Atlanta* that would be leaving at noon. She would sleep over and take a plane to *Cincinnati* the next morning. It would connect with *Cleveland* in the afternoon. When Asher returned from the golf course, Corazon was already gone, Grace explained.

"What next," he mumbled to himself? "For a woman who'd sworn she'd never go near snow again, she'd gone north mighty fast," he thought. Cory was playing with blocks on the patio. Asher opened a beer, walked out and sat down on the tile next to him. "Can I play too?" he asked. "I'll show you really good stuff."

Chapter 30

Predawn, navigational twilight, and with a faint glow in the east, the second mate prepared his sextant. Black waves, crowned in white, rushed the starboard beam. They are opposed by a long northerly swell. Josh, the second mate braced himself, and swayed opposite the ship motion. He brings the star to the horizon. He cries mark. A dizzy plunge and the mate turned his shoulder to the bulkhead, as he's thrown against it. Spray, coming hard with the wind spattered him; salt stung his eyes, coated the lenses and mirror of the sextant.

"Son-of-a-bitch!"

The words came through the captain's porthole with the cool air. The motion of the ship was immoderate. In cross-seas, east of *Ponto do Calcanhar*, the ship would first pitch, then she would roll. At times she did both at once, plowing headlong into an oncoming wall, and falling on her side with a shuddering crash. Lying in the troth of her propped-up mattress, the motion seemed less severe to Connie than was the fact. An hour before, feeling the need to relieve herself, she was forced to crawl to the head, a mere twenty feet to starboard. She wasn't seasick, but she was miserable. The freighter had been plowing into this since *Rio de Janeiro*, three days back.

Connie managed to doze again. She was awakened by the sound of the shower, and then the clinking about in the head as her husband shaved. She only realized he was gone when the door banked shut. The motion seemed less now; it seemed slower.

The hands of the clock indicated seven fifteen. Connie had to decide: was eating breakfast worth the ordeal of getting to the officers dining area? Her appetite won out and she carefully swung her legs over the side of the bunk. She showered, and then sitting on the floor with her back to a bulkhead, dressed.

The motion was easier and as she descended the stairway to the officer's dining room, it became no more than moderate. Connie took her place at the captain's table. The tablecloth had been wet down to keep the dishes from sliding, so rather than get her sleeves wet, she kept one hand on a pillar just to be safe. A mess man brought her coffee the way she preferred it.

"Has Captain MacArt been to breakfast this morning?" she asked.

"No ma'am, and Mister Higgins don't eat breakfast, so except for the third engineer, you're the first. Do you want to order, ma'am?"

Connie smiled up at him, "I'll wait for the captain, thank you."

Grey and Rudy Rankin, his Chief Engineer came in together a few minutes later. They greeted Connie and sat opposite each other. The first assistant appeared as they were ordering. Seconds later the first mate came in. Everyone exchanged pleasantries and the deck and engineering officers exchanged work lists. The food began to arrive, and they ate as they worked.

Turning to his wife, Grey asked, "How did you sleep, honey?"

"Well enough." she answered. "The weather seems improved since dawn. At least I can move around."

The chief cracked a smile. "Was a little rambunctious, wasn't she, ma'am?"

"We're past *Calcanhar*," Grey said. "I had Higgins alter course. We're on a more westerly course now, toward the *Guianas*. We'll make better time inshore, particularly when we enter the *Northeast Trades*."

Connie finished her coffee and smiled. "If that puts us on flat water, captain, I'm all for it."

"Oh, that will get us in flat water all right," the mate interjected, "There's a lot of coastal traffic to bother with, though."

"Hey, Gary! What's this about the radio shack generator?" the first assistant said, holding up the work sheet. "We fixed this last month."

"Sparks told the third mate it won't start. Go see him; I'm just passing it on, Geordie."

"He's probably flooding the carburetor."

"Hey, Geordie," the chief said, "Get the baseball scores from Sparks while you're up there."

"Sure, but first I gotta start my boys changing out the brake on the port boat davit. Drum's all scaled up with rust up chief."

"Here's a question, Geordie. You want number five cargo boom rigged and up— how, with us rolling like this?"

"When it flattens out is what I meant, Gary. I have to hoist that old refrigeration unit up on deck before we get into port. It doesn't matter when, just as long as you give me a day."

"Dave, one thing," Grey said to his chief engineer, "Let's not string out that work on the life boat davit."

"Overtime on Sunday!"

"Just do it. There is no overtime paid on safety gear," Grey said tersely.

"You heard that, Geordie? By the way, Captain, we're still on twelve burners. If you're planning to go to sixteen, give me a heads up."

"No, we're making a steady fifteen knots. I'll see the swell down before we push her up to eighteen. How much lead time do you want?"

"Two hours if it ain't an emergency."

Connie sat and listened as the senior officers discussed the day's work. She listened as she had for the last two weeks. The various officers knew what to do, and each had his own territory, which no one touched without invitation. It was an interesting form of diplomacy. A sort of an on-going negotiation in which, only the captain over-ruled everyone.

Each person on board had his schedule and duties, except for her of course. She was reading a lot and not really bored. They had made one port outbound. That was *Maracaibo*, where they delivered oil-drilling equipment and bunkered the ship. Grey had taken her ashore for a nice dinner, and afterward they had gone dancing. Connie had been disappointed that there had been no chance for sight-seeing. Two days later, she'd had a look at *Trinidad* as they passed. However, her four days in Rio had been worth the whole trip. She would love to come back and extend her sightseeing. As wonderful as the shore time had been, the best part of the passage had been sharing so much time with Grey. This was the longest they had together since they'd met. She had been trying to decide when the best time would be to let Grey in on her secret. Not yet, she was having too good a time to complicate things.

The seas flattened through the day, and toward evening, the ship ran on calm water. Connie had read some and entertained her captain during the afternoon. The open ocean, it seemed, was quite an aphrodisiac. Feeling very much pleased; Connie did her hair up and dressed for Sunday dinner. It was a splendid meal and one that the officers cleaned up for. The steward played music on the phonograph and no one spoke of work.

"Mrs. MacArt," the First Assistant said. "You grew up in *Miami*. Are you acquainted with either of Kohl sisters? My older brother married Diane Kohl; her sister is Bonnie."

"As a matter of fact, I went to high school with them. Diane was the quiet one; she was a year ahead of me. Bonnie was a real hellion in her senior year. Married a Frenchman I heard."

"There's a story behind that. You might find it amusing," Geordie said, and began to relate it.

Grey beckoned the mess-man and asked what the steward had for desert. A short time later, Connie was enjoying an egg custard, when the radio officer entered and passed her husband a message. Grey excused himself. Ten minutes later, his voice came over the intercom.

"Attention, this is the captain speaking. I'm with Sparks and we're picking up both Morris and short-wave radio messages that affect us all. A little, over an hour ago naval aircraft of the *Japanese Empire* initiated a sneak attack on army and navy bases in the *Hawaiian Islands.* As far as we can tell from radio traffic, the battle is still going on. It's a good bet that we're in the war now. Men, it means were fair game for subs. I doubt if there's any Jap subs in the *Atlantic*, but I dam'd well know there's plenty of German subs, and for anyone who doesn't know it; the Japs have a deal with the Germans and Italians. It's a military pact. That means they're signed up to fight each other's enemies. That means this ship will soon be a target for German subs — if it's not already," he added. "Dusk to dawn, I want a blacked-out ship, and there will be extra look-outs. Each deck officer will brief his watch on what to look for. Thank you, and officers' report to the bridge.

The chief stood to leave, then turned back to Connie and said, "This is one of those very few times that it's good to have an ex-navy man for captain, Ma'am."

Connie sat, stunned at the turn of events, shocked, frightened and at some emotional level, hurt that her husband had not taken a moment to reassure her. "You're being childish," she told herself on an intellectual level, but at the same time, the inner child trembled. Food had always been a solace to Connie, and she ate two more of the cook's egg custards before leaving the officer's dining room.

Uncomfortable below, she went topside and sat in a lounge chair on the boat deck. She watched the sunset. The sun was settling on the port bow. The sky was profuse with reds and oranges, and squalls marched like titans along the horizon. Just forward, one of the black-gang was working on the lifeboat davit. An ordinary seaman was going from port to port, placing blanks over the glass.

When he got to Connie's chair, he said, "Scuse me, Ma'am,"

Apologizing, she got up and pulled her deck chair back. The sun was now below the sea, and it was rapidly becoming black. Restless, she paced and after a few minutes, walked forward and climbed the steps to the bridge. Grey was discussing smoke with the Chief. The firemen were to pay close attention to the burners to avoid making smoke. When the chief left, Grey took Connie out on deck.

"How does it look for us?" she asked in her straightforward manner.

"Good, for now," he answered. "We're in the *Pan American Neutral Zone* and were south of the equator. I don't think the Germans have any boats out here, but they'll be on their way. They'll be all over the *Caribbean* and *East Coast* within a few weeks, and we have to transit that area. With luck, this ship can make port before the U-boats get on their patrol stations."

"But the Germans haven't declared war on us."

"Well, a dime can get you a dollar that Congress is going to declare war on them, if they don't first. The outcome is the same. Even if a state of war doesn't officially exist, it probably won't mean much to a sub commander. Even if a U-boat commander has scruples, he could track us on the surface until it is official."

"Can they do that?" she said, feeling chills.

"Yes, but we have one advantage Sugar, our speed. This ship was designed to carry perishable cargo, fruit and meat as well as freight, and she's fast. Speed is a protection. A U-boat can make maybe eighteen knots on the surface. With all twenty-four burners fired up, were good for over twenty knots. Give us a head start and were gone. Were too fast to be worth chasing.

"I admit, I'm frightened," Connie said.

"Well don't be too worried, Sugar; I'm going to put you ashore when we bunker in *Trinidad*. I want you to fly home on the Clipper."

"What about you," Connie said the emotion evident in her voice?

Grey smiled and half laughed. "I'm master of this ship, Sugar. I can't just quit and go home. I am resigning when we dock in *New Orleans,* though." He saw relief come into her face and forced himself to get it over with. Better to tell her now, with the shock of war new in her mind. "I'm quitting my job to go back in the Navy, Connie. We're at war and I'm obliged to do my part as an officer. It's what I trained for. It's my duty."

She wanted to argue and throw a fit, tell him she was going to have another baby, and make him stay home with her, but she'd been a navy wife. Connie understood how futile that would be. There was no argument. An ocean of tears would change nothing. Eyes closed, she pressed her face to his chest and let him hold her. She thought of praying but had long held the belief that God didn't take sides. Instead, she took him to bed and made love. There was hope in that, hope and reassurance.

***

At dawn, the bos'n had the crew at work painting over the American markings on the ship's sides. Every bit of news gleaned from radio transmission was posted. The Japanese had attacked American bases in the *Philippines*. That afternoon they heard Roosevelt's speech and learned that war had been declared on *Japan*. The next evening as they steamed east of the Amazon and approached the *Guianas'*, news came that the British battle ships, *Prince of Wales* and *Repulse*, had been sunk by Japanese aircraft. They were at breakfast northeast of *British Guiana*, when they learned *Germany* and *Italy* had declared war on the *United States*. The third assistant, who spoke German, had listened to Hitler's speech. He assured everyone that it was official.

That afternoon, the *Wilber Lykes* entered the *Northeast Trades* and began a slow roll. It wasn't enough to make moving about difficult, so Connie decided to organize her belongings. That evening she began to pack. They would be entering Port of Spain, Trinidad by afternoon tomorrow and she wanted to be prepared.

She stood with Grey on the bridge wing as the equatorial sun slid swiftly into the sea. A squall was passing to windward, and the moisture-laden breeze chilled a little. "Night falls so quickly here," she thought. She was used to a longer, lingering sunset.

As dark closed around the ship, a full moon began to lift in the east. Grey went into the pilothouse to check the second mate's new position. Connie went into the captain's cabin to pack. As she folded clothes, she listened to the sounds of the ship. On the other side of the bulkhead, she could hear Bob Higgins taking the mid-watch. An AB called out the course, as he was relieved at the wheel. She was trying to latch a suitcase stuffed with souvenirs when the Port lookout called out.

"**Torpedo, broad on the port bow**."

She started. Then she remembered that this had happened twice the night before. It had been dolphins rushing in to ride the bow wave.

"Left full rudder."

"Left full," the helmsman responded."

That had been her husband. She grabbed hold of the dresser as the ship leaned violently to Starboard. Everywhere was the sound of sliding crashing gear.

"Meet her and steady."

"Two-sixty degrees, Captain."

The deck leveled and someone, Higgins she thought, yelled, "Clear to port."

The engine order telegraph rang full ahead and was answered from below. The general alarm began to ring, and men were running, shouting.

Terrified, Connie opened the door into the chart house. The radio operator dashed past the chart table and plunged through the door into the radio room. Grey's broad back was ten feet from her.

He spun, "Douse that light," he shouted.

It came loud, harsh like a slap, and she slammed the door realizing her mistake, for she had blinded everyone with the cabin lights. She could hear the radio operator keying, SSS ("attacked by submarine") then SOS and the position, then SSS

SOS. "My god, this is real," she thought and yanking open a locker, she began to put on her life jacket.

Grey stuck his head out the pilothouse door trying to see clearly ahead. He was amazed at their luck in maneuvering on the torpedo. His mind raced as he tried to apply everything he knew about destroyer doctrine to a freighter. He should now be heading directly for the sub that had tried to sink him. He knew his doctrine. Do not offer your side to the sub. Do that and he will torpedo you. Go straight in and drop your depth charges. Well, he had no depth charges, but it's hard to torpedo a ship coming straight at you, bow on.

To the lookouts he shouted, "Watch for anything dead ahead and on both bows." He thought, "If he doesn't surface, I will pass over him, and then I can outrun him. If he stays down just a little while, I can run out of range. What if he did surface?" Grey asked himself. "Were not heavy laden; we can take a few shells, maybe. Maybe he'd miss."

The voice tube squealed. Higgins listened and spoke excitedly. "Chief said everything's lit. You'll have top speed in five or six minutes."

"*U-boat*, starboard beam," An AB shouted.

Grey's head jerked around. The *U-Boat* was surfacing inside a quarter mile, and he wouldn't have time to run out of the range of its '88mm' deck gun. "Threaten to ram and force it back down," he thought. "Could he close them fast enough," he wondered?

"Starboard full rudder," he ordered loud, but below a shout.

"Starboard full rudder," the helmsman echoed.

Again, the ship heeled but more severely than before, Water poured over the port rail. The ship shook as the propeller began to cavitate. Griping a handrail, Grey crossed to the helmsman, "Meet her, he said quietly, "Steady up on the *U-boat*, Butch. Keep her bow on the *U-boat*."

"Jesus, Captain."

"Follow them as they move, Butch, lead them a little."

"Sweet Jesus," the helmsman groaned, fully understanding that he was to be the instrument of an act of insanity. Sweating, he steadied up on the sub's bow, lined her up and held her.

"Higgins, the searchlights, hit them with the search lights, blind them."

The ship was running straight now, gathering even more speed and in the glare of the searchlights, he could see the Germans were passing a shell into the breach of their deck gun. The gun was coming around. Two Germans were clearing the anti-aircraft guns. The sub was gathering headway, angling away from the *Wilber Lykes*, but the freighter had gathered over twice its speed. From the Radio shack came the sound of the operator's key tapping. The course change of the sub was making a hard shot for the sub's gunner. A flash, the whoosh of a shell, and the mast exploded, peppering the stack and after decks. The '20mm' machine gun, aft the sub's tower opened up. Glass shattered, and men dove to the deck, crawled on their bellies. One search light exploded. A second shell tore into the bow at the haws pipe, lifting the anchor winch up and at right angles to the deck. There was a clattering roar as ten shots of chain ran into the depths at breakneck speed. The *U-boat* was close, almost under the Wilber's charging bow, attempting to turn to starboard but the drag of the anchor-chain assisted the ships rudder and the *Wilber Lykes* was turning inside her. The '88mm' deck gun fired again, this time at point blank range. The ship's starboard side erupted; twisted steel and the forward hatches blasted upward into the night; plate torn loose by the blast was ripped aft down the side of the ship by the force of her headway. The subs diving horn was going as its men scrambled for the hatches. They had misjudged the speed of the merchant ship, and the desperation of its crew.

The *U-boats* foredeck was already submerged when the *Wilber Lykes* bow struck her aft. She was caught in the anchor chain and spun round under the ship. She rolled on her side, her propellers beating against the *Wilber's* bottom. Her rudders bent over as she slid aft along the ship's hull, and the freighter's propeller took off the starboard diving plane. Mauled, the *U-boat* bobbed in the wounded ship's wake.

Bow down, listing to port, the *Wilber Lykes* plowed ahead. She bucked and trembled, was shaken like a leaf by her damaged propeller. Grey pushed the telegraph lever back and forth, stopping on slow ahead. It was answered from below and as the ship slowed, the shaking continued, though it was less. The clinometers indicated eighteen degrees list. Bright flames climbed up from number two hatch. Screams and groans drifted out of the dark. The chief mate was standing by, and Grey ordered him to take his team forward to fight the fire.

Higgins was leaning against the flag locker. He looked dreadful, bleeding from several places. Grey asked, "Are you okay, Bob?

"Just cuts, the glass, Captain."

"Can you sound the tanks for me?"

"I can, and sir; take a look; one of the Starboard boats is shot to hell. The other's peppered."

Grey looked behind him on saw the second mate was fixing their position. Grey was, for an instant, woozy. He touched his scalp and it was wet, bloody. He moved out onto the wing and looked aft. The sub was on the surface about a mile back. It was dead in the water and down by the stern. The distance was growing. "Out of range soon," he thought, "not that it mattered, for the Germans apparently had dire problems of their own.

"Sir, your positions on the chart table," the second mate said, instantly gaining his attention. "And Mister Dobson is dead sir, killed when the top of the radio shack blew down on him."

"And the radios?"

"Junk sir."

"See what you can do for the wounded and report back," Grey said. The fire forward was raging, blowing back on the fire team. He turned to the helmsman, "You okay, Butch?" The man nodded, and Grey had him swing further off the wind. He rang dead-slow. At that instant, the chief burst onto the bridge and Grey remembered his wife. He yanked open the door to his cabin, but she wasn't inside. "Have you seen my wife?" he half shouted at the Chief.

"She's helping the steward with the wounded, but we got serious trouble, Captain. The shaft alley is flooded, and the hulls breached in the boiler room. Geordie's down there trying to stop it off with wedges, but I don't give it much chance. We're going to lose power if the water rises another six feet and its coming. Captain, I'm going to have to vent steam or she'll blow when the water reaches the boilers."

"Rudy, the main deck is only a few feet above the sea forward; if were flooding aft too, it doesn't look good." Grey paused and thought for a minute, trying to do the math in his head. "Higgins is sounding tanks. I think she'll capsize long before she sinks. Do you think she'll float if we counter flood and the other holds are tight?"

"To be honest, no, not even if we could keep the machinery going. We're screwed, Captain."

"That's it, then," Grey said flatly. "Butch, come left to two-twenty and steady her, then go to your boat. Rudy, this course will keep the fire off us for a few minutes. Get your boys up on deck," Grey ordered. He rang all stop, finished with engines. He waited a moment, for the third assistant was venting steam. When the noise lessened, he rang abandon ship on the general alarm. The chief was going out the door as Grey sounded abandon ship on the whistle. He sounded it twice. He took his pistol from its locker, snapped it to a lanyard and holstered it. With the ship's log in one hand, he went to look for Connie. He found her splinting the second cook's leg and knelt beside her.

"Is it over?" she asked.

"The shooting's over but the ship's sinking. We're going to the boats now; I want you to stay near me." He kissed her and stood. A squall swept down, the cool rain spattering the deck.

Gary, the chief mate, had managed to lower the after starboard boat, but it was shot up too badly. It swamped within minutes. He and the bos'n were now trying to swing out the after-port boat against the list of the ship. Grey directed all hands to push the stern of the lifeboat past the ship's side, and the bos'n paid off on the after falls until it hung only from the forward davit. When it hung only from the forward falls, they lowered it stern first. It swamped to the seats, but floated buoyed by its air tanks. Four men boarded and began to bail. The mate hung a cargo net over the rail, and men began to board as the others set up to launch the forward boat.

The ship's list increased by the minute, and the angle was making the lowering of the second boat even more difficult. They managed to get the boat's stern clear, but the falls jammed, and it would not drop. Frustrated they could only cut them away. The boat's stern fell away; it swung like a pendulum on the forward fall which abruptly carried away, plunging the boat forty feet into the sea. It floated, but upside down.

"Everyone in the boat," Grey yelled.

The rest began descending into the last boat. The Chief mate was lowering the second of three men, too severely wounded to climb when the ship began its roll. The top fluke of the wheel was already exposed, and a second came into view. The bow of the boat began to lift as the sea painter tightened.

"Cut away; cast off," Grey yelled.

The bos'n slammed his hatchet through the line and the bow fell back. The bottom of the ship began to rush past like a waterwheel drawing them in toward the riveted hull. Metal scraped, and sparks flew up from the gunnel, as men the fended off with oars. The chief mate ran down the ship's side like a lumberjack on a giant log, to end standing on its upturned bottom. Water poured through several gashes in the lifeboats side, and Grey ordered men to stop them, others to bail. The Chief Mate dove into the sea, swam several strong strokes, and climbed into the crowed boat.

"Lost the cook and an oiler," he said panting.

"Boat's holed all down the starboard side," Grey told him. "We'll pull clear of the ship, then we'll see if we can wrap the boat cover around the hull. Slow the water down until we can seal the leaks. You there, Griggs, Butch, Kaplan, and Joe Snyder, fix your oars. Bob, lend Gary a hand forward there."

Slowly the boat moved out from the capsized ship as the mates worked to pass the canvas under the floundering lifeboat. Two hundred feet off, they stopped rowing in order to pull the canvass tightly against the side. The water was slowed, but not stopped. It was up, almost to the benches. Again, the mate dove overboard and feeling through the canvass, he inspected the hull.

"Seams are split behind the float tanks." Gary was breathing hard. "No way to get at them."

One of the firemen said, "Can't keep up this bailing captain."

Grey considered the problem. Nothing could be done in the dark. Save our strength and access things at dawn. There was always the chance of a passing ship.

"Tie off everything that can float away," he ordered. "Her buoyancy tanks should keep her up, and we'll take turns overboard if necessary. Keep an eye out for useful wreckage, anything we can make a raft out of."

Soon they gave up the bailing, and the boat wallowed with men clinging to its sides. It took an hour for the ship to sink, and a great deal of flotsam drifted down on them. In the dark, they managed to find a steel fuel drum and a bench, which were used to lift the boat a little higher. Some dunnage and a wooden skylight were retrieved and lashed together. Three of the five wounded died and were set adrift. Two others lay in the bow of the boat, as it drifted down wind on the black sea. The seas built. Black clouds raced past the moon.

Dawn came blood red behind a squall. The rain rinsed the salt from their upturned eyes, and the sun dried their faces. New salt began to form. Their heads baked, and their bodies puckered, as the equatorial sun climbed. Grey sat in the stern sheets holding Connie. He watched bubbles rise from the air tanks. The mate and bos'n were still trying to plug the leaks, but the tanks were rusted, and the attempts often made it worse. They were lower in the water now.

"Have we a chance," Connie said softly in his ear?

"There's always a chance, Sugar. We're only about a hundred miles out from Georgetown and the winds are pushing us toward shore, but I can't guess where the currents will take us. *Orinoco* runs to sea west of here. We might drift fast enough to reach shore in a few days, but with the currents?" He sighed.

"It will be awful if Cory loses both of us," she said.

"I'm sorry about this, Sugar. I should have listened to your grandfather."

"I wanted to come, and I didn't listen to grandpa, either. This wasn't the first time."

"I could have tried to surrender to the *U-boat*. They might have given us time to abandon."

"It was bad luck this boat was stove in Grey. Another minute before the ship rolled and we would be half way to the coast by now. My god, you actually knocked out a *U-boat*. Grey MacArt. That was at once the most frightening, and the proudest moment of my life. All that's happened after has been dreadful luck."

"Now I know why I married you,' he whispered. "I knew I'd need reassurance someday."

"I love you, too, and you've been a good husband to me. Whatever happens though I hope it happens quickly. I've always hated the specter of a lingering painful death. She shifted her position and snuggled against him. He gently kissed her cracked lips. She sighed as he rubbed his cheek against her head. "If there's no hope Grey, none at all, you won't let me suffer, you'll promise."

"You have my word, Sugar. We have a good chance though, at the coast, or a ship might spot us. Our radio message might have been heard."

Connie listened and thought, "I won't tell him I'm pregnant. If I don't survive this, it won't matter, and he won't have borne the guilt." She grieved for all the sweet things of life she might never again experience. She thought of her grandparents and her sister and wondered which would raise Cory. No, she would not think that way. Her speculation would change nothing anyway. The steward was passing a tin cup, six ounces to each of the survivors. Connie sipped hers and passed the cup back feeling revived.

That afternoon they spotted more planks and a few pallets. Men swam out to retrieve them, and they began lashing them together for the boat was almost submerged. With hatchets, they cut two benches and the straps to the only tight air tanks. As the tanks popped up the boat disappeared into the depths. The raft held six of them. The others clung to its sides and they traded places in shifts.

Sunset and rain, they lifted their mouths to the sky and drank drops. Another oiler died, and they put him in the sea. In the undulating dark, men groaned. Connie whimpered in her sleep: Grey caressed her cheek. Later, she held his head while he slept, and she prayed for strength to accept God's will.

Daybreak, four men had slipped away in the night. The sea was calm, and they could see a great way off. All day the sun beat down on the long smooth swells. It had become a ball of brilliant heat, and with the fresh water gone, they suffered.

At dusk, the first shark came unseen. It was a tiger shark, large and powerful. That it took Connie first was fate. Grey clutched her with a superhuman grip as it pulled them clear of the raft, and he struggled back with her when the shark broke off. She cried out to him in terrified agony as it came again. When she screamed, he held on again, this time drug outward fifty feet. When it released her torn body, blood swirled red around them. Eyes burning with grief, Grey pulled his pistol. As the shark closed again, he cradled her head; he whispered, "I love you Sugar," and shot her behind the ear. A second shark took him before he reached the raft.

Stars shone out of a clear, black sky.

Chapter 31

All along the south shore of *Lake Erie*, snow had been falling since dawn. It seemed strange to Corazon to see snow falling out of a clear sky, but Mrs. Palmer explained that this was due to the wind picking up moisture from *Lake Erie.* The fields and buildings had a fresh dusting, and it was all beautiful in spite of the cold. Corazon sipped her coffee and watched as Angel marked the calendar.

"Twelve days till Christmas," Angel announced.

"It will be my first Christmas in the north," Corazon said.

"And it will be white, grandma."

"Have you heard from your husband, honey?" Mrs. Palmer asked. "Will he be home for Christmas?"

Angel sat awkwardly down at the table. "He wants to be here of course, but with the training schedule it's not a sure thing. Have you heard from your sons, Phyllis?"

"No, not since Don's phone call the day they signed up with the marines. They don't let the boys call home for a month, or so I hear."

"Jed's an officer and he hasn't called every day," Angel complained. "He's arranged to have someone come to take all the dairy cows, and I have no idea who. They were to be here yesterday."

"It's the weather, honey," Mrs. Palmer said, looking over her shoulder. She started to stack the dishes in the cupboard and continued, saying, "Mr. Palmer's done the same, culled our dairy herd. With the boys gone and no help—" she sighed. "The trucks are yet to pick the cows up. It was Mr. Tonaburger over near *Akron* that bought the lot, you know. They are some of the sweetest natured cows."

Angel listened and wished she were up in her studio painting. She cared not the least for cows or any other animal on the farm. She would be glad when they were gone, so she didn't have them to worry about. Most of the help in this area had joined the military within a few days of *Pearl Harbor*. Others had been called to National Guard and Reserve units. The girl who was to have been a live-in helper had run off to *Toledo* to be married, and now Angel had only one old man, who came over each day to feed and milk. Of course, there was Mrs. Palmer, who already had her hands full on her own farm. Of course, her grandmother knew no more about farm animals than she did.

Angel recognized she was cranky. She hadn't slept well for the past two days. It was difficult enough with Jed away, but she was filled with so much anxiety. Grandma blamed it on her being pregnant, but it was somehow different, another thing altogether. She sensed something strange with Connie, something frightening.

"Would you mind if I rode into down with Phyllis this morning," Corazon coughed raggedly. "My! Excuse me. There are a few things I'd like to buy."

"Of course, I don't mind."

Mrs. Palmer said, "I'll be ready to leave in a few minutes, Cori, you bundle up good. The heater in that old truck's seen better days."

In her room, Corazon put on long underwear and two pairs of wool stockings. She buttoned up her sweater and buckled her boots. When she put on her mink coat, it still smelled a little of mothballs, but after all these years at least she was getting some use out of it. When Corazon came out, Mrs. Palmer was buttoning her hooded coat.

"Well, here we go. Hope we don't get stuck," She said.

They sloughed out to the farm truck and climbed up in the cab. The ride into town was bone jarring, for the muddy ruts of a week past were frozen hard beneath the new snow. Mrs. Palmer parked in the center of town, and the women walked through the slush toward Kroger's grocery. At the door, Corazon asked her where the pharmacy was.

"Just around the corner, next to the bakery," she said, "And Cori, let me tell you they have the best cream puffs for a nickel. You might bring home a few for that granddaughter of yours."

"Why thank you, Phyllis. I won't be long."

Corazon walked up the street, stepping gingerly on the ice and stopping occasionally at windows to look at Christmas decorations. Rounding the corner, she passed the bakery and entered the drug store. She passed up the soda fountain and magazine racks, going directly to the pharmacist.

"Do you have something good for a cough," she asked. "It's settled in my upper chest and made my throat a little raw."

"Those Smith Brothers cough drops might soothe your throat, ma'am, but to loosen up that cough you might want to use some medication in a steamer while you sleep. There are some good Eucalyptus cough syrups I can mix up, if you have a few minutes," the pharmacist offered.

Corazon returned to the front of the store and chose a newspaper and some magazines from the rack. War headlines shared the cover with --

Federal convicts' riot and burn New York prison.

The magazine seller took her money and saw her glance back at the headline.

"Darn fools set the prison on fire while they were locked inside. Feds over in *New York* will be sifting bones for some time, trying to figure who burned up and who got away."

"How awful," Corazon said.

"It serves em right," the man said, and counted out her change.

She picked up her medicine and a vaporizing contraption and went to the bakery. The cream puffs looked wonderful. She bought several and ate one on the spot. The grocer's boy was loading the truck when she rounded the corner. Mrs. Palmer waved happily.

The snow was falling harder, and the sky had become overcast as they drove out of town. On the country roads, the snow was growing deeper, but at least it cushioned the ruts a little. Corazon sucked on a cough drop and wondered how people could live in such a dismally cold place. With the cold in her chest, she was a little under the weather. When they arrived, she hurried happily into the warm house and showed Angel the cream puffs. Angel had coffee perking, and once the grocery bags were inside, they each had a pastry with the freshly perked brew.

Afternoon passed to evening and as usual, Mrs. Palmer went home after supper. The two of them listened to music on the radio, and then to the news hour. Not much of the news was good. The loss of life at *Pearl Harbor* was over two thousand, and in the *Philippines*, the Japs were pouring ashore. *Guam* had fallen, and the *Malay Peninsula* was cut in half by invading troops. At home, the Germans torpedoed a tanker on the *East Coast*, and over a hundred inmates and staff had died in the *New York* prison fire. Gasoline and food rationing was being considered. Sabotage was suspected in several west coast fires, and there were reports of German agents sneaking into the country.

Corazon had been listening carefully, waiting for President Roosevelt to speak, but Angel seemed oblivious to what was being said on the radio. When Corazon looked closely, her granddaughter was quiet and sickly pale. "You're so pale, darling; aren't you feeling well?"

Angel looked up and with incredible sadness said, "She's gone grandma; I can't feel her."

"My God, Angel," she said, thinking of the baby, "Should I call the Doctor?"

"No, grandma," tears were forming, "You don't understand; Connie's gone. I felt her for a moment, absolute terror and then nothing. There's nothing now. It's like an empty place."

"Angel, you've had so much happening lately. It's only your nerves darling, imagination."

"It's not imagination. We've always sensed each other," she said blankly. Tears streamed down her face, but her voice held neither hysteria nor doubt.

Corazon did not want to believe, but her own experience pushed her toward the precipice of belief. Too many times during her life, impossible intuitions had proven true. She remembered the news report; a tanker sunk right off *Miami Beach*, and feared for Grey's ship far at sea. Cold chills ran up her back, and goose bumps covered her skin. She sat on the sofa beside Angel and they clung to each other. "I will phone Asher," she thought to herself. "He may have gotten a telegram or a phone call. He could contact the shipping company."

***

Asher received the troubling call from his wife shortly after dark, but it was too late to reach the offices of Lykes in *New Orleans*. He was able to reach an agent whom he had dealt with before, and he got the home number for the company's port captain. He introduced himself and inquired about the *Wilber Lykes*. The man was uncomfortable, but straightforward with him. The ship was indeed three days overdue at *Port of Spain*. The last radio contact had been on the tenth. Asher had thanked him. The port captain had promised to phone the moment he knew anything.

Very worried, Asher put down the phone and poured a tumbler of scotch. He walked into his library and sat in his leather chair. On the wall was a model of the *Biscayne*. Fine ship, but shelled by a German sub, she had gone down in a few minutes. A shame, she was new and without a speck of rust. Asher had resented the loss of that ship for over twenty years. He sipped the scotch and frowned at the waste of war.

Well, they had brought it to us this time. Twenty-three years ago, like fools, the government had jumped into the mess, and lost a lot in the process, lost too many men ashore and at sea. He thought back on what it had been like in a small open boat seven hundred miles offshore. A week or more in the boats trying to make Ireland, touch and go. That was pure seamanship with no one knowing if they were dead or alive. Well, most of them had made it. Grey was a good seaman. If it can be done, he'll bring my little girl home — if it can be done.

"God's will be done," Asher said aloud, and picked up the phone to call his wife.

***

The constant worry added to the severity of her chronic cough and by Tuesday, Corazon found herself too ill to leave her bed. Mrs. Palmer called Doctor Boise out in a growing winter storm to attend to her. He examined her and explained to her that it was bronchial pneumonia. He gave her a host of pills, an ointment for her chest. In her room, he set up a hot plate, with a large pot to serve as a steamer. Mrs. Palmer and Angel were advised to see that she breathed deeply twenty times each hour. He would have a nurse out to look after her if she had not improved by tomorrow. He examined Angel and suggested she have a little wine each evening to help her sleep. Satisfied that he had done all that was possible, he bid them good afternoon and struggled out into the wind, headed for his next house call.

Asher called that afternoon and when asked, did not betray his growing concern about the *Wilber Lykes*. Instead, he reminded Corazon of the weeks it had taken him to reach shore and of the difficulty in getting word home when the *Biscayne* was lost. Privately, he was distraught and on the brink of chartering a small vessel to search the coastal islands southeast from the *Orinoco River*. Had he known how ill Corazon had become, he would have gone immediately to *Ohio*, but she was sheltering him from worry, as he was her.

That evening he took Cory to the new Disney movie, *Dumbo*. Corazon and Angel listened to the radio after dinner, and for a short time, each of them forgot their worries.

Chapter 32

Sleet, mixed with rain, had coated all the roads along the lake the day before, and with new snow drifting across the ice. Highway 20 was more than treacherous. He had ended up in a ditch early that morning. The five-ton cattle truck he was now driving was a piece of junk, but it did plow right through the snowdrifts. That afternoon, the light flurries became a heavy snowfall and then a blizzard. He had already turned off at *Geneva*, headed toward *Harpersfield*, when the north wind had picked up. There was almost no visibility at all now. Snow coated signs and vehicles materialized out of the white and vanished quickly. After *Harpersfield*, he had to ask directions from the yokels a dozen times before he found the place.

There was a letup in the snowfall as he pulled up on the farm road that led past the place. He looked at the photo and studied it for a while. He wanted to be sure that it was the right farm. It was almost dark, and a farm truck was coming out of the place. He looked closely as it lumbered out onto the road and pulled past him. The fat woman at the wheel was no one he knew. After it drove out of sight, he put the big truck in gear and realized it was stuck. He got out, cursing as the wind took the door from him. The wind cut like knives, and the biting cold numbed his fingers in the time it took to tuck his scarf and button his coat. Hunched against the gale, he walked toward the invisible house, in the tire tracks left by the other truck. By the time, he was half-way there, the tracks had filled, and the snow topped his boots. Blasted by the wind and half blinded by driving snow that encrusted his eyelashes and face, he was thirty feet from the house before he saw it. Back to the wind, drifts poured snow around each corner of the house, but the door stood clear. He reached out from his pocket, knocked with his left hand.

***

It took a few moments for Angel to reach the kitchen door, for she'd been in her grandmother's room, on the far side of the living room. She gasped at the man who was a living snow statue. Her first thought was that he must have driven off the road. "Oh my," she said.

"I got stuck. Anyone here that could pull me out?" he asked, in an unusually high male voice.

"I'm sorry, but my husband's away," she said looking at him curiously, as the snow melted. "I could phone the Palmers at the next farm."

"I can get help from my brother. Mind if I use your phone?"

"Oh, help yourself," she said, opening the door wide, and pointing toward the wall phone.

Walking with a slight limp, he crossed to the phone, lifted the receiver and tore it from the wall. Angel gasped in surprise, but only when he turned, pistol in hand and laughed, did she realize it was Paul Benetti. He had become pudgy and his face was as hairless as a girl, but the evil in his eyes, was if anything, more menacing.

He looked around the kitchen and laughed a second time. "You've come down in the world babe. This is a real no-class dump."

Angel, mute with astonishment, backed against the counter. Her mind raced. How had he gotten out of prison? How had he found her? Why did he look and sound so different?

His eye fell on the stove, on the coffee pot and he pointed with the pistol, "Pour me a cup of that java there. You know how I like it, lots ah sugar." On the table, Paul saw half of a pie under a glass cover, and pulling back a chair, he sat. "Pie looks good. What else you have to eat? I skipped lunch and supper today." As she poured the coffee, he grinned again and said, "Anything will do. Over the last few years I learned not to be squeamish."

She spooned sugar into the coffee, and rapidly she reoriented herself with the old lessons of survival. She must not show fear. That fed his cruelty. She must be polite so as not to make him angry. She must avoid eye contact when she spoke, to avoid challenging him.

"I have cold ham in the refrigerator," She said, setting the coffee on the table.

"Get it," he said, reaching for the coffee.

The door opened toward the table, blocking his view, and he failed to catch the adroit move of her hand, as she slipped the carving knife under her apron. Turning, she pushed the door shut with her hip, and put the platter on the table across from him.

Angel's mind raced. "Had her grandmother heard them or was the radio muting their words?" she wondered. He still wore his coat. She didn't think she could stab through it." Her primal fear was drawing out of her a desperate strength, an assessment of her options and the calculation of odds.

Paul swallowed a chunk of ham with gusto and said, "Got any booze?"

She turned and reached for a bottle of wine used for cooking. There wasn't much left. "It's only a table wine," she said.

Paul pulled the cork and sniffed it. He finished the few ounces in a swallow and sat the bottle down, and said, "That tastes like crap." He began to unbutton his coat and shrugged it off his shoulders onto the back of his chair. "Finally getting warm," he said. "You have any other booze in the house?"

"Some hard cider," she offered.

"Bullshit! A lush like you with no booze in the place," he leaned back in his chair, "Give me a break, hard cider, my ass."

Paul looked her up and down, pregnant again. He thought, "*This Russell hick, must be knobbing her nookie very regular to keep her out in the sticks like this.*"

"You're a happy farm wife. Looks like your hubbies got the stuff," he said pointing at her stomach. "Where is he? Got a girl in town now that you're knocked up, huh?"

"He's an army officer," Angel said. She wanted to say other things, but she knew he was baiting her. She must not slip. Paul's high girlish voice was disconcerting. Why he was mimicking a woman, was beyond her. She tried to stay calm. She must be careful and watch for her chance, her one only chance for her baby. She thought, "*Is grandma aware of what was happening*?"

"Yeah, like he's in the barracks every night." He snorted. "You know, babe, smoking and booze are among my few pleasures since your granddaddy's boys had me altered." He saw her puzzled expression and sniggered. "You didn't know they had me trimmed — mutilated that is — they whacked my wang. Hell, babe, they sliced off my nuts too. I do have to admit, your granddaddy is nothing, if he's not thorough. You don't think this smooth chin is from spending extra time with Burma Shave and a razor, do ya? Hell, before the prison burned down, I was singing high soprano in, choir." He laughed again. "Too bad I died in the fire. You sure you don't have just a little booze, Angel?"

"None, my husband seldom drinks," she said, with the realization he was working himself up to something. Had grandpa really done that? She didn't know. She did know Paul wasn't just mean, he was crazy. She looked for other weapons, saw an iron skillet and she remembered there was a shotgun in the living room, but she had no time to reach it. Maybe if she could slow him down. His pistol was on the table. She thought, "*What if she could get to it?*" She trembled as the adrenaline coursed through her veins.

"Too bad," he said, and took another bite of pie and swallowed. "I'm jealous, you know. It's not hardly fair, you with a new man, having a baby and me not able to even jack off. You can understand how much that hurts me Angel. For a long-time you know, I've been thinking about how to approach this problem. I decided that a razor cuts both ways." He turned, leaning back to reach into the pocket of his coat for something.

In a single fluid motion, Angel grasped the skillet, spun and slammed it against the side of his head. His chair went over backwards, and she grabbed for the pistol. The first time she fired, she missed. The second bullet hit him in the foot as he scrambled under the table. The two clicks that followed seemed more thunderous than the pistol's two reports. It was empty. She ran but his hand locked on her ankle, and she fell forward on one side, protecting her stomach. Cursing in his high-pitched voice, he dragged her back to him. The knife slash across his left eye came as a complete surprise. Red haze squirted, and clutching his face, Paul inadvertently allowed her to scramble away.

He felt for a towel, a rag, anything and heard the bang of a door. There was a mirror. He grimaced at the deep slash. The bitch put out his eye. He howled like a wounded animal. He would kill her slowly. Nothing else mattered. He fumbled for something to batter down the door. He grabbed up the oak bench from the foyer.

Corazon had jerked awake at the first pistol shot. She was alert, if confused, by the second shot. She heard a foul-mouthed woman swearing and a short scream. She was already out of bed when her bloody, wild-eyed granddaughter came scrambling through the door. Angel paid her no attention until after she had bolted the door.

"Help me, she," cried as she tried to slide a big dresser.

"What's happening/" Corazon said beginning to push.

The dresser bumped into place.

"He's going to kill us, grandma," Angel hissed. "Quick, get dressed," she said, running toward the wardrobe for her coat. "We have to go out the window," and from somewhere in the house came a piteous howl of rage.

Corazon reached for her coat as cold chills ran up her spine; "Who?" she said.

"Paul, grandma," Angel said, struggling into her coat, Paul's here. She ran to the window and pushed up on the sash.

"But, he's in prison?"

"I don't know." Desperately, Angel banged her palm against the wood, and it slid up to reveal hard packed snow. "Nooo," she groaned in despair.

"What," Corazon said trying to get her feet into her boots.

"Snow drift, we're trapped."

There was a loud crash. The wall shook, and plaster fell. Two more blows and the dresser jumped.

"He's getting in." Angel sobbed.

Corazon became ever so calm. She whispered, "Does he know I'm here?"

"No," Angel said, shaking her head rapidly.

"Ssssh! Stand there and be ready to run," Corazon directed, her pointed finger indicating a place that would be in full view of the open door.

Taking a towel to insulate her hands, the old woman picked up the boiling pot from the hot plate and backed against the wall. Again, the wood shattered, and the dresser jumped inward. Paul grunted as he pushed back the dresser.

He crooned, "I'm coming, babe."

The dresser toppled, and the splintered door swung inward. He saw Angel in front of him, and pulling his straight razor, he started for her. The scalding water wet him from head to waist.

"Run," Corazon shouted as she pushed him over the toppled dresser.

Even as they fled, they could hear him thrashing on the floor. They burst out of the kitchen door into the arctic cold. They were thirty feet from the house when the rush of the wind pressed against their backs. Another fifty feet and the whole world, up and down, became blowing white. Snow drifted along the road, and they skirted it until a gate caused a break in the drift. Behind them, there was a dim flash, and a muffled gun blast. He'd found Jed's shotgun.

"This way," Angel shouted.

She pointed past the gate and they moved to their left. Leaning to the wind, they ploughed ahead through knee-deep snow, circling drifts, pushing as hard as their bodies would go. Angel led, keeping the wind to her left cheek, she sought landmarks. Gripping her grandmother's hand, she pulled her doggedly in the direction of the Palmer farm.

Buffeted, wrapped by the intensely cold wind, Corazon's lungs were heaving. Each time she inhaled, she sucked in snowflakes. Each gasping breath was a labor that burned like a knife. The cold had begun to penetrate her clothes, sink like daggers into her body. At first her feet had burned, now they were numb. The muscles of her thighs ached, and finally her knees buckled.

"My legs won't work," she said apologetically, against Angel's ear.

"It's only a quarter mile to the Palmer farm," Angel urged. "He's not far behind."

"I can't," she wheezed. "Go child, you're my future," she said weakly, and leaned forward on hands and knees. "Please, think of your baby. Go ahead, send help back for me."

"I won't," she cried, her tears freezing as she tried to lift her grandmother. There was a mound near the fence, a haystack and she pleaded, "Just a little way, grandma, please. Try to crawl," she begged, pulling, half-dragging her grandmother toward it.

Angel burrowed for at least six feet. After the first foot, the hay was not frozen, and it became easier. She made a tiny cave of sorts and covered the old woman with hay. She kissed her and promised she would return quickly. Outside, the bite of the cold struck like a club, as she hurried to cover the entrance. Backtracking to the fence line, she brushed her tracks with hay, and again set out for the Palmer farm.

Her hands turned red; they were burning with the first nip of frost, and she jammed them her inside her coat as she trudged ahead. Several times, things caused her to fall: rocks beneath the snow, barbed wire, a ditch, and finally, a plow. Anything covered by snow tripped her. Each time she found herself on her feet again, without understanding where the strength to rise had come from. She had never imagined the glacial cold of this Christmas blizzard. By the time,

Angel saw the lights, her numb legs no longer wanted to carry her forward. With pure will, she pushed them through the thigh deep snow.

"Only a little way," she mumbled to herself.

***

The tracks had been clear, but the pain in his foot had slowed him down. At first, the cold had soothed his burns. He had overshot their trail, when they cut left at the gate, but he found their tracks easily when he backtracked. The cold had helped his foot. Paul no longer felt any pain where the bullet had passed through, but the cold was killing him. It had gnawed its way through his coat and was freezing his wet shirt. The wind blew with such force that it had erased the tracks. He'd wandered back and forth in the general direction, until he picked up the trail again, but it seemed like only one set of footprints. On dead feet, he hurried stiffly ahead on a trail already broken for him.

Paul stumbled over a plow and dropped the shotgun. Angrily he grappled for it in the drift and brushed it off with clumsy hands. He saw the lone figure ahead of him in the field. He raised the shotgun and with his one good eye sighted down the barrel. It was hard to make his senseless finger curl around the trigger. When the gun discharged, it surprised him. The figure pitched forward in the snow, but when he reached the spot, he saw no body, no tracks. Paul floundered back and forth, searching for the body. Nearly spent, he stumbled over the shot riddled scarecrow.

Rage pulsed through him, but his mind had become too dull with cold to act. He tore the coat from the straw-man and held it over his head. His tracks led in every direction, and he wondered which way he had been walking. Confused, he sagged down to think about it. He was still tired, but his slowing brain told him he was getting warm.

Chapter 33

The call had come from Mrs. Palmer before they found Corazon. Mr. Palmer and several neighbors were out in the blizzard searching with only Angel's blind directions to go by. They had torn a dozen haystacks apart before discovering which one Corazon was under. The roads were so drifted over that they had not gotten the women to a *Cleveland* hospital until late the next day, but these farmers lived in the cold and knew how to treat its injuries.

Asher had tried to leave immediately, but the winter storm was severe, and no passenger planes were flying north of *Chattanooga*. He had taken the train, the *Atlantic Southern,* north to New York and boarded a plane there for *Cleveland*. There was so much snow, he had arrived only a few hours behind Jed. As the taxi's tires crunched and spun through the ice and slush, new snow was beginning to fall into the canyon of the road. A snowplow was at work somewhere ahead, and as they drove the pavement cleared, and the walls of snow grew higher.

"Hell, of a storm for this early in the season, got down to twenty below," the cabbie said. "Only thing moving yesterday was sleds."

"I can imagine," Asher said, and maintained his tense silence until they reached the hospital.

He paid the driver ten dollars for a four-dollar meter and hurried in out of the cold. The antiseptic smell was pervasive and awoke too many sorrowful memories of other hospital arrivals over the years. A large, square-featured man, in the uniform of an Army Air Force Captain, was standing in the hallway outside the two-bed room occupied by Angel and Corazon. They shook hands firmly eye to eye. It was Asher's first meeting with Jed Russell, and the man's calm demeanor impressed him. He quickly informed Asher of what he knew, and of the condition of the women.

Angel was coming along fine. She was more exhausted and distraught than ill, and the ordeal had not seemed to affect her pregnancy. It was Corazon who laid deathly ill with a private nurse in attendance. Her hands and feet were being treated for frostbite and her bronchitis had developed into full-blown pneumonia. Asher could, in no way, have prepared himself for the appearance of his wife. When he entered her room, she was in an oxygen tent. Through the opaque material, she seemed gray and withered. Her chest rattled when she breathed.

He sat between the beds and spoke with Angel as Corazon slept. Every few moments Angel would break down, softly sob, and then containing herself, would continue. Asher heard it all, moment for moment, and realized that Angel blamed it all on herself. She had analyzed each day and each moment and dammed herself for everything that had not gone well. She had compiled a mental list of her deficiencies. They included her first involvement with Paul, surviving his first attack, and coming back from *Europe*. She said that if she hadn't remarried it would not have happened. She was crazy, allowing her grandmother to stay in a harsh climate. Missing Paul when she tried to shoot him was stupid; not killing him when she had a knife was inexcusable. Leaving her grandmother out in the cold alone bore down on her more than the rest, and she had a guilty list that went on and on.

No one could convince her that she had accomplished heroic things while confronting impossible odds. She recognized only what she perceived as her shortcomings. Jed had quietly asked the nurse to sedate her, so she could rest.

Asher listened; he confronted his own demons as she spoke. When Angel fell into a sedated sleep, he analyzed his own missteps. He had the chance to see Paul Benetti dead, and he had passed it up. He exacted his own revenge and turned what was left of Benetti over to the state for justice. Tully had warned him; had said the only smart thing was to see Benetti dead and done, but he had let Benetti live, left him for the state to execute. His foolishness had come back to his loved ones as injury. In this respect, Dan Tully was a wiser man than he was, but to whom could Asher confess it? In his old age, Asher had learned another valuable, if painful, lesson concerning choices. He dozed for a time and woke as Corazon's doctor entered on his rounds.

Doctor Simmons was the hospital's pulmonary specialist. With his stethoscope, he listened to her heart and lungs; he took her blood pressure and studied her chart. He made notes on the chart for medication and brought them to the nurse's attention. Outside the room, he expressed his concerns to Asher. The buildup of fluid in Corazon's lungs was placing a strain on her heart. He thought that a procedure to remove the fluid would most certainly be necessary. If her condition did not improve quickly, he wanted Asher's permission to perform it. As he explained the details of the procedure, Asher grew pale. Weak with worry, Asher returned to Corazon's bedside and placed his hand on her wrist.

Some-time later, he felt a slight movement and realized she was awake. When she spoke, he could not hear, and he leaned close, placing his head and shoulders inside the tent.

"I'm so glad you're here," she whispered. "I've dreamed of you, missed you."

"I came as quickly as I could. I had Shawn drive Grace and Cory up to his grandma's."

She smiled. "Have you heard anything of Connie and Grey? I've been so worried."

Asher shook his head. "There was no word of me for weeks, darling. They could turn up any time."

"Angel knew," she said softly. "After dinner, she just knew, and I've come to accept that Connie's gone. It saddens me that our lives have been visited by so much death. We had such beautiful children, if only you'd had more time with them." She hesitated, and then said, "Asher." Fixing his eyes, she continued. "You take special care of Cory. He deserves your time and your heart. Connie is gone and he's her only tomorrow, and Asher, he is yours. He deserves the things of value, only you can give." She coughed, no more than a shallow rattle, and caught her breath.

"Darling, you mustn't tire yourself," he said with concern. "And don't distress yourself about Cory. We're both going to be caring for him."

"All I do is sleep," she said. "You've been here for a time Asher, tell me." She coughed again. "Angel seems to be doing well?" It was a question.

"She's good, but she feels responsible for you," Asher said, lifting his eyebrows.

"She's always been critical of herself. She's becoming strong, though." Corazon smiled with pride. "My God, the fight she put up and darned near won. The girl half carried me through that blizzard before I gave out. She had the presence of mind to save us both, anyway. She saved us when that brute couldn't save himself. When her baby comes, she will be complete. She will have something beyond her own misgivings to occupy her. How I wish May had lived to know her girls. May would be so proud, and you should be proud of her, darling."

"I am Cori, I am. Both of the girls have become extraordinary women." Asher was feeling strange and realized it must be the oxygen. With healthy lungs, he was getting too much. He smiled and pulled his head out of the tent."

"Ask the nurse to help me," she said, a little embarrassed.

Asher stepped out while the nurse brought a bedpan and attended her. He was light headed. She had dozed again by the time the nurse finished, and he went with Jed to get a bite to eat.

***

The men spoke a little about the hospital and Angel's surety that Connie was dead. They tried not to sound as if they took it seriously, but neither would disparage Angel's belief. Jed told Asher that Benetti's body had been found inside a quarter mile of the Palmer place. It looked like the women had done a job on him, and the blizzard had finished it. The Sheriff had given his shotgun to Mr. Palmer. She would hold it for him until he got back home.

"It will be hard on Angel to stay out there all alone, won't it?" Asher asked.

"I'm planning to sell or lease the place," Jed said. With the war, I did not want her alone out there anyway. We both thought it would be better to wait until after the baby came before we moved, but now I'm going to get a place in town straight away. Money's not a problem, and I don't want Angel going back out there. She can stay in town with my mother and aunt, at least until we get a place we like. We'll figure it out from there," he said.

"I'm just relieved that Angel wasn't hurt again," Asher said. "I hope she can get past this."

"Your granddaughter is a far more resilient woman than she realizes, sir. She'll come around after our babies born."

The men finished their meal, and in the gathering dark, they went back to the hospital. Jed took Angel out to the lounge in a wheelchair, so they could visit without disturbing her grandmother. Asher sat by Corazon's bed. Perhaps an hour had passed, when she woke again. She smiled when she saw Asher and made a kissing motion with her lips. She shifted her shoulders painfully.

"Are you uncomfortable?" Asher asked.

"My chest is tight," she said, with difficulty. "I can hear my heart beating."

"I'll get someone," he said, starting to rise.

"No, stay a little, first."

He slipped under the tent and kissed her on the forehead. Her skin was hot. He whispered, "I love you -- more than all the other things of my life."

"*Querido,*" she whispered to him, "Beloved."

"Do you feel better?"

"No, worse I think." She coughed again and moved a bandaged hand to her chest. The coughing tired her, and it took a moment for her to speak. "I had hoped to see Angel's baby," she sighed. "Perhaps I've been greedy, my love, but I had hoped to hold it."

"We hope together," he said. Most of all, I hope for you."

Her eyes were closed. Weakly, she smiled and said, "Take courage my love."

His hand beneath the tent, Asher stroked her hair, and again she slept. He gently held her poor cracked, blackened hand. When finally, he slept, it was leaning onto her bed, his head pressed against the fabric at her side. In the hours before dawn, a doctor squeezed his shoulder to wake him, to tell him she was gone.

Chapter 34

Corazon was buried among the graves of her children and grandchildren. Scores of her family attended. Her cousins came down from the *Carolinas*, her sister, nieces and nephews up from *Cuba*. The Byrans were pioneers of *Miami*, and Corazon was known throughout the community. Hundreds filled the church, and more gathered for the service at her grave, but amidst this crowd, Asher was alone.

When the mourners had gone, Angel sat late into the night, talking with her grandfather, sharing memories of her grandmother. There was much they spoke of, and more they left unsaid. Each knew the guilt of perceived failures. Each found it impossible to forgive him or herself, for the mistakes that had caused the other anguish. Jed coaxed Angel to come to bed around midnight.

"Would you rather stay here than up north," Jed asked, as they prepared for bed. "You always told me how much you loved it here."

"Yes, but there are too many ghosts here now, she replied. All I have here is grandpa, and every time I see him, I want to cry. Grandma was his only real friend, and he's going to have to find himself again." She sat on the bed, the bed she had slept in since she was a child. She could picture her mother, her grandmother and her sister. She could hear the echoes of their laughter. Angel turned to her husband and said with a gentle passion, "I have my life with you Jed. I need to be where we are going to build our lives darling. We can travel, we can visit, but I cannot live here again, not in this house. *Hurricane Road* has far too much loss, far too many memories for me to endure."

He turned out the light and pulled her against him, "There's time to decide," he said.

"I'm sure," she said sadly.

Jed's emergency leave was up the day after Christmas. He needed to get Angel settled before he returned to duty. He took Angel north the morning following the funeral. Clare MacArt caught another train early that afternoon. When Fedrico Vega left for his office, Asher was very aware of being alone.

It was the last day of school before Christmas vacation, and the day of class parties. Asher saw no reason to keep little Cory home. Without him, the house was quiet. Of course, there were the servants of Hurricane Road tiptoeing about, but no one needed to call out just for the pleasure of hearing his voice. No one looked for him for the simple joy of seeing his face. His and Corazon's room was silent. Alone, he stood inside the door. Only Asher's breathing, and the steady beating of his heart disturbed the quiet of the room. It was a different kind of alone. Different than when he had been away at sea. It was nothing like when she had been away visiting. Then there had been the knowledge of her existence. In the past their companion spirits had been separated by a mere measured distance. Two points in a fixed plain of existence, which could be traversed, one to the other. Now the veil of death parted them. In privacy, he wept.

She had once asked him; would he forgive her if she died first? She had told him that it would be more than she could bear, living without him. Asher had given his permission so lightly, so long ago. It had not seemed possible then that she would leave him behind, alone in life.

Asher went to his library. He poured a drink and sat in his chair, looking through photo albums. His mind wandered from one memory to another, and his melancholy grew with the turn of pages. He remembered Corazon's last words, "Take courage my love." He needed to do that, but not just now. He did not know where he would take the courage from, from her memory perhaps.

What of Connie? He must deal with her non-death. Logically she had preceded her grandmother. It hung above him, unacknowledged. How long before he must abandon the sanguine attitude toward her disappearance. When should he officially recognize her death and mark a place for her and Grey among those, who had gone before. Soon, he must tell Clare.

Gone missing, such a superficial term to express such pain and suffering. How long had the 'gone missing' taken to die? How long had their suffering lasted? Did some still linger? At least Connie had her husband with her in the end, a comfort and an agony, but better together than apart. To perish alone at sea, it is a thing of unbearable woe. The waste of war, Asher despised it.

An unexpected clamor, punctuated by childish giggling, drew Asher from his gloom. Without doubt, Cory was home from kindergarten. The little boy entered the library in full flight with Grace in apologetic pursuit.

"Save me, pap, save me," he yelled, flinging himself into his great-grandfather's lap.

"I's so sorry disturbing you're mourning, Cop'n Asher. He got clear away."

"Leave him, I'm fine," Asher said, smiling.

Cory had burrowed under one of Asher's arms, and pulled it around himself. He stuck out his tongue at Grace. Asher reached around with the other hand and latched onto the little tongue.

"This here tongue is for talking and eating Cory. You go sticking it out, especially at your elders, and old pap is going to have to nip it off. Sticking out tongues, why it just isn't proper, boy. Do you think I should let you keep it?"

"Eth 'ir," he said with difficulty.

"Glad we worked that out," Asher said, turning loose. "Now where's that slippery thing belong boy?"

"Tongue belongs in my mouth, Pap."

"Glad we agree on that, Cory boy." He adjusted the five-year-old on his lap and asked, "You hungry?"

"Yes sir, I'm super hungry."

"It's early for supper, but I think cook has some pumpkin pie," Asher said standing with the boy in his arms.

As he walked to the kitchen, he looked around the house. He noted the draped windows, the funeral atmosphere. Two days until Christmas and no tree; it was a crime to be this close to Christmas and have no tree, with a five-year-old in the house. He sat the boy at the table and cut two pieces of pie. He got the whipped cream from the refrigerator and smeared on a thick coat.

"Think you can eat all that," he asked?"

"Yes sir."

"Well you do, and then we're going to go buy a Christmas tree and decorate it."

"That's keen, Pap."

"I want you to think about what you want for Christmas. You ain't gonna get everything, Santa's got a lot of kids to deliver presents to, but you think about it."

"How's Santa gonna know Pap?"

"Well Cory, were gonna go to Sears Roebuck tomorrow because Santa is supposed to be visiting. He does that just to hear what little boys want. Good little boys."

Cory swallowed a bite of pie. Earnestly, he said, "I'm a good little boy."

"Then Santa will bring you something."

When they finished, Asher put the dishes in the sink, and got the car keys. He asked Grace to have Shawn bring in the boxes of Christmas ornaments. Asher put Cory in the car, and drove down *Twenty-*

Seventh Avenue, looking for a lot. The selection of the tree was presented as a serious matter. Cory's opinion was sought in getting one that was perfect. Once they had chosen, the boy was allowed to pay, and he danced around tree until the merchant tied it on the car.

They began to decorate after dinner. It was very late for a little boy when the star topped the tree, and by then, even excitement could not keep Cory awake. Asher carried him up to bed, pushed the limp arms and legs into his pajamas and tucked him in. He looked down on his great grandson and switched off the light. It had been a good evening.

He surveyed the tree critically, as he descended the stairs. This was the first tree he had decorated without Corazon's direction. It certainly lacked artistic proportion. The tinsel was uneven, as were the lights. Cory had fun hanging the stuff and was delighted with it. That was what was important.

The night was cool, and Asher wandered outside. Restless, he wandered to the bay, where he sat on his boat. In the dark, the *Constance* was a mix of blues and grays. The tide had ebbed, and the air was heavy with the odor of fish and seaweed. A sliver of moon hung in the east, and the sea whispered against the boats hull. Asher lay back and gazed at the sky. He was sixty-four years old, yet he didn't feel it. He was, in his own estimation a youthful sixty-four. Corazon, except for an act of evil, might have shared another twenty years with him.

"We get what we get," he mumbled to himself, and his eyes burned. He sniffled, wiped his eyes, and thought of the living.

He thought of Angel. She would be fine. She had her life now, and it would be a good life if Jed lasted out the war. He was a training officer, so his chances were favorable. Angel and the children she would have, they would all be fine. He'd visit and help them as he could. Cory would be his responsibility and his life. Clare would want to have the boy, and he would see to visits, but Cory would stay with him. Cory would get the attention he had never had the time to give his own sons.

Asher had always appreciated the Greeks, in their belief that the best in men was brought out when they were mentored. What years are left to me are Cory's. It was a less a pledge than a recognition. Corazon had told him that the boy deserved not only his time, but also his heart. It was truth. His wife had always seen the human aspects of life clearly. Asher rose from the deck. As he stepped off onto the dock, the ketch rocked slightly. He had a great deal to give the boy. The difficulty would be in deciding which things were worth giving. He looked to the sea, back to the shore; he sighed, and walked up the coral ridge toward *Hurricane Road.*

Chapter 35

Eleven years later, near twilight, the wind fell off and *Utila* lost headway. Canvas rustling the old Barque drifted south of the *Tortugas*. As the night deepened, the light sweeping twenty miles out from Loggerhead Key reflected from her rigging. In the silent calm, Asher could hear a pod of dolphins blowing. In the chart house, his great-grandson worked at fixing their position. Celestial navigation was the measurement of distance, in degrees, between celestial bodies and the visible horizon. The sixteen-year-old knew his work. Asher already knew his position. This was useful practice.

Asher had hoped to make *Tampa Bay* by tomorrow evening, *Ybor City* by Wednesday noon. Unless they picked up a good breeze, it seemed unlikely they would be on schedule. Cory was due in *Green Cove Springs*, and he was going to be late. No way to tell Clare MacArt, and Clare would get herself all worked up; worried that she had lost Cory to the sea. After a father, a husband, and two sons who failed to come ashore, Asher could not blame the poor woman, but they'd actually succumbed to the war and disease. Her men had merely had the mischance to be at sea when it happened. Clare was a good woman, but hard for Asher to deal with.

Forward, there was a disagreement. He couldn't see much from where he stood, but the sounds were telling. There had been bad blood between two of his crew. A woman in *Belize* had lived with one and favored the other, not exactly a new page in human history.

Cory had come out of the chart house and followed the mate forward. Asher walked to the break of the deck for a better view. José Hernandez knocked Wilcox to the deck. They had fought with fists, and though smaller than the Jamaican, Hernandez was the better boxer. From the deck, Wilcox vented his rage.

"Sponish mon. Hey! Sheess, you Sponish fella, thinks you take my woman." Wilcox scowled, threatened, "Sheess! You look, me waitin' all time. Hey, Som' time I gib you what you doan see comin'."

"*Comemierda estupido* 'stupid shit-eater'," the Honduran said and with a wave of distain turned his back.

Before Hernandez had taken a step, Wilcox came at his back with a knife. The cook shouted; Hernandez tried to turn and block. The knife sliced the fabric of his shirt and bloodied his shoulder, but he locked the Jamaican's wrist. He forced the blade back on him. Asher could see there was an instant when Hernandez could have taken the knife. Instead, he forced it up under the Jamaican's ribs and into his heart. Hernandez looked Wilcox straight in the eye as the man's knees sagged and let him slide to the deck. He stepped back and spit, for the man was a coward in his eyes.

July 6, 1953, 21:18 hours, Peter Wilcox, able bodied seaman, died while attempting to knife another man in the back.

Asher continued to write, logging the circumstances of the death and the names of the witnesses. It was self-defense and no charges would be filed against Hernandez.

***

They committed Wilcox to the deep next morning. The ship was reaching on an easterly breeze and making good way. Asher finished his log and called to Cory to fetch a cup of coffee aft. Cory returned shortly, and his great-grandfather pointed to a chair.

"You saw a man die last night Cory. Not a good thing, but who was in the right?"

"It seems like it wasn't right for José to take Wilcox's woman, Pap."

Asher took a sip of his coffee, then a gulp. "Let's consider this boy, and then I'll ask you again. A woman is not property in our part of the world and should not be anywhere. Of course, a man in our culture or another culture might disagree. That aside, it is a woman's right to change her mind, and ally with a different man. When that happens, men tend to get very emotional, if you get my drift. Well, women, too, Cory, men and women are both naturally possessive of each other. However, they do not own each other. They loan themselves to each other. Some loans last a lifetime, others a single night." He drank more coffee. "Now, who was in the right," he questioned?

"Sir, I guess neither could claim anything then. They plain did not like each other. Wilcox was jealous and started the fight. He was angrier when José whipped him, so he tried to knife him in the back. José had the right to defended himself, didn't he?"

"Every man has the right to defend, Cory, but what about killing." Asher looked at him and waited. "Killing and defending yourself ain't necessarily the same thing," he continued. "Did you see a point when José could have taken that knife, let Wilcox live?"

"Yes sir, right after Wilcox cut his shoulder, sir. José had Pete's wrist locked, but it was mighty quick."

"Was he right to kill him — when he could have taken the knife away?"

Cory didn't answer.

"What would you have been thinking if you were José?"

"Scared he'd kill me the next time sir."

"Kill you right then or some-day Cory?"

"Both, sir, sooner or later, and Wilcox said as much; he had a nasty temper sir."

"And there lies the dilemma boy. We're supposed to spare a man when we got him beat, but there are those men, who are just pure evil, or just too stubborn to be spared. Odds are, they will come back at you, or your loved ones, time and again, and you, Cory, if threatened, will have to make that decision just like José. Then you have to live with it. If you kill a man and you're caught, the law might just decide you're wrong. They might make you pay. If you don't, he might come back at you or yours when you ain't looking, like Wilcox did."

"It seems best to avoid fighting in the first place, sir."

Asher finished his coffee and leaned back in his chair. He considered what he'd say next.

"Cory, you're more a man now than many that are twice your age and size. Age does not make a man though, and no man is all good or all bad. Men are just men who choose to do good or bad and often disagree on what good or bad is. However, we all have to learn and make our judgments on the rights and wrongs of life. What you experience, what you chose from life's lessons, to keep for your own is how you form your character. How you apply that knowledge to make difficult choices, and to acknowledge what is correct, that is being a good man or bad. To see a thing through because it is right, or because it is necessary that is character and the mark of a good man. This is particularly true when there is no profit in it. Choices like that; they make and define a man, Cory. We all have to fight. The trick is choosing the right fight and the right side in that fight, and at times the difference can be a dam'd hard do see."

"Yes, sir."

Asher smiled and waved him out. "You have work boy, and when you finish, remember that your Latin grammar stinks. You best work on it and leave off reading novels."

"Yes sir," Cory said rising.

"And Cory, remember — we don't always get to pick our battles be they with man or nature. Consider what might happen in every circumstance and plan for it. Never be surprised."

The boy smiled and nodded. Asher sighed as he disappeared up on deck. There was a lot more to the world than when he'd been that age. Another year and the boy would be off to college. It would be hard to let him go.

Cory snatched the sextant from the chart house and compared his watch to the ship's chronometer. From the starboard quarter, he brought down the sun and marked the time. Back in the charthouse, it took only a few minutes to work out the line of position and advance the dawn position for a running fix. The ship had advanced forty-two nautical miles since dawn. Eleven knots over the bottom. They were making up time.

As Cory left the chart house, Ramos, the second mate gave him the hard eye. Cory understood, and yet he didn't. Ramos resented that a kid knew the arcane science of spherical trigonometry as applied to navigation. The resentment was only because Ramos lacked that skill. In all other things, Ramos was able. Cory wondered why the mate had not taken the trouble to learn.

The fact was, Ramos had been forced to sea with only five years of school, and he was fortunate to remember fractions. With time, these things would be apparent, but Cory still had much to learn. For the moment, it was Latin grammar

.

Chapter 35

Captain Thompson had met the ship as planned, and they had come ashore. Cory went to his grandmother MacArt's, and great-grandpa went on to Aunt Angela's in *Ohio*. Pap had promised to be there for Janice's birthday. Cory would like to have gone to her ninth birthday and play around with his young cousin

Alex. He'd wanted to visit at times when Pap went up, but he always got stuck with Grandma MacArt.

July passed slowly. His grandmother was the original worrywart. She didn't even want him swimming in the river unless someone was around. Flowers and table manners were all she thought of that, and the possibility of him drowning. He did like grandma Clare's cooking. She knew what he liked best and made sure that it was on hand. Hot bread and different kinds of pie were his particular weakness. He played a lot of baseball too, and even got in some studying. When August rolled around, Cory was ready to go. He caught a train south and met Pap in *Miami*.

***

They had planned to sail down to *Knights Key* and then over to *Cay Sal* and load up on Langosta. Cory thought one tasted the same as another, but Pap thought the crayfish there had a special flavor. Cory spent a day getting the *Constance* stored up and he put in a new battery for the engine. Next morning, they waited for a good breeze, and by mid-morning, tacked out toward *Key Biscayne.*

"Whatever happened to those PT boats they used in the movie, *They Were Expendable*, Pap?"

"That dam war movie?" Asher replied.

"Yes sir."

"They burned one PT up making the movie. I know two ended up as charter fishing boats. One is running out of *Haulover Cut*, as I recall. I couldn't tell you about the others."

"I liked that movie. It was fun watching them film it, the explosions and stuff."

"I'm glad, because they killed half the fish in *Biscayne Bay*. The fishing wasn't the same for two months." Asher looked down into the water. He could see the bottom eight feet down, but cloudy. "You know, the water was still crystal clear ten years ago. Remember what I say; in ten more years, you won't be able to see the bottom in four foot. There are too many people for nature to deal with, and more are coming. Everything here is going to change for the worse. Cory, you think about that some-day, and then you decide how you fit in to these future problems."

"There's a lot of open space out here Pap," Cory said, not wanting to disbelieve.

Asher chuckled, "Boy, civilization knows how to deal with wilderness and open space. Knock it down and fill it up."

"Doesn't everything grow back when civilizations die? Like Maya, it's all jungle now."

"Modern man's getting better at surviving. Man's more successful and he doesn't just live in this world, he changes it. You know, before the turn of the century, man was hard pressed to grow enough food."

"But there was a lot of empty land, and there's lot more people now Pap."

"It's all about natural balance and upsetting the works. You see, we're messing with the adjustments, upsetting nature's scales. The problem with the food was not lack of land; it was lack of fertilizer. There wasn't enough of what plants needed. Farmer had a finite amount of natural fertilizer. Had to have ammonia to make chemical fertilizer, and there wasn't enough supplied by nature. A smart German figured how to make synthetic ammonia, and now we got all the plant food we need but in the future what will all that extra ammonia do? More food, yes but that upsets the balance, and now we're getting too many people. I swear boy, we're told God's got a plan, but whatever it is, well it's beyond me."

Cory pictured the planet filled with people, shoulder-to-shoulder people. He did some mental math and figured it would be getting pretty crowded in the Twenty-First century.

The *Constance* was close on *Key Biscayne*, and he brought her around on a port tack. The jib sheets thrashed, and he hauled in and tied off. *Constance* heeled and gained speed.

"Talked myself thirsty," he said. "I'll take the wheel if you'll pass me up a beer."

"Sure, Pap," Cory said and dropped down the hatch. "Want some pretzels?"

"Surely."

A squall to windward obscured *Fowey Rocks Light.* A building wind on the port bow curled sheets of spray up over the deck. In the sunlight, the salt and droplets glitter like gems. Rail down, the *Constance* flies; braced, Asher puts a few spokes on the wheel. He grinned, while Cory popped the cap on a beer bottle and climbed on deck.

"Wanna reef, sir."

"Nah, we'll let her haul. She'll take care of herself in this little breeze."

Cory passed the beer and pretzels and took the wheel. Above, the sail's leech cracked in the breeze. The bow wave foamed outward, rushed down the ketch's run. The sun blinked out and cool rain begins to drum the deck. His back to the rain, Asher sheltered his pretzel, and bit off another chunk. The rigging hummed and Cory, stripped to his shorts, laughed into the driving rain as her, tightened the outhaul on the main.

The waters of *Featherbed Banks* are roiled by the squall's winds, and they pilot by marker sticks. Mid-afternoon and they anchor north of *Pumpkin Key*. As Cory dove for conch, Asher watched a sport fishing boat running toward *Angelfish Creek*. Conch fritter, rice and beans for supper. They read until twilight.

Asher turned on the radio to catch the news and weather. No hurricanes. There was comments and gossip about movie stars and scandals. Local businessmen had been complaining bitterly about loss of business, due to Senator Kefauver's investigation into the mob and gambling. Now business on the Beach was getting better again. There was more trouble in *Korea* and talks with the *Chinese*. President Eisenhower was talking tough. The Russians had tested another hydrogen bomb, and people were frightened. Asher turned the radio off.

"It sounds bad, Pap. You have to wonder why God lets it happen."

"God gave us rules and free will Cory. Men seldom follow God's rules, and they bring misery on themselves. God watches, and he weeps."

"The world seems to be going bad pretty fast right now, Pap."

"Cory, the world has been going to hell since man was put here. There are more of us now, so it's going to hell a little faster. Your worrying won't speed it up or slow it down. I doubt you'll be around for the world's arrival in hell." Asher stretched and yawned. "I'd like to have the anchor up and be underway first light. Let's us get some sleep."

"I prefer reading for a while."

"Suit yourself."

Cory lay on deck, staring at clouds that drifted across the stars. He was reading a novel. The characters were young lovers, a pioneer couple, struggling alone in the wilderness. As they faced danger and impossible obstacles, they knew they could rely on each other. In the cold cave where they had taken shelter, they were short of food, but they had warmth, loving companionship.

"Yeah," Cory said quietly. He would love to have a beautiful girl to share things with, a girl to take care of. The kissing and stuff would be great, but just knowing she loved you back would be best. His thoughts became dreams and he slept smiling on deck.

Dawn came with the flight of a thousand squawking birds. With wind abeam; *Constance* skirted the upper keys with trolling lines strung astern. Close to dark, they anchored off *Marathon*; Cory cooked. It was good. Grilled dolphin, rice and peas, canned peaches for desert, and stuffed, they lay back watching the shore lights.

"How'd you know you'd like Great-grandma when you met her, Pap?"

"Where'd that thinking come from Cory?"

"From a book I'm reading. It says love at first sight, but I don't think that makes sense. How do you love somebody you don't know?"

"Will you don't, but that somebody may look pretty good. I saw a dish of food in a British restaurant once, and it looked very tasty. Well, Cory, I ordered some up. Most disgusting food I ever tasted." Asher shook his head, making a face. "Women are the same, they can look really tasty. It's wise to get to know them, sample their company for a while, see if you can get along before you marry into that company for a lifetime."

Cory grinned and said, "Did great grandma look really tasty?"

Asher closed his eyes, and picturing Corazon as a girl, said, "When I saw your great grandmother for the first time, she was a thing of beauty. Then she disappeared. Poof, like a puff of smoke, and I wondered if she'd ever been there. The next time we met, I run her down as she was coming out of an elevator in a *Tampa* hotel. Knocked her flat and tripped on her dress. I exposed her legs right up to her underclothes, and you just didn't see a lady's legs in those days." Asher leaned forward, and he said as if he were passing a secret, "Cory, in a long life, I was never so embarrassed before or after. And then I was seated at the next table. I choked on my food."

"That's not much of a start, Pap."

Asher leaned back and continued. "Well, it got better. I was properly introduced a few weeks later, and I conversed with her for a while without appearing like a complete fool. She was on my mind after that, day-in, day-out, even though I never expected to see her again. Six months later, we met by chance, middle of nowhere. I mean the middle of nowhere, on a country road in *Santa Clara Province, Cuba*. Figure that? I began courting her. Cory, I swear— courting a woman is the most painful experience a young man can suffer. After a few months, we concluded that we wanted each other as husband and wife, and no one else would do. It must have been love at first sight. She looked really tasty but it took a year getting to know each other to be sure. Love at first sight comes after the fact sometimes. You see how it works boy? Choosing a wife is the single most important thing a man does in his personal life. It will influence all the other things and all that follows. You remember, pretty is only one consideration."

"Did you get married right away, Pap?"

"No. To tell the truth, Corazon's family took a severe dislike to me at the outset, and there was a serious unpleasantness that followed. Corazon's daddy forbade her to see me, but she took it upon herself to travel to my Aunts house in *Charleston*. We married there. The O'Ryans was angry as hornets, but they came around after a few years. They're good people Cory and it's time I took you down there to spend some time with them. Your great-grandma's sister is still alive. You haven't seen your Aunt Esmeralda since you were seven, and you must have a hundred cousins by now."

"We could run south from *Cay Sal Bank*," Cory suggested. "Stop in *Cuba* before we go home."

"Not a bad idea. We'll see." Asher sighed. "Perhaps, better to get snazzed up and take a plane. They go in style down there, you know."

***

With morning came a fresh southeast wind, and *Constance* beat to windward across the stream. They steered in turns, read their books, and ate bread smeared with corned beef or spam. The low Islands quivered on the horizon by early afternoon, and Cory fell off toward the south end of the chain. Bering up west of *Elbow Cay* tower, they anchored *Constance* in eight feet, over coral sand. Shallow coral shelves were on all sides. Cory was over the side, and back in minutes with a dozen lobsters.

Asher smacked his lips when the last bite was gone, "Cory, my boy, the feast was worth the waiting."

"I ate too much," Cory confessed.

"Rest a while. We'll clean up later.

"What are we doing tomorrow, Pap?"

"Poke around on shore. We might find some old Scotch. There's still a lot that was buried by the hurricane of twenty-six. The seas took out several of the bootleggers' warehouses. Bottles washed all over the cays. Never know when one might poke its way up out of the sand."

"They made a lot of money, I guess."

"A lot of people made money, Cory. Every time a government, or as far as that goes, a preacher, tells people they cannot do a thing, they just naturally want to do it more. Human nature ain't rational — it just is."

"Were you a bootlegger?"

"I'm ashamed to say I dabbled at it, a protest of sorts — I've come to regret. Your granddaddy Fred, he was the real thing, though. Fred was very successful, but then, he could have been just as successful at most anything. Fred had a mean streak when he was young, and the danger of the business, well, it appealed to him. I believe he would have outgrown it if he'd lived."

"How'd he die, Pap?"

"He died protecting his children, Cory, your mom and your aunt Angela. There is no higher call to a man than the call to protect his children. A man must stand ready to rescue anyone in need, but his own, his wife and children above all. Your grandpa did this without hesitation, he succeeded, and he fell in the effort. That's a story best left untold for now. Those were mean hard times." Asher lay back and sighed, "Getting tired quicker than I used to."

Cory picked up his book and went back to reading. At one point, he pictured the girl in the story as Sally Kenny, who was in his English class. She was super pretty and smiled at him sometimes. Her brother was a year ahead of him in football. Pete Kenny was a jerk, a cheater and a bad sport to boot. Cory hated a cheat. He finished the book by lantern-light and went below to sleep. Pap was snoring. Cory fell asleep anyway, picturing Sally Kenny in tennis shorts.

The next afternoon when they returned from beach combing, *Constance* had a foot of water in the bilge. Cory dove overboard and inspected the bottom. It appeared that worms had eaten through the planks near the forefoot. The problem wasn't serious, but pumping was a nuisance. Asher decided to patch it up when they reached *Anguila Cay*. At high tide, they would put her on the beach, and haul her over with tackle.

Dinner finished, they played chess. Asher won the first game, Cory the second. They were both being cautious in the third. Asher had found a bottle of twenty-five-year-old Scotch and decided it should not grow older. He sipped at a second glass, enjoying it even more because it had cost nothing. He set a fine trap for the boy but found his own Queen in it. Cory had an eye for the unusual tactics. Asher felt a mix of pride and aggravation.

"Ah," Asher said, "You left your knight unprotected, and I'll have your rook next move."

It was true. Cory grimaced. Asher took them in succession.

"Check Mate," Cory announced, with a smug expression.

"Dam it!" Asher exclaimed, recognizing he'd been snookered.

"One more game, Pap?"

"I've suffered enough at your hands for now. Put it away." He leaned back and sipped his Scotch. "Want to play poker?"

"It's not much fun with only two playing."

"Poker ain't about fun; it's about observation and math."

"But I know all your giveaways, Pap, and the math is boring."

"What are you going to do, read another romance novel?"

"I'm reading Victor Hugo, a collection of his short stories, sir."

"Any you like?"

"The about a small French naval vessel, the *Corvette Claymore*, it's pretty deep."

"What did you get from it?" Asher asked with interest.

"A man must stand responsible for his mistakes and his crimes. If later, he performs a good deed or courageous act it should be acknowledged, but that does not excuse him. He must accept responsibility and punishment for his earlier crime, sir."

"That's it Cory. You will find Victor Hugo good company when you ponder human ethics. Hugo has a far better understanding of humanity than most of us. The religious thinkers are too narrow. In my opinion, most holy men have an axe to grind. You might try Conrad's work when we get ashore. A dark gloomy writer, but he has a genius for guilt and ethics. '*Lord Jim*' is a fine example. He'll show you that what is ethical in one culture is not necessarily so in another. When you move about in the countries of the world, you must look out from the heart of the native, as well as your own. Remember, there are many conflicting truths Cory and they're all valid."

"I'll remember sir."

"Well, get to your reading then. I've talked myself dry."

Asher woke to the whoosh thump of the pump. Cory had brewed coffee. Pouring a cup, Asher climbed up to the cockpit, sat and worked his left shoulder to relieve the charley horse. The black silhouette of palms stood against the dawn's pale glow. He watched as the colors deepened and shadows shrunk eastward. Cumulonimbus pillars stacked over the banks, and sea birds soared outward on their daily hunt. Asher sighed, "Ah Corazon," he thought, "a perfect dawn if you were sharing coffee at my side." Forward, the racket stopped, and Cory came aft to hoist the mizzen.

"Morning, Pap, sleep well?"

"I did, thank you. Do you need a hand?"

"Anchor's already short sir," Cory said throwing his weight against the halyard. "I'll handle things just fine."

Asher watched as his great grandson hoisted the sails in succession and brought the anchor home. It was smooth, effortless, and the work of a seasoned hand. He trimmed sail and set up his course anticipating the shift in wind that would come as the sun climbed. The mark of a true seaman was in sail trim, and the understanding of the winds shifts. Asher was satisfied with the boy in every way. He'd been raised differently than his parents and grand-parents. He'd been given what he needed, rather than what he wanted, and he'd been taught to work for the extras. What Asher had lavished on him, was time, love and wisdom gleaned from hard lessons, learned in a long life. He had lavished on the young man an understanding of the valuable things that made men sound. When he went to college, Cory would be fine.

Underway, with a building breeze, *Constance* rounded the south end of *Elbow Cay*, and tacked east for *Anguila*. Breakfast was cornflakes with canned milk and pears. Asher took the wheel while Cory cleaned up. Mid-morning, the breeze fell off and *Constance* ghosted along over her shadow.

Asher lay back on the cabin top. Though his mind was young, his body felt old and full of aches. When he looked in the mirror, the old face never failed to surprise him. Even stranger, his oldest memories were the sharpest. He had recalled his favorite memories each day for years, shuffled them like a deck of precious cards, and relived the moments one by one, as he turned them up.

We look back down the road when we grow old and not ahead, he thought. All there is ahead is a wall of mist, and it's not too inviting. He sighed, our life is over our shoulder when we become old, and a memory becomes a fine place to visit. "Corazon," he thought, "to visit with you my love." He closed his eye and saw her on that dancing Arab mare of hers. He saw her on that day, on the hot Cuban road when she had challenged him with a laughing glance over her shoulder.

That had been the beginning of his life. She had ridden like an Amazon, and he had followed, matched her, full out, racing side by side. In truth that had been the day of their union, that day that moment, that race through the cane. He smiled as the vision ran through his mind, and he slept, and, in his sleep, he raced after her, his love, his Corazon.

Anguila Cay rose above the sea. The *Constance* closed to a hundred yards. With her sails luffing, she slipped along a jagged, rocky shore. Cory called to his great-grandfather, but the old man could no longer be wakened.

End

A Change of Times **#4 of Hurricane Road.**

Next, venture out into the islands with Cory. In **A Change of Times,** not knowing he's heir to millions, Cory MacArt sets off into the Caribbean to win his fortune and wins the girl of his heart instead.

Novels in this series

1   Hurricane Road
2   Florida Straits
3   Valuable Things
4   A Change of Times
5   Lies and to the Wall
6   Implausible Deniability
7   Paths of War

Other books by author

To Stalk the Hydra
Truth and Other Precious Things
Racing for Pride and Profit

Made in the USA
Middletown, DE
10 January 2022